HOW TO STOP A VAMPIRE WAR IN SIX EASY STEPS

VAMPIRE INNOCENT
BOOK ELEVEN

MATTHEW S. COX

How to Stop a Vampire War in Six Easy Steps
Vampire Innocent #11

Cover art by: Alexandria Thompson

ISBN (e-book): 978-1-950738-32-8

ISBN (paperback): 978-1-950738-33-5

CONTENTS

1. Great, Our House is the Creepy One 1
2. Birthday déjà vu 12
3. Shadow Politics 24
4. Dare 36
5. Left Field Question 43
6. Forgiveness Is Easier than Permission 49
7. A Little Recreational Decapitation 57
8. Did Anyone Order Zombies? 69
9. How to Avoid Being Grounded 76
10. Un Chaton Errant 83
11. Maximum Overkill 92
12. Do Vampires Dream of Undead Sheep 100
13. Timeout 106
14. A Personal Reality 113
15. Undetermined Origin 124
16. Nature Girl 133
17. Behold the Power of Spite 146
18. Friends in (Very) Low Places 158
19. Keep it Believable 165
20. Sore Spots 174
21. Out of the Frying Pan, Into the Weird 192
22. The Mother of Nightmares 199
23. Nothing Can Truly be Absurd until the Government Gets Involved 212
24. Fire in the Sky 217
25. Dutiful 230
26. A Bit Too Much for Mom to Handle 234
27. Surprise Tentacles are Never Fun 246
28. Bloodbath 251
29. Vast Interdimensional Non-Space 256
30. A Brittle Alliance 262
31. No Longer My Problem 266
32. The Walking Derp 272
33. Sorta, Almost, but not Quite Canine 279
34. Somewhat Less Cordial 284

35. Father Daughter Project 289
36. Mission Highly Improbable 292
37. Calories are for Lesser Mortals 301
38. They're not Ready Until They Stop Snarling 307

Acknowledgments 311
About the Author 312
Other books by Matthew S. Cox 313

1

GREAT, OUR HOUSE IS THE CREEPY ONE

Adapting to existence after death is something of an ongoing project.

No one prepares you for how to handle being murdered at all, much less discovering vampires and all sorts of other 'myths' really exist on the same day. Considering everything the universe dumped on me all at once, I'm coping about as well as an eighteen-year-old can be expected to cope with a surprise gift of immortality. Wait, I'm nineteen now. Technically.

I hit the ground running in the sense of breaking vampire tradition. My lack of concern for the 'way things are done' is hardly unique. Vampires before me have bent the rules… often way worse than what I did. Ever notice some actors or game show hosts don't seem to age much over a span of like fifty years? Yeah… they're vampires who couldn't give up the limelight, using makeup to appear to age a little on screen. They hang around until it would become too obvious, then they retire, maybe fake their death. Nothing *that* dramatic for me, thanks. *My* way of breaking tradition is strictly low-key.

On my first full night as an undead, I only went home.

Apparently, telling mortals we're real is a big deal to some vampires. They think the world would stop spinning if our families knew we still existed. Makes no sense to me why they have a problem with it. Kinda sounds like they're jealous. Not going to rub their noses in it, though. If I'd done the traditional thing and run off with Dalton, allowing my family to believe I'd been killed, and I found out decades after my last relative died I had the option *not* to make them think they lost me—I'd be pissed.

Some people obey rules simply because they're rules and don't question it.

Hello, world. I'm Follows Rules Girl.

Or was… anyway.

I still sort-of am. Most of the time. Unless the rules are dumb. What can I say? Death gave me some confidence. Also, Dalton Ames wasn't the most methodical sire a vampire could ask for. He somehow managed to lose track of me long enough for the authorities to collect my body, thus setting everything in motion. Had I woken up in a basement somewhere right next to him instead of being alone in a body cooler at a morgue, who knows what might've happened. Possible I'd have still gone home. No, it's *probable*… but not a guarantee. Anyway, can't break a rule intentionally if you don't know it exists. Point being, Dalton wasn't there when I woke up to tell me going home is frowned on. If I'm honest with myself, it's doubtful he'd have tried to talk me out of it, anyway. In fact, he regards my going home as a bit of a relief to him since he didn't have to take care of me for the first few months of vampirism.

Aurélie stepped up to be my mentor. Dalton's far too flighty and irresponsible to care for a child—and I mean that in terms of a 'baby vampire.' He's like the cool uncle you can leave the kids with for a weekend, but trusting him with long-term care isn't wise. Basically, Dalton's the 161-year-old who had a kid but can't raise her, so he gave me up for adoption—to my actual parents. Plus Aurélie. She's essentially my 'vampire mom.' Though, this whole undead deal doesn't come with a user's manual. Whole lot of winging it going on here. My Dad would be awesome at vampire. He never reads instruction manuals. Ever. Is that a guy thing, a programmer thing, or a dad thing?

Speaking of defying vampire traditions, I'm presently doing something no vampire has ever done before. (At least I sincerely hope so.) Today is Thursday, March 22, 2018. On this day, I, Sarah Wright, have become an 'honorary tween,' participating in my sister Sophia's eleventh birthday party… or at least the tail end of it. Mom's been making jokes about drinking heavily because of having *two* eleven-year-olds in the house. The woman is, of course, totally kidding. I've never really known her to have more than one glass of wine a day—except for a few occasions when Uncle Hank happened. She really didn't like Dad pointing out they will eventually have three teenagers under the same roof. Technically, four, since I'm permanently eighteen despite what the calendar says.

So, yeah. I'm stretched out on the living room floor in pajamas with Sophia, Sierra, and three friends. Megan Scheller, the somewhat chubby girl Sophia met in dance class, has finally gotten past worrying Sophia only made friends with her as a cruel prank and has accepted my sister is sincere. I swear the girl would jump in front of a bullet for Soph. My littlest sister is a scrawny little shy twig of a kid, but she's legit screamed at people for teasing Megan. Considering the way my unlife is going, I probably shouldn't joke about anyone jumping in front of bullets.

Nicole Pierce, our few-houses-over neighbor, has been friends with my little sisters for a while now, going on four years, I think. Maybe five. If 'normal suburban kid' had a picture in the dictionary, she'd be it. The girl's a bit like me at the same age, terrified of getting in trouble but willing to do just about anything as long as they have a 110-percent chance of not being caught. Okay, not exactly me. I didn't break the rules because I felt bad about doing so. Nicole couldn't care less about rules; she mostly doesn't want to be punished. Also, she won't do anything malicious or mean. She's a good kid, but has no issues with some harmless rule-breaking.

Priya Chawla, Sophia met in school. If life were a video game, Priya is basically a palette swap of Sophia's avatar. Highly similar personality, similar size and build, similar long hair. Thus far, Priya hasn't shown any signs of having magical abilities. Given my sister's newfound talent, she's become a little more confident. This leaves Priya as the most timid of their group. She's shy, polite, and doesn't usually speak to people she doesn't know.

Right after they got home from school, Mom took Sophia, Sierra, and their friends out to have fun. They hit some Chuck-E-Cheese like place. Sure, Sophia's a little old for it, but she wanted to go. Megan, Nicole, and Priya didn't seem too embarrassed. For obvious reasons, I didn't go out with them during the day. When they got home, we had a tamer version of a birthday party like something parents would throw for a six or seven-year-old kid. It would have been *exactly* a party for six-year-olds if we had her entire class screaming in one room and twenty parents in the kitchen doing shots of vodka and price gouging each other for foam earplugs.

After dinner and cake, the girls went into sleepover mode. Sophia insisted I join them. Nicole didn't mind because she knows me, but Megan and Priya kinda regarded me more like Sophia's second mother. At least to them, I look old enough to be a responsible adult. Go figure, the first time someone doesn't mistake me for a kid, post-vampirization, it's annoying. This must be the universe mocking me for being annoyed by adults mistaking me for anywhere from fourteen to sixteen all the time.

No big deal. A minor mental poke adjusted their opinion of me from 'parental narc' to 'tall tween.' I'm not here to make sure the kids don't do anything bad. Hanging out with a bunch of girls this age isn't even my idea. Sophia insisted. We're having fun for Sophia's birthday. Seriously, there is no way in hell *Sophia* would ever do anything even remotely bad on purpose. She's even expecting to go to sleep on time. I mean, come on. This is a girls' *sleepover*. Sneakily staying up past bedtime is required by international law, even on school nights.

My sister still can't handle scary movies, so we've got *Zootopia* playing on the TV, mostly for background noise. The girls are talking more than anything, and—except for Sierra—doing each other's nails. Sierra's not a big fan of nail polish. Proof I'm no longer a tween is quite obvious in my inability to meaningfully participate in most of their conversation. I don't recognize half the TV shows or bands they mention. I have no idea what 'Poppy' is or why *she* is creepy as hell—but somehow cool. Both Priya and Soph are terrified of her. Sophia misses some of the TV references, too. She tends to read books for the most part. Admitting to this gets Nicole checking her forehead temperature for a fever.

For the most part, I sit back and exist here for Sophia's benefit. She'd always been a little clingy and attached to me even before my death. In my opinion, I'd never been mean, cruel, or overly dismissive to her… just normal. Honestly, what sixteen-to-eighteen-year-old wants to spend hours hanging with their kid sister who's eight years younger than them? I had friends of my own, schoolwork, summer jobs, all sorts of stuff pulling at my attention. Yeah, maybe I could have made more time for Sophia, but it's not like I screamed at her to get out of my room whenever she tried to talk to me or told her she's annoying.

Despite our relationship before having been relatively ordinary by most standards, I do feel guilty for not giving her more attention. It's as irrational as a teleporting kitten who steals things. Oh, wait. She has one of those. Any girl who thinks their monthly visitor sends their emotions into wild overdrive should be glad they haven't tried dying and coming back. I don't recommend it.

Yeah, small uses of mind-control aside, we're having a fun night.

Priya seems a bit on edge, though. The poor girl keeps looking around like someone is watching her. Then again, she *is* sitting ten feet away from a vampire.

Most of us don't trigger 'prey reactions' in normal people since we don't need to kill in order to feed. Sure, some vampires out there get off on drinking their victims to death. Rumor has it literally sucking the life out of a person is, to a vampire, what taking a hit of a powerful drug (like heroin or something) is to a mortal. Assuming, of course, doing heroin legit made people stronger, faster, and more powerful for a little while. Vamps who routinely kill-feed have an entirely different presence. You know how when looking at some dogs, it's possible to say 'yeah, he's definitely going to pee and poop on the rug every chance he gets'? Same for vampires. The ones who kill-feed radiate malice.

I radiate the urge to hug bunny rabbits.

Sigh.

Could be worse, though. Can't complain.

Priya keeps looking around like a PUBG player in their first match. The girls are in the middle of calling Justin Bieber 'old' and teasing Megan for liking his music. I wisely keep out of the conversation and take a peek into Priya's thoughts.

She's on edge, feeling nervous for no specific reason. The dark living room is scaring her all on its own. At least Priya's not afraid of *me*. Hey, it might be a little petty to be happy about not being the focus of a kid's fear, but there isn't much left for me to be afraid of other than turning into a monster and/or the effect it would have on my family if I had to go away forever or died for good.

Maybe Blix—my little brother's imp friend—is spying on us. Or… she senses the hellhound in the backyard. Or maybe Coralie, the ghostly oracle, is drifting around the house. Or this kid is picking up on the energy thrown off by whatever's taken up residence in Sam's closet. Things have been getting progressively crazier ever since the mystics tore Sophia's soul out of her body and borrowed it as a spy. She's done all sorts of odd magical stuff in her bedroom. Also, Dalton and Glim—two reasonably powerful vampires—have been in and out of the house somewhat frequently.

All of it must be imprinting some serious weird energy in the walls.

Yeah… I guess slowly but surely, we're morphing into a dorkier version of the Addams Family. Won't be long before our home becomes *that* house all the kids avoid on Halloween. Probably shouldn't joke about it out loud or Sophia *will* enchant the place to be scary so we have more leftover candy.

Thinking about scary houses all the kids avoid going near gets me thinking about Mr. Niedermeyer. He lives in the last house on the left side of our cul-de-sac. The man's been a butthead to kids ever since I was little. Probably before, too, but my memory only goes back so far. He's been really quiet after our little war. Jackass tried to call the cops on the Littles for selling hot cocoa with the intention of donating the money to a veterans' support group. So... I did the only thing reasonable in my situation: I sicced Blix on him. Exactly what went on inside the house, only he and Blix know. Not gonna ask. My only conditions were not to cause physical harm or kill the guy. Imps are wicked pranksters, and they definitely have a malevolent streak. Their mayhem almost always leads to injury and death, the more painful, the more hilarious they find it. However, Blix is an oddity. Somehow, he made friends with my little brother and got hooked on the PlayStation. Guess imps don't have video games in whatever alternate dimension they come from.

I could probably write a thesis on nurture vs. nature if discussing imps wouldn't get me laughed out of college. As far as I can tell, Blix doesn't have the same streak of 'gleeful evil' I observed in the others of his kind. This is entirely the reason he's still alive. Odd as it is to say, I trust him. So does Sam. In a weird sort of way, it's reassuring Blix is always with him. He's small and no real threat to most people or supernatural beings, but he's got plenty of tricks he can use to keep my little brother safe. Sierra is morbidly terrified of someone shooting up her school. No, there haven't been any threats, but her school does drills. Swear, those drills scare the shit out of the kids as much as a real guy with a gun would.

With Blix around, a miscreant would have a *real* bad day.

So, yeah. Sophia's eleven... and she's overdoing the cute today. The girl's nowhere near as extra as Aurélie, but she's rocking a frilly pink dress. Or was. Now, she's in cat pajamas. No, she's not so bad she has a onesie with a hood and cat ears. I saw this video a few months ago about a woman who's like almost thirty but dresses up like she's an eleven-year-old anime character. Fake neon hair, wild outfits, colored contact lenses, face paint even. Hard to tell from a short video, but she seemed *way* immature. The woman thought it cute. I think it's heavy on the creepy and probably a sign of some serious underlying mental issues. Cosplaying at a convention is awesome, but living 24/7 dressed up like an anime girl and baby-talking to everyone is... eek. I mean, having fun is one thing but that's some serious Kardashian level denial of the real world existing.

Fortunately, I don't think Sophia is going to be anywhere near as bad. She doesn't act overly childish, more shy-slash-skittish-slash-girlie. Even though having literal magic is giving her a modicum of bravery, she still won't watch scary movies. Hell, even *Gremlins* gave her nightmares. It's a good thing Blix is grey-and-black. If the imps had been green, she'd have lost her damn mind.

Whoa, I wonder if the writers for *Gremlins* encountered real imps?

So, my little sister isn't *overly* childish, but she is a little immature. Sure, they went to Chuck-E-Cheese, which I guess isn't entirely for five-year-olds. Sierra didn't mind it as much due to them having a ton of arcade games. Sophia's party at home felt a bit juvenile, but not as much as it did last year. Whether her (modestly) increased maturity is a result of age or magic, I'm not sure. Me participating in the sleepover portion hadn't been in my plans, but I couldn't say no to her begging.

Sierra's not showing visible signs of separation anxiety. She hasn't touched the PlayStation at all. A day passing without random explosions in the living room is a rarity. It's sad to think an *actual* random explosion in the house wouldn't freak me out too much these days. She's got a new obsession lately: swords. Rather, learning and practicing how to fight with a blade. It hasn't consumed her to the same extent as video games, but it gives her something to think about when she's unable to have a controller in her hand.

It's nice to have some quiet time with the family—as much as my sleep schedule allows.

Peace makes me nervous. It shouldn't, but it does. Can't help but expect the universe to sense me having somewhat of a normal life again and rushing to action to fix the problem. All things considered, my family is doing well. Mom got a little promotion at work and her job is totally secure... unless the VP she reports to quits or is fired. Then I'll have to mentally influence her new boss. No, Mom's not doing anything shady. She's where I got the rule-following gene. Just a small tweak for job security in a world of random corporate layoffs and VPs cutting half their team to save their own butts.

Dad's excited about a new work project he's doing programming for. Nothing exciting like a video game, only some boring business software, but it's a big paycheck. Sierra's doing great at her sword class. The weird presence in Sam's room hasn't caused any problems… and oh yeah, we have a hellhound in the yard.

It's huge for a dog—as well as invisible—good thing.

Mom would totally freak. She nearly lost her mind when she found Sophia had a kitten. In Sam's defense, he didn't *make* the hellhound or summon it. The critter simply showed up. When most little boys say 'he followed me home, can we keep him?' they're talking about a puppy, not a 300-pound infernal canine.

When Zootopia is over, Sierra decides to test the waters by putting on *Troll.* It's one of those movies some people think is scary, others laugh at. It's meant to frighten small kids, which means it's going to scare Sophia. The girls take a quick break before the second movie starts to run to the bathroom and make more popcorn. I'd slip out for a snack, but it's not worth changing out of my *Buffy the Vampire Slayer* pajamas. Yes, Dad got them for me. Yes, Dad has a weird sense of humor.

Yes, my father is a dork.

Unlike the first movie—which all five girls have seen before—this one's from Dad's Eighties collection. Only Sierra and I have seen it, and it enthralls the other girls. Even Sophia, but in the sort of way someone can't help but stare at what they're afraid of. She's handling it better than expected. However, the movie has definitely shifted the mood in the room darker. None of the girls are talking anymore, all staring at the screen, mesmerized.

Priya, who'd already been on edge, looks so frightened now I'm tempted to suggest they put on the *Care Bears* movie or something similar. It's probably going to take Sophia telling her the truth about a harmless ghost and/or imp in the house to convince the poor girl to set foot inside this place ever again. She has to be spiritually sensitive, similar to how Sophia was before the mystics whammied her from afar. Hmm. Telling her the truth might not be the best idea. I promised not to use my powers on my family, but my oath doesn't include school friends. Protecting secrecy is vitally important to the entire concept of my parents and siblings being able to continue existing in peace. Vampires like Stefano Bianchi and Paolo Cabrini would exploit any potential 'risk' to make trouble for me.

An instant before I reach out to nudge her so she makes eye contact with me, Priya screams and leaps to her feet, flailing her arms and staring at the spot she'd been sitting. Her sudden scream sets off Sophia, Megan, and Nicole who also scream.

Sierra cringes, and pauses the movie. "Dude… this isn't even a scary part."

"S-something pulled my hair!" Priya points at her sleeping bag.

Sophia's eyes go wide in a 'whoa, really?' expression. She stares, both hands clamped over her heart.

Megan fans herself.

"Stop lying," grumbles Nicole. "You're just trying to freak us out."

I glance around. Blix is probably being naughty. Easily frightened kids watching a scary movie is too much temptation for any imp, even one as (relatively) nice as him. He *is* still an imp, after all. Pranks are in his nature. Thankfully, he doesn't try to cause actual harm. Blix wouldn't draw blood or break bones from kids, though he'd find it funny to make them soil their pants. Oddly, I don't see him anywhere. Video game noises from upstairs tell me he's probably in Sam's room. Even though my boyfriend's kid brother Ronan has been using the mirror to go back and forth from home, it's unlikely he's here at this hour, especially on a school night.

Hmm. Maybe Blix pulled Priya's hair, maybe Klepto. Hard to say. Probably Blix being naughty.

One cheap laugh for an imp is a therapist buying a new car.

I make a show of looking around and finding nothing responsible for a hair pull.

"Did she really feel it?" asks Sophia.

"Why are you asking her?" Nicole gives me side eye. "Like she'd know."

Sierra makes a 'she really would' face, but keeps quiet.

To save the girl from therapy—and prevent her from becoming permanently scarred by our house—I dive into Priya's thoughts. She really did feel something tug on her hair. Could have been the gap between sofa cushions as easily as an imp. Whatever. It's playful and not making me concerned. I do a little tinkering in her mind to take away the fear. She is still aware our home has an 'unusual energy' to it, but after my adjustments, her opinion of the mood is reframed to be reassuring. It's kind of like setting the tare weight on a scale. She's experiencing our baseline of messed up. If something new and dark shows up, she will notice.

Sierra and Sophia both stare at me, wondering what I'm doing to their friend.

Relax guys, I say telepathically. *Priya might be slightly sensitive, psychic wise. She's aware everything isn't exactly normal here. Just helping her calm down so she's actually willing to come over a second time.*

Sophia fake-wipes sweat from her forehead.

Sierra tugs at her hair, raising an eyebrow.

Yeah. She felt something. Probably Blix, maybe the sofa cushions. Dunno.

"Girls, time for bed," calls Mom above and behind us.

All of them—except Sierra—scream.

"Can we finish watching it?" asks Sophia. "Only like a half hour left."

Mom's voice floats down the stairs. "All right, but I don't want to hear any complaining in the morning."

"Thanks!" chimes Sophia before leaning against me and whispering, "If this movie freaks me out, please help me fall asleep."

I grin. "No problem. Got'cha covered."

2

BIRTHDAY DÉJÀ VU

The thing no university brochure or recruiting department ever tells you is: college is a lot of damn work.

Some students rely on coffee. Others drink an unhealthy amount of those little energy shots. I went extreme and resorted to becoming a vampire so I could stay up all night studying. Not really… the vampire situation fell on my head unexpectedly. In the interest of full disclosure, becoming a vampire isn't something I would have voluntarily done. This isn't me complaining, merely being realistic. Based on how I used to think—trust me, I'm an expert on this since I was there—pre-vamp Sarah would have been too frightened to take the plunge.

Vampirism is like Clamato. Looks horrifying on the outside, but once you've tried it, you realize it's awesome. Okay, no, I'm kidding. My Dad likes Clamato. He's the one who said the thing about liking it only after trying something apparently horrifying. If you're not sure what Clamato is, it's tomato juice with clam juice added. Yes, someone out there has *way* too much free time on their hands to think this stuff up. Who looks at tomato juice and thinks it needs a hit of clams? Probably the same weirdo who first got the idea to try eating a lobster. Ooh, giant sea cockroach, let's cook it!

So, yeah. Even with the ability to stay up all night every night and not feel the slightest bit off the next day, school's gone into high gear and is kicking my ass. It's not taxing or frustrating me, merely sucking up a lot of time. School in general is imposing its demands on my entire family. Between the Littles' after-school activities and homework, it's amazing we still manage to be home at the same time for dinner. It's the one thing Dad really puts his foot down about. If it's any clue how serious he is about family dinner time, he's given me permission to use mind control to make the Littles stop using their phones at the table.

I haven't needed to do it, and to be honest, the four of us aren't completely sure he meant it seriously. According to my father, most of the country's problems are due to American families being fragmented and not having dinner together as a matter of routine. If you ask me, the problem is more the way money has shifted to a small concentration of people and families are forced to have both parents working full time jobs in order to survive. Not like I'm in any position to complain, though. My family's doing okay money wise. Far more so now, since a leprechaun gave me some gold.

Seriously. Yeah, I know how it sounds. Long story.

It's weird and nice to exist in a state of relative normalcy. Except for going out to bite people a few times a week and random flashes or weird sounds from Sophia's bedroom, things are almost like they'd have been if I never died. Enough time has passed to where my friend Ashley's prediction I'd have gotten too homesick being in California and come home might've come true. The main difference being night school. Only reason late classes are happening is because the sun's a fiery little bitch who hates me.

Another thing my father says is 'don't pick a fight with celestial fireballs thousands of times bigger than Earth unless you know you can win.' Kidding, he didn't say it, but he probably would if he heard me referring to the sun as an adversary. Really, though. I don't think of it as an enemy as much as an annoying, obnoxious roommate who does whatever they want and has no regard for anyone else's comfort or feelings. Sure, the sun *could* kill me, but it's kinda like a lazy assassin standing still while holding a poison dagger waiting for me to walk into it. I'd have to seriously mess up to get in its way. Big perk of being an Innocent.

Unlife's been sweet—if mundane.

Enter Thursday, April 12th.

No, it's not the apocalypse… or even Arthur Wolent having a moment. Being allied with one of Seattle's more prominent elders is both good and nerve wracking. While I am technically still Aurélie's protégé—and she's older than him—she's also a non-political figure. It's pretty rare for a vampire her age not to care about having any sort of political power or influence over the goings on, but she is content to simply be. She also happens to be friends with Wolent, making them allies I suppose. It's not a conflict for me to be involved with him. No, not like that. I'm 'involved' with him the way an employee is involved with their boss.

Grr, still sounds perverted.

Whatever. I work for him. If vampires are royalty, I'm the young kid fresh off the farm in the silly outfit who gets sent to deliver messages to other nobles. So far, I've done a handful of 'jobs' for him. All but one required me to deliver messages to other vampires in the area. Not all the meetings went off cordially, though other than being thrown in a dumpster once, I can't call them violent. It kinda scares me how Wolent's reaction to the Mercer Island crew's tossing me in the trash involved several pounds of plastic explosives. The blast itself didn't scare me… it's how I felt vindicated. Like, Wolent got *pissed* at them for being nasty to me.

So, the one job where I didn't have to deliver a message ended up being attending a social event as his representative. He even gave me a red evening gown and shoes to wear for it since they held it at this super formal banquet hall. Unofficially, of course… after hours. Talk about weird. Despite me being the youngest person in the room—both visibly and as a vampire—everyone else there treated me like an adult. Any vampire past a certain age can 'smell' newbies, so there's no way they mistook me for being older. Guess I wore Wolent's name as a badge of respect. I'd say it's awesome he trusted me for something like that, but if I'm not sugar-coating things, the meeting *was* boring as hell and largely pointless. Pretty sure he asked me to go because his more senior people would have been wasted on it.

Not complaining. Gotta start somewhere, right?

Yeah, doing vampire jobs does cut into study time, but it's not like I'm running errands every day. Seriously considering changing to an English major or something less mathy. Maybe I could write a series of 'how to' books for new vampires. Undeath really should come with an instruction manual. Could even get super meta… like publish them under the guise of fiction novels, but it's all real information. Best way to hide is in plain sight, after all. Nah. If the vampires don't kick my ass, the Persons in Black will. Stefano and Paolo would *not* appreciate me attracting attention.

Anyway, back to it being April 12th. It's Sierra's birthday. The brief period of time between March 22nd and April 12th when both my sisters are the same chronological age, is over. March-to-April is like birthday Armageddon. Sophia not long ago, Nicole Pierce—their friend from a few houses over—on April 6th. She's twelve now, too. Mom's got an aunt or something with a birthday like on April 27th or something, and Michelle—my friend—turned nineteen on April 3rd.

It totally sucked all we got to do was go out to dinner. She had to work, what with it being a Tuesday. Apparently, law firms aren't big on 'it's my birthday' as a reason to get a day off. Yay for being grown-ups. Sigh. You know what? Ashley's turning nineteen on October 7th. Still a ways off, but dammit, I'm going to throw her and Michelle in a car and surprise them by going to Chuck-E-Cheese, like a pack of kids.

Or maybe not. Sounded better in the instant. Less cool the more I think about it. Whatever. I'm going to do something fun and somewhat childish for her birthday. She'd adore it. Anyway, Dad is going overboard with 'dad-ness' today because Sierra's age is the same as the day of the month. She's turning twelve on the twelfth. Weird number things make him happy. He always points out if he looks at a digital clock at 12:34. Or weird date stuff like September 9th 2009 at 9:09:09. The man has a framed picture of the Sentra's dashboard showing the odometer at 123,456 miles. Sounds like a lot, but the car is ten years old. My friend Michelle's uncle works as a driver for a car service. His Lincoln is past 300,000 miles already and it's only five years old.

Okay, the number deal is kinda cute of him, but repeating digits in dates don't thrill me. I mean, I literally had my ex-boyfriend's severed head in my hands. Worse, *I'm* the one who ripped it off him. Takes a little more than numerical synchronicities to get my blood flowing. Perhaps it's a sign computer programming isn't what I should be studying.

Sierra's birthday always feels like déjà vu since Sophia's is so close. I'm kinda glad my sisters aren't twins, mostly because it prevents Dad from making jokes about Mom clicking the 'print' button twice instead of being patient. Okay, he *still* makes printer jokes about them, but calls it 'serious network latency.' As in the second 'copy' of a girl child didn't print out for almost a year.

Sigh. Nerds, right?

Myself included. I have to admit to laughing the first time I heard it.

And really, why *do* people click the button like 500 times if their document doesn't print?

In another moment of déjà vu, Sierra's birthday *also* falls on a Thursday this year. Unlike Sophia, Sierra doesn't go out of her way to make friends. She's content playing with herself. Whoa. Ack. I mean PlayStation. Gah! That *totally* didn't sound right. Good grief. I mean, she is perfectly content with her own company. The girl isn't antisocial as much as she doesn't feel like she needs to surround herself with a crowd of friends to feel validated as a person… or something. I remember her having school friends over like once or twice. Mostly, she hangs out with Nicole and Sophia, and now Megan and Priya.

Sam and the boys are at Darryl's house. It's like boys have this deep primal instinct to flee the scene whenever too many females gather, like they sense the estrogen and don't want to be caught up in whatever powerful supernatural forces we unleash. Maybe seventy-five percent of the time, Sam and his friends hang out here. They did the same thing on Sophia's birthday, too. No sign of a little boy for miles around the house until bedtime—unless Dad counts.

Speaking of Dad, he's scrambling to finish a section of his work project by the deadline. Today is pretty similar to Sophia's birthday. Right after school, Mom took the girls out. Since it's Sierra's day, they're going to the VR gaming place instead of the Chuck-E-Cheese. Sierra's not a clothes horse or a mall rat, so it's anyone's guess if they'll wind up at the mall after. With the Littles being a bit older now, rather than get a birthday present ahead of time and wrap it, the 'rents take them out somewhere to buy a reasonable gift. The 'big stuff' waits for Christmas. They figure doing it this way prevents disappointment. It also ruins any joyful surprise, but no one gets something they aren't interested in. Besides, getting the gift you've been dropping none-too-subtle hints about for weeks isn't exactly a surprise either. The Littles haven't figured it out yet (though maybe Sam has) but I believe the 'rents budget a certain amount for each kid's 'gifts' per year, and whatever we get for our birthday comes out of our Christmas haul.

So yeah… I've got the house to myself, except for Dad. So, no wild parties for this girl.

As if.

The universe has a painful sense of irony. Of all the kids in my high school class, I think I'm perhaps the only one who could've gotten away with throwing a house-trashing party while the parents went away for a weekend and *not* ended up permanently grounded. All I'd have to do is wear the *Risky Business* underwear plus sunglasses or make a *Ferris Bueller* reference and Dad would love it. He'd see me as recreating some of his favorite movies. High school kid throws wild party in the parents' absence is totally Eighties, right?

Mom, however, would not be pleased.

The irony comes in where I'm totally not the sort of person to throw parties like that. Probably why the Universe let me have the parent who wouldn't lose their mind. Between my 'rents, I'd most likely be required to do all the clean-up myself and wouldn't get in *too* much trouble as long as nothing irreplaceable broke. Can't do it now with my new friends. If a party involving vampires gets wild, walls come down. Besides, the wild party thing doesn't fit my schedule anymore.

After grabbing a shower, I spend a few hours doing homework and researching another damned paper I have to write… and lose track of time. I'm still wrapped in a towel when the house above me fills with tween girl squeals. My vampire powers do not include the ability to see through solid ceilings/floors, but I can assume Klepto did something unbearably cute based on the tone of the voices. Maybe curled up on the arm of the sofa with her paws in the air.

It's been a while since Sophia made the kitten, and she hasn't gotten any bigger yet. Either Klepto is not going to change, or she's somehow linked to my sister, growing up at a more human pace. Doesn't really matter to me either way. I'm sure Sophia wouldn't object to having a perma-kitten either.

"Sarah," says Mom from the kitchen doorway. She's on the opposite side of the basement at the top of the stairs and speaking at a normal volume since she knows I can hear her. "We're going out for Sierra's birthday dinner. You are planning to join us, right?"

My mother does not have vampire hearing, so there's no point in me replying. Even screaming, she still couldn't understand me from this distance behind a closed door. Hmm. Birthday dinner… I throw on a nice but not overly fancy turquoise dress, grab the matching flats from my closet, and head upstairs. Sierra is not a big fan of dresses, but she's less a fan of formal boys' clothing. Whenever we have to go somewhere 'nice,' she suffers a dress. Sophia had her birthday dinner home, by request. It's honestly kind of strange Sierra didn't make the same request since she wouldn't have had to put on a dress for it. Maybe she wants to give the parents a break from having to cook?

Mom's in the kitchen when I emerge from the basement stairs. It's uncomfortably light out, but what's a little mild incineration for my sister's birthday? At least it's not *so* bright smoke's peeling off me. My mother's on the phone. From the sound of it, she's telling Sam to come home ASAP so we can go out to eat. She sees me 'dressed up' and nods once in acknowledgement. Sophia, who lives in dresses, is already prepared for dinner. One by one, Sierra, Megan, Nicole, and Priya come downstairs in dresses nice enough to go to a restaurant where people get kicked out for wearing T-shirts. I'm sure they didn't go to the VR place like that, so the girls must've brought a change of clothes with them.

The 'rents can't help but smile at Sierra, but they manage not to say anything. She's uncomfortable enough as it is. Mom and Dad let her do her own thing fashion wise, but they don't hide how happy they are when she impersonates a girl. No, it's nothing deeply psychological. My sister is a major slacker. She hates dressing 'nice' for anything, even her own birthday. Sometimes, I think the girl popped out of the womb already in a T-shirt and jeans. If we'd been kids in the Sixties, Sierra totally would've gone full hippie.

Only, she wouldn't have liked the Sixties. No video games.

"All right, see you soon," says Mom. She drops her cell phone in her purse and walks into the living room where the rest of us are waiting. "As soon as your brother is home and changed, we'll go."

The girls nod.

"Jonathan?" calls Mom.

Dad emerges from his office wearing cargo shorts and a tuxedo-printed T-shirt.

The girls burst into laughter.

Mom frowns.

"Not formal enough?" Dad pretends to grab the lapels of the fake tuxedo.

Mom taps her foot.

Sam rumbles down the stairs. He stops short at the bottom, still in a T-shirt and jeans, sees us, and blinks. "Who's funeral? And is Dad supposed to be a birthday clown?"

"We're going to a nice place." Mom makes a shooing gesture at Dad. "Go change to something nice."

"Umm." Nicole points at him. "How did he get here so fast?"

Priya and Megan stare at him in awe.

Ack!

I jump in front of the girls and… crap. My powers are offline. Can't force them not to pay attention to Sam being in the house literally two minutes after hanging up the phone. "He was already walking home when Mom called. He's messing with us."

"Oh." Priya nods, then laughs at Sam.

He and Dad hurry upstairs to change.

Mom presses her hand to her forehead. "That man…"

"Would have been worth it to see the look on the restaurant guy's face when he tried to go in wearing a fake tuxedo shirt," mutters Sierra.

The other girls snicker. Mom sighs again.

SAM PUT ON A BUTTON-DOWN SHIRT AND DRESS PANTS, BUT HE SKIPPED socks.

Dad cracked *Miami Vice* jokes the whole ride to the restaurant. When we arrive at Shogun West in Kenmore, it makes sense to me why Sierra is not complaining about wearing a dress. She's a huge fan of anime, and by extension, all things Japanese. She's not a weeb, but we don't often get to go out for Hibachi, so when she had the choice of where to eat, it took her all of a half-second to come up with this. Dad's a fan, too. Mom gets nervous around the flashing knives and open flame. Last time we had hibachi, I'd been alive. Come to think of it, the big blast of flames might be uncool. Hopefully, with me expecting it, I won't have a vampiric panic attack.

I'm still gonna have dinner here. This food's too good not to.

The nine of us neatly fill one hibachi table. Since we don't have to wait for total strangers to take the last few seats this time (thanks to us bringing three extra kids) it's not long before the chef pushes his cart over to us and introduces himself as Jimmy. There's about as much chance of the guy's name actually being Jimmy as Sierra re-enlisting in the Girl Scouts. Is 'enlist' the right word? They're pretty militant about cookie sales, but I'm not sure they take things *that* far.

Predictably, 'Jimmy' sizes us up for the prank soy sauce bottle. I'm safe, since I'm not the youngest female at the table. Hibachi chefs tend to 'attack' the guest they think will have the most extreme reaction to a fake squirt of soy sauce (black yarn). Sam's not significantly younger enough than any of the girls to stand out. My money's on Priya or Sophia. Priya's got a generalized air of nervousness around her all the time. Sophia, well... she's Sophia.

After his warm up routine spinning a spatula around and preparing the grill, Jimmy makes his way around everyone at the table confirming our orders. Chicken and shrimp for me. Dad, of course, gets the filet. Sierra opts for full shrimp. The other kids all get chicken. Mom ordered steak and chicken. The smells in here are going to drive me insane—good insane.

Sure enough, when the time comes for soy sauce, Jimmy grabs the fake bottle and thrusts it at Sophia as if he's squirting it all over her. Also, predictably, she squeals and almost jumps out of her chair. Once she realizes she's not covered in soy sauce, she fake-laughs, though it looks like she wants to cry. The instant she notices a bunch of other people looking at her, she blushes.

A few minutes later, the guy stacks up a bunch of onion pieces to form a 'volcano.' He squirts oil in, then a boatload of sake. I brace myself for the moment he lights it and sets off a huge blast of flames. The fire, I'm ready for. The fire being bright neon green, not so much. Fortunately, no one notices me jump back and yell 'whoa' because everyone at our table does it, too.

Even Jimmy stops in his tracks, staring at the jet of lime colored flames shooting out of the top of the onion volcano.

I shoot a look at Sophia. Revenge?

She holds her hands up innocently, shaking her head in a 'wasn't me' gesture.

Dammit. I start looking around, wondering what sort of paranormal cheesedickery is about to come my way. Not sure how I'd explain having to fight an udon demon in front of fifty witnesses. Blasts of neon green fire kinda feel like something a Japanese monster would use as an entrance, right?

Don't see anything obvious... the screams of terror haven't started yet.

So, hibachi cooking takes a lot of training and is highly ritualized, but it doesn't usually rip open a breach in the planar boundaries. Something else must be going on here. Aha! I spot Blix perched on Sam's shoulder giving 'Jimmy' the finger. Whew. We're not under attack. Blix is taking revenge for him scaring Sophia. Great, if shrimp start crawling around on the cooking surface, the chef is going to snap.

Everyone, Jimmy included, appears to decide the bright green fire didn't really happen and proceeds to continue with dinner as normal. Blix hops down to sit in Sam's lap and occasionally swipes bits of food from his plate. The boy doesn't seem to mind. Neither does anyone else, primarily because the imp is invisible to them. Sam can see him, as can Sophia. Priya keeps giving Sam odd looks. The lack of screaming tells me she can't *see* Blix, but does sense something odd.

Dad leans close to Sierra and whispers, "Want them to do the birthday stuff? I know you think it's embarrassing."

"Yeah, but it's not as bad here like the other place with the stupid saddle thing. If you and Mom want pictures, go ahead. I'll deal." Sierra smiles at him.

"Your choice, hon." Dad pats her on the shoulder.

"Go for it. You'll enjoy having the pictures when I'm grown up."

He sighs, gets misty-eyed, and pulls her into a hug.

Once we're done with our meals, the restaurant staff goes 'birthday crazy.' This involves flashing lights, loud music, and a crew putting weird glasses studded with blinking green lights on Sierra. They also sing a bizarre rock music version of happy birthday. Yes, she blushes, but doesn't hide her face the way Sophia would totally do in the same situation.

Mom looks impressed.

Darn. My near miss with death has made my kid sister aware of the concept of her own mortality, or at least how she's going to grow up and the parents will be alone. She's tolerating this for the pictures so Mom and Dad will have memories. It should make me feel a little maudlin, but my only thought is: 'dammit, I hope they survive to adulthood.'

And it's got nothing to do with the crazy world, school shooters, or whatever else. My anxiety is entirely based on paranormal stuff. Maybe becoming a vampire has made *me* keenly aware of how close we all are to losing everything, and it's not my mere existence putting my family in danger. I argue with myself all the time over staying home instead of going away. There has to be some reason vampires, as a matter of tradition, allow their mortal families to assume them dead.

Oh, right. Ancient people burned things they didn't understand. That'll do it.

Couple centuries ago, if I'd have gone home to my parents and told them I'd become a vampire, they'd have tried to kill me. Society has become a lot more progressive in terms of undead tolerance. We haven't quite gotten to the 'go out openly in public' level yet. Not sure anyone's even trying. Revealing actual proof of supernatural beings would totally freak people out. I mean, we still have potatoes out there who think the Earth is flat. Tell them vampires are real? They'd probably spontaneously combust.

I grin at the look on Sierra's face. The manager's standing behind her, swaying side to side with her while singing. Those light-up glasses are completely ridiculous, as are a dozen restaurant workers all singing in different keys to music so loud we can barely hear any of them. Other diners join in, clapping along with the incomprehensible words. At least the melody reveals it as 'happy birthday.' The 'rents take a bunch of pictures with their phones. A woman in a kimono snaps one of Sierra using an actual camera (as opposed to a phone)… and she gets a take-home ceramic 'shogun.' It's a bizarre sort of 'glass' they normally serve alcoholic drinks in, but they gave her a Shirley Temple on the house.

Yeah, it's cheesy as hell, but sometimes, the best memories are.

3

SHADOW POLITICS

Mondays have been the bane of human existence since the advent of the day job.

First world problems, amirite? Not only does Monday bring the dreaded end of the weekend, it bears another inevitable reality… at least in Sophia's case: dance class. Dad and I did rock-paper-scissors for choice. He took Sam and Sierra to taekwondo. Mom got stuck late at work—prepping to defend against a lawsuit—so I'm driving Sophia to the studio.

It's not a 'Monday' thing for my sister. She adores the class. Her new magical pursuits may or may not interfere with how long she keeps at it. Sophia never had any plans to try 'going pro' as a dancer, or aspirations of becoming any sort of star working on Broadway or in music videos or whatever. She might stop going once she's in high school and has more of a demand on her time from homework. Then again, for the same reason Sierra likes sword lessons, Sophia might keep with dance to stay flexible. She did dodge imp attacks like a pro.

I take a seat among the parents. The two cougars are in the front row, having coffee and chatting about their pool boy fantasy plus an annoying neighbor who evidently thinks eleven at night is an awesome time to do yard work with power tools while singing in off-key Spanish to whatever music is playing on his headphones. Ugh. I've brought my biology book to catch up on reading while the class runs. Probably won't finish the chapter I need to review before the class is over. No big deal. I'm making the most of my time.

No way could any meaningful reading happen at the taekwondo place. *Way* too loud. Sure, they play music here sometimes, but it's much easier to tune out music than a crowd of tweens and younger children screaming their heads off. Screaming occasionally happens here, too… but only when one of the kids takes a spill or the instructors announce a new recital in the works.

Before I know it, Sophia is standing politely beside me, waiting for me to notice her.

"Over already?" I ask.

"Yeah. Must be a good book."

"Ehh. More heavy than good. It's dense and takes a lot of concentration."

"Oh. School stuff?"

"Yeah." I stand, pack up, and follow her to the exit.

Sophia pauses at the door to look both ways before venturing out into the parking lot.

I raise an eyebrow. "Expecting a speeding golf cart to come wheeling at us down the sidewalk?"

"No, hipster vampires," she deadpans.

"It's still light out."

"Oh, duh." She fans herself. "Sorry, out of breath and a little loopy."

"You okay?"

"Yeah. Every time we're here, I remember those idiots." Sophia heads around to the passenger door of the Sentra.

I sigh. "Sorry."

"Not your fault. *You* didn't do anything. Eleanor's bad and Dalton made a mistake." Sophia swipes her hair off her face. "I put all the blame for my mental scars on Eleanor."

She makes it sound almost cute, but I can't laugh. Eleanor St. Ives is still on my bad list. Doesn't mean anything more than 'avoid at all costs.' I'm not the sort of vampire to hold grudges or want revenge.

I've seen enough Eighties movies to know where a drive for vengeance leads—lame sequels. It's an endless cycle. Bad guy does something, good guy exacts revenge. Bad guy takes revenge for the revenge, and before you know it, Jean Claude VanDamme is getting his ass kicked, then there's a training montage, and more ass kicking in the other direction. Of course, the win results in more revenge, but they have to squeeze it into another whole movie.

On the ride home, I try to reassure Sophia that Eleanor St. Ives has no reason to come after me. As far as I know, Dalton hasn't stolen anything else she wants, I haven't relocated any other mummified remains, and my nose has been far away from her business. Except for Wolent sending me around as his messenger and Aurélie taking me to those fancy soirees, my involvement in the vampire world is as minimal as possible. I'm keeping a low profile to protect my family, but also because I'm not a fan of social politics. I hated it in high school and it's not appealing to me in vampiredom either.

"... and she's an Academic. The woman has zero emotional investment in anything. As soon as doing anything no longer offers her measurable benefit, she stops wanting to do it."

"Weird." Sophia exhales. "So even though you guys stole the spyglass thing from her *and* didn't give her Coralie, she doesn't care about you anymore?"

"Ugh. No. Dalton didn't steal the spyglass *from her*. He stole it from this other guy who owns a night club. She wanted it, but we didn't give it to her."

Sophia blinks. "She got mad at you for not giving her something stolen from someone else when it wasn't even hers?"

"Yep. Well, not mad. She simply wanted it and harassed us while I had the thing. Since Wolent's got it now, she has no reason or desire to bother me."

My sister seems slightly reassured, though she can't quite understand how someone can be like St. Ives and operate purely on logic and cost-benefit analysis. The scientist type Academics are creepy as hell, basically like AI androids. Mystical Academics go the other way... pretty much all eccentric or straight up nuts.

Great. Now I'm going to spend the rest of April worrying about Sophia going nuts. The mortal mystics of the Aurora Aurea didn't seem too crazy. Little offbeat, but not nuts. At least not the 'nuts' the way Aurélie described vampire mystics. Or 'mystic' rather. She only knew of one. Maybe I shouldn't assume they're *all* bonkers because of one dude who acted like Merlin on lab-grade LSD.

Sophia runs inside as soon as we get home.

This is one of those annoying moments where I have too much time before class to leave for school right away, but not enough time to really do anything. It's about quarter after six, and today's English lit from seven to ten. Once-a-week classes are a slog. According to my phone, sunset is going to happen at 7:57 p.m. Grr. Means I have to drive in. Can't even say 'first world problems' complaining about having to drive instead of fly.

Screw it. Can't do much with like twelve minutes. Might as well go to class now. I run inside to grab my books and hug the family, then head back to the car.

Oh, drat. Need gas. Maybe those twelve minutes *will* come in handy.

WITH SUFFICIENT MOTIVATION, PEOPLE CAN DO A LOT IN FIFTEEN minutes.

One thing I can accomplish in fifteen minutes—during a class break—is head to an adjacent building and grab a quick snack. The second break happens after dark. If I can find someone to bite here, it'll give me more time for homework after class lets out. People don't tend to sit outside alone once it's dark, which forces me to be a little creative. Really hate following people into the bathroom, so I avoid it whenever possible. Rather take twenty minutes out of my night after class than develop a mental association between toilets and eating. Trust me, public bathrooms are ten times worse when you've got a vampiric sense of smell.

Luck is with me tonight. I catch a dude sprinting down a hallway, likely late for a class. Sorry, man… need a few minutes of your time. He stops short as I basically crash into him while pretending to be lost and ask where Room 401 is. Before he can process the question, I'm in his head and encouraging him to follow me into a dark space between vending machines in the nearest lounge room. His blood hits me over the head like a giant meatball Hot Pocket. No time to ponder what about this guy made me conjure the flavor. He's in a rush, and I have a time limit. Maybe the flavor of Hot Pockets came from being in a hurry?

When I'm done feeding, I buy him a candy bar from one of the machines and send him on his way, giving him the urge to munch on it. Still dunno why blood donation places always give out orange juice and cookies, but there's gotta be something to it.

The instant I step out of the other building, a weird sense of ominous dread falls over me. My English class is half a block away from here. Even though the world doesn't appear dark to me, looking at the mostly deserted street fills me with the same sort of dread mortal me would have felt about walking anywhere alone at night in the city.

I hate it. I *really* hate feeling scared and vulnerable. It pissed me off as a mortal, but couldn't do much about it other than travel in packs, take karate, or carry a gun—the second two options never ended up happening. This present fear has no basis in reality. Which means one of two things is happening… either something supernatural is bearing down on me, or something supernatural is forcibly changing my emotional state. Okay, option three: I'm still sleeping and this is a dream.

No, not the vampire thing. Going to class now. But, can't be. Class had too much detail.

I slow my stride to spite the fear and look around. The mood changes to one of ambient hostility. An urge to turn the other way draws my attention to a pale woman in a dark blue top and shiny black leggings lurking at the corner of the building. She's part runway model, part porcelain-skinned psychopath. As soon as we make eye contact, I recognize her: Petra Stanovaya.

This bitch is the exact opposite of Eleanor St. Ives. Petra *will* carry a grudge. She'll rent a 700-square foot storage space for her grudge and never be late on a rent payment. We *did* try to kill each other. The only thing keeping her off me is a threat from Glim—and the Shadows—to shred her if she bothers me. Our truce didn't explicitly forbid menacing glares from fifty yards away, though.

Still, it's unusual to see her sapphire-eyed rage coming out of nowhere.

Shit. Now what? Something happened.

Screw it. Hopefully, she doesn't realize the strength and speed I had when we last tore each other apart came from Dante, a local Lost One who loaned me a bit of his fury. Vampires can give each other temporary use of some powers unique to certain bloodlines. Furies can give greater strength. Academics can let people borrow whatever weird powers they have, like turning into wolves or whatever. Aurélie could loan me charm powers from hell if she ever wanted to. Me? I let Glim drink beer sometimes. I can share the ability to tolerate food. That's me. Total badass.

Not complaining. Honest. Just poking fun at myself.

Petra has to have figured out by now I'm an Innocent, thus zero threat. Then again, this is a woman who considers the gradual ruination of someone's life to be art. She wouldn't hesitate tormenting anyone because they're weak or (comparatively) helpless. It's not a contest of strength for her at all. She adores the emotional destruction that comes along with destroying someone's entire world.

In short, she's a sick bitch.

She's also proof people can't judge anything by appearances. Petra looks like a French runway model or a Hollywood actress. Early twenties, sleek. Black hair and piercing dark blue eyes. She *appears* pretty and harmless. If the Universe had any sense of justice, she'd be so hideous, Shadows would say *daaaaaamn.*

Don't have time for her BS now. But… I'm not turning my back on her. Only one thing to do here. I march over to her. Her reaction is to fold her arms and smirk at me. Yeah, she's totally vibing like the popular cheerleader about to get all snooty and condescending at the nerd she's bullying. Only, I'm a stealth nerd. Never got picked on in school because I didn't 'look' like a nerd. Dad says we're more geeks than nerds. Nerds go to college at age fourteen and save poor countries from drought by age sixteen.

"Petra." I nod an insincere greeting. "Don't really have time for anything at the moment. Need to get back to class. Are you looking for me or is this a Marcellus Wallace moment?"

She blinks, evidently caught off guard. "What? Who's Wallace?"

"Never saw *Pulp Fiction*?" I raise an eyebrow. "Dude sitting in a car, just happens to see the guy he wants to kill walking in front of him by chance?"

"Oh. No. I am not here by chance." She unfolds her arms, tea-kettling her left hand on her hip, other one pointing at me. "I'm here for you."

Sigh. "What for? We have no further business."

"Playing dumb? At least stick to what you're good at."

"Seriously. I have no idea why you would possibly be looking for me."

She narrows her eyes. A little tingle at the front of my brain says she's trying to read my mind but can't get in. The gap in our age isn't quite big enough, but it's close. Hah. Perfect. She will never be able to read my mind. Might come in handy someday, but at the moment, I truly am baffled. "The attack?"

I hold my hands up. "The last thing I'd ever think of doing is starting a fight with a vampire turned in 1920. If someone attacked you, I had nothing to do with it."

She jabs her finger into my chest. "Don't play me for a fool. I know you've joined Wolent's little social club. Since you're one of 'his people,' he sent some palookas to my home."

"Umm. He never said anything about it to me. How am I responsible for what he does? Even if it *was* him, which I doubt, I never asked anyone to act against you."

Petra folds her arms again.

I fold my arms as well. There. Take that. "Yeah, I object to you keeping guys as pets and trashing innocent people's lives, but we came to an agreement to pretend each other doesn't exist. I don't want the headache it would cause to start messing with you."

"You expect me to believe this?"

"Yes, assuming you care about actual truth and aren't just imagining an attack as an excuse to come after me for revenge." I thrust my arms out to either side. "Ask any Shadow. They'll know."

"Oh, of course. They're on your side and will say whatever you want them to."

I facepalm. "Ugh. Really? Are you serious? You're over a hundred years old and don't understand? I've figured it out already and I'm two months short of a full year as a"—I drop my voice to a whisper—"vampire."

"What are you rattling on about?"

"Shadows. They aren't on *my* side. *Glim* is on my side. *One* Shadow is my friend. He made an arrangement. If I broke it by attacking you, all the other Shadows in Seattle would be pissed at me and hold him responsible for me breaking the agreement. He'd get in a crapload of trouble, and I can't do that to him even if I was stupid enough to pick another fight with you. Seriously. I did not do anything."

She stares at me.

"What happened, anyway?"

"As if you don't know."

Sigh. "Whatever. I'm going to be late for class. If you want to keep brooding at me, I should be done by ten. Can we pick this up later?"

"Four vampires showed up at my house several nights ago. They broke in and caused a significant amount of damage, left several threatening notes warning me it would become worse if I didn't leave you alone."

Say what? I gawk. "Uhh, seriously, Petra. I had nothing at all to do with it. Unless you've been up to something I haven't noticed yet, you *have* been leaving me alone. Why would I risk setting off a crapstorm? You know the situation with my family. It makes zero sense whatsoever for me to antagonize you, or ask someone to antagonize you on my behalf. Not only does it put my family at risk, it would get the Shadows pissed at me, probably infuriate Wolent, too... and Aurélie would lose her mind."

Petra cringes ever so slightly at the mention of her name. Heh. Aurélie is another case of appearances being deceitful. She looks delicate, harmless, and innocent. While she *is* nice, she's not harmless... and she is certainly *not* innocent—in any sense of the word.

Jealousy seethes behind Petra's deep blue irises. She glares at me the way the schoolyard bully looks at their victim when the teacher's standing right next to them and they can't do anything. She totally hates me having Aurélie's protection. "You are wrong about one thing there, girl. Wolent wouldn't object. You forget how much contempt he has for those outside his circle."

Oh, right. She's a Sybarite, not literally a Lost One, but she acts like them, stays outside the political scene, considering herself above it. Honestly, someone as warped as her wouldn't be welcome among the other vampires.

"Look..." I raise a 'hang on a sec' hand at her. "I understand you're angry and jumping to conclusions, but anyone could have done it and left messages to set off a problem. Any of them would be concerned about someone who causes destruction and risks attracting attention to our existence."

She scoffs. "I am hardly a brute leaving a trail of corpses in alleys."

"No. You're not. You are highly intelligent and methodical in what you do. But... sooner or later, someone might start wondering why so many people in a particular area commit suicide."

"My dear, Seattle's got a reputation for that already." She examines her fingernails as if to imply it's her doing.

"Pointing the finger at me is a weird twist, but maybe it's someone who wants *me* dead and they're trying to use you to do it."

She keeps tapping her foot.

Argh. Time running out. "I really have to get back. If I kicked in someone's door and wrote your name on the wall, would it prove you sent me? Stop and think. Someone who knows about both of us is trying to stir some crap, but it isn't me."

She fixes me with a stare. "You… are either quite skilled at lying or telling the truth."

"I'm a horrible liar."

"Firebombs through my windows. Only minor damage… this time."

I exhale. "Someone's messing with me, too. Maybe those LA vampires. Only people I can really think of who'd want to send you after me like a guided missile. Look, if you won't rip my head off for making contact, I'll let you know if I find out who attacked you and why."

Petra looks me up and down. She doesn't seem thrilled, but nods once. "All right."

As soon as she starts walking away, I hurry in the other direction. Hopefully, no one notices me zoom by way faster than people can run. For a moment, the only thought on my mind is getting back to class before I'm late. Alas, I *am* late, but only by like thirty seconds. Professor Kendall hasn't even resumed teaching yet. Four other students arrive after me, so whew. I'm not the one who'll stand out in his mind as being late.

After melting into my seat, it occurs to me I've made a deal with the devil. Or at least with his little sister. Well, maybe not a *deal*. Any conversation with Petra Stanovaya that doesn't end in blood flying everywhere feels like I've compromised my morals. Ugh. I am *way* too nice. How can I be civil with such an evil person?

Oh, right. I don't want my family to end up slaughtered. Also, if I initiate crap with her, it puts Glim on the outs with other Shadows. Not sure exactly how their internal politics works. Maybe they'd only give him a big, creepy frown. Regardless, he's a friend who's gone out of his way for me multiple times. If not for him, Petra would have destroyed me. No way am I going to be reckless and ruin his standing with his 'people.'

Don't even want to think about what sort of vampiric shitstorm would roll over Seattle if I started a fight. Maybe not so bad considering Petra's outside 'polite society.' Most of the vamps who attend the soirees don't have high regard for Lost Ones. Some even call the ones who reject ordered society 'anarchists' because they're not all from one bloodline. There are even a handful of legit Lost Ones who go to the meetings. As long as any fighting doesn't draw the attention of mortals to vampires, the elders probably wouldn't care at all if someone got into a fight with the anarchists. However, they don't consider me a 'baby' anymore, Stefano and Paolo aside. Baby in the sense of how kids can do stupid stuff and get away with it for not knowing any better. I'm 'official' enough now to be held responsible for whatever I do.

It's kind of like being in the Mafia—or at least my impression of them from watching movies. My actions reflect on Wolent. Even if he had nothing to do with my screw up, he'd be blamed for 'not being able to control me' if I stepped out of line. If someone is out there trying to make it look like I'm 'shit-stirring,' things are going to get ugly.

Grr.

Paying attention in English lit is difficult enough during a three-hour class when I'm *not* worrying about who is trying to set me up. Obviously, my first thought is Stefano. He thinks I'm a disrespectful brat for no reason other than I decided to stay with my mortal family and bring them in on the secret of vampires. Kinda hard to live there and not share such an important detail. It would make it really hard to explain why I needed to move my bedroom into the basement and someone would accidentally give me a face full of sunlight. Makes no sense to me why he's got such a bug up his butt about it.

Then again, some people are mortally offended at the mere existence of LGBTQ people. No, I'm not claiming to be anywhere near as vulnerable or oppressed as them. Just saying how random and stupid it is for Stefano to have such a problem with me when my existence has absolutely zero impact on his unlife. It's like having a meltdown someone ahead of him in line at Subway ordered a turkey sub because he doesn't like turkey.

Question is, is he so fanatic about his idiocy he'd try to trick Petra into killing me? Whoever did it knows enough about me to understand the issue I had with her months ago. They'd have to also understand she isn't really the 'hands on, claws out' type of vampire. She'd destroy my family—and everything I love or even like—slowly over months, driving me to the point of self-destruction. While I doubt Stefano or Paolo would shed any tears if I decided to fling myself into the sun, it's a little too cruel and involved for them to use Petra as a weapon. As traditionalists, they certainly wouldn't lose any sleep over Petra being destroyed since she is outside 'society.'

Maybe I'm thinking about this wrong. What if it isn't *me* someone's trying to get rid of? If Petra lashed out at me, both the Shadows and Aurélie would be after her blood. Neither Stefano nor Paolo would bat an eyelash at sacrificing me to destroy a more important vampire they didn't like. They might be doing this to set *her* up to be potentially destroyed by Aurélie. However, back to her being outside society. Unless she is attracting the attention of vampire hunters, they'd have no reason to care about her enough to do this.

Argh! So frustrating. Deep breaths. Okay, Sarah. Find Zen. Put this issue aside for now. Pay attention in class and stop wasting Mom and Dad's money.

Learn now, vampire political BS later.

4

DARE

I mentally give a middle finger to the Universe.

Not only is some strange vampire political crap going on that's probably going to end with blood on the ground, Professor Kendall hits me with another writing assignment. At least this one isn't a presentation in front of the class. Gotta do a research paper on the contributions of a major author or poet of the nineteenth or twentieth century. We can choose the person to write about under two conditions: they have to be dead now and also a big deal.

Might as well do Poe… or Mary Shelley. Half the class is probably going to do Shakespeare. Writing about him has to be the English lit version of playing *Stairway to Heaven* in a guitar shop. Professor Kendall must be sick to death of reading about William Shakespeare. He's probably also kinda worn out on Poe, too, but whatever. He said the writer has to be a big deal. Obviously, most students are going to go for big names. Mary Shelley basically invented science fiction. Can't do Jane Austen, too old. Tolkien? Maybe. Ray Bradbury? Hmm. My junior year teacher in high school English had a serious hardon for Ray Bradbury. We spent a whole month dissecting *Fahrenheit 451.*

Good book, but after putting it under a microscope so much, I'm sick to death of it.

I wander back to the parking garage, tossing author names around in my head.

It's distracting to let my thoughts drift. Way too much so for me to have ever done as a mortal walking alone in the dark. A young woman has to pay attention to her surroundings at all time. It sucks *so* much, but it's true. Anyway, the parade of famous author names circling around in my head is so distracting I don't notice the creep coming for me until after he's tackled me to the floor.

My brain goes blank for a second at the sheer audacity. This guy's about to get a rude surprise. Guess it's true what the cop said during the presentation he gave at my old school. A woman who looks like an easy target unaware of her surroundings ends up being targeted.

A second man darts over and grabs my legs as the dude who tackled me shifts his weight and tries to grab my arms.

"Hurry it up," whispers Leg Man. "Stefano wants it clean and permanent."

In an instant, I go from annoyed to freaking out. These are *not* garden-variety creeps.

Snarling, I wrench my arm loose, twist myself over, and slug the guy hovering over me in the side of the head with everything I have. A wet *crunch* accompanies my knuckles mashing into his head in front of his left ear. He goes flying off to the side like a human torpedo. His head not exploding proves he's a vampire. We're a little bit tougher.

Leg Man looks up, startled. He gives me this cocky smirk and grabs my throat, pinning me to the concrete. Growling, I extend my claws, sink all ten of them into his upper arm, and rake downward, using his whole arm as a scratching post. He lets off a horrible scream like I'd clamped a red-hot waffle iron closed on his nether bits. Yeah, vampire claws *sting*. It's worse than lemon juice and salt in a paper cut lit on fire.

He goes limp, in momentary shock from the unexpected agony. I take the opportunity to throw him off me and scramble to my feet. By the time I swipe my claws at his face, he's recovered enough awareness to duck. The dude's maybe late twenties. Undead pale, longish hair. A leather jacket and jeans make him look like he ought to be playing bass for a band who graduated high school six years ago but still hasn't played a gig larger than the bar down the street from where they live—because his parents' friend owns it.

Head smash guy is wearing a MASH-era olive drab Army jacket, also longish hair. He hasn't tried to get back up yet. Either he's finding the concrete floor tasty or I hammered him hard enough to knock him senseless. Good chance my middle finger broke, so his skull is likely cracked.

Leg Dude stares at me, specifically my claws, making a face like someone seeing the monster in a horror movie face to face for the first time. He doesn't seem to understand some vampires have claws. Got a little blood on my shirt, but nowhere near as much as a normal person would bleed from such a wound. I basically shredded ten two-inch-long razor blades all the way down his arm. One sleeve of his leather jacket has become a fringe skirt wrapped around strips of loose flesh. Vampires like blood. We don't like bleeding. Our blood tends to pool in wounds and not fall out unless the wound is huge—like decapitation or a severed leg.

"What's Stefano doing?" I ask, glaring at Leg Dude.

His friend moans, gradually pushing himself up onto his knees. "Get her."

Leg Dude hisses in pain. The flesh strips, formerly his muscles, twitch in response to his attempt to move the limb, but they twist around like a drunken octopus who forgot how to work his tentacles. That is nasty as hell. I cringe away.

"What the shit is this?" yells Leg Dude, gesturing at me with his remaining functional arm. "You didn't tell me she's got freakin' *claws.*"

The other guy swivels to look at me. I cratered the side of his head. Bone fragments stick out the skin of the opposite cheek. Blood dribbles from both his ears. A dimple the size of my fist remains on the left side of his head, which seems visibly concave. Yeah, his whole skull has to be cracked inside like a hard-boiled egg dropped on the floor. It's astonishing the guy's not unconscious. Can't be much actual brain damage if he's still sorta awake. He's about halfway between comatose and flat earther, far from counting as entirely conscious. The only way to knock a vampire out cold is to do enough penetrating damage to the brain to kill a mortal. We get back up from it, but it can take a few hours. Heck, even decapitation doesn't kill us. It's seriously annoying though.

"Tell me what Stefano is doing or I'm going to rip your little vampire off and stuff it down your throat."

Totally graphic and over the top, yeah, but I have no intention of doing it. Three quarters of intimidation is talking a good game. They don't have to know I'm too squeamish to follow through. Mashed-Head rushes at me in the wobbly gait of a drunk at a bar fight. He's fast and strong, but still loopy from the head wound. The punch he throws for my face probably would've missed if I stood still, making it easy to slip under it and rake my claws down his back, shredding the heavy material of his Army coat easily. He shrieks in pain, whipping back at me with an elbow I'm a little too slow to fully avoid.

The glancing shot knocks me on my ass without doing serious damage.

Both guys sprint across the parking garage and dive over the side. Considering this is the third floor, I'm guessing they can fly. Part of me is too lazy to chase them since it could take hours. Another part of me is worried about bait goblins. Either those two guys are as new at vampire as I am, or they're acting like fools, pretending to be clueless, so I chase them into some kind of trap.

I look down at my shirt. Not so much blood it won't wash out with enough effort. I sacrifice a moment to feeling proud of myself for walking away from a fight without my clothing ending up in tatters. Vampire combat is not friendly to fabric. Speaking of which… I retract my claws before anyone happens to walk by and notice me. They're a bit long and pointy to pass off as a tragic false nail mishap. No one would believe me if I said I got fake nails from Wish.

Yeah, I don't buy it. Me kicking ass? No way are those guys total scrubs. I'm less than a year old as a vampire, plus an Innocent. Okay, maybe I'm overplaying the Innocent part a bit too much. We're not inherently weaker than vampires as a whole, we simply don't get the really cool extra powers. Like, when I'm 400 years old, I'll be able to kick as much ass as Aurélie using claws, martial arts, or whatever. I'll just never have her charm powers or be able to throw cars around like a Fury or jump into the Shadow realm. I keep hearing some vampires can turn into wolves. If it's true, I *so* want to see it happen… but it'll never be me.

Right, so a one-year-old (basically) Innocent isn't really at a disadvantage in a fight against any other vampire of similar age, except a Fury. Evidently, being stupid strong is an easy power to develop. Personally, I don't think it's worth the side effect of their bloodline—random fits of irrational anger. Better than Beasts, though. They sometimes lose control entirely and do serious damage. Beasts are commonly kill-feeders but not because they want to be. It's easy for them to lose control to whatever darkness powers vampirism and let it take over.

Yeah, I'm totally happy being what I am.

Anyway… no point standing here like a tool. I retrieve my backpack, run to my car, and start the drive home. Being stuck in the car at night instead of flying is kinda frustrating, like being stuck on the road behind someone driving thirty in a sixty-five zone. The longer trip home gives me unwanted time to think about what happened in the parking garage.

I'm not totally freaking out, but I am freaking out somewhat to hear Stefano has so flagrantly given Aurélie's protection the finger. He obviously sent a pair of new guys to rough me up, planning for me to get away. Does Stefano know I have claws? Maybe not. Not every vampire has them. No idea what the percentage is, but those two definitely did not expect me to be armed. Stefano might assume claws are unlikely for an Innocent, but he's taking the name too literally. My jury is still out regarding if I turned into one due to my personality or the circumstances of my death. Actual innocence or niceness may or may not have anything to do with it. Dalton's a Lost One, which means I should have been one, too. Only, Aurélie explained (due to Dalton not being around) a vampire's bloodline isn't guaranteed to pass on to any others they make. Some lines, like Shadows, have a much higher chance of producing vampires of the same type.

The opposite is true for me. If I ever made someone else into a vampire, they almost certainly would not be an Innocent… unless whatever circumstance dictated it for me holds true for them. Aurélie said me not wanting to become a vampire, plus my age, plus the circumstances of my death, and general personality is why it happened. Mercy-Transferences aren't too common. Could be the only thing required to produce an Innocent is the recipient not asking for it, and the Transference being given as an act of kindness.

Anyway… I'm going off on a tangent. Stefano, prejudiced dick he is, would take Innocent too literally. He wouldn't think I'd have claws. Makes sense. Both he and Paolo see me as an irritating, bratty little child thumbing my nose at tradition. However, even if he didn't expect those two to abduct and destroy me, sending them to attack me is basically taunting Aurélie.

Since I did nothing to provoke him, her decree of protection obligates her to respond. If she doesn't attack Stefano, she appears weak. If she *does* attack him, all hell is going to break loose. Might be best not to tell her about it. I don't want to be responsible for starting a vampire war. Heh. Yeah, right. The idea of me 'not telling' Aurélie anything is laughable. As soon as I'm anywhere near her, she's going to know everything I'm mentally dwelling on. As easily as I can read the minds of mortals, she sees into my head—and heart. Meaning, she's tuned into emotions. Everyone around her basically has their current emotional state scrolling across their foreheads in marquee text. She'd know instantly something bothered me, then read my mind to find out what I felt super guilty about not telling her.

Given the reason I'm inclined to keep quiet, she wouldn't (I hope) be mad at me. My silence gives her an excuse not to act. I could also tell Wolent what happened… or simply ignore the attack altogether.

Grr. I drum my fingers on the steering wheel, staring out at the highway. Stupid road doesn't have any answers. Ignoring this is only going to invite more problems, like telling Stefano he can do whatever he wants to me. However, taking any action in response could also be exactly what he's hoping for. Feels like either option is him winning.

"Dammit!"

I stop myself before breaking the steering wheel.

Is this jerk trying to turn me into the 'little girl who runs to tell mommy' about every problem? Even if I talk to Wolent in the most detached manner possible, giving him the story like a reporter describing an event happening to someone else, it could set him off. Wolent is a Fury. I saw the man throw a chair out a closed window… and it landed like a hundred yards away. Their fits of anger are irrational. Something as random as a person wearing the wrong color shoes can piss them off. They could get mad over shoes, start yelling, and the person saying 'yes, you're right, I shouldn't have worn these' could set them off even worse. Even keeping silent might enrage them. It really is Russian roulette. Fortunately, most Furies understand—once they calm down—and don't hold grudges. The trick is surviving the short but intense rage long enough for them to become rational again.

The last thing I need at the moment is the stress of an unprovoked vampire attack. The school year is getting close to over. Two more months and I'm done for summer break. Finals aren't too far off. I really can't waste the time on vampire politics. Dammit, how do normal college students handle the pressure of immortals trying to kill them?

Oh, wait. They don't.

Sigh.

Screw it. I'll worry about this later. Gonna go home and get started on my 'Poe attempt at a research paper.'

Poe attempt.

Ugh. I bang my head on the steering wheel.

"Dammit Dad! These are your genes!"

5

LEFT FIELD QUESTION

Biology tests are surprisingly distracting.

I couldn't focus on the issue of vampires trying to kill or kidnap me last night knowing I had a test in bio today. Had to put the Poe research on the back burner for the time being. It's probably quite silly of me to be stressing out over grades within an hour of flaying most of the flesh off a dude's arm. Maybe it's not upsetting to me because I know in an hour or so, his arm will be back to normal. Oh, wait. Claws. More like a week. Probably be sore for a month or two. Still, it makes me cringe to think about. Know how every man who sees another man take a hit in the balls winces? Yeah. Same thing with vampires and claw wounds.

Well, that's what he gets for grabbing me by the throat.

Anyway, biology test.

It's Tuesday night, about twenty after seven. I'm in Professor Connolly's class staring at my test paper. Merely having a momentary case of wandering brain, not stuck. I *did* actually study for this test. At least it's still light out for another maybe half hour or so. One of the few times being offline is better for me. No incredibly sharp vampire hearing treating me to a deafening serenade of body functions and annoying noises. One guy two rows over on my left and back a seat is trying to play a Kenny G solo with his butt. Don't need supernatural ears to notice him as the room is mostly dead silent. Seriously, I understand people don't fart on command, but the guy thinks it's *way* more hilarious than it is.

Maybe it's nervous laughter from the inappropriateness of it. Couple years ago, we went to a funeral for one of Mom's tangential relatives we'd never even met. A great aunt or something. Maybe a hundred people attended, most of whom we didn't recognize. This one guy came in a little drunk. He didn't really make a scene so much as let out an unrepentant belch. While everyone else stared on in horror, Sam cracked up and couldn't stop laughing. Dad needed to go outside with him. Honestly, I think Dad cracked up once he got outside, too.

This dude's butt sounds more like a depressed saxophone player warming up rather than a traditional fart. It *is* kinda funny. Even Professor Connolly seems to be struggling to keep a straight face. Guess boys really never do grow up. Connolly is a bit of a comedian. Wouldn't put it past him to make a quip about 'biological processes in action' or 'we could do without the live demonstration.'

Again, I try to read the question on the test paper, but my mind is stuck on Stefano. It's been driving him crazy to watch me becoming part of Wolent's… whatever it's called. 'Political machinery?' I'm not even working hard to ingratiate myself to vampire society, merely doing what's asked of me as quickly as possible so I can get back to my 'normal-but-screwy' life. It is kinda weird to have Wolent smile and back-pat me like I saved him a million bucks for something as basic as taking a message across Seattle. Feels like I'm stuck in one of Sierra's video games doing the level one missions. The way it's going, I half expect Wolent is going to send me to a particular address to steal a rare car, eventually.

Grand Theft Bloodsucker.

The whole 'vampire politics' thing isn't as different from the normal world as one might think. Despite being undead, they're still mostly obsessed with money and power, only they have to take their power behind the scenes. For example, Wolent owns a corporate entity that owns other corporate entities that own corporations and businesses. It's kinda like how the same three companies own ninety percent of all branded consumer products, even though they're sold under a hundred or more different brand names. Wolent's name doesn't appear anywhere a mortal could find it, but he has decision making power over like forty percent of Seattle's economy.

He doesn't really *do* much with it other than have the power. The ability *to* control appeals to him more than constantly 'working the levers' so to speak. I guess many people who become vampires take advantage of their newfound abilities to seize all the wealth they couldn't have as mortals. Even as young as I am, it's easily possible for me to bend the world around me to my will, albeit on a much smaller scale than an elder. I have no need of a mansion or a stupidly expensive car. Don't really understand the appeal of yachts either. Not like vampires can go out to enjoy the sun on the water. Cruising at night is kinda scary, though perhaps less so since it wouldn't be dark to us.

Whatever. I'm happy with our home as is. And no, it wouldn't bother me at all to use my powers to keep the house if need be. Holding on to what's ours is different than stealing from someone else.

Right, test.

It's amazingly difficult to avoid thinking about the Stefano situation, but I force myself to proceed answering questions. Tests have always made me a little bit anxious no matter how much studying happened. I'm not the slacker Sierra is, so except for one time when I had a bad flu, I've never gone into a classroom on test day feeling unprepared. Doesn't stop me from being worried about a random blank-out. No amount of studying will fix mentally seizing up at a critical moment.

Ashley shocked the heck out of me once when she quipped about trying to get up the nerve to go down on her then boyfriend. Said she was afraid she'd choke at the last minute. At that point, I realized she was making a joke. Couldn't believe *Ashley* said something so bawdy. Coming from her made it ten times funnier. Like a sweet little old lady dropping an F-bomb.

Thinking about Ash grinning once I caught her double entendre helps me stop worrying about Stefano and concentrate on the test. For a few seconds between each question, I end up second guessing myself all over again about the whole 'going to college' deal. Yeah, it helps me feel normal and it's good for the 'rents mental health, but it's starting to feel like it's getting in the way of vampire stuff. Or is vampire stuff getting in the way of school? Should I put this on hold until Sam turns eighteen? If Stefano is coming after me so brazenly, he might do something to hurt my family. Or not. He's too worried about attracting mortals' attention. Most likely, he plans to destroy me and mess with my family's memories to erase me from ever having existed. None of them have any real defense against a vampire's mental powers.

Coralie hasn't warned me of anything yet, so I'm holding it together.

Again, I stare at the paper. Nah. If I keep going, I'll finish college before any of the Littles make it to eighteen. Sierra just turned twelve. She'll be sixteen when I finish a four-year degree—assuming I do. Maybe seventeen, considering night school. I can't cram as many credits into a schedule as day classes. Still, an extra year is a triviality to a vampire. The sun, less so.

One thing I *have* decided on is, computer programming is not doing it for me. Choosing a major because it's what my dad does for a living was a mistake. Still can't figure out what I *should* major in. Seattle Central College doesn't exactly offer an 'unlife skills' program. Suppose there's always the idea of doing something entirely academic, like philosophy or anthropology or whatever, pull a Professor Heath. Except, I don't want to become a teacher and honestly, I *can't*. No one would take me seriously, especially at the college level, since I literally look like a kid. Well, not a *child*. Anyone over the age of twenty mistakes me for anywhere from fourteen to sixteen. People my age tend to guess seventeen-ish. Actual kids under say, thirteen, all think I'm 'old.'

So, yeah. No way could I teach college classes. Students would think I'm the professor's daughter there on 'take your kid to work day.' Besides, too public. I may be defying vampire tradition and staying home with my actual family, but my preference is to stay out of public view as much as possible—which is a fairly traditional vampire opinion. The fewer times I'm seen, the easier it is to keep my secret. As Sophia would say, the best way to avoid setting off traps is not to go down the corridor at all. Or, as Sierra would say, send the NPC first. Sam prefers the 'fireball' method of trap clearing.

I think people would frown at me for setting off random explosions in the real world.

Question thirty-six finally gives me brain lock. What's the function of the systemic circuit? I stare at the paper for a long few minutes. They say it's better to skip questions where the answers don't come to you right away and come back to them, but… ugh. Something about oxygen. Oh, duh. I *did* read this. It distributes nutrients and oxygen around the body to cells. Okay cool. Back into the flow…

Until question forty.

If the DNA sequence is 5' GCCTCC 3', what is the sequence of the primer that begins replication?

Well, shit. Might've been able to select right for multiple choice, but Connolly likes fill-ins. Yeah, uhh, no. I don't have the first clue on this one. I shift my gaze up, peering over the shoulder of the guy in front of me at the professor, sitting at his desk reading a book. It's possible for me to pluck the answer out of his thoughts in another few minutes once the sun goes down. Wouldn't take much effort on my part.

Sigh.

Nah. I'd feel guiltier about doing it than shredding the one dude's arm. It would bother me way too much. I don't really *need* straight-As. Getting a degree or not won't have much impact on my future. Also, missing *one* test question isn't a big deal. I'm certainly not trying to become a genetic engineer. Who the hell cares if I can't figure out gene sequencing?

Eyes back on the test.

Yeah, I don't have to ace it and get a perfect score. I *do* have to keep some integrity.

6

FORGIVENESS IS EASIER THAN PERMISSION

Careful not to make a sound, Sierra slipped out of bed and hurriedly traded her nightgown for a T-shirt and jeans.

She crouched to pull her sword case out from under the bed, opened it, and lifted the sheathed blade. Nervousness at getting caught imparted an irresistible shake to her hands, but it would pass as soon as she made it outside. Risking getting in trouble seemed a small price to pay for preparedness. Not like she intended to go far from home... merely the woods behind their backyard.

Having Sarah's old room to herself was awesome. She didn't really mind sharing a bedroom with Sophia for most of her life, but the girl woke up at the slightest noises. No way would sneaking out of the house after bedtime have been possible if they still shared a room.

Sword clutched tight, she padded over to the door and gingerly turned the knob, keenly aware of every little squeak. She mentally prepared herself for Sam or Blix coming out of nowhere for a late-night bathroom trip, so she didn't scream if they surprised her. A scary loud creak came from the hinges as she eased the door open.

No big deal. They'll think I'm going to the bathroom.

Sierra stuck her head into the hall. Seeing it empty, she stepped out, eased her door closed, and hurried to the stairs. Trying to be quiet here probably wouldn't matter if Sarah was in her room. Big sis might not come upstairs to investigate her wandering around. Going downstairs could be something innocent like needing to use the bathroom because the upstairs one already had someone in it. She'd definitely know who came downstairs. Sarah had the unnerving ability to tell who moved around based on the sound of their footsteps. Recognizing Sam didn't take supernatural powers. The boy made more noise than a dead body tumbling down the stairs. But, Sarah could even tell Sophia and her apart by ear, which baffled her. If Sarah happened to be home, she'd *definitely* come looking to see what went on once she heard the patio door slide open.

At the bottom of the steps, she picked her sneakers up from the area by the front door and carried them across the house to the kitchen. The instant she reached the sliding glass patio door out to the deck, a strong feeling of being watched came over her.

"Hi, dog," whispered Sierra. "Just me."

Somehow, they'd managed to keep the hellhound in the backyard a secret from the parents. It had to be nice—or at least nice to their family—since Sophia had no problem with it. Sierra held her breath while tugging the door aside at a snail's pace. Despite it making no noise she could hear, she kept staring at the plain white door to her right, the one leading to the basement stairs. Any second, Sarah would appear, wondering who the heck wanted to go outside in the middle of the night.

The kitchen remained silent. No hurried footsteps coming up the basement steps.

Maybe she's out feeding... or soaking in the tub. Cool!

Sierra stepped outside, cringing slightly at the chilly, damp deck under her bare feet. After sliding the door shut, she leaned the sword against the wall long enough to pull her sneakers on, then grabbed it and crept across the deck to the stairs. As soon as she reached the ground and didn't need to be quiet anymore—Sarah probably couldn't hear someone running around outside from her bedroom—she sprinted to the rear of the yard, jumped the fence, and wandered a short distance into the woods.

Dalton had agreed to meet her tonight for some training. Mom and Dad *probably* wouldn't mind her learning. It would, however, bother them she went outside after midnight. They'd never have said yes if she asked, but any punishment would be mild if they caught her.

Where is he?

Sierra paced around, eyeing the shadowy trees. She'd never admit to being afraid of the dark, instead pointing out the technicality of being afraid of what might be hiding in the darkness, not the absence of light itself. She hated being scared all the time. As much as she made fun of Sophia for Fuzzydoom, Sierra used to believe something hairy lived under her bed and would grab her leg if she tried to go anywhere before morning. She hadn't worried about the creature since like second grade when a new monster took over her fears: dread some idiot would show up at school with a gun. All the teachers and parents thought her 'mature,' but she really kept quiet so she could pay attention to her surroundings. School no longer felt like a safe place. Why would teachers bother training them how to react to a shooter if they didn't think it would happen someday?

Everything went crazy after Sarah turned into a vampire. Now, Sierra had to worry about monsters like the five-headed spider wasp thing, of Dad being silly and not taking a weird creature or situation seriously enough, of vampires trying to kill them… and she *still* dreaded someone would bring a gun to her school. Knowing how to use a sword wouldn't help much against a crazy person waving a gun around, but it helped her deal with the other stuff. It made no sense, but a blade seemed like a better option for dealing with supernatural monsters than a gun.

Too many movies or video games. Guns never work on the weird stuff.

A snap came from the darkness in the direction away from the house. They lived beside a small patch of untamed woodland, maybe a thousand feet across, surrounded by houses. It didn't seem too likely for a pocket of forest in the middle of suburbia to have bears. However, deer made much less noise than what moved around in the dark.

Is Dalton sneaking up on me?

Sierra bit her lip in worry. The gift he'd given her had mostly faded away. Being normal made her feel slow and weak. True, nothing had happened recently that required her to possess modestly superhuman agility, but she feared as soon as she didn't have it, she'd need it. Mr. MacDiarmid, the main instructor at the sword place, noticed her slowing down and wondered if she'd been getting enough sleep. Danae—the only woman student there and her perpetual sparring partner—noticed, too.

Grr. Sierra gripped her sword tight. Alone, away from everyone who might make fun of her, she let her fear out in the form of a few tears. Sarah *had* to know how she felt, but she still couldn't bear to cry in front of her… except for the day her big sister had come back from the dead. Death got a pass on dignity. Everyone, even Dad, cried over death.

I'm not going to be a little kid forever. I won't have to be scared anymore. Gonna protect Soph and Sam.

Another snap made her jump.

Something's out there. She gazed into the darkness, half tempted to pull the sword out of its scabbard. *Please let Dalton give me another sip.* Sierra cringed. His blood tasted utterly vile, but she'd deal with it for the benefit. A few months of turning into an almost literal superhero was totally worth it. She wanted to be 'ready' if anything happened.

Motion in the shadows drew her attention to a human figure wobbling out of the trees in her direction. The near-total darkness concealed his appearance except for the general shape of an adult man in a baggy hoodie with the hood up. Two other men ambled along behind him, all as unsure on their feet as if they'd had too much to drink or hit the weed way too hard.

Not Dalton.

Sierra crept to her right, moving out of their path to take cover behind a tree. Despite the darkness, all three men veered to their left, continuing to walk straight toward her. Unnerved, she scurried even farther to the side… and they followed.

Uhh... the heck?

"Umm, what's up?" asked Sierra a little over a whisper.

The men said nothing, continuing to approach in no great hurry. Sierra jogged left, circling around until it became obvious the men clearly saw her and intended to follow.

"What do you guys want?"

None of the men spoke. She stepped backward, staring up at the three taller figures closing in on her. Spooked, she stopped, drew her sword, and pointed it at them.

"That's close enough. Stop chasing me."

A heavy *thud* came from the direction of her house. She chanced a quick peek back over her left shoulder, but couldn't see anything unusual except darkened trees. Her next breath drew in the rancid smell of chemicals and bad meat. Sierra whirled to face forward and stared up into the eyes of a man who didn't look right at all. Under his navy-blue hood, his cheeks had no color, eyes milked over, gaze unfocused, mouth not fully closed.

The man on the left also wore a hoodie, albeit pink. Despite him being black, his skin had an unnatural ashy tinge. Guy number three sported a red hoodie. All wore the same style of plain grey sweat pants. None had shoes. Their clothes didn't fit them well, a little too large.

"You guys know you look silly, right? Are you like the 'hoodie' gang, or trying to start a hip-hop group?"

All three men continued walking toward her.

She took another step back, gawking at the horrifying realization none of the men appeared able to bend their elbows or knees fully, teetering along like bad Claymation puppets. Her next breath tasted like the frogs in science class smelled, the *dead* frogs preserved in formaldehyde. A flash of moonlight revealed a small bullet hole above the left eye of the guy in the red hoodie.

Crap!

"S-stop! Don't come any closer!" Sierra waved her sword at them while backing up.

The lead man lunged, trying to grab her. She yelped, ducking to the side as the clumsy dead guy almost fell on his face. Bullet-head took a swing at her, trying to punch her in the chest. Sierra flung herself to the left. Knuckles grazed her back, launching her off her feet. She landed on her chest and slid a few feet, gasping for air once she stopped in a mound of dead leaves.

What little speed she still had from Dalton's gift probably saved her life.

Damn, they're strong. If they hit me, they're going to break me in half like a twig.

A series of heavy thuds coming from the direction of home grew louder.

Red Hoodie charged while the other two spun in place as if they'd lost track of where she went. Sierra scrambled to her feet, dodging another fist trying to take her head off. Circling, she clutched her blade in both hands, staring at Red, hesitating, unable to bring herself to swing her sword at a person.

He's not a person! He's already dead!

Navy Hoodie ran (sort of) at her, reaching out to grab her shoulder.

"Eep!" Sierra leapt backward, slicing defensively at the incoming limb—and severed his hand at the wrist.

It landed a few feet away with a soft *thump*. No blood leaked from the stump. She gawked at the flat end of his forearm, more shocked at the man showing no reaction whatsoever to losing a hand. No scream, no change to his facial expression, not even a grunt.

"Oh, no way. Freakin' zombies?"

Red Hoodie rushed at her.

Sierra darted around Navy Hoodie. Red's fist connected with the other man's chest, knocking him tumbling. Pink Hoodie swung his arm in a wide, telegraphed attack like he had a baseball bat sticking out of his shoulder. Sierra ducked under it easily and maneuvered to get behind him—but tripped over a root, landing on her right side. Pink hoodie grabbed her ankle.

He started to haul her into the air by one leg. Sierra hacked her blade into his forearm, cutting one bone, but the sword stalled on the second. Pink Hoodie lifted her up in the manner of a fisherman showing off a giant tuna. Sierra dangled upside down by one leg for a second before the remaining bone in the partially cut arm snapped. She tumbled to the forest floor, kicking her leg rapidly to dislodge the disembodied hand.

Navy Hoodie ambled into a charge, but took only two steps before stopping short for no apparent reason. Two holes appeared in his chest, one by his shoulder, one at the stomach, each as big around as Sierra's wrist. The dead guy sailed into the air, thrashing back and forth as if in the mouth of a giant, aggressively playful dog. Bones snapped and cracked from the force.

Sierra got her legs under her and ran to her right in a circle, avoiding Pink Hoodie's grab. The guy with an obvious bullet hole in his forehead chased her, having more agility than his two buddies. Navy Hoodie's body slapped into the ground. Something huge and invisible pounced Pink Hoodie flat. Sierra ducked another punch from Red Hoodie, flowing smoothly into a slash across his chest. Like the other man, he didn't bleed, at least not blood. Clear fluid oozed out of the slice.

She momentarily regretted ruining an obviously brand-new hoodie, but considering it had been on a dead guy, figured no one would want to touch it, anyway. Whoever put it on these corpses already wasted the clothing. Snarling and crunching continued behind her on the left as she dodged and weaved around Red Hoodie's continued attempts to crush her skull. Finally, he committed to a lunging grab. Sierra darted under his arms, then spun back to face him, holding her sword high in both hands. After a split second to aim, she took his head off with a downward chop.

More clear fluid gushed from the neck.

The body hit the ground inert, not even a single twitch.

Sierra backed away, trying not to breathe the nasty fumes.

A short distance from the headless corpse, a canine-shaped creature faded into view out of invisibility. Black armor plating like a crab covered most of its body in between swaths of inky fur. A ridge of small horns ran down the spine to the tail. Its face sorta resembled a wolf's. Despite his glowing red eyes and smoke peeling between giant teeth, he gave off a note of friendliness. He also stood at eye-level to her.

Whoa. He's big. She glanced down at the man she beheaded. "So much for Little Red Riding Hoodie."

The hellhound breathed fire on the other two bodies, spitting a stream of burn as intense as a flamethrower.

Sierra cringed slightly at the blast of light and heat. "Guess the wolf wins this time."

The hellhound looked at her. He appeared to be giving off a vibe somewhere between 'this is what happens when you sneak outside at night' and 'are you okay?' Before she could say anything, he abruptly shifted its attention to the left, snarling.

"More?" asked Sierra.

He nodded once.

She raised her sword. "Let's get 'em."

7

A LITTLE RECREATIONAL DECAPITATION

There has to be someone out there who would find it ironic for a vampire to be researching Poe. Or would it be more ironic if I'd picked Bram Stoker? Eh, too meta. It's not terribly unusual for a college student to take a break in the middle of doing their homework for a snack. Few college students have an irresistible itch to consume blood, though. I'm in a rare minority along with business majors.

So, I took a break from reading for a quick flight to Seattle downtown. It doesn't burn too much time for me to get there, and downtown is my preferred feeding ground. Big cities are ideal, since it's easy to select people who will never see me again in their lives. Ambushing my neighbors isn't wise. Not only does it increase the chances of someone who knows me catching me in the act, I usually need to eat more often than a small population can support without health complications. A good safe rule is not to feed from the same person more than once every eight weeks. I'm basing it on the guidelines for donating blood. Obviously, if I don't drink as much as they take during a donation, it shortens the re-feeding time, but it's still safer to avoid biting anyone twice at all.

Tonight's meal is a security guard I notice standing alone in an alley behind a high-rise office building. He's a bit on the heavy side, his body pear shaped—not too surprising for a dude working security who spends ninety percent of his time behind a desk. I land unnoticed at the end of the alley and walk toward him. A weird smell of raw potatoes hangs in the air, mixed with something fruity—probably his vape wand. Ugh. Potato-berry? Eww. I sneak up on him, opening with my usual, "Hey, what's up?"

The guy's in the middle of sucking a hit of vape juice when I break the silence. Startled, he inhales a giant breath through the thing and lapses into a coughing fit, spraying fog from his nose and mouth.

As soon as he turns to face me, I recognize him: Bobby Archer. He was in my class from kindergarten straight to the end of high school. The 'potato' smell makes sense now. For some reason I never understood, he just smells like raw potatoes. Always has. The berry is totally coming from his vape. Bobby's had a few extra pounds on him his whole life, but the security job has clearly gone straight to his butt.

"Sarah?" he gasps in between coughing. "From school?"

I dive into his head, deleting his memory of seeing me tonight. Already here, so no point skipping a meal, but I can't let someone who recognizes me remember. Easier to replace with a random, nondescript brown-haired girl he thought was me… wait, no. Eliminate any hint of me. Blonde.

Bobby's not a bad guy. Little quiet, but can't blame him. Kids teased him for his weight all through school. Okay, I gotta know. Why the potato smell? Oh, ack. His mother and grandmother are hoarders. Their garage is full of vegetables in various states of rot. Looks like he finally moved out. The potato smell on him now is all in my head from memory due to some weird subconscious association. Apparently, I recognized him before realizing it. Poor guy. Also, he's trying to stop eating junk food but has no willpower. Hmm. Is it unethical of me to help him out? I mean, he *wants* to… just can't. Oh hell. Least I can do for the guy for feeding me once is help him out.

I bite him, totally 'shocked' to taste blood flavored like French fries.

Once the feeding is done, I stare into his eyes and implant a compulsion to listen to his inner voice and stop eating five or six cupcakes, Twinkies, or blueberry pies a day. Not easy to cope with the environment he grew up in. Suppose snack cakes are a better vice to fall back on for comfort than drugs, but still. Maybe giving him a little push will help. I'm not forcing him to do anything he doesn't already desire, merely helping him overcome a lack of willpower.

"Thanks, Bobby. Take care of yourself." I pat him on the arm and leap into the air while he's still lost in a mental fog.

Drat. Now I want actual French fries. Might be a fast food place open at this hour, but hunting for one would waste time. Besides, my wallet's at home. I'd have to compel a clerk to give me free food, which would attract attention and probably get someone fired. Yeah, Follows Rules Girl strikes again. I'm the world's lamest vampire. Of all the nefarious deeds an undead immortal is capable of committing, stealing one order of fries isn't exactly high up on the badness scale. Me? I can't even move statues around as a prank without feeling guilty.

Whatever.

I fly toward home debating the right or wrong of harmless pranks. The statue thing isn't *exactly* harmless. Normal people can't simply pick those things up and lug them around. Putting them back where they belong would likely cost money to hire a crew, so not entirely harmless. However, flying gives me the ability to TP the hell out of a house—or hang Christmas lights. Sigh. Thanks, Dad.

Did I mention what his great idea was this year coming up? He wants to go full Clark Griswold and have me put a ton of blinking lights on our roof since I can fly. He's tossed the idea of roof lights around for years, but Mom shot it down. Dad plus ladder plus electricity equals *bad* things happening. And crap. If he gets Sophia in on it, turning our lights on *will* black out all of Cottage Lake.

Maybe it's time to break my promise—slightly—and delete the idea from his head.

A flash catches my eye below me on the ground. Out of curiosity, I look—surprised to see five men in nice suits swinging swords at two guys and a woman in ordinary clothes, if a bit 'grunge.' The blonde woman is easy to recognize—Amy, one of the 'Seattle Lost Ones' as I call them. Considering it's her, I assume the two men are Dante and Luke. You know, the same Dante who loaned me his Fury power so I had a chance against Petra?

I'm reasonably certain The Matrix hasn't sucked me into a real-life simulation of *Grand Theft Auto* and random well-dressed corporate heavies are not supposed to mysteriously appear with swords. Dunno who these creeps are, but they're trying to kill three vampires I consider my friends. The thugs having swords tells me two things: one, they know they're dealing with vampires. Two, they're most likely intending to *kill* my friends. Thanks to Dalton, I also know a third fact: the suits are completely unskilled in how to use blades, hacking away like they're swinging baseball bats.

Dante's handling three of the five suits on his own, but only managing to keep himself alive. One of the guys on him has long, blond hair. He's like a cross between the lead singer of a hair metal band and an Eighties pro wrestler who's stuffed his bulging muscles into a suit not made for him. The fabric's about to rip at any second. A guy chasing Amy around—ugh. 'Chasing Amy.' Sigh. Dad joke and didn't even mean it—sports the slicked-back hair of an old-school mobster. The suit trying to kill Luke has a little grey in his brown hair, seems to be the oldest in his middle forties. Amy and Luke dart around in circles, avoiding a constant series of clumsy sword strikes. Luke's holding a handgun, which appears to be empty. Can't tell on the black suit, but the older dude swinging a sword at him probably absorbed a few shots to the chest. Yeah, guns are more irritating than dangerous to vampires, barring head shots, which are knock-out hits.

Mr. Mafia kicks Amy's legs out from under her, flinging her onto her back, then steps on her chest, raising his sword to go all *Highlander*. Grr. I dive at him, accelerating as much as I can in the relatively short distance between me and the ground. A cool—and presently helpful—aspect of vampire flight is total silence. The dude doesn't notice me coming until I dive-bomb-tackle him to the side, plowing him into the rear end of a red sedan. Our impact crumples the trunk and shatters the back window, setting off a few car alarms nearby.

Oh, that's a broken rib. Owwie. Maybe my collarbone, too. I hate to say it, but after having my spine broken in two places, a single rib (and possibly collarbone) barely register on the pain scale. Yeah, I need serious counseling.

Sudden, rapid lateral acceleration from zero to a hundred miles an hour in an instant is enough to daze even a vampire. He emits a disoriented moan. I grab the cutlass from his hand. Mine. Hmm. Not bad. Little heavy, single-edged, slight curve. Not too long for me. Balance is decent. Wow, this sword is 'real,' not a Home Shopping Network fake. While he struggles to pull his arms out of the bent remains of the car's trunk, I separate his head from the rest of him.

And, ouch. Yeah. My collarbone went. Can feel the two pieces grinding against each other. At least it's the left side. Not affecting my sword arm.

A fair amount of blood sprays up from the neck stump… but nowhere near as much as *should* come out of a body—proof he's also a vampire.

"Right on!" yells Amy. "Thanks!"

Luke gurgles.

I spin. The older dude has rammed the cutlass into Luke's stomach.

"Luke!" I yell. "Use the force!"

"Not funny," gurgles Luke.

Amy rolls her eyes at me.

Growling, he punches the suit in the jaw, knocking him into a backward stagger. The smallest of the three guys on Dante breaks away from him, seeing an opportunity to double team the injured. I run to intercept his attempted cheap shot at Luke's back, raising my borrowed sword to block. Our blades meet with a loud *clank*. Nice. This cutlass feels beefier than my katana. It's definitely better for the style of fighting Dalton gave me. Might just hang onto it. Luke jumps away, spinning to keep Old Dude and this guy in sight.

Headless dude charges me. Fortunately, his head is facing away from the fight, so the body's nowhere near on target.

I stare at the guy in front of me. His light brown hair is short and neat, bit of a goatee going. "Wow, is someone ordering henchmen from Dudebros R Us?"

Frowning, he dismissively slices at me. I parry and cut a slash down his chest, destroying his blue necktie. He chops overhead in a super telegraphed maneuver so basic even Sierra could parry it. Wait, she's actually fairly good. I keep forgetting Dalton brain-zapped her, too. She could totally have parried this moron—but at her size, would've gone flying anyway. Let me rephrase. He chops overhead in a super telegraphed maneuver even Sophia could parry. I knock his blade aside and swipe at his throat. Dudebro leans back, reducing another beheading to a half-inch-deep slice across the front of his throat. Dark blood seeps down into his shirt. He grabs the wound, blood oozing between his fingers. Takes him a half second to realize his head's still attached.

Speaking of detached heads, the headless corpse lumbers by again, grabbing at nothing.

Amy trips him.

My maneuver appears to piss Dudebro off. He growls, attacking me as fast as he can slash, each successive swing coming faster than the one before it. Fortunately, he has about as much finesse in his technique as Rian Johnson directing a *Star Wars* movie. Our swords clash six times before I seize an opening to disarm him—by cutting off his thumb. His cutlass falls from his grip and clatters to the parking lot. Not sure where the thumb went. He backs up, stuffing the thumb-stump in his mouth. I grin at him, wagging my eyebrows in an 'I win' gesture while he makes this stupid bewildered face at me.

Amy pounces on the severed head, sticking a knife into it. The rampaging blind body promptly falls over.

The blond 'wrestler' dude goes flying across the parking lot, embedding headfirst into the side of a van. Ooh, they finally hit Dante's Fury button.

"Sarah?" yells a guy. "What the hell are you doing?"

I point my cutlass at Dudebro's neck in a 'you stand right there' motion, and glance toward the voice. The fortyish-looking man who stabbed Luke is gawking at me with the same horrified/bewildered expression Uncle Hank uses on us for wearing casual clothes at Christmas dinner. Or the look on a judge's face if the defendant arrived in court wearing a T-shirt saying 'F the police.' It's about the same level of offended disbelief.

"Helping my friends. Who the hell are you?" I shout back.

Old Man swings his cutlass back and forth in a gesturing motion at Amy, Luke, and Dante—who have mysteriously stopped fighting. It's like all of them had merely been playing a super high contact version of football and a time-out got called. "Wolent wants these anarchists wiped out."

Oh, shit. Double shit. I glance down the length of my cutlass at Dudebro. Already, a quarter inch of new thumb has sprouted from his right hand. If he *is* one of Wolent's heavies, it might explain why he's just standing there making sour faces at me instead of either running or trying to smash me.

"Are you serious?" I ask. "You guys really work for Wolent? Crap!"

"Wait." Amy stares at me. "Seriously? Are you really going to help them kill us for Wolent?"

I blink at her. "Of course not. I'm just... shocked. This can't be legit."

"It is," says the older guy who stabbed Luke.

"Hey, Siri," I say in a loud voice. My pocket beeps. "Call Arthur Wolent."

"Dialing Arthur Wolent," replies my phone.

The remaining four suits lower their weapons, evidently waiting for me. Uh oh. If the bit about them being here at Wolent's behest was a lie, they would be running away now... or at least appearing worried at me *calling* their bluff—literally.

"Sarah, good to hear from you," says a somewhat muffled Arthur Wolent.

I fish my phone out from my pocket. It's on speaker, so I switch it to normal. "Umm, sorry to bother you, sir. Did you send some guys to destroy Lost Ones?"

"I sent some associates to deliver a message. Attacks on my interests will not be tolerated."

"Umm." I shift my gaze to Amy and Luke. No point trying to talk to Dante at the moment. He's Fury raging. Wrestler Man's back on him. He left a hole in the van where his head went through the side. He and the other suit I'll call Dudebro2 are trying to hold Dante down and are almost managing to do so. "Did you guys mess with anything Mr. Wolent controls?"

"No." Amy scoffs. "Why would we? All that political stuff is BS."

"Naw, girl." Luke shrugs. "You know us. We just hang out and relax. Ain't got time for any agenda besides what concert's up next. Need them tunes."

Dante's response is a noise similar to what I'd imagine would come out of a moose if someone shot it in the balls.

"Uhh, sir, I think your people made an error," I say. "They're attacking some Lost Ones I know, and it's pretty unlikely these three are the vampires responsible for messing with you."

Wolent remains quiet for a few seconds. Amy, Luke, Dudebro1, and Old Guy all exchange uneasy glances. Dante lifts Wrestler Man and Dudebro2 off their feet, swinging them around. Neither loses their grip on him. The spin costs Dante his balance. He topples over sideways, the two other vampires dragging him down and attempting to pin him again. Fortunately, they've had to drop their swords to keep hold of him and no longer appear to be interested in doing anything worse than holding him down until the Fury fades.

"Sarah," says Wolent. "Are these friends of yours willing to tell me to my face they are not involved in the attack?"

I look at Amy. Obviously, Wolent knows he's old enough to be able to read her mind, or at least assumes he can. She's been a vampire for fifty years, so there's a good chance he *can* read her mind. Little fuzzy on the gap needed, but it's either 100 or 150 years… unless some vampire out there is as gifted with mind-reading as Aurélie is gifted with charm. One thing I've learned as a vampire is not to trust anything to be true unconditionally. There are exceptions to every situation.

"Guys, he wants to know if you'll meet with him in person and tell him you aren't involved in whatever happened."

"Yeah, no problem." Amy flaps her arms in a motion part 'whatever' part shrug. "We're not involved."

"Sure." Luke rubs his stomach. "If we can trust him."

I nod. "You can. Since you guys didn't do anything, he won't have an issue with you."

Dante grunt-growls from the strain of lifting the two vampires pinning him.

"I'll take that as a yes, too." Smiling, I move the phone close to my mouth again. "Sir, they are all willing to tell you in person."

"Speakerphone please," says Wolent.

"Sec." I hit the button, then hold the phone up on my palm. "Go ahead, sir."

"Clark?" asks Wolent.

"Here, sir," replies Old Guy.

"Please escort Sarah's friends back to the estate so I may speak with them. If they are cooperative, treat them like guests. If they are not involved in the events at the warehouse, they will not be harmed."

"Yeah, cool," shouts Amy. "We're fine talking to you. We had nothing to do with any attack."

Wolent chuckles. "You'll have to tell me sometime how you ended up there, Sarah."

"Luck, sir. Was flying home after feeding. Saw the fight from the air. A bunch of guys waving swords around in a parking lot isn't exactly… uhh, subtle."

He pauses. I picture him pinching the bridge of his nose and thinking the men he sent are morons for doing it so publicly. He sighs. "All right. Tell Clark to bring your friends by the mansion. I'll make it right by them if they're not the ones we're looking for."

"Yes, sir." Since it's on speaker and Clark obviously heard him, I simply hang up and stuff the phone in my pocket.

Dante finally calms down and lays there glaring at the sky.

Wrestler Man, who Dudebro2 calls Jay, goes with him to pick up the headless body they refer to as Virgil. I sheepishly walk over and retrieve the head, carrying it back to the black Chevy Suburban they drove. Jay and Dudebro2 (Donnie) toss Virgil in the back.

"Uhh, here. Sorry." I hold out Virgil's head to them. "Don't usually offer strange guys head, but I'll make an exception in this case."

Jay rolls his eyes, takes the severed head, and sets it back on Virgil's neck.

I cringe and put the cutlass in the truck, too. Darn. Wanted it, but it belongs to one of Wolent's guys so I can't steal it. "Sorry. Sense of humor is from my father."

"How the hell did you do that?" Dudebro1 walks up to me.

"Do what?" I ask.

He blinks as if confused by my question. "Uhh, not get hit and make me drop my sword."

It takes all my self-control not to whistle in awe. Seriously?

Jay wraps duct tape around Virgil's neck, then pats me on the shoulder. "Don't mind Stan. He's cognitively disadvantaged. If you're going to explain anything to him, use small words."

Stan glares at him.

Wow. The guy's named Stan. No offense to other men named Stan, but *this* guy *looks* like a 'Stan.' His expression makes me half expect he's about to say 'Mongo like candy.'

"Umm. I dunno. Got lucky, I guess."

"Heh." Jay adds a little more duct tape to keep Virgil's head in place. "She must've been on her school fencing team. Guessing she actually knows how to use a blade. Pretty rare skill for a kid these days."

I shrug. "Had a little training."

Jay shuts the Suburban's rear hatch. "Only a little?"

Technically, I didn't lie. Dalton only gave me a brief amount of actual training. Most of the knowledge, he just kinda uploaded into my head. The other four vampires, plus Amy, Luke, and Dante, crowd around me.

"So, uhh, what happened?" I ask.

"Some nimrod thought it would be funny to toss a couple Molotovs through the windows of one of Mr. Wolent's properties," says Jay.

Did I mention this guy is *tall*? I'm head level with his pectorals.

"Wow. What made him suspect Lost Ones?" I glance sideways at Amy. Despite her 'Nirvana inspired' outfit, she's the picture of blonde, blue-eyed innocence.

"Security cameras," says Donnie. "Bunch of punks. They moved too fast for mortals or to get a good look at 'em. Mr. Wolent was unable to determine the origin of the attacks, so it had to be anarchists operating outside the system."

"We're not the only ones in Seattle who ignore politics." Amy rubs a sore spot on her arm.

"Any idea who might've done it?" asks Jay.

She stops short of laughing. "We don't keep attendance records or have weekly check in meetings."

"Right, come on." Jay motions at the door. "Sarah, you coming with us?"

"Umm. I've got a ton of homework, but…" I glance at my three friends. It would be pretty lame of me to bail on them, and I'm not sure if Mr. Wolent would consider it bad form for me not to be there. So… yeah, might as well. "This is important."

A Suburban has a lot of room, but nine people is still pushing it a bit. Since I'm on the small side, I end up in Dante's lap. He's cool. Total big brother type situation. Jay drives. Hopefully, this won't take too long or end with me obligated to do a long, tedious mission for Wolent. If he's trying to track down anarchist vampires, who may or may not be actual Lost Ones, the 'sweet suburban girl' is *not* the right agent to use. Let's just say I don't blend in among those circles. Had I been a goth, a pothead skateboarder, or a punker, sure.

So, some anarchists decided to firebomb Wolent's business interests. Just like Petra's house. A Molotov through the window. No one really knows how many unaffiliated vampires are in Seattle. Heck, Dalton's technically one of them, as he doesn't pay any attention to politics.

Oh, crap. I stare at up at the roof. *Please* don't be Petra. She's not the most patient individual. If she sent some idiots to poke Wolent out of revenge, it's not going to end well for her. Can't say I'd lose much sleep if she ended up removed from the world. The woman might be evil as hell, but she's not an idiot. Can't see her benefiting in any way by antagonizing him. Now Stefano, on the other hand, would totally be interested in creating a situation where he could 'dethrone' Wolent and take over as the de facto 'head vampire' of Seattle. He's around 250 years old. Wolent's only 175. It probably annoys Stefano to have a 'kid' calling the shots. Paolo is even older. I think Aurélie said he's almost 300.

Going to meet Wolent. Shit. I hope he doesn't look into my head and see those two morons who attacked me for Stefano. Knowing him, he'd probably connect some dots and think the warehouse arson is also part of the same scheme.

Ugh. Maybe I should've bailed and gone home. I'm sure Wolent won't hurt Amy, Dante, or Luke. However, my being here increases the chances of this ending peacefully. Dammit. No idea what's about to happen, either in the next twenty minutes or few days, but I *am* sure it's going to be messy.

Probably *very* messy.

8

DID ANYONE ORDER ZOMBIES?

Sierra held her sword in both hands, staring at the smear of chemical on the blade.

Formaldehyde is poisonous. I shouldn't touch or breathe it.

The hellhound stalked off into the woods, shimmering back to invisibility. Branches and small trees seemingly moved on their own out of its way. She ran after it, holding her breath until she couldn't smell the fumes from the 'juicy' zombie.

Weird the one guy didn't leak at all, not even blood. She narrowed her eyes. *Vampires must have killed them... but why refill the dead guys with formaldehyde? Who the heck puts that stuff in people?* She scrunched her nose. *Oh, duh. Like funeral homes, right?*

Sierra, her siblings, and friends sometimes played in the small patch of forest inside the circle of houses. Sam, Daryl, and Jordan got more use out of it than the girls, but she still generally knew her way around. Even if she got lost, going in a straight line for a thousand feet would definitely bring her to civilization. It didn't look the same at night, but she had a feeling she headed north toward 169th Place.

An invisible 'branch' pressing across her chest made her stop. She grabbed at it, finding a partially furry, partially chitinous tail blocking her path like a gate at a parking garage.

He's telling me to stop here.

She nodded.

The tail dropped away. A zipper sound came from ahead.

Sierra crept three steps forward, taking cover behind a tree and peering past it at two people in the clearing outside the forest between two houses. They appeared to be gathering empty body bags and bundling them up. The woman looked Hispanic, dressed like a punk rocker, her hair dyed sky-blue. Beside her stood a guy who looked like almost everyone she'd seen at Dad's office. Thirtysomething, slightly chubby, white polo shirt, glasses.

Bet that guy has twenty alts all at level cap in WoW. She grinned to herself. *Not judging. Just, he looks like he belongs in front of a computer, not releasing zombies into the wild.*

"So damn creepy," said the guy. "Watching the dead sit up."

The woman rolled her eyes. "Hello? Vampires? What do you think *they* are?"

"Yeah, I know." The guy pointed a rolled-up body bag at her. "But they don't *look* dead. Or moan. Or stagger around like drunk Muppets."

"Hah." The woman laughed. "What the hell does a drunk Muppet look like?"

Uh oh. Vampires.

Arms came around Sierra from behind, grabbing her in a bear hug. A man lifted her off her feet, carrying her out into the open. Sierra fought back the urge to scream from being surprised, channeling fear into anger. Warm breath blasted her in the back of the head. Body heat seeped through her T-shirt, confirming she'd been grabbed by a living dude.

"Lookie what I found," said the guy holding her.

The blue-haired woman raised an eyebrow. "I think she's one of them."

IT Guy clutched the body bag like a teddy bear, seeming afraid of her… or possibly not wanting to be part of hurting a kid.

Sierra grunted, forcing her arms outward. The relatively skinny man holding her gradually lost his grip as she overpowered him.

He strained, fighting to keep her arms pinned, but couldn't hold her. "What... the... f—"

"Grr!" Sierra slipped loose, dropped to her feet, and spun, ramming her knee into his groin.

"Ay!" The man flew back a few feet before crumpling to the ground in a heap, cradling his balls and whimper-gasping.

IT Guy pointed the body bag at her. "Crap. She's enthralled."

"Look who's talking." Sierra narrowed her eyes at him. "Horde or Alliance?"

"For the Horde," said the guy.

"I knew it. You're a Tauren main, aren't you?"

"What the hell is she babbling about?" asked the woman.

Sierra folded her arms. "Probably plays a female shaman."

IT Guy scowled. "What's wrong with that?"

"*So* much," said Sierra. "I don't have time to get into details."

The woman smiled at her. "Okay, sweetie. Put down the sword and come along quietly."

"Uhh, how about 'no.'" Sierra pointed the blade at her. "You're planning to kill me, and I have serious objections."

"What makes you say something so mean, dear?" The woman batted her eyes.

Sierra pointed her left thumb back at the woods. "You set loose a pack of zombies who tried to eat me. Operative word there being *tried*."

The woman bowed her head, sighing. "Fine." She pulled a handgun out from behind her back and aimed it at Sierra. "Let's try this again. Drop the sword and come with us."

A twinge of fear tickled along her spine. Nothing new. The front doors at school had the same effect on her as a handgun every time she saw them. One day, the active shooter drill wouldn't be a drill. She had plenty of experience acting brave while frightened. The moment she'd dreaded so much for years finally stood in front of her with blue hair. Some crazy person pointing a gun at her. Better here than at school with other kids around.

"You really don't want to do that." Sierra casually rested her sword across her shoulder. "You guys aren't vampires, so it would mess me up in the head to kill you… or to watch you die. I'm also gonna guess you're doing this against your will, kinda like me selling Girl Scout cookies two years ago."

IT Guy blinked. "The vampire forced you to sell cookies? Okay… twisted."

Sierra rolled her eyes. "No. My parents did."

The woman sighed at the sky. "No, Dave, she's being sarcastic. Her master didn't force her to do anything."

"You guys…" Sierra rolled her eyes. "I don't have a master."

"Stop stalling." The woman held the gun higher. "Move."

"Seriously, bad idea to threaten me." Sierra shook her head.

The woman and Dave laughed.

"C'mon, kid, just drop the sword. We're not gonna hurt you," said Dave.

"Yeah, right."

A low, rumbling growl came from the trees behind Sierra.

The woman glanced at Dave. "What the heck did you eat?"

"That noise didn't come from my ass," said Dave.

An even louder growl emanated from the forest.

"What *is* making that rumbling?" asked the woman.

"Ooh." Sierra raised her left hand. "I know the answer."

The woman stared at her.

Sierra lowered her hand. "It's the reason you two shouldn't hurt me. Stop pointing the gun at me right now and maybe he won't eat you."

The woman "Oh, the hell with this. Brat, you—"

A blurry beige smear fell out of the sky, crashed into the woman, and zagged to one side, resolving into Dalton swinging the blue-haired punk around and slamming her back against a tree, one hand on her neck, the other controlling the wrist of her gun hand.

Dave screamed.

The man on the ground continued gasping for breath, cradling his balls.

"Sorry I'm late, luv," said Dalton. "Got a bit tangled in a messy affair, and not the cheaty kind of affair."

Holy crap. Sierra's heart nearly jumped out of her chest. *Not* having a gun pointed at her made her want to collapse in a heap of relief. She settled for exhaling hard. "No problem."

Dalton lifted the woman up a little higher and stared into her eyes. "Hmm. Someone loyal to St. Ives sent them to… oh my."

"Yeah, zombies," muttered Sierra.

"Technically," moaned the guy cradling his groin, "animated corpses. Aww, God. I think you cracked my pelvis."

Sierra held her chin high. "Don't grab people from behind then."

He moaned.

She turned to look at him. Dave appeared harmless enough. Any grown man who mained a Tauren female didn't scare her. "What's the difference?"

"I need my pelvis," rasped the guy.

"No, dork. I mean what's the difference between a zombie and an animated corpse. Aren't zombies and animated corpses the same thing? Dead people moving around due to outside forces?"

"And she calls me a nerd," muttered Dave.

"I didn't say I wasn't. However, I'm not a cow shaman."

Dalton raised an eyebrow. "I feel I've missed a withering insult there."

Dave looked down, grumbling to himself. "Stupid Night Elf Hunter."

"Oh, please." Sierra rolled her eyes. "I have *some* self-respect."

The man on the ground gasped again. "Zombies are mindless creatures that just kinda do whatever regardless of what goes on around them."

"Oh," said Sierra. "Warlocks… or noobs."

The blue-haired woman gurgled, struggling to pull Dalton's hand off her throat.

"Huh?" asked the man on the ground.

"Mindless? Like people who've never played *Call of Duty* before.

Just run around blowing random crap up no matter what's happening."

"Uhh, whatever, kid." He took a few rapid breaths and pushed himself up to sit. "These aren't zombies. They're more like remote control toys."

"*Were.*" Sierra smiled. "They're gone now."

The woman passed out. Dalton dropped her on the ground and collected the handgun.

Dave tried to run, but took only four steps before Dalton appeared in front of him. He didn't even have time to yelp in surprise before he went glassy-eyed and fainted.

"Aww, crap. That friend of yours is a vamp, isn't he?" asked Ball Kick Guy.

"Yeah." Sierra walked around the guy, who still lay curled up on the ground. "I'd say it's pointless to try running, but I'm not sure you can right now."

Dalton walked up beside her. "What's going on here?"

Fear melted out of her. Between the hellhound watching over her and Dalton right next to her, she felt protected. Nothing against her parents, but neither one had the abilities of a vampire. She may or may not freak out at having a woman point a gun at her later, but for now, she kept herself under control. "Thralls, I think."

"Hmm." Dalton grabbed the man by the shirt and pulled him upright, gazing into his eyes. Within seconds, he groaned as if something hit him in the groin, too. "Oh, my." He coughed. "These poor sods aren't thralls. Merely mortals compelled to be delivery drivers. UPS is far too expensive for shipping undead minions."

She chuckled.

Dalton dragged him the rest of the way out to the road, over to a rental van. "This man should probably visit a hospital. He's in a great deal of pain. His figs may have burst."

"We're letting them go?" She peered up at him.

"Aye. They're merely pawns."

"They wanted to kidnap me… or worse."

He fidgeted, which told Sierra 'worse' had been on the menu.

"Seems Eleanor has a grudge after all. Someone programmed these three with exactly where you live and sent them bearing rather rotten gifts."

"Great..." Sierra rolled her eyes. "Dad's gonna freak. Guess I'm busted for being out late."

Dalton patted her on the head, smiling. "It's not as though you intended to be a miscreant. You are merely looking out for the best interests of your family. I am certain your parents will appreciate you hearing a disturbance in the backyard and going to check it out."

Wow, really? She grinned. "They're going to be upset at me for running outside instead of waking them up right away."

He held one finger up. "Waking them up is precisely what we are about to do. One moment. Let me send these three on their way."

Sierra nodded, then exhaled out her nose.

I'm probably gonna get grounded, but it's better than being shot.

9

HOW TO AVOID BEING GROUNDED

Wolent ended up being surprisingly reasonable.

Not surprising to me, more to Amy, Luke, and Dante. Okay, maybe a *little* surprising to me, but not because he treated them fairly. I expected him to. I hadn't expected to be done so fast. Fortunately, he didn't dig into my thoughts, or if he did, he's not revealing he caught me worrying about Stefano Bianchi's creeps trying to take me out. Still not sure how to handle it. Talking to Aurélie could start a war. Talking to Wolent about it could start a war—and potentially bite me in the ass if it ends up being Petra's fault.

Like, those idiots openly said Stefano wanted me dealt with permanently. Call me cynical, but it's like something goons in a bad movie would say. Sure, Stefano *is* the kind of butthead who would want me to fully understand *why* two guys were about to feed me headfirst into a woodchipper, but something feels off about it. I could totally picture Petra sending a pair of baby vampires pretending to be Stefano's people to rough me up, knowing they'd fail. Even *she* thinks I'm a whiny little kid who'd run straight to Wolent or Aurélie crying.

Yes, she is definitely petty enough to still be mad at me for ruining her 'art' project by saving Alex Parrish from killing himself due to her systematic ruination of his entire life. Sybarites are pathologically into their pursuits, be it art, singing, sex, whatever. Their passions can vary, but it's generally something creative or pleasurable. Like no Sybarite ever would get passionate about checking groceries or doing hard labor. Sports maybe. I think the sex-addict Sybarites kinda bridge the gap between pleasurable activity and sports.

Guess I've figured out what the opposite of 'casual sex' is.

Wonder if Sybarites have like bracket-ranked competitions with championships. How do they keep score?

Whatever.

Point is, Wolent apologized to Amy, Dante, and Luke once he looked in their heads to discover they didn't attack him. He offered them a favor as a token of apology and a ride back to wherever they needed to be. Wolent seemed surprised to see me, but I got the sense he appreciated me sticking around.

As soon as he declares the matter over, I'm out and flying home.

Losing about a half hour isn't *too* big a deal. I expect to get done what I need to get done for tomorrow's classes before the sun comes up and have time left over for researching Poe. What I *don't* expect is to see lights on in the house when I land on the back deck—or catch the smell of… *guh,* that's awful. Chemical, rotting meat, blech. No idea what it is, but it probably causes cancer to breathe too much of it.

Sliding door is locked. Grr. Annoying. I walk around to the front of the house and let myself in.

Dalton, my parents, and Sierra are having a conference in the living room. The 'rents are still in their pajamas, Mom in a bathrobe, Dalton and Sierra are dressed except for shoes. It's almost funny to see him respecting my mother's rule about shoes in the house. However, at almost one in the morning, it is *not* normal to see Sierra both awake and *not* in her PJs.

Also, Mom looks about ready to have a meltdown. Dad is somewhere between panic and 'oh, cool.' The expression on Sierra's face tells me she's expecting to be punished for something. Dalton, as always, is Mr. Casual, hands stuffed in his pants pockets.

"I assume some manner of foul play is at hand?" I ease the door shut behind me.

"We were merely explaining to your parents the details of a slight incident." Dalton glances over at me.

"This... this is just *too* much." Mom grabs her head, shaking it.

I kick my sneakers off.

Sierra sits on the sofa next to her. "Relax, Mom. They're not *actual* zombies. Just like some vampire guided missile thing."

"Wait... what?" I blurt. "Did you say zombies?"

"Not exactly," replies everyone at once.

Dad chuckles.

"St. Ives sent some dead people to kill us." Sierra pats her sword. "I got rid of them."

Mom glances at her. "They couldn't have been too dangerous."

"Gee, thanks." Sierra rolls her eyes, sighing. "I had help."

Mom and Dad smile gratefully at Dalton... but Sierra's thinking about the hellhound as having helped out on zombie detail, not him. He pounced on a woman pointing a gun at her. Oh, crap. I watch the scene replay in her memory. Ooh, she snuck out of the house to meet Dalton for sword lessons. Sierra shifts her gaze to me as if she's aware of what I'm doing. She doesn't know I've read her mind, but the look she gives me at the exact moment I become aware of their meeting feels like it. Having Dalton teach her doesn't bother me, but sneaking out after midnight is dicey, even if it's only our yard—or the woods behind it. Apparently, Dalton already smoothed the situation over with the parents, encouraging them to believe Sierra heard something and went down to check it to make sure she didn't imagine it before waking the parents up.

And by 'smoothed it over,' he's used mind control on my parents to keep Sierra from getting in trouble for sneaking outside after midnight and having a sword fight with zombies. Honestly, I'm not sure which one would bother Mom and Dad more. At least she didn't wear shoes in the house. Yes, I know it's irrational. Mom has this weird thing about germs and dirt. She's not like a germophobe who can't touch elevator buttons without using a tissue. Something about shoes, though.

Dammit. The 'rents don't know what really happened, and think the fight occurred literally in the backyard, not the woods 600 feet away from the house. Eh, semantics. It's astonishing enough they appear to be completely at peace with the notion of Sierra fighting off a group of zombies using a sword. Yeah, that's totally normal for the suburbs, right? Not going to disturb this. Mom and Dad don't need the stress over events well outside their control. I may talk to Sierra later. Not gonna get her officially in trouble, but I'm not above playing 'mom' to protect her. If she wants Dalton's help, she'll have to squeeze it in between sunset and bedtime. Then again, if she hadn't been awake, the zombies might have gotten into the house and—no, the hound would've eaten them.

Remind me to get him a Milk Bone or something. Where am I going to find a five-pound dog treat?

"Back up. Zombies? What is going on?" I zoom over to them.

Sierra explains a version of events where she went downstairs upon hearing an odd noise, bringing her sword for protection, and got ambushed by the zombies in the backyard. She claims to have killed one—which is true—and Dalton dealt with the other two. The parents haven't questioned what made him show up, and it seems neither she nor he are inclined to mention it.

"Didn't you deal with this St. Ives problem?" Mom makes a face at me like she's annoyed I forgot to do laundry.

By the way, I've never forgotten to do laundry. Put it off, yes. But I didn't forget about it. "Yeah. It's kinda weird she'd be coming after us. Academics are basically emotionless machines who get super fixated on one thing at a time and care only about whatever's going to benefit them in the near term. Once something no longer concerns them personally, they forget it like it never happened or mattered."

"She works for Fox News?" asks Dad.

Mom throws a pillow at him.

Dalton snickers.

"No, Dad. I mean, once I no longer had anything she wanted, St. Ives regarded me as a non-issue. It would be a waste of resources to pursue any sort of revenge. Even if she thinks of me not giving her the spyglass or Coralie's body as 'stealing' from her, she's not emotionally invested at all. Just looks at it from a cost versus benefit perspective."

"Oh." Mom stares at the ceiling. "I know a few people like that at work."

"Hi, sweetie," says Dalton for no particular reason.

I glance over and catch sight of Sophia crouching on the stairs, watching us.

"Seems we made too much noise." Dalton winces apologetically.

Dad stands, pacing. "So now we have to be on the lookout for these puppet things."

"Possibly." Dalton nods once. "However, if another vampire was controlling them like drones, they'd have seen Sierra destroy them. If I were they, having an eleven-year-old destroy my minions would forever make me consider those minions worthless."

"I'm twelve," grumbles Sierra.

"Oh, all the difference." He winks at her. "Sorry, luv. And no, they don't know you are—" He fidgets. "You have advantages other children your age do not."

Hmm. He's either talking about giving her a little bit of blood power or the hellhound. Neither one would go over well with the parents.

Mom looks up as if about to ask what he means.

"How many children her age know how to handle a sword?" asks Dalton.

"Ugh. My child killed someone?" Mom grabs her head in both hands.

Dalton, Sierra, and I say, "No" simultaneously.

The parents look at us.

"You just spent fifteen minutes explaining how my daughter chopped up a bunch of zombies." Mom pulls Sierra into a protective hug.

Normally, the girl would squirm or frown, but she doesn't. Uh oh. Gotta look. Crap. The woman pointed a gun at her. She's freaking out inside. I give Mom a mild encouragement to keep holding her until she squirms to get away. Sierra needs it. Otherwise,

Mom would let go fast since Sierra is not usually a huggy sort of person.

"I'm splitting a hair here," says Dalton, "but she didn't kill anyone. Those creatures were already dead. What she did was no worse than slicing up a pot roast."

Dad coughs.

"Perhaps mildly more disturbing than slicing up a pot roast." Dalton raises a finger. "Concede the point. Pot roasts don't generally moan in existential agony when sliced."

"You've never seen Dad cook, have you?" asks Sophia.

Mom covers her mouth to hold back a laugh while Dad puts on this 'fake offended' look.

"Only got one." Sierra squishes her toes into the rug. "Had help with the other two."

"I feel a bit weird." Mom stifles a yawn. "Did either one of you mess with my head?"

"Just got here, and you know I won't, Mom." I glance up at Sophia who's still watching us from the stairs. She looks suspicious, but too tired to question anything.

"Certainly not." Dalton smiles.

I know the smile. Fortunately, my parents don't.

Relax, luv. Just helped them accept Sierra's story, says Dalton's voice in my head. "Anyway"—he claps softly—"the one responsible for these ambulatory pot roasts would have seen a child destroy them. They are likely convinced such a tool is useless. I'd advise caution, but they will probably not try that again."

Pacing, I grab two fistfuls of my hair and emit a frustrated snarl.

Someone is attacking Petra in hopes of making her mad at me. One of Wolent's properties got firebombed. Men claiming to work for Stefano tried to abduct me… and now we have zombies coming from St. Ives. I want to blame Stefano for all of it, but it would be too easy. It's also super flimsy. Gotta remember I'm dealing with *vampire* politics now. It's not completely beyond possibility for Wolent to arrange a fake attack on his own stuff to blame someone else. No, I don't think he did it in this case. He seemed genuinely angry over the warehouse. Doesn't mean he didn't send some fake 'Stefano goons' after me. But, nah. Not his style. Arthur Wolent is, to my young naïve opinion, a straightforward dude. I don't think he's the type to hide behind proxies.

So something else is going on. Maybe multiple somethings else.

Good freakin' grief. Did Seattle declare war on my family?

Screw it. Don't care how it looks. I need help.

10

UN CHATON ERRANT

I made a mistake.

Sometimes *not* doing something is every bit as much of an error as actively screwing up. Fortunately, this oops happens to be small. It hasn't killed anyone yet. My lapse is assuming Aurélie would go off like an intercontinental ballistic vampiress the instant I told her men attacked me and name-dropped Stefano.

I mean for eff's sake, *I* think it sounds shady. No way would she be convinced enough from looking at my memory of the attack to fly out the window and go tear Stefano's head off ala *Mortal Kombat*. Though, I wouldn't put it past her to swing someone's head and spine around as a fashion accessory for a little while if they really got on her bad side.

So, yeah. Like I said, time for some help.

Leaving my parents to talk Sophia back to bed, I hurry out the door and fly to Seattle, specifically Aurélie's place. She's got a huge, and awesome, penthouse apartment in a high-rise downtown. Basically, one entire floor of the building is hers. I am not jealous, honestly. Doesn't mean I can't admire it even if it is *way* too extra for my taste.

As she so often does, my mentor appears to know I'm on the way before I get there. The patio door is open and she's waiting a few steps inside, wearing an expectant look as well as a frilly white-and-gold gown. Aurélie's also holding a matching collapsible fan adorned in metallic gold filigree. She looks like the queen from a ridiculously expensive Louis XIV-themed chess set. At least wearing a costume so over the top goes with her copier-paper-white skin. Like any vampire other than Shadows, she *could* alter her appearance to be more lifelike. For me, it's an automatic process, like breathing or blinking for mortals. Other vamps have to concentrate on it.

Apparently, it's kinda draining, too. Faking lifelike qualities is as much of an energy burn as a serious fistfight using boosted strength. Totally makes sense why she doesn't bother. I mean, everyone who had money back then painted themselves white anyway, so she looks the part without even trying.

And yeah, she's beyond beautiful. Even knowing a good portion of it comes from radiant charm powers doesn't make her any less captivating. I've come to learn her 'subconscious' aura has different effects based on the attitude of the observer. Men, or women who'd find her sexually attractive, do so to the Nth degree. Women, like me, who aren't attracted to other women, find her captivating in a 'whoa… what is she going to do next' sort of way. It's hard to take my gaze off her. Sophia wanted to 'collect' her like a big doll. Despite being a kid, Sierra's reaction is about the same as mine. Awestruck staring. She made Sam blush. No, he's too little to be attracted to her. He basically thought she was 'powerful and awesome' and wanted her to protect him. He blushed because it made him feel childish.

Anyway…

By the time I walk up to Aurélie, she's already seen most of what's on my mind. Still, it's rude to assume mind-reading.

"Hello, *cheri.* What troubles you?" She walks around me like a mother studying their child upon the kid's return home from school. "You are most definitely troubled."

"That's putting it mildly." I rub my hands down my face. "For starters, St. Ives sent some manner of 'zombies' to my house to—I assume—kill my family."

Aurélie hardens her gaze. Her entire presence changes from enthralling to 'find somewhere to hide, now.' Despite her looking entirely calm, it feels like I'm standing next to a warhead about to launch the upper fourth of this building into orbit. "Do you have proof?"

"Nothing solid, no. Dalton read the minds of a few mortals who dropped them off. He said the people had been grabbed randomly off the street and mind-controlled into believing they had to kill my family. When they saw Sierra, their 'programming' somehow made this woman want to kidnap her and bring her back to the vampire."

"Interesting." Aurélie purses her lips.

"Dalton thinks the woman's actual personality surfaced a little when she saw my sister. Couldn't bring herself to shoot a child… so the control changed plans and compelled her to kidnap instead."

"Hmm." Aurélie paces around, mumbling to herself in French for a moment. "This is something different than ordinary compulsion. It is closer to making a servitor."

I cringe. "Oh, yeah. Sounds ominous as hell. Like, slave?"

"Somewhat. In the realm of vampires, there are several methods by which a mortal can be turned into a servitor." Aurélie lowers herself to sit on the couch.

Right. She wants to talk at length. I shut the patio door and hurry over to sit next to her.

Aurélie smiles. "All vampires can put commands into the minds of mortals. They are simple and do not change. If you compel someone to do something, they will do it."

"Right."

"A servitor is more complicated. The vampire conditions the mortal to *want* to serve them, so they remain capable of thinking for themselves. Always, the command is there, guiding what they do, but *how* they do it is up to their experience and skills."

"Sounds like an awful lot of trouble to deliver a truckload of zombies." I whistle. "Is this something St. Ives can do? How many different vampires can make someone into a servitor?"

"I possess one such way. It tends to produce *le flagorneur,* which I find irritating."

Umm. Maybe it's time for me to work on French.

"Oh, what is the English?" Aurélie snaps her silk fan open, waving a light breeze over her face. "Sycophant."

"Aha. You can make people love you so much they trip over themselves to do whatever you want."

She frowns to the side. "*Oui.* They are too obsessed and lose focus. Cannot do complex things. They will literally run into walls trying to please me fast enough. Not only are they essentially useless, I find it cruel, no?"

I nod.

"St. Ives… she is *Académique.* Scientist." Aurélie fans herself idly. "If she were to 'ave the ability to turn a mortal into a servitor, they would most assuredly be like her. Robotic."

"Doesn't sound like what Dalton described. Is doing this to mortals one of those neato advanced powers Innocents don't get?" I lean forward, elbows on my knees… and stare down at my toes sunk into the carpet. "I don't want it… just wondering how many suspects are on the list, what bloodlines it could be limited to."

"Mmm. Most except Beasts and Innocents, I believe." Aurélie stops fanning herself and snaps it closed. "They'd 'ave to be at least a century old. What did Dalton do with them?"

"He said he removed the command and sent them home."

Aurélie quirks an eyebrow at me. "Not servitors then. The process is somewhat lengthy, and permanent… or close to permanent. It is possible to undo, but not in a few minutes."

No point asking what happened if not the servitor thing. She's already thinking. Besides, she knows I want to know.

"It could be a particular gift of compulsion." She taps the fan, her nails clicking on the gold filigree. "Occasionally, one of us possesses a unique strength in a more common ability."

Right. Like how she's so potent with charm. There could be a vampire out there who gets more mileage out of the standard mental compulsion power. Maybe his order to kill us failed when the woman saw Sierra, so the command rearranged itself into a less objectionable form to achieve the same result. If she'd brought Sierra to whatever vampire brainwashed her, she or he would certainly have harmed my sister.

Aurélie nods once in response to my reasoning. "I do not believe Eleanor possesses such a unique talent. It would certainly be known by now. There is more bothering you."

"Yeah." I explain the attack in the parking garage as well as my meeting with Petra and the incident involving the Seattle Lost Ones and someone firebombing Wolent's warehouse.

"I am glad you brought this to my attention." Aurélie leans closer, patting my cheek. "I am touched you feared I might become so enraged at someone trying to 'arm you. Sarah, *cherie,* you are precious to me, and I would certainly not 'esitate to show my displeasure should anyone threaten you undeservedly."

"Hopefully, you never have to show anyone how upset you are. Sorry. You're right. I shouldn't have assumed you'd go nuclear right away. We don't even know for sure who is doing what."

Aurélie reclines in such a casual, commanding way she looks like a model in a painting worthy of hanging in the Louvre. Any other woman draping herself on a sofa would merely be loafing on a couch. She makes leisure artistically regal.

"What about these 'zombies?' Sierra said the one guy she nutted made a big deal about them not being zombies, rather remote-controlled corpses."

"Nutted?" Aurélie blinks, staring at me for a second. "Ahh, I see. A crude way to deal with a problem. But, alas, effective. Given her age, I do not blame her."

Yeah, Dalton's blood still gave her a bit of a boost. My sister had the strength of an adult man packed into the little bony knee of a twelve-year-old. Poor guy. Yeah, I know they tried to hurt my family, but it hadn't been their idea.

"Though I am aware of the existence of less pleasant techniques, their use is not something I am well versed in. Eleanor does not possess the necessary skill set to reanimate corpses in the way you describe. True, she is an *Académique,* but *very* few of them are what you would call mystics."

"Whoa. Wait." I stare at her.

She flutters her fan. "Hmm?"

"Are you saying only a mystic could do the walking corpse thing?"

"Non." She smiles. *"L'Ombres, Académique,* some *Traditionaliste* can do something similar, but the wretches do not last long and they are not, as you say, 'remote controlled,' mindless creatures not even as useful as rats. Disgusting and pointless. You are thinking some vampire manipulated these corpses the way you control the little people in your video games."

"Yeah. Dalton's explanation made me think of that. He said whoever made them could see out of their eyes and control their every motion."

"If he is correct, it must be mystical in nature… or perhaps an unusual twist of a *L'Ombre.*" Aurélie pauses her fan. "I do not think it is a Shadow. Your associate, Glim, would have objected and likely warned you."

"Definitely… if they didn't hurt him." I scowl at the floor. Great. Yet another thing for me to feel guilty and worried about. "Something stinks about the two idiots at the college. Way too obvious in letting me 'accidentally' hear they worked for Stefano. Sounded fake as hell. It's almost like someone else is trying to trick us into starting a war."

Aurélie nods. "I am 'aving similar thoughts. We must be careful. If they act too openly to create the appearance of 'ostility, I may be forced to respond, lest others doubt the sincerity of my decree of protection over your family."

A knot tightens in my gut. Ugh! I hate politics! Even if she knows it's suspicious, she might have to do something to Stefano or St. Ives. Obviously, if they're not really involved, they'll see whatever she does as an unprovoked attack. Not sure what to do if the poop hits the fan, especially if there's so much poop it knocks the fan over.

"There has to be a way for you to hold off until knowing for sure who did what." I rake my hands through my hair. "What if it *is* Stefano? I know it sounds really stupid, but maybe he's expecting us to think 'no way would he be that dumb or obvious' and not blame him. Could he be trying to see if I'm going to 'run to Mommy' and tell on him? Maybe he's finally tired of being subordinate to Wolent and this whole brewing crapstorm is a power play for the entire city. If he goads you into attacking him, it's going to be Stefano, Paolo, and their people all coming after you, me, and my family. Would Wolent involve himself?"

"Perhaps, as you are in his circle now." Aurélie smiles sideways at me.

It's part approving smile, part curious to see how crazy things get. She's happy I didn't try to be immature or selfish and ignore the existence of vampire society. American vampires don't really do the 'king of regions' thing like in Europe, but Wolent is close enough. Becoming an official vampire generally required becoming part of his empire. The only other option would've been going Lost One or declaring loyalty to Paolo—fat freakin' chance—or maybe St. Ives. Again, a big no. Technically, all the elders are part of Wolent's domain, even though they could theoretically be rivals. It's similar to nobles in medieval times all having their personal land, armies, and estates while officially following one king.

I'd totally have joined 'Team Aurélie' if she cared about politics. But, honestly, her philosophy is perfect for me, too. Officially part of 'polite vampire society,' but no political aspirations. I'm sure Wolent would expect her to help out if any serious threat to his power came to be. Would she be able to claim neutrality and simply nod loyalty to whoever 'took over' in the event Wolent fell? The two are friends, so I think she'd help him. Also, pretty sure every other vampire in Seattle is afraid of her. Compared to other elders, she's not *that* deadly, but it's hard to fight someone who charms you into calming down and going away like a nice little boy every time you step within fifty feet of her. It would simply be too frustrating to attack her.

Aurélie giggles. "You are not considering the other option."

"Other option?" I sit up straight.

"We do not know for certain the men who attacked you—or the

vampire who sent the corpses—are who they say they are." Aurélie points her fan at me. "All you have is their word."

"Yeah." I lean back into the sofa, folding my arms over my chest. "But who else would attack me? St. Ives isn't exactly a fan, but she wouldn't go to the effort of coming after us if she didn't have a specific goal in mind. Unless she wants to toss the Innocent in a lab and experiment on me, there's no reason for her to use up time, energy, or resources on me."

Aurélie taps her foot on air, thinking. "Perhaps she has discovered Sophia's talent and wishes to study her?"

"Ack. Damn." I start to freak out, but catch myself and stay—mostly—calm. "Going to say 'probably not' there. Those corpses were sent to kill, not abduct. She'd have a much easier time kidnapping one of the Aurora Aurea than Sophia, plus they're more practiced than my kid sister. Also, grabbing one of them doesn't come with the political baggage of pissing you off."

"Hmm." Aurélie gazes up at the ceiling as if watching a ghost dance by, her gaze tracing off to the left. "Eleanor also likely would have asked you if she could borrow the girl. The woman is nothing if not direct."

I grumble. "Yeah… and she wouldn't have any hesitation over referring to a child as an object to be used or tested."

Aurélie sighs. "Such a tragedy for them, to lose all feeling."

"So… if it's not St. Ives, and you don't think Stefano sent those men after me… who are we looking for?"

"Someone who knows 'ow the traditionalists feel about you. Someone who knows about your 'istory with Eleanor." Aurélie fans herself again. "This may not be the same party. We should be cautious before assuming everything is related."

Grr. "Everything happening at once is no coincidence."

"I agree, but it does not prove a connection, merely bad timing." Aurélie gestures to the side. "Are you thirsty?"

"Sure." I'm not starving, but I have room. Not sure where she gets her blood from, but it's amazing. I feel awesome after having a glass.

Usually tastes like Shirley Temples or cherry soda. Yeah, the flavor thing is entirely coming from my brain, but still.

Aurélie stands and crosses the room to the mini-fridge concealed in an ornate wooden cabinet.

Oh, wow. Blood doesn't ordinarily keep long enough to be tasty to vampires in a fridge. Like those blood packets at donation places? Blech. Even without the preservative stuff they add, blood that's been out of a body more than fifteen minutes or so is horrible. Proof the 'nutrition' is more spiritual than anything physical about the blood itself. Whatever energy lingers 'in vitae' as Dalton says fades away reasonably fast. The blood coming from Aurélie's fridge is yummy, which means she preserved it—by adding a drop or three of *her* blood.

This explains a few things. She's quietly giving me a little power boost.

Aurélie smiles to herself as soon as I realize this.

Wow. It's gotta be a rare honor for an elder her age to take such an interest in helping someone like me. Not sure what I did to deserve it, but there is no way I'm going to turn down the help.

"Here you go, my *petit Cherie.*" Aurélie hands me a wine glass filled with blood. *"Je ne peux pas résister à un chaton errant."*

I take the glass, smiling despite having not the first clue what she said, and clink it with her in a toast. "Think it's an outsider?"

"It may be. Or..." She sips from her glass, flaring her eyebrows. "Perhaps we have an agitator in our midst."

11

MAXIMUM OVERKILL

Sophia fired off a text message to Darren Anderson, the leader of the local Aurora Aurea.

Nicole, Priya, and Sierra, seated around her at the lunch table, talked about random normal stuff. Megan didn't go to the same school, living closer to Woodinville. Fortunately, she had awesome parents who didn't mind giving her a ride so she could come over. Sophia went to Megan's house a few times as well. The first time she showed up, the girl's parents didn't do a good job of hiding their shock. It almost made Sophia cry to see them so surprised their daughter really *did* have a friend and hadn't made 'this girl at dance class' up.

Some kids, she understood why they didn't have friends. Smelled bad, acted bad, didn't *want* friends, had crazy parents who didn't allow them to have friends, or something. Megan expected everyone to make fun of her for being a bit heavy, plus tended to be quiet. Nothing about Sierra's looks would get her teased, but she, too, tended to be quiet—and didn't have any friends outside the ones Sophia made. Unlike Megan, being alone didn't bother Sierra. Also unlike Megan, Sierra *couldn't* really be alone. She had three siblings plus Sophia's friends constantly around.

Beyond fixing her friends and siblings' social lives, Sophia had a new mission: stopping zombies.

Her twice-a-month 'classes' at the lodge hadn't yet gone into any practical applications of magic for the purposes of destroying undead or shielding a house from mindless fiends—probably too advanced. When she'd texted Mr. Anderson last night asking how she can keep 'mindless fiends' away from her home, he replied 'having a problem with Jehovah's Witnesses?'

Dad laughed his head off when she asked him what that meant. He still hadn't explained it.

Obviously, Mr. Anderson intended the remark as a joke, so she pressed. She didn't have time during class to explain what Sierra told her about the attack. Having to swear on her stuffed unicorn not to tell Mom and Dad the truth about her sister sneaking out of the house hurt, but she did it. Knowing Sierra broke a big rule and got away with it sat in her stomach like a piece of bad hamburger. Her promise to her sister got into a fight with her guilt over lying to her parents.

At least Sierra accepted a compromise. Sophia wouldn't say anything unprompted, but if the parents ever directly asked her about it, she'd be honest. Most likely, Sierra figured if Mom or Dad were asking about it, they already knew—so no point forcing Sophia to lie.

Lunchtime offered the first opportunity for unrestricted texting with some degree of privacy. No teacher would run over, grab her phone, and see stuff they shouldn't see. Teachers didn't handle talk of magic and zombies well. They'd probably send her to see a counselor. Lying made her feel so guilty she couldn't even convincingly say she talked about a book or video game. She had to keep any teacher—or other kids—from seeing her talk seriously about mystic stuff.

He responded with ‹Researching. Call when you are home.›

Whew. Sophia exhaled in relief and closed the message screen before stuffing her phone in her bag.

"Welcome back to Earth," said Nicole. "How's your boyfriend?"

Priya giggled.

"Not my boyfriend. He's a tutor my parents are letting help me."

Nicole tilted her head. "What do *you* need a tutor for? You're like the smartest kid in the entire school."

"No way. Maybe I'm kinda smart, but I'm definitely not the smartest." Sophia picked up half of her turkey sandwich. "And everyone could use a tutor. Learning is cool."

"Are you trying to get into high school at twelve or something?" asked Priya, still snickering.

"Not an academic tutor." Sophia bit into her lunch.

"Drama coach," said Sierra. "She's working with him to help get over stage fright."

"Oh." Nicole shrugged and shifted the conversation back to Mr. Rose farting in math class.

Sierra, a grade ahead of them and no longer in his class, thought it hilarious. Priya and Nicole, predictably, called it gross. Sophia shifted her gaze off to the side so Nicole didn't notice her expression. Sierra took care of the lying, but the guilt still showed plain as day on *her* face. With any luck, her friends would interpret it as disgust at the math teacher exploding from the butt.

Her gaze landed on a group of older boys surrounding another eighth-grade boy. They subtly shoved him back and forth while muttering. Sophia couldn't hear them across a crowded, loud cafeteria, but the way they grinned at the other boy gave away they bullied him. The picked-on kid had on a dingy, shabby shirt and ripped jeans, also filthy. She didn't know the boys, them being three grades ahead of her. However, simply from looking at him, she assumed the recipient of the bullying probably smelled bad due to his dirty clothes. Even an eighth-grader couldn't be responsible for something like that. She figured he had some big problems at home, not his fault. What kid would *choose* to be filthy?

Other kids picking on Megan angered Sophia enough to scream at them, but she didn't quite have the nerve to directly confront six eighth-grade boys. Still, she couldn't sit there watching him get picked on for something out of his control. Yeah, a kid his age could probably do his own laundry, so maybe he shared some responsibility. Still, if his parents didn't buy detergent or the machines didn't work…

Sophia stared at the group of boys, wanting to help the kid out, but in a subtle way. Using magic at school could be risky, but how much trouble could trying to clean and repair some kid's clothes possibly cause? Two ideas orbited around the urge to release a spell: stealth and fixing the boy's outfit. Energetic tingles ran down her arms, creeping into her hands and gathering as a sense of warmth among her fingers—then faded.

The boys continued to pick on the dirty kid.

Umm... nothing happened.

A faint *pop* came from inside her backpack, about as loud as a kid clapping once. Neither her sister nor her friends appeared to notice. Sophia pretended to take a bite of her sandwich so she could look down at the pink backpack between her feet. The main zipper eased itself open, revealing a strange eight-inch tall creature. It resembled a little old man with a thick body and spindly limbs. His onion-sized head, half the size of his torso, sported a long, pointed nose and equally long pointy ears. Amber-colored faerie wings sprouted from his back through holes in a brown tunic halfway between court jester and medieval peasant. Scraps of gossamer white hair stuck out from under a cloth cap like something a commoner from the middle ages would've worn.

Uh oh. He looks like a winged brownie, only smaller and not as round. Sophia bit her lip. *Hope I didn't mess up.*

The 'faerie' gave a diminutive grunt of exertion and pulled himself out of the backpack. He peered up at Sophia, looked at the boy being bullied, then made a hat tipping gesture at her before flying straight up into the air. Sophia squeaked in alarm, but no one noticed him despite his hovering in grabbing range of Sierra's face.

Hmm, said a high-pitched, creaky voice in her head.

Sophia jumped at the unexpected telepathy. *Whoa... is this what it's like for Sarah? You, umm can hear me?*

The little man nodded.

She peered past him at her sister. *Sierra? Can you hear me?*

Sierra returned the look, raising a questioning eyebrow. "What?"

Say peanut butter if you can hear this.

"Why are you looking at me weird?" Sierra reached across the table to feel her forehead. "You okay?"

"Yeah, fine." Sophia sighed. *Guess it's only because I summoned you.*

The strange little faerie shrugged.

Will you please fix that kid's clothes? He's all dirty and probably smells bad. It's mean those other boys are picking on him.

He glanced over at the kid, still trapped against the wall surrounded by other boys. For some reason, the teachers hadn't done anything yet. Maybe they assumed the boys were friends and simply horsed around. The faerie looked back at Sophia, nodded once, and grinned… with a little too much mischief in his eyes.

Uh oh.

The cafeteria exploded into a mess of flying food, milk, and sprays of condiments. Screaming came from all sides as spaghetti, salad, hamburgers, cheese-steaks, squirts of mustard, and other half-eaten food items smacked kids in the face, splattered on shirts, or hit the windows at the far end of the room. Nicole and Priya screamed along with everyone else. Only two people in the entire cafeteria remained calm: Sophia and Sierra. Eighty percent—give or take a few points—of the flying food launched itself in a siege barrage at the bullies, chasing them off in a pelting of tomato sauce, melted cheese, and nachos flung like shuriken. Rachel Cartwright, two tables over and down a few seats, went wide-eyed as a strange gurgling noise came from her cup. She peered into it—and unsweetened iced tea exploded upward into her face.

The girl screamed.

Amid the disorder, the faerie zoomed over to the disheveled boy, who cowered against the wall trying to shield his face from the hail of food. With everyone focused on the flying mess, no one noticed a whirl of glowing gold light spiral around the boy. His torn, stained jeans, equally grimy T-shirt, and rotten sneakers changed into nice shoes, some manner of Aeropostale style pants, and a D&G sweater.

Sierra grabbed the collar of Sophia's dress and pulled her forward slightly. "What did you do?"

A basket of thankfully ketchup-less French fries smacked into the side of Sierra's head, scattering over the table.

She snarled.

"Uhh..." Sophia stared in horror as the weird little faerie zipped across the cafeteria and disappeared through the main set of double doors into the school. "Crap."

"Crap?" Sierra shook her. "Soph. Focus. What happened?"

"I just wanted to help!" Sophia teared up.

Sierra glanced around briefly. "Scream. Now. Before we stand out."

Sophia shrieked in a reasonable attempt to sound like every other kid in the room dodging 'thrown' food. Sierra also shouted, slipping under the table and pulling Sophia to safety with her as half-eaten lunch items continued whizzing by overhead.

Sierra grabbed her by the shoulders, forehead to forehead, and stared into her eyes. "Why?"

"Umm." Sophia smiled cheesily. "Some kids were picking on this boy for having dirty clothes. I just wanted to help him."

"So you start a food fight?"

Sophia shook her head. "I, umm... it didn't exactly work like I was hoping."

"No kidding." Sierra rolled her eyes.

Silence fell over the cafeteria a few seconds later. Sophia pulled herself out from under the table, looking around at a mustard-and-ketchup covered wasteland of stunned, confused children. An ice cream cone stuck to Mrs. Reynolds' head, making her look like a one-horned demon. She, too, appeared equally as bewildered as the kids.

"Umm," whispered Sophia, cringing at the mess. Her guilt worsened because no one looked at her as the responsible party. "Oops."

Sierra crawled out and stood beside her. "Imp?"

The ice cream fell from Mrs. Reynolds, splatting on the floor. Several hamburger patties stuck to the ceiling unpeeled and hit the floor one after the next.

"Not exactly." Sophia continued gazing around in mortified awe.

"It looked like a mix of faerie and brownie. Did what I asked him to do and now I think he's run off to do bad stuff."

Sierra facepalmed. "*Why* did you summon a destructive creature?"

"I didn't mean to!" yelled Sophia.

A few nearby kids stared at her.

"Oh, no! Grab me." Sophia looked around, increasingly freaked out and ashamed of herself. Emotion boiled until it burst out of her in a wave of raw magic.

Flickering purple-teal light flooded the cafeteria. Sierra clamped her arms around Sophia and held on. Roaring like a thunderstorm of screaming children caught in a tornado played backward raged from wall to wall. In a flash, the cafeteria reverse-videoed back to being clean and orderly. The eighth graders reappeared surrounding the formerly dirty boy, but he still had his clean, new clothes. When the rewind stopped, time held still. A cafeteria full of kids sat motionless like a three-dimensional painting of an ordinary lunch period. Sierra let go of her, scrambled under the table to the other side, and took her seat. Sophia sat in her place as well.

"One problem fixed." Sophia 'wiped sweat' from her forehead.

Sierra looked around. "More than one… nice fix. Is anyone gonna remember?"

"No, because it sorta didn't happen. You will. I left you out of the rewind. The boy's clothes stayed nice, so the thing I let loose is still out there. Spell kinda messed up. I only wanted to fix his clothes, but I kinda overdid it."

"You know what Dad says." Sierra grinned. "Anything worth doing is worth *over*doing. How dangerous is this monster you set loose?"

Sophia grimaced. "I dunno. He's probably not *dangerous,* but he's definitely going to cause trouble. Gotta find him."

"Can you leave time stopped?"

"Nope. It's only this room… and it's gonna wear off soon. Just enough for us to sit back down."

The world resumed like a movie coming off pause.

Sierra exhaled. "At least you saved a ton of food from being wasted."

"Yeah. Wow… I hadn't even thought of that until you said something." Sophia grimaced. Wasting all that food *would* have made her feel awful.

A scream came from the hallway outside the cafeteria.

Sierra twisted around to look at the double doors. "That didn't sound good."

"No…" Sophia sighed. "No, it didn't."

12

DO VAMPIRES DREAM OF UNDEAD SHEEP

Okay, so when I got home last night, I Googled 'chaton errant.'

It's the only part of what Aurélie said to stick in my brain. Yeah… stray kitten. No idea what she actually said, but my guess is she sees me as a stray kitten she couldn't help but take care of. Maybe being an Innocent isn't the most uber of bloodlines, but if my 'powers of cuteness' are strong enough to convince an elder like her to take me under her wing, they're pretty epic.

No, I'm not too proud to object.

She's 397 years old. I've been a vampire for ten months. I *am* a kitten.

Also, I'm not beyond putting up with ridiculous tedium in video games for an advantage. If repeating the same little area over and over and over ends up giving my character a boost, I do it. She already explained to me—when I freaked out over Dalton giving Sierra blood—drinking an older vampire's blood doesn't do anything creepy or weird like make them subservient mind-slaves or anything of the sort. Well, it *can* if the older vampire happens to be a user of blood rituals. However, only Academic-mystics can. Aurélie is not one of those.

Neither is Dalton. The worst possible side effect I could suffer from drinking this is less resistance to her being able to see into my head.

Considering our 396-year age gap, my 'resistance' to her is about the same as holding up a sheet of paper to defend against being shot by a bazooka. So, I'm not losing anything. Doesn't really feel like she's giving me major 'power-ups' either, but it's probably a gradual thing. Not like Popeye sucking down a can of Spinach and turning on god mode. And hey, I did basically kick the butts of those two idiots at the parking garage.

Maybe they weren't total scrubs after all and she is having an effect on me.

But I still have questions. Like... who is messing with us? Who sent the zombies? Why is Petra such a psychopathic bitch? Why don't women's clothes have pockets? Why do chickens have that flappy red stuff on their faces... and why the hell am I standing in a cubicle farm?

In all directions except behind me—which is a doorway to a small break room—stretches a seemingly endless field of office cubicles and workers. It's not a business casual sort of place. Everyone's dressed in professional attire, no polo shirts anywhere in sight. As strange as me being here is my outfit. I'm wearing a skirt suit that's a bit big on me, but not too ridiculous. It's also nothing I own. More like stole from Mom's closet. 'Funeral director grey' isn't my style.

Wow, I feel like the girl in *Dead Like Me* on her first day at the temp agency. Some people are just not made to wear skirt suits and rock them. George from the TV show looked like a skinny teen who got a cheap skirt suit from a thrift store. I look like a little kid playing dress up. Workers going back and forth smile at me in varying degrees of patronizing from 'oh just go home already' to attempted civility. No one throws off overtly hostile vibes, but it's beyond obvious they aren't happy to see me for some reason. Or maybe they're jealous. Of what, I have no idea. Certainly not my looks. No one's jealous of the girl next door. I'm no Aurélie. Hell, I'm not even a Bree Swanson. Considering they're all like old—thirty plus—they might be jealous of my age. That would make sense... certainly more sense than me randomly appearing in the middle of a giant office building with no memory of how I got here.

The last thing I remember is going home after leaving Aurélie's and doing school work until…

Oh, crap. I have to be dreaming.

Right. Let's see where this crazy mental rollercoaster goes. Hopefully, Ego is driving and not ID.

I proceed down the aisle with no particular destination in mind. People who notice me continue giving me these 'what the hell is *she* doing here' looks. Weirdly, all of them feel like vampires. Whoa, trippy. I'm stuck in some kind of weird mash up of *The Office* and *Dracula.* Is this *What We Do in the Cubicles?* An entire company staffed by vampires. Wild.

Kinda creepy how everyone's staring down at me, but this is a dream… so it has to be my feelings of inadequacy making me short as like a metaphor or something. Crap. Nope. Superego is driving. The more I walk, the taller the grey fabric cube walls get. I soon feel like I'm stuck in a literal minotaur's labyrinth of corporate process.

Shit.

Random wandering brings me to a cube in the corner with high walls and no accessible windows anywhere nearby. For most office-dwellers, not having a window would be dreary. I don't mind. Post-It notes and other bits of paper are all over the various cabinets and soft walls of 'my' cube. A weird sense of familiarity makes me think I've been working here for years, even though on an intellectual level, I understand this is neither real nor actually familiar.

Apparently, I'm a programmer.

Whatever, dream. Do your worst.

I hop in the chair and poke the mouse. The screen is full of computer code that's simultaneously something I wrote and foreign. Somehow, I'm aware of working on a super-mega important project, deadline looming, but I can't remember what the software does or who it's for. The vague, indefinable fear of a looming deadline gets me to start typing. I'm writing lines from programs I wrote in school. Stupid, basic learning type things. Certainly nothing a high-end software company would be paying anyone to create. The input from the keyboard doesn't match what's on the screen. As a test, I randomly mash keys. Code appears on the screen much faster, but it's no different from what appeared when I tried to type actual instructions.

Yeah. Definitely dreaming.

Hey, this is a step up at least. I'm not naked in a morgue cooler or seeing the Littles as vampires this time.

It occurs to me my feet aren't on the floor. I peer down at myself. My skirt suit appears even frumpier, like it's become far too big on me. I grab my chest, pressing the billowy white dress shirt against epic flatness. Not even angry bee stings remain of my boobs. Great. I'm a kid. Aww, crap. Explains why everyone here is looking at me like I don't belong. I slide off the chair and walk out of my cube into the aisle again.

Yep. I'm not surrounded by giant vampires. I'm like ten. Or, technically, dreaming about being ten.

A man in a blue tie hurries over to me. "Hey, Wright. Mr. Smith wants to see you. He's been looking for you for an hour at least. Not the best day to take too long on lunch."

He gives me this fake-as-hell smile that really says 'I hope you get fired so I can have your cubicle,' then walks off acting overly pleased with himself. Grr. Douchebag.

I tap my foot. Aww, I have cute little kid-sized high heels.

What the hell is wrong with me?

Okay, think, Sarah. Am I a child because Aurélie called me a lost kitten? Is this some internal insecurity about me feeling like I'm not ready to be a 'grown up vampire'? Did the guy I fed from last night have LSD in his system? Probably not. The stuff's kinda rare around here.

Another question. Do I really want to subject myself to being verbally reamed out by a boss I don't have at a job existing only in my imagination? When people say 'dream job,' this isn't what they mean. The absolute worst part about being a teenager working a summer job is getting a manager who thinks people under the age of eighteen are like Warcraft peons they can abuse whenever they feel like it. At fourteen, I worked briefly at an art supply store in the mall. My first day, the manager—a total dick named Steve—told me to spend the whole four-hour shift wandering around to familiarize myself with the layout, so if someone asked where something was, I could answer them. Fair enough, right? Anyway, while I was roaming and staring and complaining in my head about how slow the clock moved, something happened with one of the other employees. He ended up yelling at her, calling her stupid or a moron… I forget exactly the words. Everyone in the place thought Steve was inches from hitting her. The poor girl locked herself in the bathroom sobbing. Called her father for a ride home and refused to come out until he got there to protect her from Steve. Yeah, I didn't go back.

I'm expecting this Mr. Smith to be a chimera made from the mixed-together memories of various butthead bosses.

Oh well. Should probably get this over with. I head down the aisle, hook a left, and walk to the opposite end of the floor to the giant, fancy corporate office. The man sitting behind the desk is sorta Paolo Cabrini with Stefano's hair, Wolent's jaw, and Steve the art store guy's weaselly nose.

The second I'm in the door, he starts yelling at me—not literally shouting, merely scolding—about missing deadlines. My projects are all late. He's finding errors. He's questioning how I ever managed to pass a programming course and get a degree. Well, gee, numbnuts, let me guess. You hired someone for a programming position who's taken *one* intro to computer science class and hasn't even finished it yet. Think I found your problem.

Wow. Most people have nightmares of monsters. I guess monsters have nightmares of day jobs.

"Do you have anything at all to say?" asks Mr. Smith.

"Yeah." I set my fists against my hips and stare at him. "Why the hell do I look like I'm ten years old?"

The room flashes away to blinding white light.

NEXT THING I KNOW, I'M HOME IN THE UPSTAIRS HALLWAY.

No more skirt suit too big for me. I'm wearing a tank top and short shorts, barefoot, my toenails painted pink. Alas, I still seem to be ten. Wait, no… maybe closer to eleven. Mom's right next to me getting ready to clean the windows. Sunlight streams in, bathing us in warmth—not the least bit uncomfortable.

Okay, I used to love doing this with Mom. No, not the cleaning part. Only insane people *love* cleaning. Normal people tolerate it. Normal people love having a clean house, not so much the process of doing the cleaning itself. Anyway, I loved spending time with her. She'd always been busy with work, so time to hang had been kinda limited.

Everything's moving in slight slow motion, highlighted in a surreal glow.

Yeah, Ego is trying way too hard. This is like the 'everything is awesome' cut scene in a lame Eighties movie. I really freakin' hope St. Ives or Stefano isn't about to burst through the wall and shred Mom to pieces.

Nah, the vibe in the air is too calm.

Hmm. Am I insecure about something? No… they say insecurity and worry cause naked dreams. Perhaps this is simply my brain going overboard with the whole 'day job never working out for me' thing.

"Hey, hon." Mom smiles, handing me a sponge.

Or… this could be the opposite of a nightmare. I'm still allowed to have a nice, happy dream, right? Hell, the real world is basically a nightmare at the moment. Someone needs to make a word for the opposite of a nightmare—a really amazing, warm, happy dream. Time to stop worrying and just enjoy this escape for as long as it lasts.

"Hey yourself." I grin back at her, take the sponge, and start washing the window.

And yeah. Screw Mr. Smith.

13

TIMEOUT

Sophia stared down at the completed vocabulary test on her desk.

Worrying about the creature she set loose in the school made her take a little longer than usual, but she still finished the test in six minutes. She sometimes didn't know how to pronounce some words since she'd only ever read them, but her functional vocabulary—according to her parents—matched that of a high school student closer to graduating. Language class felt like a breeze. She had to be the only kid in the room who read books for fun all the time.

Mom let her read pretty much anything if it didn't have 'icky stuff' in it. Didn't make too much sense to Sophia how people kissing was 'icky' but monsters being sliced in half or gore flying everywhere was fine.

No one got in trouble for throwing food, but the critter is still loose.

She twirled her fingers around an imaginary small sphere, able to detect a thread of energy connecting her to the weird little faerie she'd accidentally summoned. It didn't feel the same as Klepto. No, the kitten she'd *made*. Permanently. The faerie's energy resonated like temporary magic. Mr. Anderson and the mystics had taught her the basics of spells.

Some happened in an instant and stopped—like making a lock open by itself. Some spells lasted for a few minutes or a few hours, then stopped on their own. This faerie summoning didn't feel like a true summoning. She hadn't gated in an actual creature from another place. No, she'd molded magical energy into a fake creature, but it didn't give any sense of having a time limit. The invisible thread connecting her to it acted like a power cable. As long as she let it 'run,' the spell would continue.

Except for what mischief the little goober might cause, the worst it could do to her would be to make her so tired she collapsed wherever she happened to be. Getting detention for sleeping in class would stink, but she dreaded what the critter would do to other people more.

She concentrated on her hands, trying to 'unplug' the connection to the spell so it stopped. Force built up inside her. Resisting the urge to grunt in an otherwise silent classroom, she mentally pushed at the want to shut the spell down.

A blast like a small firecracker went off with a sharp *snap* two desks to her right.

Rachel Cartwright screamed.

Almost everyone jumped.

The girl who often teased Sophia for being 'too nice' sat at her desk, covered in blue ink from her exploded pen. She looked as if someone hit her with spray paint. All over her face, sweater, desk, the floor…

Crap. I can't concentrate in here. Too many people watching me. I'm scared of being caught.

A few kids nervously laughed.

"Uhh, Mrs. Hooper?" asked Rachel in a timid voice. "My pen exploded. Can I go wash my face?"

The teacher nodded, waving her to go.

Rachel slipped out of her seat, picked her test up off the desk, and brought it to the teacher. "The whole paper's blue. I'm sorry. Can I have a new one when I get back?"

The teacher stared at her, and the paper for a long moment, clearly baffled at the unusual way the pen had burst. "All right, dear. Go wash your face before it dries."

Loud heavy metal music erupted over the school's PA system.

Her classmates might have screamed, but she couldn't hear them. Mrs. Hooper nearly fell out of her chair.

Uh oh. I definitely messed up. How the heck did a fix spell turn into a weird not-summon? It's not gonna wear off like an enchantment. Drat! I really need to send it back.

Sophia jumped out of her desk, grabbed her completed test, and jogged to the teacher. She set the paper down and mouthed 'bathroom?'

Mrs. Hooper glanced at the paper, raised both eyebrows in an expression of impressed surprise, then nodded.

Sophia thanked her, then ran out into the hall. She rushed past Rachel, heading for the school's front office. The blaring screechy music cut out to silence two seconds before she got there. Both office women stood by the control desk for the announcement system with their backs to the glass wall and door. Sophia cringed. Something pink fell down from overhead, striking the floor in the middle of the office. She gawked at the ceiling—covered with random objects. Staplers, two vases, a paper clip holder, books, papers, and one umbrella clung to the white foam tiles as if superglued.

I made an imp... just without the mean streak.

She raised her arms, pointing both hands at the office, and cast a dispelling charm.

All the stuff abruptly falling to the floor startled the women into screaming.

Sophia rushed away before they noticed her, following a vague sense of direction toward the magic. Commotion in a classroom halfway down the next hall on the left sounded suspicious.

"Ow!" yelled a girl. "Stop pulling my hair!"

"Now what?" muttered Sophia. She crept up to the door and peered in at a seventh-grade room.

The teacher lay asleep across his desk, snoring. Half the students also napped. Two girls with long hair in the middle of the room had been braided together so their skulls touched. Every kid with laced shoes had them tied together. Pens, books, backpacks, papers, and other various junk had floated up to the ceiling and stuck.

Oh no!

Sheer terror at getting in so much trouble they expelled her hurled a time stop spell out of Sophia as instinctively as yanking her hand back from a hot pan. Everything inside the seventh-grade room stopped moving.

She ran in, tossing dispels at all the pranks, starting with the girls braided together. Merely looking at them hurt. After the magic detangled them, she dragged the standing girl around like a department store mannequin and stuffed her into the empty desk behind the girl she'd been braided to. From there, Sophia dispelled levitating objects, knotted shoelaces, and so on.

A snarl came from a bookshelf in the back.

The not-faerie zoomed into the air, jabbing its finger at her. "Stop ruining everything!"

"I can't let you prank the whole school. You have to stop."

"No deal. Already paid the tax."

She furrowed her brow. "What tax?"

"Did your favor. Passage!" The not-faerie puffed out his chest. "Now free to have fun."

"You aren't a real… whatever you are. Just a spell running. Magical energy doesn't pay taxes or make deals."

He folded his arms.

"Sorry, but I have to end the spell. If you were a real… faerie-goblin, I'd totally make a deal with you, but you're just loose energy."

"No!" wailed the faerie. He pointed at her, sending a tingle across the tops of her feet.

She peered down. Ballet flats didn't have shoelaces to tangle, a fact the faerie appeared not to notice until after attempting to trip her up. Sophia raised her hands toward the errant magical creature. Her hair wrapped around her face like a Nerf headlock.

"Gah!"

Sophia pulled her hair down from her eyes in time to see the faerie disappear out the door. Grumbling, she ran after him, still fighting to get her hair back to normal. The instant she left the room, the time freeze effect stopped. She didn't wait around to be seen or observe what happened.

Not far from the classroom, the faerie darted into an open locker, slamming the door after itself. She skidded to a stop and yanked the door open. The faerie hovered in the middle of an otherwise empty—unused—locker. He backed up, cowering against the wall. Again, Sophia raised her hands and began to cast a dispel. The faerie launched himself at her face. Instinctively, she ducked. Before she could stand, a force hit her from behind and threw her into the locker, which slammed.

Blind panic took over. She burst into tears, pounding on the door while a momentary nightmare of being stuck there until late at night when Sarah showed up to look for her played out in her head. After a moment, she collected herself.

"I'm being stupid."

Two deep breaths later, she focused on the mechanism and cast an unlock spell.

The metal door flew open.

Growling, Sophia jumped out into the hall, looking left, then right both ways.

Quiet.

A faint hint of magic seemed stronger to her right. Grumbling, hands balled in fists, she fast-walked down the corridor until noticing a clamor coming from the alcove leading to the cafeteria. She'd already gone past the point of having to explain what took so long for a bathroom break, so she figured better to finish this. No point getting in trouble *and* failing to stop the mischief she set loose. Maybe she could get out of trouble by claiming a bully shoved her into a locker and closed it.

Technically, not a lie. She didn't need to specify the bully wasn't a person.

Metal clattering and shocked gasps led Sophia across the cafeteria to the kitchen.

She stopped short at the door, frozen in utter horror at everything being gooey brown. Gloopy slime coated four kitchen workers, the walls, floor, ceiling, and tables. Once her nose informed her the terrifying substance consisted of nothing more disgusting than chocolate pudding, she relaxed.

The weird little faerie hovered in the middle of the chaos, back turned to the doorway, laughing his butt off at the reactions of the cafeteria workers to the pudding-splosion. Sophia leaned into the room enough to get her arm through the gap in the swinging plastic doors, trying to be as silent as possible.

Sorry little guy. Thanks for helping that boy, but I gotta send you home.

She thrust her hands at it, invoking a dispel.

The faerie emitted a pained wail, then popped into a burst of glowing sparkles. Its energy returned to her, running up her arms as a tingle. Her sense of channeling power into an active spell stopped.

Whew.

"Mary?"

"Yes?" asked another woman.

"What just happened?"

"I'm still trying to work that out."

"We are covered in pudding," said an older-sounding woman.

Slurp. "Chocolate."

Crap! Rewind! Rewind!

She threw magic into the kitchen.

In her haste, she didn't exactly do what she wanted—rewind time—but instead, rewound the pudding, which reverse-exploded, peeling away from everything and compressing back into the giant cans from whence it came. She'd undone the destruction, but all four women remembered everything.

Stunned cafeteria workers exchanged bewildered glances.

The nearest woman turned to face the others. "Did you see pudd—?"

"I saw nothing," said a grandma-aged woman with reddish hair. "Nothing."

"Yeah," replied the third, a tall, older woman whose large nose and skinny body made her look a bit like a bird. "We've just been working way too many darn hours."

Sophia backed away from the doors before they saw her and slouched in relief.

Whew. No more summoning at school. I got so *lucky.*

14

A PERSONAL REALITY

Sam stared between his knees at the television, gripping the PlayStation controller tight.

He lounged in an extreme slouch on his bedroom floor, more lying down than sitting, head resting against the side of the bed. Blix perched above him on the edge of the mattress, little daemon feet dangling on either side of Sam's head. They co-op played *LEGO Marvel Superheroes,* taking a break from beating each other up in *Street Fighter 5.*

Weirdness happened at school earlier. He vaguely remembered taking a flying plate of spaghetti to the face and seeing an ice cream cone stuck to the side of a teacher's head, but it seemed more like a daydream than reality. Blix explained Sophia did something hilarious, barely able to speak due to how hard he laughed while describing a massive explosion of food flying all over the cafeteria.

Sam didn't think the imp lied, but it also didn't sound anything like Sophia to start a food fight. Most likely, she tried to do something else and screwed up. He would have preferred to remember it, but she probably panicked and didn't think to leave him out of the rewind. Good she undid it, though. The teachers would have given the entire school detention if they couldn't figure out who started it.

Ronan sat on Sam's left, absorbed in the PSP, a bowl of pretzels and chips on the rug between them. They'd worked out a rotation for PlayStation time since he lacked a third controller or any games three people could play at once. Ronan didn't notice—since time flew while playing—but he got longer time slots than Sam or Blix took. Sam could play video games whenever he wanted since he lived there. Blix often stayed up super late to game with headphones while Sam slept. Even though Ronan's mom got him a PS4 for Christmas, Sam hadn't bothered changing the times. The only real difference is they could hang out at Ronan's house and play as well. The boy had a giant house, but it kinda fell apart in places, which made it like an adventure. Sometimes, they stayed home and gamed together virtually. Everyone using separate PlayStations also let Darryl and Jordan join in, usually for *Destiny.*

His other friends both had to go home earlier since they didn't know about all the cool stuff or the mirrorverse shortcut. Ronan basically stayed over until bedtime or his mom demanded his return. Whenever Darryl and Jordan came over, Blix had to stay inconspicuous. Even though the boys couldn't see him, he lurked in the closet or under the bed with the PSP and headphones. They'd notice a PS4 controller floating in midair.

Blix did allow Ronan to see him, though.

Sam loved having one friend who knew about the secret, awesome stuff, even if it occasionally resulted in near death experiences for both of them. His newest friend almost getting stuck paralyzed for years to demonic venom scared him more than having a vampire grab him by the neck. His big sister had basically become a superhero. Everyone called vampires 'monsters,' but Sam didn't think of them as any worse than people. The bad ones just had more ability to do bad stuff—like supervillains.

Turning into a vampire hadn't changed Sarah much. If anything, she'd become *nicer*. Problem being, some other bad vampires out there didn't like her being nice. He wasn't going to let anyone hurt his big sister—if he could do anything about it. Making friends with a few demons wasn't a big deal. Mom didn't really like it, but she also didn't like kittens. Well, she didn't have an issue with kittens in general, simply didn't want one in the house—at least initially. She no longer minded Klepto.

It's more likely Sarah will scratch up the furniture than the cat, said Dad in the back of Sam's memory.

He grinned.

Even if associating with demons put him at risk, he didn't mind. Having a vampire in the house already put them at risk. A nine-year-old boy couldn't do very much to protect his family without something like a gun, but Mom would totally freak out if he touched one. She'd probably object more to a gun in the house than a demon. Also, guns didn't work well on vampires, ghosts, or butthead wizards possessing people from across town.

Besides, vampires and demons had a lot in common. People misunderstood them. Sarah proved vampires aren't any more evil than ordinary people. The Aurélie lady made him feel all sorts of weird whenever he saw her, like a faerie tale princess who wanted to love and protect him. Honestly, he blushed thinking about how she made him feel. Sam wanted to *do* the protecting, not be a protected child—even if he *was* only nine. Almost ten. He didn't have long to wait until June 19th.

He frowned, worried his parents would be sad in June, since Sarah had 'died' on the 25th last year, exactly one week after her last day of school. Since she didn't stay dead, he hoped Mom and Dad would not make a big issue out of her 'death-i-versary.' If anything, they should celebrate it as an 'unbirthday.' As in undead.

While guiding his LEGO Wolverine down a street, Sam daydreamed about being a vampire and flying around doing nice things for people. Like everything else cool in the world, going vamp would have to wait until he got older. Then again, he didn't *really* want to do it—mostly because he had to die first and it would make his parents sad. Still, he could pretend to be a vampire.

"Sam?" whispered Ronan. "There's something in the closet. I heard it move."

"Yeah, I know." Sam mashed a button to beat up a pack of bad guy robots. "Just a voice."

Blix shot the pack of robots from above using Cyclops' eye beam laser. All sorts of colors flashed on the screen from the crazy battle. Somehow, Sam managed to keep track of it all, knowing which baddies had the lowest health, and even predicting when they'd attack. He'd played the game enough to see through their routines. After four hours, he understood the AI did the same basic things.

"No, something moved."

Sam glanced sideways at his friend. Ronan was basically the boy version of Sophia—meaning a little short, a lot skinny, and easily scared. That he also had long blonde hair only strengthened the comparison. He didn't wear it anywhere near as long as Sophia, only to his shoulders. Dad called him 'Hanson' as a joke for some silly reason. Sam hadn't cared enough to Google or ask about it.

Assuming his friend had seen Klepto or something not really scary, he shrugged. "Probably the cat."

"Serious, dude. Something in the closet moved."

"Okay," said Sam. "Let me know if it starts trying to eat us."

Ronan exhaled, seemed to find the courage to ignore the closet, and resumed playing the PSP.

Sam steered his LEGO Wolverine into a building to rescue some people.

Blix emitted a strange warble Sam understood to mean "Don't slice the hostages."

"I won't."

Tiny imp feet tapped him on the head. "I know you know. Wolvie's got multi-hit arcs when he swings. Can hit the good people by accident."

Sam held back the urge to sigh. He knew this. Blix knew he knew this. The imp liked to feel important and point out obvious things.

"What'd he say?" asked Ronan.

"Wolverine's claw attacks are big sweeps that will hurt hostages, too."

Ronan gawked. "Whoa, really?"

"Yeah, really. We've been playing this game for a month and you didn't realize his claws hit everything around him?"

"I knew they hit every bad guy in front of him. Didn't think they'd score hits on hostages though." Ronan rolled his eyes. "So stupid."

"Not stupid. They want players to be careful and use the quick stab." Sam headed right for the supervillain boss. "I'll deal with this guy, you mop up the henchmen."

"On it!" chimed Blix.

"Uhh, Sam?" asked Ronan, once again sounding worried.

"Yeah?"

"My feet are warm."

"So, take your socks off."

"Didn't wear 'em. Uhh, your closet's glowing."

Sam paused the game, earning a startled, "Ack" from Blix. He looked left, past Ronan, at his bedroom closet door. Orangey-red light shone out from under it, almost as if a blast furnace raged inside. He shifted one foot closer to Ronan's. Sure enough, warmth radiated from the closet strong enough to feel from here.

"Interesting." Sam raised an eyebrow. "It's never done that before."

"Uh oh," said Blix.

"Is your closet on fire?" Ronan looked back and forth from the glow to Sam.

Sam sniffed. His room smelled the same as normal. "I don't think so."

He set the controller on the rug, stood, and crept over to the door. The closer he got, the warmer his toes became… but not painfully so. Standing right outside the closet felt like he'd stuck his feet under a baseboard heater. Definitely not a fire. Fire burned *way* more. He tested the doorknob by tapping it. Normal, not even warm. Curious, he grasped the knob and turned it.

"Wait!" yelled Ronan.

Sam didn't.

His closet looked normal—except for a huge hole in the floor leading to a tunnel of black basalt rock. It appeared to be a portal ringed in brilliant red-orange energy, containing a relatively short downhill slope to a much wider cave.

"Whoa," whispered Ronan.

Sam entered the closet and stuck one foot past the opening. The stone floor felt slightly less hot than a sidewalk in the summer. Exploring strange alien cave systems barefoot didn't sound like a great idea, but the doorway might disappear if he ran downstairs to grab his sneakers. Going in *might* also be a bad idea... but curiosity pulled at him. Also, he had a strong, unexplainable feeling it wouldn't be dangerous.

"C'mon." Sam took another step.

"You wanna go into a fire cave without sneakers?" asked Ronan.

"Like sneakers would matter if we stepped in lava."

Ronan chuckled. "Yeah, but the rock *near* lava is gonna be too hot to walk on."

"Okay, fine." Sam looked at Blix. "Would you please grab my sneakers from downstairs? This gate might close if we all leave the room."

Blix gave a thumbs-up and disappeared.

"I left mine home." Ronan sighed. "Guess I'll wait here."

Sam leaned back, looking at the door to the hall. "Klepto, you here?"

The kitten appeared in the doorway amid a flash of purple light. "Mew."

"Can you please do us a huge favor and grab Ronan's sneakers? He left them home."

Klepto nodded, then vanished.

Blix appeared, holding Sam's sneakers, which he held out.

"Thanks, man."

"No problem." Blix grinned.

"Your mom's gonna yell at us for having shoes on in the house."

Sam pointed at the opening in the closet floor. "I'm not technically in the house. This is another dimensional reality. Doesn't count for Mom's rule."

Klepto reappeared in a flash, one sneaker in her mouth. She dropped it in front of Ronan and disappeared again.

"Dude, your sister's cat is awesome." Ronan sat on the rug and pulled his left sneaker on.

"Yeah. Totally."

"Can't believe you haven't told Darryl or Jordan about all this stuff."

Sam raised one hand. "I can't. You know we can't. Only told you for two reasons. One, your big bro is dating Sarah. You guys are basically family now. Two, I trust you not to tell anyone. Sarah will get in a buttload of trouble if anyone finds out."

Klepto reappeared with Ronan's other shoe, which she dropped. "Mew!"

Sam scooped the kitten up and hugged her. "Thank you!"

"Mew." Klepto purred for a few seconds, then disappeared.

"C'mon. Hurry up. Sophia's about to run in here and tell us not to go." Sam stood, jumped into the hole, and slid down the stone ramp into the cave.

Blix glided after, pulling up at the last second to land on Sam's left shoulder, curling his tail across his back for balance.

Ronan followed less confidently, stumbling to a halt beside him. The closet door closed, seemingly on its own, but the portal remained open. All the items on the closet floor appeared to be floating on a glass plate above the hole. Knowing Sophia would panic and whine at him to come back out, Sam darted off down the cave before she opened the door. If she didn't see him, she couldn't guilt him into turning back.

"Sam?" called Ronan uneasily in the distance. Seconds later, the scuff of running sneakers hurried up behind him. "Why are you afraid of Sophia?"

"'Cause. The kitten's her familiar. Whatever Klepto sees or hears, Sophia knows about. If she found us before we went in, she'd threaten to tell Mom if we went in." Sam grinned. "She's not going to follow us inside."

Ronan looked around at a giant cavern of charred rock. Horn-like protrusions stuck out of the walls everywhere. "Umm. Maybe going in here *is* something she should tell on us about."

"Nah. It's safe." Sam resumed walking down the cave, which continued straight into the distance as far as he could see without turns or branches.

"Dude… We are definitely *not* in Narnia." Ronan jogged up alongside him. "This place looks like a map in *Diablo*."

Blix laughed. "It's a demi-realm."

Ronan glanced at the imp. "What did he say?"

"He said we're in a demi-realm." Sam traced his fingers along the wall on his right. Warm, not hot. The air smelled kinda like the oil-fired furnace in Grandpa Sheridan's basement.

"Demi-realm?" Ronan scrunched up his nose. "What's that mean?"

Blix extended his little arms out to either side. "An in-between realm. It's a personal reality. The one who cured Ronan lives here."

"Oh." Sam nodded, feeling a measure safer. "Should we be here?"

Ronan kept glancing sideways at them as he walked. "What's he saying?"

"This isn't Hell or even a real world. Think video game. We clipped off the map and we're in the grey area under it. The being who cure-poisoned you lives here." Sam patted him on the arm. "Chill."

"I can't chill. It's too hot here." Ronan gave a weak laugh.

"Naw. Just warm."

Ronan whistled.

"What?" Sam punted a little rock out of his way, watching it skitter down the cave.

"It's more than 'warm.' Feels like the middle of August… in California. I'm already sweating. And…" Ronan gestured around. "How are we even able to see? This is a cave and there are no lights."

"Uhh, magic?" asked Sam, chuckling. "We're in some other plane. I don't think they have electricity here, so they gotta get their light from something else. Be glad gravity is pointing in the normal direction."

Ronan fanned himself.

They explored a network of caves, chambers of varying sizes, and all manner of awesome rock formations. Some rooms even had frozen 'rivers' of shiny black rock, maybe cooled lava. Eventually, they found their way to the edge of a massive three-story-high chamber. Dozens of rounded, lumpy columns like molten black candle wax stretched off ahead and to the right. Not far away on the left, the stony floor ended at a cliff overlooking a vast field of grey silt under a crimson sky striated in black clouds. Miles away to the right, a bubbling black lake so vast it might be an ocean stretched off as far as he could see. The chamber continued straight ahead for about three football fields before reaching a wall where a small rounded tunnel led deeper into the strange world.

"Wow… this is… so weird," whispered Ronan. The normally timid boy walked toward the cliff, but didn't get *too* close. "Sam, check it out. We're up high."

Sam hurried over to stand next to him.

The ceiling extended only about ten feet past the edge of the floor, forming a roof overhead, making him feel as though they stood on the balcony of a bizarre castle. Straight down past a hundred or more feet of inky-black stone, a huge lava river ran along the base of whatever mountain or structure they inhabited. Several dark islands broke up the glowing orange flow. The magma river extended left and right to the horizon, as did the black wall.

Sam felt a bit like a bug sitting in a long crack on the side of a house.

"That's lava…" Ronan leaned forward and spat over the edge.

Sam leaned a little too, in order to watch the tiny white dot fall to oblivion.

"Aww. Didn't see anything."

"Too far," said Sam.

"So, this guy who lives here… is he a demon?" whispered Ronan.

Blix nodded.

"Yeah." Sam poked the imp in the stomach. "But he's like you."

Blix tilted his head.

"Technically a demon, but cool. Not mean."

Grinning, Blix gave a double thumbs-up.

A blast of blackish-crimson smoke erupted from the ground right behind them.

"Exactly why I helped you," said a booming deep voice.

Sam whirled, as did Ronan.

A strange man stood an arm's length away, as tall as a pro basketball player. Long horns sprouted from either side of his bald head, stretching straight up two feet in a gradual reward curve to smooth points. Dark crimson skin and a black goatee definitely added to the 'demonic' look. Five skulls of varying size adorned a heavy black leather belt, the largest in the center, growing progressively smaller to either side. His skirt of golden chain mail armor gave off a faint clinking as he moved. He had the legs of a giant goat, each hoof larger than Dad's head. Shiny black bracers on each forearm bore glowing red runes in an indecipherable language. Two great dragon-like wings sprouted from his back, hanging like folded up umbrellas close to his body.

Ronan backpedaled. "That's—aaaaaah!"

The demon's glowing yellow eyes went wide—in concern.

Sam spun, jaw hanging open at the sight of his friend falling backward off the cliff.

"Oops," said the demon in an impossibly deep voice. "Perhaps appearing suddenly in a blast of smoke might have been unwise."

Blix shot off his shoulder like a missile. Sam rushed to the cliff edge, staring helplessly as the imp intercepted the falling boy, clinging to his back and acting like a parachute… or a set of clip-on wings too small to allow flying. The tiny imp managed to get Ronan oriented upright before steering him to a crash landing on a football-shaped island in the midst of the lava river about twice the size of Mom's GMC Yukon. Despite the great height, the landing didn't look too much worse than taking a spill off a bike.

Sam cupped his hands around his mouth and shouted, "Ro!"

Blix babbled frantically, explaining Ronan hadn't been hurt, but the landing knocked the wind out of him and he couldn't talk.

"Whew." Sam slouched. "Ro, you okay?"

Eventually, his friend stood, dusted himself off, and waved both arms as if he signaled an aircraft for help. "Yeah!"

Grinning, Sam pointed down at him. "It's over, Ro. I have the high ground!"

"Not funny!" shouted Ronan. "Get me outta here."

15

UNDETERMINED ORIGIN

It's not often people leave a happy dream behind for a nightmare.

Okay, sometimes it happens, but usually not because the person woke up. No, I'm not referring to my unlife as a nightmare. It's the combined weight of a bunch of schoolwork plus studying plus multiple unknown supernatural entities trying to kill me and my family—or at least stir up some shit with the elders.

According to my iPhone, it's 2:39 p.m. Roughly average for me insofar as wake up time goes. Haven't had my ass kicked recently, and the day must be reasonably overcast. Strong sunlight days tend to keep me zonked a little longer, even in a windowless basement room.

I lay there in bed staring at the ceiling and trying to make some sense of everything going on. Talking to Aurélie helped ease my mind. Stupid of me to assume she'd go off like a bomb merely from hearing me tell her someone attacked us. A vampire doesn't make it to her age without a certain degree of care in everything. Even someone like her who has no lust for power and does her best to avoid getting in the way of other vampires' plans needs to tread with caution. If another elder is unhinged enough, they could completely misinterpret her actions and get pissed.

Real talk time. If Stefano or Paolo *genuinely* wanted my family dead, they wouldn't send a pack of mind-controlled mortals with Walmart zombies. It's naïve of me to think men in their position wouldn't be able to arrange 'accidents' or set up a hit man to redirect blame away from themselves. Since neither of my parents are involved in anything shady, it would be highly suspicious for someone to show up out of the blue and bomb our house. Girl Scout cookie sales are competitive, but the girls aren't cutthroat enough to hire bored military contractors to rough up the competition. So, no one's going to blame the Littles for having angered the local underboss and brought the wrath of organized cookie sales down on their heads.

Still, men like Stefano or Paolo would play the long game. They'd set Mom or Dad up for some conflict the mortal authorities would link to the attack and package everything neatly so society as a whole never suspected the existence of the paranormal. Vampires adore setting up complicated schemes. Look at JFK. All this time and it's *still* unclear what happened exactly. Humans cannot keep secrets so perfectly. Every person involved in a conspiracy is a potential leak. The more people involved, the greater the odds someone's going to slip up and say something. Once more than three people are involved in a project, the chances of secrets being kept are lower than one percent. Professor Heath didn't tell me the what or why of it, merely implied vampires had been involved in orchestrating the assassination. Jimmy Hoffa, too… whoever he was. And some Black Dahlia thing.

Not totally sure if Professor Heath pulled my leg, but he basically said every high-profile murder where people never figured out what happened involved vampires or something similar. By 'something similar,' he likely means mystics. Mind-control powers make it easy to get away with crimes. Having the literal ability to warp reality is even worse.

Fortunately, the number of people on Earth who can do magic powerful enough to be worried about can be counted on one hand… or so believes Darren Anderson. He's not lying. If the information isn't true, he doesn't know.

Anyway… thinking about all this Mafia and vampire conspiracy stuff makes me feel better. It seems less and less likely for this to really be the work of Stefano, Paolo, or Eleanor St. Ives. None of them would be so sloppy. Well, maybe Eleanor, but in her case, it wouldn't be sloppiness but 'efficiency.' She'd take the fastest, most direct route to achieve what she wanted, lacking the patience or finesse to fully obfuscate her involvement.

I mean, the last time she genuinely messed with me, she sent some of her hipster minions to rough me up, making no secret of where they came from. So, if a pair of vampires jumped me in the parking garage and said they worked for Eleanor, I'd be inclined to believe them.

Sure, the remote-control corpses had her name somewhat on them, but there exists the larger problem of her not having the ability to create such bizarre 'weapons.' Sierra described one of the not-zombies as leaking formaldehyde. Maybe it hadn't been actual formaldehyde but some 'sciency' serum she made paranormal to animate a corpse? Nah… the other one she cut didn't bleed, nor did it release chemicals. I'm thinking someone stole the bodies from a funeral home, one post-embalming, one perhaps in the middle of it. I don't really know how the process works. Do they drain all the blood first, then pump a body full of chemicals or do they just start pumping chemicals in and stop when the outflow stops being blood?

Whatever.

Doesn't matter where the bodies came from.

The more I think about it, the more it feels like someone is trying to play us. Could also be multiple unrelated antagonists, but too coincidental. Also, whoever it is knows enough about me and the vampires in the area to understand which names to drop in hopes of setting off a war. My next thought both comforts and worries me in equal measure. Someone going to all this trouble would have to know the elders wouldn't immediately start mashing each other's faces in the moment I went crying to mommy about Stefano's friends being mean to me. It doesn't make any sense for someone to even do this. Are they incompetent, testing us, or intending this to seem ridiculous to us in the moment, but on top of what comes next, turns into 'proof?'

Grr.

I have hours of daylight left before it's time to worry. I head out into the basement, hook a left, and go to the mini bathroom for a quick shower. Once I'm dried off and dressed, it's time for homework and research.

Minutes after I start studying, the Littles get home from school. Murmured conversation between them and Dad goes on for a few minutes before Sam thunders up the stairs. The girls follow, making *far* less noise.

Everything sounds ordinary, so I stay focused on killing the homework beast to get it out of my way. *You did this to yourself.* College is tedious—at the moment due to my paranormal worries—and pointless, due to my paranormal existence. No, not gonna quit. I'm allowed to be frustrated. If I didn't have a 'secret admirer' out there, this work wouldn't bother me at all. After my dream of being stuck in a cubicle farm surrounded by deadlines, I'm *seriously* rethinking the computer programming major. Meaning, I am now definitely committed to changing it. Just don't know to what yet. Not a big deal since I'm still in my first year. Credits from this class should count for electives or something on a different academic path.

I'm soon serenaded by random explosions from the PlayStation in the living room. No idea if Sierra's already done her homework, has none, or is putting it off until later. She has a habit of working on it during slow classes, so it's mostly done before she's even out of school. Totally defeats the point of homework, which is, of course, to suck the joy out of children's lives. Can't go allowing them to actually be kids and have fun. Nope. They've gotta be trained for the workaday world where eighty percent of their awake time is spent grinding away on some tedious task simply to continue to exist in society.

Yeah, being a vampire is cool. I found a trapdoor out of the rat race. Cost a little more than a lottery ticket, but no complaints.

An hour or so later, the superhero voices occasionally shouting trademarked catch phrases in Sam's bedroom loud enough for me to hear over Sierra's *Call of Duty* in the living room stop. Probably paused the game to grab a snack. Maybe he's switching games or doing homework.

I keep studying.

"Klepto?" calls Sam.

Huh. Odd. The boy doesn't usually invoke the stealth attack kitten. Fortunately, Sam is Sam, so I don't worry at all he's abusing the critter to steal a new video game or do something nefarious. Maybe something in his bedroom moved and he's wondering if the cat did it.

By the time the smell of cooking food makes it down here, I've about had my limit. My brain absolutely needs a break from studying. Between the stress of school and the stress of Vampy McDerpface out there, I'm taking a night off no matter who I have to mind control. Okay, it's a Wednesday and I still have classes to go to, which I'll deal with. But after I'm out, it's Hunter time.

Decision made, I close the books, pack my comp sci and calc books up for later, then head upstairs.

Dad's cooking. Despite the running joke about my father's efforts over a stove being somewhere between necromancy and a CIA project of questionable ethical standing, he's not bad at it. Problem is when he gets near a grill. He thinks 'char' is another food group. Mom's at the kitchen table typing away on her laptop. Personal laptop, so she's either emailing the grandparents or doing budget type stuff for the house. I creep down the hall to check the living room. Sierra's sitting on the floor, leaning against the sofa while shooting people in *Call of Duty*. Klepto orbits her head like a tiny, fuzzy blimp. Floating kitten. Yeah, my house is totally normal. Sophia's reclining on the couch nearby, reading her Kindle.

"You eating with us tonight, hon?" asks Dad.

"Umm." I glance at the clock. "It's almost 5:30 and still light out. Gotta drive in, so… can't. I've got about eight minutes to leave before I'll be late."

"Come all ye minions," bellows Dad. "Thine gruel has reached an acceptable level of warmness."

"Sec," whispers Sierra. "Two minutes left in the match. Is it okay if I finish it?"

"Yeah, sure. It'll take your brother that long to get down here." Dad chuckles, then yells, "Sam?"

Mom closes her laptop and moves it to the counter, off the table.

Sophia runs to take her place at the table. About a minute later, Dad walks to the base of the stairs and calls for Sam again. No response. I'm offline up here in the living room, so I can't tell by listening. Damn windows letting in sunlight. The nerve.

"Has anyone seen Sam?" asks Dad.

"Did he go to Daryl's or Ronan's?" Mom scratches her head.

"He's in the closet," chimes Sophia.

Dad rubs his chin. "Hmm. He did seem rather comfortable wearing a princess gown."

Sierra snickers.

Mom rolls her eyes.

Heh. I hold up a finger. "I believe Soph is being literal. Sam's closet has been giving off some weird energy."

The 'match over' music fills the living room. Sierra's team won. Good, she'll be in a pleasant mood for dinner.

"There's a portal in there." Sophia huffs. "I tried to stop them, but I didn't get there fast enough. They were already gone."

"They?" Dad raises both eyebrows. "Which they are we talking about."

"Sam, Ronan, and Blix."

Mom turns to face her. "Sophia! Did you summon another interdimensional gateway in your brother's closet? We talked about this!"

Sierra logs out of the PlayStation and jumps to her feet.

"No!" wails Sophia. "I didn't make this one. Promise!"

"Mom. Mom. Mom." I pull at her like I'm trying to hold an attack chihuahua away from a fight. "Chill. This isn't Soph. Remember when we had Ronan stuck to the bathroom wall and he got poisoned by this demon stuff that would've paralyzed him for months? Blix asked *something* for help removing the poison from Ro.

Whatever the 'something' is, it's been hanging out in Sam's closet ever since."

Dad blinks. "So, the boy's got a literal monster in his closet?"

I make a so-so hand tilt gesture. "More of a supernatural entity of undetermined origin than a monster."

Mom stares at me. "Are you making a political correctness joke?"

"Erm…" I bite my lip. "Not intentionally."

"Ugh." Mom rubs both hands down her face. "I really ought to start smoking weed again."

Say what? I raise both eyebrows. *"Again?"*

"She hasn't touched it since college." Dad winks. "Your mother was wild."

Mom blushes. "You know I'm kidding. I'd lose my job if they tested me."

I grin. "No, you won't."

"Good grief, Sarah. I shouldn't be hearing you talk about this." Mom flails. "It's a conflict of ethics."

"Oh, and having an interdimensional portal in Sam's room is fine?"

Mom stares blankly at me.

Dad's face turns red as he tries not to burst out laughing.

A purple flash on the sofa beside Mom precedes Klepto appearing out of thin air. "Mew."

My father gestures at her. "And we have a teleporting kitten. Don't worry about the weed, hon. Lots of things seem normal compared to cute furry creatures who disregard the laws of reality at their whim."

"I used to work with a guy who could be described the same way," deadpans Mom. "Except for the cute part."

Heh.

Dad smiles. "And now we have dimensional gateways cropping up in closets."

I can't help but laugh nervously. All this crazy stuff going on and my father's wisecracking. Hopefully, he hasn't lost his grip. Gotta check. I step into the little toilet closet in the first-floor hallway so I'm out of direct sunlight enough to come online, then focus on him. He notices me look at him and tilts his head in question. Eye contact, and

I'm inside. Wow. Okay. No. He's not going insane. Well, not going *more* insane than he was before. Merely ordinary 'my dad' level nuts. To him, we're somewhere between playing Jumanji and being in one of his D&D campaigns. He doesn't believe any 'zombies' Sierra—a level one character to him—could kill are a serious threat to the family. The idea of a portal in Sam's room strikes him as something straight out of a cool Eighties movie. He's imagining my brother and Ronan having an awesome adventure in some alternate world and fully expecting them to arrive home safe—just like in the movies.

Aww, Dad. I'm the young woman. I'm the one who's supposed to be naïve.

I can't break his bubble. There's nothing he can do about Sam other than worry himself to death until the boys return. *If* the boys return. And, whoa. Dad's thinking it's not a big deal because Coralie didn't warn anyone about anything. Okay, a fair point. But… we shouldn't place so much weight on her. Yeah, it's not like she's going to get old and die on us, but she's also a ghost. There is no guarantee she'll remain inclined to help us forever and we might never know the moment she decides to go elsewhere for good. Also, her abilities aren't perfect. However, it's only been months since I liberated her mortal remains from the mystics. She's most likely still interested in keeping an eye on us.

Besides, she likes popping in to talk to Sophia or me. Ghosting is lonely. Non-ghosts who can see and talk to her aren't common.

Crap. Sam. What did you do?

I zoom upstairs and fling his closet door open, not sure what to expect.

It's normal. No gaping maw into another dimension… just the usual assortment of toys, games, clothes, and some laundry that really ought to be in the basket. The frogs stare eerily at me from their terrarium. Or maybe they're staring at the closet and I happen to be in the way. Swear those things are intelligent beyond frog normal. Or a Beast is spying on us. Apparently, Beast vampires have the ability at some point to control animals, or talk to them, or see through their eyes. Yeah, one of those neato powers Innocents never get. I'm cool though. Not jealous. The cost of admission to Team Beast is *way* too expensive for me.

Hmm, the boys left the PlayStation on, paused. Wolverine is frozen in mid jump. Looks like he's having some serious issues with a bunch of bank-robbing robots. Something must have happened in the closet to distract them away from the game.

At least Blix is with them, so the boys aren't entirely defenseless. Not saying an imp is going to help them fight any monsters. They are, after all, pretty weak. Blix can guide them around and keep them from running into worse things.

Dammit. Stomping on the rug inside the closet doesn't open any doorways. If Sam and Ronan went somewhere, they're on their own. This closet portal is totally unrelated to what's going on, but it's becoming increasingly obvious I am in over my head. My little brother vanishing—even if it's a harmless sort of supernatural excursion—is one more thing I really *don't* have the bandwidth to worry about at the moment.

I'm going against my opinion of Dad's flawed logic here, but Coralie didn't warn me about Sam. He's basically having an adventure like one of the boys from the old movies my father adores. *Explorers* or *The Gate* or some such thing. Well, hopefully not *The Gate*. That one ended with the entire house being destroyed. I'll keep my fingers crossed for somewhat lower scale destruction. Maybe a single pair of sneakers on fire.

Fingers crossed he's going to be okay.

16

NATURE GIRL

Traffic, for once, did not become another thing adding to my stress level.

Yeah, despite my brother's absence, I went to school for two reasons. One, Mom insisted. Two, I couldn't think of anything within my power to make contact with, rescue, or retrieve Sam and Ronan. Standing around the house instead of going to class would've left me with idleness and a wandering mind going down every dark scenario imaginable.

Sam is not an idiot. If he willingly entered the portal, he trusted it. I'm going to assume the gate is somehow related to the entity responsible for curing Ronan of the mirrorworld poison. It is probably about as benevolent as a demonic being can be, or it wouldn't have cured him. My knowledge of occult subjects, specifically demons, is a bit weak. Various human religions have ideas about them, but who knows which ones are right, which ones are wild guesses, and which ones are straight up the result of eating too many of the wrong kinds of mushrooms.

It's tempting to tune out in computer science and charm my way to a passing grade since I've already decided to change my major, but I respect Professor Garcia too much. She's pretty awesome. Doesn't stop me from quietly texting Darren Anderson to ask his opinion on my brother disappearing into a possibly demonic portal created by an unknown entity previously responsible for assisting us.

He says a whole bunch of stuff about bargains and terms, suggesting the boys may or may not have made a deal with something to cure Ronan earlier and he, she, or it now wants payment. I really do not like the phrase 'wants payment' as it applies to a demon and my nine-year-old little brother. Something tells me an infernal creature wouldn't be looking to take a rare baseball card. Probably wants his firstborn, or his soul, or maybe some freaky Disney-level mermaid stuff like taking his voice. Sam's not stupid. He won't agree to any bad deals.

Or maybe the entity *does* want a baseball card. Hell, Blix is cool and likes video games.

There's a weird thought. Did my brother 'tame' Blix? Could the imp have gone into his room to mess with him and… something else happened? Coralie mentioned a while ago my brother had a 'strange relationship' with demonic beings. We've also had a hellhound living in the backyard, and no one's ended up dead or mildly incinerated. In fact, it protected Sierra.

Usually, demons aren't the ones doing the protecting when innocent children are involved… as much as Sierra counts as innocent. How many 'innocent' little girls scream 'die you sons of bitches' while machinegunning people, even if it is happening in a video game? Okay, I'm teasing. She's got a good heart, so she counts. She didn't want to stab any of the live humans who brought the zombies and she also charged headfirst into a crowd of like twenty imps to protect Sophia. I shouldn't equate a lack of being 'brittle and girly' with not being innocent. It's not true. A girl can appear 'tough' and still be innocent. Trust me, Sierra will argue for hours about her feelings on the patriarchy.

A text from Darren suggests my brother (and Ronan) will most likely return unharmed, but may have a demonic attachment or be possessed. He suggests I 'check their thoughts' at the first opportunity. Can do. It'll be my first time looking into the head of someone who's possessed. Not sure how to tell, but I'm guessing anyone who *is* possessed would have multiple distinctly different voices talking in their head at once. If I hear a bunch of people talking, good chance he's possessed—or maybe just an author.

I send a text to the family group chat to let everyone know the mystics are mostly confident Sam will be okay, then proceed to pay attention for the remainder of my two classes tonight. My second class, philosophy, gives me a chance to talk to Professor Heath during each break. He's a vampire, but largely isolated from the outside world. The man never leaves school grounds, or even this building really. He's oblivious to who might want to be stirring up trouble around here.

We get stuck debating if Stefano is really uninvolved or thinks he's being clever by making it seem fake enough to sow the seeds of doubt… and we run out of break time. I'm in too much of a rush to get home to bother him after class, since he's contributing only additional doubt to my already overburdened load of it.

I'm out the door of the school at 9:52 p.m. Professor Heath is the exact opposite of Dr. Mercer. He usually ends class a few minutes early. In the interest of maximizing my Hunter time, I leave the Sentra in the parking garage and fly, making it to the Mi Tierra restaurant at three minutes to ten.

Miraculously, they haven't locked the doors. As soon as I walk in, the hostess—a new girl about my age—comes jogging over to me. We're about the same height, though she's a bit heavier. Meaning, she has a normal figure. Same shade of brown hair as me. Fuller cheeks, too, but she's got *way* too much foundation on.

"Sorry, hon. We're closing up."

"I know. Not here for food. My boyfriend works here. Is it okay if I chill and wait for him?"

"Oh. Umm." She bites her lip.

Cheating time. I dive into her head. She's new, only been working here four days, and doesn't know what to say. I prod her to think it's not a big deal. Kim goes from confused to smiling, and waves me back with a 'no problem.'

Hunter comes out of the kitchen. He looks so dashing in a raspberry button-down shirt, black apron, and jeans. I get a 'one sec' smile as he hurries over to a table carrying a small piece of cake. Figures, the only two customers left in the place are his. At least the older middle-aged couple is on dessert already.

I meander down the hall to the kitchen area and do my best to stay out of everyone's way. Anyone who gives me too much of a challenging look receives a mental prod to accept my presence as normal. Some may consider the use of mind control in this manner to be a bit cavalier, but it doesn't bother me. I'm not here to do anything wrong… though, this one guy—chef's assistant maybe—smells too good to resist.

Thank you, storage closet.

He's a little heavy, shorter than me, and doesn't know much English. High school Spanish is enough for me to coerce him into a secluded place and feed. Imagine that. Simple phrases being good for something. No, I did not ask him where the library was. After erasing our momentary aside from his memory, I leave him with the thought he stepped into the closet to inspect it, then resume waiting for Hunter.

I'm not *so* impatient the last two customers need to be mentally prodded out the door. Hunter clocks out at 10:12 p.m. and promptly sweeps me into an embrace. I'm momentarily self-conscious about him smelling the assistant cook on my breath, but he doesn't. Or he doesn't react to it, knowing the only reason I'd be near another man is food.

"You okay?" asks Hunter. "Seem tense."

"Just a bit. Lot going on." I exhale hard. "I *really* need to have a peaceful night. You're not swamped with school stuff, are you?"

He shakes his head. "Not swamped. Got some stuff to finish, but I can do it tomorrow morning."

A giggle of glee almost comes out of me—until I remember I'm no longer twelve. Sweet! A whole night with him. Even if it is basically only two hours. Can't keep him awake past midnight or the guilt will bother me too much. Don't care if we reinvent the Kama Sutra, simply cuddle while fully dressed, watch a movie, or throw tiny pickles at each other all night. I just need to be with him and think about nothing for a while.

We head out via the back door to the parking lot.

"So, what's bothering you?"

"Umm, stuff. Some people are creating trouble for some other people I associate with and a giant poop storm is brewing over Seattle." I grimace-smile, hoping my exceptional vagueness gets the message across to him while keeping any potential eavesdroppers in the dark.

"Sounds… complicated."

"It—" A scuff from above and behind sounds like an aggressive vampire jumping off the roof to ambush me. I whirl into a defensive stance.

Nope, I'm wrong.

It's *two* aggressive vampires jumping off the roof to ambush me.

The one on the right crashes into me before I have time to do more than process the sight of them jumping off the roof at us. He tackles me over backward, grabbing me by the shoulders and trying to pin me under his body. The other dude is a traditional thug, having a full head of black hair instead of an apocalyptic wasteland blue mohawk. He lands on his feet and throws Hunter aside like a child, bouncing him off the wall of Mi Tierra.

No! Not now. No vampire bullshit tonight. This is Hunter time!

I sprout claws and thrust my fingers into the sides of the dude on top of me, curling them around his ribs like I'm grabbing the handlebars of a bike. We lock stares. He looks freakin' ridiculous, shaved bald with a neon blue mohawk. Vampire claws might be small, but they're impossibly sharp and supernaturally painful. While he's stunned in pain, gawping for air he doesn't need, I snarl and shove, flinging him up and away with enough force to toss him almost standing. He teeters on tiptoe while staggering backward, flailing his arms for balance. Doesn't matter how strong he is, dude only weighs as much as a normal person. Intending to rip his face off, I fly to my feet and start to lunge at him, but a silver flash redirects my attention to the other guy pointing a small handgun at Hunter, who lay in the bushes beside the door, dazed as if he'd been hit by a car.

Shit!

As fast as I can move, I lunge into a snap kick, knocking the second guy's arm upward. The gun goes off with more of a *crack* than a bang, blasting wood chips and dirt a few feet away from Hunter's head. Mohawk rushes at me, but I can't let his buddy shoot Hunter. I manage to score a couple shallow claw slices down the dude's back before Mohawk body-blocks me like a hockey player. I catch myself by flying before eating parking lot.

Mohawk tries to grab me; since I'm already hovering, I zip straight up over him and land by Mr. Pistol—who's still standing up on his toes in an ice bucket challenge pose from the pain of me ripping down his back—and shred him a little more. He goes to pistol whip me across the face. I duck—straight into Mohawk's arms from behind.

I swear. If I have to start carrying a damn sword everywhere…

At least the gun dude's anger at me is stronger than his want to kill Hunter. With his buddy holding me, he walks right up and puts the gun to my forehead. Apparently, he's forgotten legs exist. I punt him in the balls, doubling him over, then kick him in the head, flinging him face first into the side of the restaurant like fifteen feet away.

I growl, not at all liking the sensation of being squeezed by a damn forklift. Mohawk is seriously strong. Grunting, I pour as much vampire power as possible into making myself stronger. We spin in circles. He struggles to contain me while I'm losing my damned mind. The damn instant his grip starts to fail—I stop fighting due to the touch of a gun once again pressed to my head.

"Aww, shit."

We make eye contact.

Mr. Pistol offers a brief 'gotcha' smirk.

Hunter lands on the dude's back, tackling him off to the side an instant before he fires. The gun might be small, but it going off two inches away from my ear is *not* cool. I resume trying to force Mohawk's arms apart, and slip down to my feet. Mr. Pistol reaches up over his back, grabs Hunter by the shirt, and hurls him into the restaurant again. Hunter slaps into the concrete horizontally, four feet off the ground, with a *thud* that hurts me to hear, then falls into the bushes.

"You bastard son of a bitch!" I spin, grabbing Mohawk's crotch with my claws and squeezing as hard as I can.

His face goes from corpse pale to bright red in an instant, eyes bulging—then he rams his forehead into my face. Next thing I know, I'm flat on my back, blood gushing from my broken nose. At least, it feels like it. Vampires don't really bleed as much as mortals, but ow!

Okay, I think my face broke. There's pain in places I didn't know pain could be. Having a little trouble seeing, too. My eyes are probably pointing in slightly wrong directions thanks to bone damage. Hunter hasn't moved since he hit the wall. These two bastards are definitely going to kill him if I don't win this. Snarling, I launch myself upright and swipe at Mowhawk's throat. He catches my wrist, flipping me around in a jiu-jitsu type throw. A quarter-second before I hit the pavement, I fly forward, twisting over and kicking his legs out from under him.

My attack breaks his left knee and flings him into the air. It's enough to ruin his grip on my arm. Shit, the guy can fight. And he's scary. You'd think shredding a dude's nether bits with vampire claws would maybe stun them for a minute, but the guy's over it already. Crap. He's probably a Fury. I just pushed his buttons—literally. When the rage wears off, he's going to cry for an hour. Wait, no. I haven't been broken in half yet. He can't be a Fury. How the hell is he not on the ground crying after having his groin shredded?

These two aren't idiots like the ones from the parking garage. It's pretty obvious I'm not going to win this fight. It's physically possible for me to flee, but I can't leave Hunter defenseless. Overcome by the need to protect him—I fly into the bushes… all of ten feet away.

I grab Hunter, dragging his unconscious body upright. Mohawk jumps on me from behind again. Shit! With only a split second to come up with something, I surge forward, dragging Hunter as well as the dude holding me staggering over to the door. Mohawk lifts me off my feet as I kick it open, but not before I toss Hunter into the restaurant, sending him sliding down the hall to the kitchen.

Mr. Pistol also jumps on me. "Damn bitch."

Blur warns of an incoming punch to the face. I'm fast enough to catch his arm before he smashes my skull… but he's not punching me. He's put a gun to my forehead.

"Aww, fu—"

Crack.

EVER HAVE A HEADACHE LIKE A SEARING HOT KNITTING NEEDLE JAMMED into your skull?

I wake up with one of those. To be fair, it's not 'searing,' merely too hot like McDonald's coffee. Wait, no. Can't be *that* hot… I'm not screaming. The scent of wet earth and tree sap floods my sinuses—along with blood and gunpowder. I'm starting to really hate the taste of gunpowder. Also, whatever special little magical thing my brain does to give blood appetizing flavors does not work when it's *my* blood in my mouth. For a second, I think my eyeballs are missing, then it occurs to me the process of seeing works much better when my eyes are open.

Tree bark hovers blurrily in front of my face.

Well, now I understand why I'm smelling it, and what the rough texture against my cheek is.

My faculties gradually return over the span of a minute or so. My arms encircle a fairly thick tree. Something's wrapped around me, holding my body and legs tight against the trunk. Can't move much at all beyond a little squirming. I appear to be in the woods, far enough away from civilization for there not to be any sign of electric lights.

The tree is a little too fat to see my hands, but it feels like I'm wearing three or four pairs of handcuffs. Oh, and there's a thick tow chain wrapped around me so many times I'm basically a steel mummy.

"She's awake," says a fairly generic sounding male voice.

"Took long enough." Another man groans as if stretching.

"You *did* shoot her in the forehead."

Man two—who I assume to be Mr. Pistol—laughs. "You're complaining? She almost ripped your dick off."

"Would've done it, too if it was big enough to find," I mutter.

Mohawk walks up behind me on the left, giving my butt a condescending little double-pat. "You're about to learn there are rules, bitch. Mr. Bianchi is done putting up with your bullshit. Nothing is more important than tradition, and he won't be made a fool of any longer by a little girl. Especially one loyal to Wolent." He winks. "Enjoy the sunrise."

Okay, nothing about his butt-patting came off the least bit sexual, but it's so damn infuriating, I lose control of my anger. Snarling, I try to break loose. The men find my struggle to free myself funny, which pisses me off more.

"Let her calm down and tell us all about how we're making a big mistake and big bad Aurélie is going to kick our asses for being mean to her," says Mr. Pistol in a patronizing tone.

I stop fighting the chain, giving a hard exhale. Old habits. Not like air does me any good. "Seriously? Do you realize how childish you sound?"

Crack.

A hot lance stabs into my back.

Ouch, that's my kidney.

I snarl, growling as deep as a mountain lion.

The guys find this funny, too.

"Keep running your mouth, kid. I got eleven more bullets."

Gasping, I swallow the pain, speaking in a half growl. "Real tough when I'm chained to a tree, aren't you?"

Mohawk butt-pats me again. "Yeah, you're such a total badass, you ended up on a tree. Feel kinda sad for that kid you were with, though. Looked like a nice boy."

Hunter? Fuck! No. "Where is he? What did you do to him?"

"Bet you'd love to find out." Mohawk waves. "Chow."

"What?" asks Mr. Pistol.

"Chow, you know. It's Italian for 'see ya later.'"

"*Ciao*," says Mr. Pistol.

"That's what I said, dumbass."

The guys walk off arguing about Italian pronunciation.

"Hey! Assholes! What did you do to my boyfriend!?"

They ignore me. I keep struggling and screaming at them to tell me what happened to Hunter until a car engine starts a fair distance off behind me. Doors close, and the soft crunching of tires on forest floor trails off to silence.

Shit. Sarah. Think!

I rest my forehead against the tree bark. One pair of handcuffs, I could snap no problem. Not having any luck here. Can't tell if it's the giant tow chain pinning my arms to the tree and killing my leverage, or if breaking three pairs at once is asking too much of my vampiric strength. A little fumbling around blindly later, I realize they've used hinge-style cuffs. Grr. No little chain I could snap using my fingers. Still, they went *way* overboard with the tow chain mummification. Even if I got my hands loose, it wouldn't make much difference. I'd have to be as big as Aziz to break this. My only chance would be if these morons put the padlock somewhere in arm's reach of me… which they probably didn't do.

Can't see it. Granted, my face is mushed into a tree.

Not knowing what happened to Hunter drives me into a frenzy of pointless thrashing. I'm not sure if it's a few minutes or an hour later by the time I break down and sob. What the hell was I thinking? Throwing him into the restaurant for 'witnesses' wouldn't matter to vampires. They'd blank memories. Stefano wouldn't have any reason to kill Hunter, would he? If anything, maybe they only made him forget ever knowing me. Stefano's all about tradition and keeping the secret of vampires as protected as possible.

These two guys kicked my ass soundly. They're the kind of heavies I'd expect someone like Stefano to send. Maybe those two at the parking garage *were* idiots on purpose. Aurélie didn't believe he really sent them. So when they find my smoking skeleton stuck to a tree, she's not going to suspect he had anything to do with it. He's created the appearance someone's trying to set him up.

Even if I manage to carve 'Stefano did it' into the tree, she or Wolent would discard it as attempted misdirection. Son of a bitch. He's really going to destroy me and get away with it. I lose another block of time surrendering to blind panic and impotent squirming.

Ugh, *so* much chain. It would probably have held Garret Alder down. What the hell do they think I am, a 300-year-old Fury? I sigh at the bark in front of my face. Great. I've become a tree-hugger. Well, this *is* Seattle.

Again, I wriggle, but can't move much at all. Good thing I don't really have to worry about blood circulation. Chain digs into my body everywhere. Not being able to get away from the painful pressure is maddening.

And… shit. My nose wants attention *bad*.

The headbutt broke my face. Yeah. Nose is healing. Massive itchies.

Ow. Trying to rub my nose on the side of a tree to scratch it is *not* comfortable.

I drift from anger to fear to heartbreak over Hunter and eventually settle on despondence for my family. How ironic. I went home to spare them the grief of losing me, but doing so ended up causing it. Meh. Didn't make much difference either way. No regrets. At least we had ten more months together.

No, I'm not giving up… just… what the hell *can* I do here?

There's clearly no one around. By now, someone would've heard me screaming.

Already feels like sunrise is minutes away. I must have been unconscious for hours from a gunshot to the head. Okay, guess my panic blackout wasn't really an hour long… just felt like it. Explains why they used such a dinky little pistol. They wanted me to wake up fast enough to see the sun one last time, maybe have a few minutes to contemplate my inescapable fate.

Hang on. Wait just a moment.

Stefano Bianchi is aware I'm an Innocent. He knows the sun isn't going to incinerate me right away, if at all. It's also pretty damn unlikely he'd make sure his men told me who sent them if he didn't expect me to be destroyed. This can't be intended as non-lethal torture. Otherwise, I'd for damn sure go to Aurélie and tell her what happened.

It doesn't make any sense for Stefano to try to 'execute' me by sunlight… at least not without chopping me into tiny pieces first so my powers can't protect me. Leaving me not only intact but conscious gives me a chance. I grunt, straining to shift myself enough to look upward. The forest is fairly dense. It's not exactly an Amazon jungle canopy, but I'm way better off than if they'd left me in a California desert.

Okay, I can do this. Power of positive thinking, right?

Oh, yeah. I have a Dalton.

Doubt he can do anything in the maybe six minutes left before sunrise, but… it's enough time to make a phone call. I close my eyes and concentrate on our mental link. Every vampire has a telepathic connection back to the one who gave them the Transference. I'm too freaked out for words, so I send thoughts of where I am and everything screaming around my brain.

A tiny bullet emerges from the hole it made in my back and tumbles out of my shirt. Great, just what I needed. Another itch out of reach. I scream-growl in frustration and tug at the chains. Ashley's kinda into the whole 'being tied up' thing. Totally confuses me. I do not understand how she gets any kind of thrill out of helplessness. Being chained to a tree is about as opposite from fun as anything is possible for me to experience. Granted, Ashely's dates aren't typically trying to kill her… and she does seem to be a fair bit more adventurous after her tryst with Aurélie.

Yeah, don't get me started. All kinds of weird. It's like having a sister who hooked up with my stepmother. Exactly. I shudder merely thinking about it. The only thing keeping me from *really* freaking out over it is I barely knew Aurélie at the time, so she didn't really feel like my vampire stepmother then. And I don't mean like faerie godmother.

Well, maybe. I mean she *is* into cute dolls. She probably likes faeries, too.

Sigh.

Know what else is twisted? A woman as delicate, beautiful, and seemingly harmless as Aurélie tearing guys apart like a ridiculously gory anime movie, one where a dude just pokes another dude with a single finger and he explodes like a dynamited tomato.

I fantasize about her shredding Mohawk and Mr. Pistol.

Sun's gonna be up in a few minutes. Hunter could be dead. My family has no idea where I am.

And shit, I still have to write that paper for English class.

I hug the tree for another minute or two before my sunrise alarm goes off. Yeah, thanks. I know. Can't panic. *Have* to stay focused. As much as it's possible for someone to Zen while chained to a tree, I focus my mind entirely on the idea of not burning up in the daylight. Every bloodline has a primary power they're known for. Mine happens to be *really* good at pretending to be alive. My 'big gun' vampire power is tolerating sunlight. On paper, it sounds wimpy and boring. Not like turning into a wolf or charming a whole room full of people at once, or even being a vampire mystic capable of raising zombies.

Screw paper.

In this superhero roleplaying game Sam likes, 'water breathing' is considered a pissant power… right up until your character is chained to a rock at the bottom of the ocean. I'm presently chained to a tree in the middle of—well almost the middle of—daytime. My options are pretty damn limited. Only thing I can do is clench my jaw and hope.

This could potentially suck.

17

BEHOLD THE POWER OF SPITE

Vertigo hits me for only a second.

At the moment of sunrise, my vampire butt normally goes right to sleep as fast as turning off a light switch. It doesn't come with much sensation beyond a split-second feeling of falling, like I'm standing on a trapdoor and it opened out from under me. On most nights, I'll experience a little vertical dip and the next thing I know, I'm awake—unless I have a dream.

Vampire dreams, by the way, are super weird. They're extremely vivid, detailed, and often impossible to tell apart from reality until something unusual happens. Considering the way my unlife is going —floating kittens and all—my ability to tell dream from reality has taken a beating.

Unfortunately, I'm almost positive being chained hugging a tree is not a dream.

I'd take being a ten-year-old stuck in a day job over this any day.

Hell, give me naked in a morgue cooler.

I swear to the Universe, if I get out of this alive, I'll stand naked on top of the Space Needle.

Well, not alive. You know what I mean.

Sunlight creeps across the forest floor toward me.

It's like being in a James Bond movie deathtrap and having the laser slicing the table on its way to me. I realize the sun is not moving as fast as I think it is. I'm having some weird time compression issues due to feral panic. Think I've broken both my wrists from struggling, but I can't feel much.

The line of glow meanders toward me, simultaneously too fast for my liking and mockingly slow. Like, come on... get it over with already. I feel like a little kid at the pool for the first time, about to be shoved unwillingly into the water. Focus, Sarah. Focus. You can do this. I have dominion over sunlight.

Sunlight cannot harm me.

It bends to my will.

It—I scream in agony.

Smoke peels off my right arm. For agonizing seconds, it's like I've been flung face first into a deep fryer. I force myself not to thrash. If I shatter my wrists now, they might stay permanently broken. C'mon tree. I love you. To keep myself from self-injury, I cling to the trunk as tight as my muscles permit. Roasting dials back from a holy-effing-shit scorching to a Gordon Ramsay burn. Yeah, the meat *is* undercooked... the meat also happens to be me. Maybe once my subconscious realizes I'm not being a moron staying out in the daylight and literally *can't* go to safety, it stopped trying to punish me. Dunno if my sun resistance is a power I can 'flex' like making myself stronger or faster, but I try pouring energy into it while giving off a low scream-growl past clenched teeth. It's like I'm some kind of monk firewalking over hot coals. No matter how much it hurts, I have no choice but to press on.

No idea if it's minutes or hours before the continuous burning pain makes me consider giving up and letting the sun take me out. Ever have a headache so bad eating a bullet felt like a serious option? Expand that over the whole body. Wait, no. I can do this. I *am* doing this. What's the line from *Dune*? Something about mind over pain or fear killing minds. Only, it's not my hand in an agony box. My entire body is stuffed inside the thing the creepy witch lady is holding.

Usually, a woman has to hit like fifty or so before she's worried about randomly bursting into flames.

Sometimes the dumbest things can be a mental rock to cling to. My problems are a little more severe than hot flashes, but thinking about being too young for menopause is a focus point. And yeah, Dad's lame ass sense of humor helps. If I can almost smile while cooking alive, maybe there is hope.

Chanting 'ohmmm' does not help.

Know what else sucks? The idiots who put me on this tree didn't even have the decency to chain me to the west face so the trunk shields me from the worst of the dawn. They put me on the south, I think, since my right side's on fire and my left's okay. The tow chain is so damn tight I can't even shimmy around the trunk.

Nothing to do but weather the storm.

Honestly, I think it's working. Every few minutes, there's a momentary reprieve where the inferno seems like 'hey this isn't so bad.' It's like I'm having a colonoscopy and the doctor hits a spot where I can forget there's fifty feet of hose in a place it doesn't belong—and then he moves it and I want to just die. Never had the pleasure of a colonoscopy. I'm only eighteen. Merely going by Dad's rant. Apparently, the day they tell you it's time to have a camera shoved up your butt is the day you officially become an 'old person.' Gotta keep myself smiling here, somehow.

I hallucinate someone whispering 'what the hell?'

There can't be anyone here. I'm an Innocent and it feels like I'm barely clinging to existence. Mohawk and Mr. Pistol would be ash by now. If any normal person happened to be close enough for me to hear speaking in the middle of this agony, they'd definitely have seen me and come running over to help.

Unless, maybe, someone saw me smoking or on fire and ran away in fear.

Ugh, great.

I am not a masochist. Pain sucks. However, buttloads of pain do weird things to the mind. My consciousness drifts back and forth between an almost euphoric state and pure hellish agony. Whenever it's possible for me to collect my faculties, I chant *the sun will not hurt me* over and over in my head.

The more adamant my thoughts, the less it hurts. Hopefully, it's not my imagination and my intention is having a real effect. Focusing on defiance makes this less painful—like being yelled at in school.

Yes. I am clinging to life by the power of spite alone.

Screw those guys.

Existence is a blur of light and pain.

No, I'm not trying to be spiritual or metaphorical. I have no sense of time and can't see much due to the glare. Can't even feel my body anymore, but I'll take numbness over burning. Wait, no. I'm not *completely* numb. Good sign. Means my body hasn't disintegrated. It's like I've just belly-flopped off a forty-foot diving board and the pain's faded to a faint stinging all over my body.

Ooh. If I ever see Mohawk again, I'm going to kill him.

Anger plus spite equals win... or at least a funny fail video.

"Sarah!" shouts Dad.

Okay, now I know I'm hallucinating.

A stampede of footsteps approaches on my right. Oh, when did it become my cool side? The left is on fire now.

"Sarah?" asks Dad.

I peel my face—no it's not melted, merely drool—off the bark and look.

My father's standing five feet away, gawking at me with an expression of horrified worry—and he's wearing his red headband. Sophia's on his left in a pink dress. Sierra's on his right holding her sword and sporting a Nyan Cat T-shirt and jeans. Not sure if they did it on purpose, but they kinda look like one of those funny movie posters for *National Lampoons* painted in the style of Boris Vallejo... except Dad's got his shirt on—thankfully.

Mom's not here. Should I be surprised? Maybe 'my vampire daughter's been chained to a tree, left to die at sunrise' isn't a good excuse for her to leave work early. Wait, I really ought to be more confused why my little sisters are here.

Or not. Wow, this sounds *so* messed up to say, but I think the girls are better equipped to handle dangerous situations than my mother, though she's pretty deadly with her two-handed skillet.

"Am I hallucinating?" I rasp.

"Dumbass," says Sierra.

"That's not nice." Dad pokes her in the head.

"No, not Sarah." Sierra points at me. "Whoever tried to kill her with sunlight is the dumbass."

Dad starts to say something, pauses, then nods. "Oh, yes. Right."

"Is Hunter okay?" I don't even bother trying to struggle anymore. "What time is it?"

"It's almost five in the afternoon." Dad pats my shoulder. "He's doing okay. In the hospital with a concussion. They wanted to keep him for monitoring."

An overwhelming burst of joy gets me crying.

"Dalton called Mom like super early," says Sophia. "He said you were in big trouble, but fell asleep before he could tell her where you were. Coralie helped us find you. Only reason I'm here is 'cause Dad can't see her."

Oh, makes sense. I shift my gaze to Sierra. "What's she doing here?"

Sierra holds up her sword. "Helping you, dork. I came along in case any asses needed to be kicked."

"No Sam?" I emit a wheezy chuckle on smoky breath. "Didn't make it a family outing?"

"Umm, actually." Dad grimaces. "He's still in the closet portal."

Sierra looks up at him. "Thought I heard Ronan in his room when I was getting dressed for school this morning. He screamed."

"Uh oh," whispers Sophia.

Crap! "Did someone kidnap him?"

"I don't know." Dad examines the chain wrapped around me.

Sophia also hunts around for padlocks. "Maybe the mystics grabbed him? I got kidnapped out of my bedroom once."

"Good grief, Sarah." Dad scratches his head. "The abductions are getting out of control."

"Not sure this counts as an abduction." I shrug, making chain clink. "They tried to kill me."

"Might've been a *good* scream from Ronan." Sierra shrugs.

I let my head fall against the tree. "What the heck is a good scream?"

"Like on a rollercoaster. Or they found treasure." Sierra smiles, walking around the tree. "Whoa… three pairs of handcuffs. They really didn't want you going anywhere."

"Yeah, I kinda got the idea from the 200 pounds of steel chain mummifying me. If I still needed to breathe, I'd probably have suffocated by now."

"Any idea where the keys are?" Dad starts hunting around the area.

"Probably with the two vamps who left me here. I don't think they'd have been kind enough to leave them in a convenient, nearby location."

Sophia grins at me the same way she smiles at people who buy her Girl Scout cookies. "I got it. Can open these no problem."

"You said the same thing about fixing that kid's clothes," mutters Sierra.

"Oh, no. What did she do?" I cringe.

Sophia looks down. "Tried to help someone and set a mischief faerie loose. He wasn't a real faerie, just a weird spell. I fixed everything."

"Can't believe you aren't grounded." Sierra whistles. "So lucky."

Dad pats them both on the head. "She's not grounded because she came straight to me and told me everything she did right away. Everyone makes mistakes. I don't ask for perfection, kids. Just honesty."

Sierra mouths 'goody two shoes.'

"And… because she fixed everything and promised not to use magic at school again except for serious emergencies." Dad holds his finger up.

Sierra taps her sword at the chain. "I think Sarah's getting sick of being tied to a tree."

"Yeah. Just a bit."

"Sec. I apologize in advance if something unexpected occurs." Sophia raises her hands.

"Dad!" Shouts Sierra before diving at him, shoving him into a stumbling fall an instant before a gunshot goes off.

Sophia shrieks, whirling to look away from me.

Son of a bitch. I can't see what's going on. My head doesn't turn far enough. Dad hits the ground, Sierra on top of him.

"Get out of the way, kid!" yells a guy.

"Eat a dick!" screams Sierra. "*Vy gryaznyy khaker!*"

"Uhh, what?" asks the guy.

"I think she called you a filthy hacker," whispers another guy. "Random."

If someone wasn't pointing a damn gun at my father, I'd probably have laughed. Sierra tried to use a 'curse' she heard while playing *Call of Duty.* Sophia emits a little hamsterine growl.

Three men all scream at once, sounding terrified.

"What the fu—aaaah!" yells one.

The WTF guy runs past me into my field of view. He's holding a bright green hissing snake like he's trying to strangle it. More hissing comes from behind.

"Whoa," says Sierra. "Nice."

The guy running around in circles in my limited field of view continues to panic for a few seconds—until the snake he's holding bites him on the face. He promptly falls unconscious, fully out cold before he can even *start* to fall over. Even though I'm undead, being around snakes with venom so potent it knocks a man on his ass in a nanosecond is *not* cool. It's *way* less cool when I can't move.

Sierra leaps off Dad and runs out of my view, shouting a war cry. Dad gets to his feet and tries to go after her, but another guy rushes him. They start brawling. My computer geek father decides to pull a Jean Claude VanDamme. As in, he's blocking every punch thrown at him with surprising ease and skill. It would be a lot better if he didn't use his face to do it, though.

Driven by sheer determination to protect us, my father flies into a furious blur of punching and grappling. The dude's obviously been in more fights than my father and appears to know what he's doing, but Dad is *highly* motivated.

They essentially stalemate and end up rolling around on the ground.

Directly behind me, it sounds like Sierra is sparring with the third man. I squirm, trying to look. Seems as though he keeps trying to get past her so he can help his buddy beat Dad up—but Sierra's not having it. She also hasn't sliced him yet, basically doing a lion tamer routine.

"Out of the way, kid."

"Touch me and you're pulling back a stump," says Sierra.

"Nice!" yells Dad in the midst of his brawl. "Who let you watch *American Psycho*?"

"No one. I'm quoting Kerrigan from *Starcraft*. You lose twenty geek points."

"Damn," mutters Dad right before emitting an *oof* as he suffers a gut punch.

Sophia darts up beside me and raises her hands.

The dude trying to get past Sierra rushes to his left, grabs Sophia by the hair, and drags her backward onto her butt.

She screams, mostly in pain from having her hair yanked.

Ooh, you freakin' bastard. Nothing makes me want to resort to violence as much as watching someone inflict pain on one of my siblings. I tug at the chains… but I'm only human strong now. Absolutely zero chance of me doing anything.

Sierra takes revenge, running up behind the guy and delivering a fairly brutal kick to the balls that knocks the man to one knee. She two-hands her sword, twisting up for a power swing, then yells, "There can be only one!"

Holy crap, Sierra!

The man screams and backpedals. Sierra stalks after him, herding the guy away from us. Oh, whew. She was only trying to scare him.

Dad gets his guy in a headlock, punching him repeatedly in the jaw. "Please tell me you were kidding."

"If he touches Sophia again, I won't be kidding." Sierra snarls. "Might not be his *head* I cut off, though."

The guy makes a dash toward Dad, but Sierra zips in his way… a little too fast to be normal. It worries me, but considering my present circumstances, I can't be upset at Dalton for giving her another little boost.

Sophia makes a series of determined faces at me. Dad and one guy roll back and forth, slugging each other. Sierra zigs and zags, keeping herself between the other dude and either Dad or Sophia. She's maddeningly fast, and the guy trying to get around her is starting to come unglued and laugh maniacally.

He reaches a point of frustration where he attempts to charge straight through her, perhaps hoping she'll hesitate.

Sierra puts the tip of her sword at his throat, pushing him back while managing not to draw blood. "Look, pal. I respect you're trying not to hurt us because we're kids, but I can't let you beat up my dad. Since you're messing with us at all, I know you're also trying to hurt my big sister. Back off."

"Almost got it," whispers Sophia.

Dad appears to get the upper hand, rolling on top of his guy and delivering a series of powerful—for him—punches to the head. At least until the guy throws him off to one side.

"Get the other brat," yells the dude by Sierra. "She's trying to let the target loose."

Ooh. I've never been called 'the target' before. Is that better or worse than 'bitch'?

The man who threw Dad wobbles to his feet, staring at Sophia. "Fred, the blonde kid is just staring at the target. Relax. What's she gonna do?"

"Oh, I don't know, Mike. Maybe *turn our guns into freakin' snakes*? Or did you already forget that happened?" Fred redirects his scowl onto Sierra. "Will you get that damn sword out of my neck?"

"Are you gonna go away?" asks Sierra.

"Maybe I could turn the chain into a snake," whispers Sophia.

"Please don't," I mutter.

Mike runs at Sophia. She screams and starts going in circles around me and the tree I'm stuck to. Sierra looks back and forth between him and Fred, hesitating. If she goes after Mike, Fred's going to jump on Dad—who doesn't look like he's up for fighting a fresh opponent. At least Dad kicked the crap out of Mike too, so he's having trouble catching Sophia.

"I can wait!" I yell. "Can't do a damn thing in the daytime anyway. Knock those idiots out or something!"

Dad intercepts Mike, dragging him away from Sophia. Fred tries to go around Sierra again. She whacks him on the knuckles with the flat of her blade.

"Ow, brat!" He jumps back, waving his hand rapidly.

Mike gets Dad in a headlock. Dad punches him twice in the stomach, breaking loose, then backs off to 'fighting distance.' Sophia emits an adorable little snarl like an angry Ewok, thrusting her hand out toward the guy.

All of a sudden, Mike barks a weird bellowing derp noise like Quasimodo stubbing his toe. He stumbles as if he's gone from zero to 'too drunk to stand' in an instant, then falls to the ground as if a puppet had its strings cut. Dad begins whomping on him, punching the defenseless guy in the head repeatedly. Two good shots knock Mike out cold.

Dad looks like he got run over by a stolen U-Haul, but he's still conscious.

Fred stares. "What the hell…?"

Sophia smiles at him, holding up her hand as if cupping a bit of powder… then blows across her palm.

He appears confused for a second, then his eyes cross. Fred falls over backward, unconscious.

"They broke the number one rule," says Dad. "Always take out the mage first."

"That's the number two rule." Sierra shakes her head. "Take out the healer first."

Dad holds a finger up. "Mages are squishier and more deadly. They have priority. Also, we don't have a healer."

"Gawd, Dad!" I yell. "You are not reducing me to a save-the-village-girl side plot from one of your D&D games."

"No!" Sophia shakes her head. "Don't take out the mage first! Bad!"

"You're only saying it because you *are* the mage." Sierra tries to ruffle her hair, but Sophia dodges, sticking her tongue out.

Dad takes a few breaths to compose himself, then walks over. Surprisingly, he isn't limping. "Nice work."

"Sorry for not stabbing the guy." Sierra looks down.

"No, hon." Dad hugs her. "It's perfect. You did great. He wasn't trying to kill you."

Sophia points at me. "They tried to kill Sare."

"With the sun. Dumb… so not really trying to kill her." Sierra sniffs at me. "She's not even burning too bad. Doesn't smell like you're failing to grill steak."

Dad frowns. "My steaks are not *that* burnt."

"Well-done is a crime against humanity." Sierra folds her arms.

"Very funny," I mumble. "Hey, guys. I'm really *quite* done with this tree. Please get me out of here."

"Okay." Sophia takes a deep breath, raises her hands, and whispers, "Please don't mess this one up."

"Soph?" asks Sierra.

"Hmm?"

Sierra grasps Sophia by the hand and pulls her around to the other side of the tree. "Might work better if you look at the actual locks."

"Oh," says Sophia. "Good point."

I brace for weird. My sister and magic haven't exactly been predictable… like *ever*.

A moment later, a ripple of clicking and clattering breaks the silence. The handcuffs pop open and the chain goes slack. Sophia emits a gleeful squeal, as if she's surprised what she wanted to happen actually happened. Granted, opening locks is—according to Darren Anderson—one of the most basic things possible to do with magic. Gravity decides to remind me how it works. I collapse in a heap. Ouch.

Dad rushes over and scoops me into his arms. "Sarah… are you okay?"

I stare into space. "I am… in a *world* of shit."

"*Full Metal Jacket*. Nice." Dad kisses me on the head.

"Umm…" Sierra grimaces.

"She's fine. Sense of humor is intact." Dad winks, then pulls me upright.

I cling to him, beyond relieved to still exist. "You guys are awesome."

My sisters hug me.

"Wow, Dad. You actually beat the snot out of him," says Sierra.

Dad points at his temple. "Never forget the headband."

18

FRIENDS IN (VERY) LOW PLACES

Sam stood at the edge of the cliff, staring down at Ronan.

It felt weird to think of him as a 'best friend' since they'd only known each other a few months. He'd been hanging out with Darryl and Jordan for years. However, having Ronan 'in the know' about the supernatural stuff allowed them to talk about things and have experiences in ways he couldn't with his other friends. Not that he disliked them or didn't want to hang out with them anymore… but Ronan started feeling more like a brother than a friend. Part of the family.

He didn't like seeing him trapped on a small island in a lava river way down at the bottom of a cliff.

Ronan probably didn't enjoy it either.

Sam considered going after him to help, but Blix hadn't come back up. Without an 'imp-a-chute' to change a fall into a gliding descent, he'd definitely go straight into the lava.

The tall demon walked up beside Sam, peering down. "I hadn't expected him to jump."

"He didn't jump. He forgot we were standing by a cliff and backed up too much. He fell."

"True."

"What's your name?" asked Sam.

"Olmaz." The demon struck a commanding pose. "I used to be known as Dal'Olmazkaggan the Bleak, Steward of the Fourth Plane of Torment."

"Why'd you change it?"

"Wouldn't fit on my Discover card."

Sam glanced up at the demon. "You actually use Discover?"

"What other card would a demon have?" Olmaz started to chuckle, but stopped at the blank look on Sam's face. "You don't really understand, do you?"

"No. My dad always makes fun of them 'cause nowhere we go ever takes it."

"Ahh yes. A delightful bit of tedium."

"You torture and torment people?" asked Sam.

"Not in the way you're thinking. My torments are more subtle. I make toilet seats cold in the middle of the night. Drain the ink from ball point pens at DMVs and post offices." He examined his claws. "Make traffic in the other lane move, but as soon as you change lanes into the one where it's going, it stops. Then the one you were in starts moving. My greatest achievement is the USB device. Despite having only two ways to orient, it invariably takes three tries to insert."

"Wow, that's… not really evil. More frustrating," muttered Sam.

"Exactly." Olmaz bowed. "My name change came about when the council realized I far more enjoyed a well-written epic fantasy novel to inciting bloodbaths."

"Ahh."

Olmaz whispered, "They demoted me" past the back of his hand.

Sam blinked.

"Hah." Olmaz chuckled. "I'm teasing you. My name is and has always been simply Olmaz." He waved dismissively while rolling his eyes. "I am not one of those self-important puffins from the Lower Three."

Sam offered a handshake. "Nice to meet you. I'm Sam Wright. It's technically Samuel, but no one ever calls me that except for my mother when she's scared or super angry."

Olmaz shook hands with him. "Pleasure to meet you, Sam."

"Same." Sam looked over at the demon. He only came up to the creature's waist, but for some reason, had no fear whatsoever of him. "What did you mean by Lower Three?"

"Planes. Demonic realms."

"Hell?"

"Some humans refer to them as such." Olmaz shrugged. "We aim to please… beyond your dimension, reality tends to bend itself to suit the expectations of the observer. If a mortal spirit enters it expecting to find Hell, they will."

"Oh." Sam nodded. "I guess the Lower Three are the worst ones? You must put all the really bad guys down there."

"Indeed. It's mostly telemarketers and those people who pester everyone about extending automotive warranties."

Sam chuckled.

Ronan wailed. Probably screamed 'help' but at the distance, his voice melted into a wordless sound.

"Wow, umm. Mom's not going to believe I met a nice demon."

"Ahh… humans." Olmaz let out a long sigh. "To be fair, my kind are not so different. Some are good, some bad, but most of us are somewhere in between. I suppose more of us are bad than humans, but we haven't exactly had the best public relations department."

"Yeah." Sam scrunched his nose. "Most people are afraid of demons."

"Humans who don't immediately condemn us for how we look are quite rare. I am surprised by you, Sam. Especially a boy your age."

Sam peered down at Ronan, worried but feeling powerless to do anything. "How someone looks doesn't mean anything. It's how they act."

Olmaz smiled.

"Saaaaam!" yelled Ronan. "It's hot down here. Help! I think my sneakers are melting."

Blix appeared to be trying to pull the boy into the air, but lacked the wing power.

Sam looked up at Olmaz. "Can you please help my friend back up here before he catches fire?"

"Would you possibly be willing to do me a favor?" Olmaz raised one brow, the yellow light in the eye under it growing brighter.

"I know you're not asking me to do a favor in exchange for helping Ro, so can we discuss it after he isn't about to catch fire?"

Olmaz bowed. "You are correct. His being down there is my fault after all."

"Thanks." Sam smiled, then cupped his hands around his mouth before shouting, "Hang on, Ro. He's gonna help."

"Please remove your shirt," said Olmaz.

Sam blinked. *Umm. This is probably going to hurt, but I can't let Ro cook.* He shrugged, then pulled his shirt off. The cave was certainly warm enough not to be uncomfortable while shirtless.

Olmaz gingerly spun him to face away and rested one hand atop his head. Two points of fiery pain pierced into his back, near his shoulder blades. He held totally still despite having demon claws embedded at least an inch deep into his body. They burned bad enough a few tears seeped from his eyes, though he didn't make a noise. Ronan looked terrified, and kept screaming for help.

A moment later, a pair of demonic wings sprouted from the claw marks in Sam's back with a leathery 'umbrella snapping open' noise. Once the burning lessened enough to where he no longer needed every ounce of concentration not to scream, he exhaled and admired his new body parts. The leading edge felt like rubbery skin, thick and probably armored, the same dark crimson as Olmaz. Membranes like bat wings between the spars appeared so black they seemed to be holes in reality. When the pain stopped entirely, Sam experimented trying to move them.

The complete oddity of having two additional limbs faded in mere seconds. He stretched the wings out, collapsed them, stretched them.

"Umm, are you making me into a part demon?"

"No," said Olmaz. "It is temporary. Think of it like a spell similar to what your sister does."

"So it's going to go crazy and do something weird?"

Olmaz laughed.

Sam grinned. "I get it. This is like a temporary conjuration buff for flight power."

"Erm..." Olmaz tapped a clawed finger to his chin. "I have existed for over a thousand years and have not the first clue what you just said."

"It's from the roleplaying game my dad sometimes runs for us. The beastmaster class has a spell to grow wings for an hour. So... am I magic too?"

Olmaz shifted his jaw to the side, still looking bewildered. "Your family line is connected to those who were once known to wield such abilities. It has been dormant for many generations."

"This is awesome!" Sam stretched his wings out to either side. "Is this just now to help Ro or can I do this again?"

"We can discuss that once your friend is no longer about to catch fire." Olmaz smiled. "Then you can hear my proposal."

Sam dropped his shirt on the ground and walked to the edge. "Okay. Be right back."

He jumped.

"Wait!" called Olmaz, reaching for him but missing. "You didn't ask me how to use them."

Screaming in glee from the sheer awesomeness of flying, Sam careened down toward Ronan. Having gone flying with Sarah several times—admittedly as little more than a backpack—the orientation and general feel of it didn't seem alien. As if he'd been flying from birth, he pulled out of the dive, circled the island over the lava river once to bleed off speed, then swung his feet down to land beside Ronan.

"What the frick!" shouted Ronan, staring at him.

"Whoa," muttered Blix. "Your Mom's going to lose her mind."

"Both you guys, chill." Sam held his hands up. "It's temporary."

"Umm, so… you're gonna carry me up?" Ronan stared at the ledge overhead. "Are you strong enough?"

"I have to be. Why else would Olmaz let me borrow wings?"

Blix folded his tiny arms. "He's the demon who drains ink from pens at government offices. He'd do it for the laugh."

"Heh." Sam chuckled. "I trust him. He felt believable."

"Hurry up. It's so hot." Ronan hopped from foot to foot.

Sam glanced around at the lava. Even though glowing molten rock passed less than ten feet away on either side, standing there didn't feel much worse than being outside in the summer. "It's not *that* hot."

"Look at me." Ronan flapped his shirt, which had drenched in sweat. "I'm about to pass out. And your jeans are smoking."

Sam glanced down at himself. Sure enough, a faint wisp of smoke peeled away from his pants a few inches above his sneakers. *Has to be the spell. I'm resistant to fire right now.* "Sweeeeeeet."

"My hero," said Ronan overacting the 'princess' and swooning into his arms.

"Ha. Ha." Sam lifted him—with some difficulty—arranging him sideways before extending his wings and flapping.

Despite looking like they'd be better for gliding than power-flapping, the wings offered a surprising amount of thrust. Sam cruised upward, zig-zagging back and forth as going straight up proved a little too slow while carrying another kid the same size as him. It took him about two minutes to reach the opening in the side of a jet-black mountain seemingly miles tall.

He landed a little hard, Ronan's weight pulling them forward into a pratfall.

"Wow. Thanks." Ronan made no effort to get up, lying there with his arms out to either side.

"Are you okay?" Sam sat back on his heels, kneeling beside him.

"Not sure. Trying to decide if I'm scared or if that was the coolest thing ever."

Sam shrugged, his wings matching the gesture. "Could be both."

The wings disappeared.

Aww. Oh well. Ro's safe.

Hooves clomped up behind Sam.

He glanced up at Olmaz, who offered him back his shirt. "My apologies, Ronan, for startling you off the edge. Sam, are you ready to hear my proposal?"

"Sure." He pulled his shirt back on, then stood. "I have room in my quest journal."

19

KEEP IT BELIEVABLE

It's amazing what a nice car ride with the family and some light kidnapping can do for my mood.

Turns out, I'd been taken to the woods east of Astoria, Oregon. It's not *too* far from home, but still a bit of a hike. Since the vampires who grabbed me had been obliging enough to leave some mind-controlled humans to watch over me and make sure no one interfered in my appointment with combustion, I had to take advantage of the situation. So thoughtful of Mohawk and Mr. Pistol to leave me snacks.

The experience drained me big time, and with the sun still out, I didn't have any more strength than a normal person. Kinda surreal watching my father handcuff and chain up three guys before he and Sierra carried them to the Tahoe. Even more surreal watching Sierra helping carry grown men. I know this isn't going to end well. Giving a twelve-year-old vampire blood is going to do *something* to her that ought not to be done. I mean they have warnings about giving kids her age too much caffeine, right?

Hate to admit it, but if Dad showed up alone, he wouldn't have been able to help me.

No point thinking about it since it didn't happen. I barely held it together when we got home. Roasting all damn day left me so hungry, instinct came close to making me pounce my sisters or Dad for food. It's scary to think about, but having those three guys close at hand and knowing food was only a few minutes away is probably the only thing letting me contain the hunger long enough to get to the basement.

Also, having three men to bite let me feed enough to recover without killing any of them.

Yeah, they attacked us, but it's not their fault. More mind-control puppets.

The all-consuming drive to feed—a blackout—breaks when I'm finished drinking from the second man. I come up for air to find my mother arguing with Dad about us kidnapping people.

"Mom, relax." I wave her off. "It's only temporary. Not planning to keep them here long."

"Oh, so only temporary kidnapping." She facepalms. "That's different then. Totally legal if you practice catch and release."

Sigh. "I needed to eat real bad after the sun bake, plus I'm going spelunking in their brains. Don't worry, Mom. They won't remember being here or seeing any of us. Besides, we didn't arbitrarily kidnap people. These are the bad guys. Well, the mind-controlled pawns of bad guys. Still."

Mom nods in her 'almost having a nervous breakdown, just do whatever and I'll try not to think about it anymore' way.

Dad puts an arm around her. "Your mother's upset at me for not calling her to come with us, but can't bring herself to say so. She's not really upset we abducted three guys."

"Jonathan…" Mom stares at the rug. "You know I could get disbarred for being part of committing a felony."

"You're not part of it dear." Dad kisses her on the cheek. "One of the reasons I didn't call you. Besides, you don't have a headband."

She groans. "I still can't believe you brought the girls."

My sisters stand there next to each other looking overly innocent.

"We couldn't have found her without Coralie's help," I say. "And for Coralie to lead us there, we needed Sophia along."

"What about Sierra!?" Mom gestures at her.

"He needed a hand kicking ass and taking names. Oops, we only got two names." Sierra nudges the third guy with her foot. "What's this guy's name?"

"Snake to the face," says Sophia. "That's his name."

"I'm going insane," mutters Mom.

I stand and grasp her shoulders. "Relax. These guys aren't going to remember anything. They'll be out of here in five minutes. The handcuffs are only until I remove their mind control. We're not kidnapping them. We're saving them. Besides, if anyone gives you crap about it, I can fix it. This is my fault… sorta, anyway. And no, I didn't do anything to cause this. It's my fault for being a vampire."

"You'll fix it." Mom rolls her eyes. "How deep is this rabbit hole going to go?"

"There's a bunny?" asks Sophia in an overly cheerful tone.

Dad cracks up.

Mom looks about ready to cry, but ends up laughing.

Obviously, Sophia meant it as a joke.

I peer into my mother's eyes. *If it's too much, I can go somewhere else. I don't want to drive you nuts.*

Mom shakes her head. *No... no. Just... I'm being hit with ethical questions I can't answer. It's confusing and nerve wracking.*

Hug time. *Mom, think about it this way. I'm using vampire powers to negate the effect vampire weirdness has on our lives. It's not unethical and it's not a rabbit hole. The only reason these guys are here is they came after me for being a vampire. Me ending any sort of ethics investigation into your knowing about it is just resetting the world to normal... without vampires.*

She nods. "Fine… Fine… just finish up what you're doing and get them out of here. Try not to get blood in the carpet."

"Where should I send them?"

"I dunno." Mom waves her arms around. "Let me go check my copy of *Serial Killing for Dummies.*"

"Mom, stop being a drama queen."

She points. "You have three men tied up in the basement."

"True, but I'm not going to kill them." I step over the third guy and crouch to feed. "Besides, they tried to kill me... and Dad."

"Operative word being *tried.*" Dad puffs up his chest.

My sisters exchange a glance of 'wow'.

Dad's posturing appears to remind Mom he got his butt kicked. She starts doting over him. Like a true badass, Dad winces and flinches whenever she prods a bruise.

"Oh, Sophia?" I abort the bite to glance over at her. "What did those snakes do? Am I going to poison myself?"

"No. Just made them sleep. Not real snakes."

"Snakes?" Mom raises both eyebrows.

Sierra points a thumb at Sophia. "The guys had guns. Sophia turned their guns into snakes. Two guys dropped them right away, but one genius ran in circles holding it like when Ashley lit a pan on fire the first time she tried to cook."

Everyone laughs.

"And it bit him *in the face!*" yells Sophia.

Nom time.

This guy's blood tastes like maple syrup pancakes. Has to be from having my nose pressed against a tree for hours, even though it wasn't a maple. Once I take my fill, I reposition to straddle him and peel his eyes open so I can stare into them.

Hmm. Interesting. In his memory, the guy's being dragged along by hands too strong to be mortal, down what's probably an underground corridor. There's no light whatsoever. They stop in a large chamber, guessing based on echoes. A hand lifts this guy's chin and red glowing eyes appear in the dark right in front of him. Before the dude can crap his pants, he's in derpville. The glow doesn't give away too much of the face, but it's definitely a man… and not Stefano. Whoever set this up has long, wavy, dark hair and a goatee. Sharp nose, cold eyes. Hard to say age from such a brief glow, but wrinkles around the eyes make me think he's in the general vicinity of fifty. At least, he'd been around fifty when he became a vampire.

Well, there's something. I know for a fact it isn't Stefano who arranged for my forced conversion to Greenpeace. Or Paolo. Unless, of course, they're hiring outside help as another tool to distance themselves should the proverbial supernatural poop hit the fan.

I check the other two, who have generally the same memories of being abducted and turned into living tools. They'd all been given a simple command to stop anyone from letting me go by any means necessary. Turns out I didn't imagine a voice. Fred expressed confusion at me not burning, but only because his compulsion told him to stay there until I burned. He became frustrated at me not doing so.

Glad to disappoint.

For once, I'm happy not to be the 'hot girl.'

It's not too difficult to remove the command and blank out their memories of having seen me. Sophia rendered them magically unconscious, so I don't have to erase the house or my family from their minds other than my sisters helping fight them.

Once finished, I stand and set my hands on my hips. "Okay. All set. So… where should I send them?"

"What do you mean?" asks Mom.

"Like… where should I make them go, so they don't get re-mind-controlled and forced to attack us again."

My parents discuss various places like Olympia, Tacoma, maybe Portland or even as far away as Los Angeles.

"What about New Jersey?" asks Mom. "A long trip should keep them busy for a while."

Dad tilts his head. "Allie, if someone claims to have a powerful need to randomly go *to* New Jersey, everyone will know they've been mind-controlled."

Mom sigh-laughs.

"Hmm. Here's a thought. I'll send them to Montana."

Dad grins proudly. "*Red October.* Nice."

My sisters both sigh.

"Are they even going to come back after us?" asks Sierra.

"Hmm." Based on what I saw in their heads… probably not. "Honestly? Doubtful. These guys appear to be random victims again. I'll just send them home."

I take a few minutes to install a mental compulsion. As soon as they wake up, they will go directly to the place they consider home and relax, having no memory of the past twenty-four hours.

Once done, I stand. "Okay, Soph. How much longer are they going to be unconscious?"

"Umm. I don't know. Maybe another hour or two." She shrugs, offering a cheesy smile. "Maybe three."

"Leave them on Niedermeyer's lawn," says Sierra. "No one will ever see them again."

We all laugh.

"Once it gets dark, I'll drag them out into the woods behind the house. They'll be in a fog until they get home, and lose all memories of today." I slouch, relieved. A nice big blood meal has me feeling pretty much normal… except for my clothing smelling of burnt meat.

Honestly, I didn't scorch anywhere near as much as expected. The tree cover helped. Maybe I pulled some super-vampiric feat of adrenaline and overamped my powers. Who knows? I'll take it.

"I could try opening a gate and sending them somewhere?" Sophia holds her arms out to either side.

"Can we not?" Sierra cringes. "I'd prefer not to be bitch slapped by a ten-ton void octopus again."

Mom makes a face like she's contemplating yelling at Sierra for saying 'bitch slapped,' but it strikes her funny.

A door shuts upstairs.

"That was awesome," says Ronan.

"Totally." Sam thuds to the floor, probably sitting by the PlayStation. "Uh oh."

"What?" asks Ronan.

"It's almost eight… we were in there like four hours."

"Didn't feel like it."

"Didn't. Nope. Time flow's different, I guess. Mom and Dad are gonna realize we disappeared and be upset."

"Guys?" I say. "Sam's out of the closet."

Mom and Dad stare at me.

"Literally." I shake my head. "As in, he was inside his bedroom

closet and is now no longer inside his bedroom closet. He and Ronan are back. I can hear them."

Dad chuckles. "I think we're beating the closet joke to death."

I make a pinchy gesture. "Just a little."

"Beating it to *un*death," deadpans Sierra. "Make the joke again and it's going to bite us."

The 'rents groan.

"Ouch. C'mon, guys." Dad smiles. "The vampire jokes are starting to get a bit stiff… but I understand what's at stake."

Mom searches the ceiling for help.

Sierra walks up to me. "Bite me now. I can't take the dad jokes."

"Careful, hon. Vampirism can be draining." Dad winks.

Sophia screams.

Before Sierra can go all *Foamy the Squirrel* on Dad, I hurry upstairs to my brother's room. And whoa… one or both of them fired off some serious egg farts. I cringe, waving my hand in front of my face.

Oddly, neither boy claims it or blames the other, just stares at me like I'm hallucinating.

"Who ripped one?"

"No one," says Sam. "Your overclocked schnoz is probably detecting the ambiance of the demi-plane we were in."

Blix babbles, points at the closet, and nods.

"Yeah, he says you're smelling the place we came from. It's probably in our clothes." Sam shrugs.

"Guys, you weren't gone for four hours. You were gone for twenty-eight. It's four hours later *the next day*."

Sam's face pales. "Oops."

"Oh no." Ronan starts crying. "Mom's gonna kill me."

Several thoughts crash into my brain at once. One is making an offhand quip about how she can't be upset over Ronan missing for a day because she's presently freaking out at the hospital with Hunter. Yeah, not gonna say it. I hate myself for even thinking it. Another thought is, yeah… his mother is probably fried. Astonishing there's no police sitting at the house. The stronger thought is 'oh, shit, Hunter!'

and a *strong* compulsion to race right the hell out the door and go see him.

Visiting hours do not apply to vampires.

Despite the storm going on in my head, what comes out of my mouth is, "I'm sure the parents will understand you didn't mean it. You're a novice at exploring alternate dimensions."

"Cool. Think so?" asks Sam, grinning hopefully.

I cringe. "Dunno. It's going to be a hard sell. Mom might still be upset at you for going into a demi-plane without asking first."

He snaps his fingers, making an 'aww shucks' face.

The parents rush in… and proceed to scoop Sam up and compete for hugs. Okay, they're so happy to see him okay he might actually slip out of this without even being grounded. Being the baby of the family does convey certain advantages.

"I'm okay." Sam hugs Mom and Dad back. "Oh, there's a portal into a demi-plane in my closet. I'm sorry we were gone so long. Didn't know it had weird time differences." Sam kicks his sneaker into the rug. "Ack." He hastily pulls his shoes off. "Sorry. We *just* got back."

"Should we be worried?" asks Dad.

Ronan kicks off his sneakers, looking frightened Mom is going to yell at him.

"Nah." Sam smiles. "The guy who lives in there is cool."

I exhale in relief. The big dog in the yard is helpful. Great. Sam's collecting demons like Pokémon. That's gotta be setting us up for a bizarre event. Just hope it's not too flamey when it happens.

"Okay…" I pick Ronan up. "I gotta get him back to his mother. And I need to check on Hunter. Not gonna believe he's really okay until I see him."

"What happened to Hunter?" Ronan's eyes go wide.

I cringe. "Some bad vampires tried to hurt me and he kinda got caught in the middle of it."

"Just a bonk on the head." Dad offers a reassuring smile.

"He's fine." Mom smiles. "Little sore, but fine."

"Are we taking a mirror?" Ronan picks up his shoes.

"Nope. Flying."

"Okay." He carries his shoes out into the hall.

I follow him to the kitchen. Once outside on the deck, he puts his sneakers on and walks around behind me so I can pull him on like a backpack. Poor little guy weighs less than the books I carried freshman year of high school. "Be home in a little while."

"Be careful." Dad says from the patio door behind us.

"I will." Sniff. "What smells burnt?"

"My shoes," mutters Ronan. "The floor was lava. Like for real."

20

SORE SPOTS

Funny thing about head injuries… they tamper with memory.

Funny thing about language… the word 'funny' can sometimes mean the exact opposite. The whole fight behind the restaurant didn't register in Hunter's brain at all. He remembers smiling at me in the kitchen and being happy to have a few hours to spend with me—then he's in the hospital and his mother's freaking out.

I never realized how much of a professional bullshitter my mother can be. Okay, considering she's high up the food chain in the legal department of Boeing, maybe I should have suspected her powers of 'creative explaining' are superhuman. She somehow managed to convey to Mrs. Lawrence why Ronan disappeared for an entire day without technically lying or revealing the truth the boys had gone into another dimensional reality via a hole in Sam's closet.

Granted, this represented one of those times where telling someone the actual truth with a straight face would have resulted in an appointment to see a psychiatrist. Last time I checked, Mom doesn't have legit powers of mind control, but Mrs. Lawrence took her straight-faced delivery and complete lack of being upset to accept Ronan slept over Sam's place and perhaps assumed it had been planned and agreed upon and she simply forgot due to her new job being busy and the chaos of Hunter getting hurt.

Not to express any sort of happiness about him ending up in the hospital, but Mrs. Lawrence going there to visit him stopped her from noticing the email from the school asking why Ronan missed a day.

Yeah, I got tasked with cleanup duty. Six teachers, an assistant principal, and one lunch lady now think Ronan (and Sam) were at school the other day. Kidding about the lunch lady, by the way. No, not about erasing a lunch lady's memory, only about it being related to Ronan and Sam missing a day of school. I caught her snooping around school grounds hunting for a faerie. While it might have been okay to leave her to a quest any rational person would consider nuts, I erred on the side of caution and erased the memory of having a ton of chocolate pudding explode all over her. Not a literal ton. I have no idea how much twenty industrial-sized cans of pudding weighs, but it's not 2,000 pounds.

The spell my sister released at school turned into the 'Sophia version' of an imp. All the pranks, none of the cruelty.

Hunter, by the way, is doing okay. He took a pretty decent whack to the head and… me throwing him into the kitchen headfirst didn't help. Whether the two jerks who grabbed me left him alone for sake of time or not wanting to murder the entire restaurant staff to cover their tracks, Hunter's being in the kitchen saved his life. I still don't know if Mohawk and Mr. Pistol wanted to kill him on purpose to hurt me or simply eliminate a witness who happened to be there. If I ever see those two again, I'll ask Eleanor St. Ives if she can extract the answer to a question from a brain Slurpee.

For the first time in my life, I fully intend to attack and kill someone without giving them a chance to even say a word. Three reasons. One: they tried to kill me already. That kinda pisses me off. Two: they tried to kill Hunter. That *really* pisses me off. Three: my best chance of winning—or surviving—a second meeting with them is to ambush them before they realize it. Mohawk threw me around like a karate instructor picking on a white belt. He knows how to fight, but I'm going to assume he doesn't know how to use a sword.

Also, it won't matter if he knows how to use a sword if he doesn't have one.

A hospital stay—they're keeping Hunter overnight—*did* allow us to have a few hours together without him having to worry about making it to school on time in the morning. We cuddled on the bed together sorta-watching the tiny little television. Even though he eventually fell asleep, I stayed with him until impending dawn chased me home. He felt well enough to make a joke about a tree not being the kind of wood I was hoping to ride last night… with his mother right there. Yes, he's on pain medication. Fortunately, no one captured the mortifying joke on video.

Thanks to the attack, I missed my Thursday class. Weird twist of fate. Thursday, I have philosophy with Professor Heath, who is a vampire. There's no need for me to come up with a wild excuse for why I missed class. Not only is it impossible for me to mess with his mind, it's totally possible for me to tell him the truth. Sure, college profs don't really care if students show up or not. At least, not in the same way teachers in high school do. No one gets in trouble for it. Worst penalty for absences is failing a class we're paying for… and possibly having a four-year program turn into five.

Still, next time I see him, he'll get the truth. Feel bad no-showing the guy. He's cool. I did email him to apologize and ask what work needs to be done for next week while remarking 'powers beyond my control' kept me away from class. He ought to get the subtle hint.

I wake up a bit late on Friday at 4:19 p.m., feeling like an Olympic bobsled after a grueling all-day practice session. Notice the absence of the word 'team' there. No, I'm not going for the 'feeling like a bunch of guys rode me' joke. My body is as sore as if I'd spent eighteen hours bouncing headfirst down a concrete chute. The prolonged battle between me and the sun yesterday hurt. Also, no. I am not complaining. Feeling as sore as a forty-year-old basement-dwelling Twitch streamer going from video games to military boot camp overnight is a *small* price to pay compared to what the sun *could* have done to me.

Added bonus: no one kept screaming at me to move my candy ass.

Shouldn't talk, really. Mortal me could in no way have handled military boot camp either.

Hi, I'm Sarah Wright and I used to be kind of a wimp.

Diary of a Wimpy Vampire, I am not.

Diary of a somewhat geeky, neurotic, rule-following vampire, maybe.

There's one cure for ouch like this. No, not weed. A peaches-and-cream bath bomb. Don't care it's broad daylight. After spending sunrise chained to a tree, walking around my house in the daytime is nothing.

I chant a mantra of 'ouch, F-you' under my breath while walking up to the second-floor bathroom. We have a little bathroom on the ground floor, but it's really a toilet closet. Sink and commode, not even a shower. Our mini-bath in the basement does have a shower stall, but my present needs transcend simple cleanliness. Today is uncomfortably warm, but the sun isn't going to get the satisfaction of seeing me flinch. Looks like it's on the brighter end of Seattle possible, one of those days where I'd never have even opened my bedroom door prior to my brief foray with Greenpeace.

That's a tree-hugging joke by the way.

Bathroom's not too bad with the curtains closed.

Even better totally submerged.

WELL, THE SOAK DIDN'T DO MUCH FOR UNDEAD MUSCLES, BUT I HAVE nice, soft skin.

And I smell like a peach orchard exploded all over a dairy farm. Not normally an unpleasant smell, but my nose is cranked up to eleven. Still not *un*pleasant. Merely not quite pleasant. Oversaturation has changed it from peach to 'obviously fake chemical peach.'. Ask me if I care.

I spend the rest of Friday's available 'me time' working on my Poe paper before saying a quick goodbye to the family and heading to school. Today, I'm using my freshman year bookbag, which is big enough to smuggle tweens into R rated movies. Why anyone would lug a hockey bag into a movie theater, I have no idea, but it's a silly metaphor to express the massiveness of the thing. Not supposed to make logical sense. It's not heavy. Still only bringing books for computer science 101 and calculus. The huge bag is to conceal my sword. This katana is *way* cooler being in my hand rather than impaled into my body. It's not the most ideal weapon for the style of sword fighting Dalton pumped into my brain, but having a sword at all beats not.

Maybe one of these days I'll pick up a cutlass, saber, rapier, or longsword even. Hasn't exactly been a priority, but recent events are changing my opinions.

Good chance bringing a razor-sharp sword to college is not going to be received well. Probably illegal, too. However, I am taking precautions. It's not loaded. Seriously, though. It's staying in the bag unless vampires come after me. As long as it remains hidden until sunset, it won't matter who sees it.

Much to my surprise, my Friday classes happen without a problem. I don't even get ambushed by missionaries on my way to the parking garage. The whole ride home, my anxiety is at peak. I'm constantly watching all angles up out of the car in case more vampires decide to drop out of the sky without warning. I make it home without incident. Hmm. Maybe whoever is doing this either assumes my butt roasted to ashes already, or they've given up. Wait, no. If the creepy long-haired dude I saw in Mike's memory is aware the whole melodramatic 'chain her to a tree for sunrise' thing didn't work, he'd totally be sending Mohawk and Mr. Pistol to grab me again for study purposes.

Then again, it's totally possible my significance is nil.

If video games have taught me anything, the first enemies are the weakest and you work your way up to progressively more difficult opponents. Could be, I'm simply the weakest vampire around, so this guy figured he'd start by messing with me.

Whatever. I'll take it.

My plans are to go to Hunter's and make up for the night we were so cruelly deprived of. However, some loose ends need wrapping up first. I leave the bookbag in my room, grab the katana, and go upstairs.

Dad's in the kitchen foraging for a snack. He glances at me emerging from the basement steps carrying a sword. "Uh oh. Where are you headed?"

"Following up on a promise I made."

"Eek," deadpans Dad.

"Relax. Not hunting anyone. When making promises to the Universe, it's best to keep them."

"Since when are you superstitious?"

I wag my eyebrows. "I'm not. This is me merely not taking the chance superstitions are real. Won't take long. But… I'm going to visit Hunter after. Probably won't be home until after you guys are asleep."

Dad walks over to hug me. "All right. Be careful. Oh, tomorrow's Saturday. *Escape from New York* and *Escape from LA*."

"Heh. Going for a theme."

"Nah. I merely heard something Russeling in the bushes."

Head tilt. "I sense a great disturbance in the force. As if a horrible pun occurred, but I missed it."

"Ooh, young padawan. Your skills are rusty. Kurt Russel?"

"Oh, gawd, Dad." I bonk my head on his shoulder twice. "Awful."

"It's not awful until you realize where I put the DVDs."

My eyebrows form a flat line. "You did not."

"I did."

"Literally in the bushes out back?"

Dad whistles innocently. "Only long enough to take a photo."

"I'm going to randomly think about this pun for a century and groan about it every time."

"My work here is complete," says Dad attempting an Emperor Palpatine voice.

I head for the door out to the deck. "Another one like that, and I might just start throwing lightning out my fingertips."

"Isn't the whole lightning from the fingertips thing Sophia's job?"

"Ugh!" I roll my eyes. "No, Dad. Lightning is dark side. She's *beyond* light side. Sophia is 'cute side.' She'd throw pink bunny rabbits from her fingertips, and pelt the bad guys into submission under a machine gun fire of squeaky nerf bunnies."

Dad laughs himself to tears as I step outside and leap into the air.

SIX MINUTES LATER, I'M STANDING ON TOP OF THE SPACE NEEDLE.

Might as well get it over with.

There's no real way to strip naked in public in any manner even close to dignified, so I don't bother caring how I look and go as fast as possible. Soon, I'm atop the Space Needle in my birthday suit, fists against my hips in a Wonder Woman pose.

"Well, okay, Universe. I escaped the tree, so here I am, just like I promised. Embarrass away if you care to."

It's probably a lame jinx bet considering no one can see me up here at night unless they happen to be in a passing helicopter, but the skies are quiet. In hindsight, making a jinx bet with the Universe probably would work better if the offered unpleasantness has an actual effect. Like, I hate Brussels sprouts. Struggled with a chemistry test my sophomore year of high school, so I made a jinx bet with the Universe to eat a big portion of them if I passed the class with a B or better.

I got an A-.

Mom laughed at my request for Brussels sprouts, but I ate them.

And yeah, they still sucked. But a deal is a deal, right?

The view of the Seattle cityscape is breathtaking. I stand there for a few minutes looking around, waiting for something to happen. It's not *so* late at night no one's in the restaurant below me, but unless some maintenance guy is here to do after hours work and comes up to the roof, it's about as private here as my bedroom. So, not the riskiest jinx bet I've ever made. Does having supernatural powers matter? Like, if I mind-controlled someone to forget seeing me streaking, does it invalidate the power of my jinx bet?

I didn't promise not to.

And how long, exactly do I need to stand here in my birthday suit to satisfy the conditions of the bet? In a purely literal sense, my promise was 'I get out of this alive, I'll stand naked on top of the Space Needle.' I am presently standing naked atop the Space Needle. Fulfilled. Didn't say I'd stand here for an hour.

Okay, cool. I'm considering myself done.

Time to go see Hunter.

Before I can crouch to pick up my underwear, the iPhone in my jeans rings. Sigh. I fish it out. Caller ID says 'stepmom.' Eep. This is probably important, so I answer.

"Hello?"

"*Allo, mon cherie,*" says Aurélie. "What are you doing, dear?"

Busted. Umm. Or maybe she's generally asking. She isn't Dalton. We don't have a mind link capable of reaching halfway around the planet. She'd totally get the concept of a jinx bet. However, for my dignity's sake, I'm going to pretend she means it in a general 'hey, what are you up to' not a 'why the heck are you on top of the Space Needle with no clothes on' way.

"Not much. Paying off a small debt. Was about to go visit Hunter. Two cretins ambushed us the other day and he got hurt."

"Oh, *non*! I 'ope he is not too injured?"

"Moderate concussion, broken rib, and a 'chipped elbow' whatever that is."

She tsks. "You are in the city, yes? I sensed you somewhat close."

"Yeah." I look around. No one is watching me. No cameras—obvious ones anyway—in sight.

"It is good you are close. There is a gathering tonight."

I stare straight up in frustration. For whatever reason, the Universe decided a night sky should still appear dark to vampires. One might think being able to fly and mind-control people is the most surreal aspect of this whole undead existence deal. It isn't. Surreal is seeing the world as bright as afternoon on an overcast day under an ink-black, starry sky.

C'mon, Sarah. Get thine hormones in check. Tomorrow is Saturday. I can spend the whole day at Hunter's. And it isn't even hormones at the moment, more being worried about him and wanting to be there for him.

"Okay."

"You seem unhappy."

Teenage girls from the Eighties had one really big advantage over me. On a phone call like this, they had a cord to fidget with. I laughed my butt off watching Mom try to convince Sierra and Sophia they used to 'tie phones to walls.' "Well, yeah. But there's a lot going on. Not unhappy about the soiree. Merely a little frustrated." I spend a minute or two talking about how my plans to be with Hunter the other night had a giant turd dropped on them, though I don't say anything in clear terms. The NSA is always listening, and they don't need to be aware of vampires.

I mean, they probably are already, but no sense risking it. Even if my Dad is overly paranoid and the NSA isn't listening to every phone conversation, still better I play it safe than wake up in a CIA lab. That's right up there with the famous quote by Abraham Lincoln when he said, 'Don't believe everything you read on the internet.'

"Do not fret, *mon cheri*. Tonight's meeting is not a soiree, but a conference about this exact problem. It will not consume much time."

"Cool. I'll be at your apartment in a minute or two."

"See you soon," says Aurélie in a cheerful tone, before making a maternal '*mwah*' kissy noise.

I hang up.

Dammit, Universe. Jinx bet satisfied. Why the second interruption with Hunter? Oh, probably because I had a little hope this wouldn't be the only time tonight I didn't have clothes on. Bad Sarah. He's hurt. We're not going to do anything in bed for a while. I send him a text message letting him know 'A' requires my presence at an important meeting with 'W,' but it's not going to take long and I'll be there as soon as it's over.

I scramble into my clothes and jump off the Space Needle.

Now *there* is a sentence I never imagined saying… or thinking.

To my absolute astonishment, I don't end up in an elaborate 1700s-era gown.

Something is *really* wrong with my life when walking into this room in normal clothing—as opposed to being a giant porcelain doll —feels wrong. Aurélie meant it when she said it wouldn't be a normal soiree. We do, however, go to the same hotel they usually hold the parties in. It's unnerving to see the other vampires in basically street clothes. There are no snacks, human or otherwise, and the mood coming from everyone is 'let's get this over with fast.'

Now, I understand what Mom meant when she described it as bizarre when she ran into Cristian Fowler at the mall and saw him in a sweatshirt and jeans. He's her boss, the VP of legal. Up until then, she'd only ever seen the guy wearing expensive suits.

Wolent's here, obviously. To him, 'street clothes' are the same nice suits he always wears for the parties. Most of his entourage is dressed like me, either in T-shirts and jeans, sweatshirts and jeans, or Abercrombie & Fitch dresses. Except for me, vampires who shop at Marshalls, Target, or Walmart don't show up for these events.

Stefano and Paolo are here. They—and their clique of traditionalists—are also all wearing black suits or evening gowns. Maybe the reason my mind keeps wanting to associate some of the vampires around here with the Mafia is due to their clothing more than the way they act. If Paolo put on forty pounds and grew a little mustache, he'd almost look like a fortyish Marlon Brando from *Godfather*. Almost. Maybe his half-brother.

The women who usually spar with Aurélie for being the prettiest in the room are completely different tonight. Both are dressed rather casually. Vanessa, the red-haired Fury, is totally soccer-momming out. As much as a woman who looks mid-twenties can soccer-mom. And no, I don't really care if 'soccer-mom' isn't a verb. She's turning it into one.

We all basically stand in a giant circle like some lame corporate icebreaker exercise my mother's constantly talking-slash-complaining about. She doesn't mind doing fun activities with co-workers to build teamwork and camaraderie, but the things HR keeps coming up with are neither fun nor do they build camaraderie. Everyone views them as tedious, patronizing time-wasters. Corporate treating adults like kids in kindergarten doesn't go over well.

Arthur Wolent starts off by announcing there are problems. He refers to the firebombing of two properties belonging to him, then goes on to mention numerous attacks on other vampires in the room, most of whom are on the older, wealthier side than me. Faces are familiar, but I don't know any of them even as well as their names until Wolent mentions them except for Henry Arnold. I *do* know his name. And that he's probably sweet on Ashton James. Apparently, they co-own a nightclub which suffered a bad case of the Molotovs.

Eleanor St. Ives points at him. "What evidence do you offer these attacks are not being carried out by your direction? And before you point out what gall I have to suggest such a thing, be aware your reputation making it seem ridiculous for you to do something like this might be the best subterfuge."

Everyone gets quiet… likely waiting for Wolent to remind us all he's a Fury.

"A vehicle abandoned at the site of an attack on my interests belongs to one of your companies." Eleanor folds her arms.

I almost interrupt to say leaving such an obvious clue behind *decreases* the chances of it being legitimate proof of Wolent's involvement, but her suspicions echo what I'd thought the other night. Making it seem like an obvious attempt to misdirect blame might allow them to pretend innocence. Might. For now, I keep quiet.

"It's not Mr. Wolent," says Stefano, nodding at Aurélie. "He's acting through a supposedly neutral party. The pink rose was a nice touch."

She quirks an eyebrow at him. "My dear Mr. Bianchi, I haven't the slightest idea of what you mean."

He narrows his eyes. "Who else in this room could have destroyed Vincenzo so effortlessly? Certainly, not your little doll pet."

Admittedly, her 'you're scarcely worth my time' tone could easily be misinterpreted as her lying in plain sight and making it obvious… but I know she didn't send anyone to attack Stefano, his friends, or his business interests. Mostly because she doesn't really *have* vampires to send… except me, and yeah—not happening. Again, I didn't know Vincenzo well. Only that he'd been one of Stefano's inner circle and over a hundred years old.

About half the room makes faces at us, like they're wondering if Aurélie's 'supposed' disinterest in political power is really a lie covering her true intentions… just like Wolent's reputation for being blunt and direct could be a lie covering his scheming in the background. I fully believe if Wolent intended to mess with St. Ives, he'd tell her to her face. Yes, vampire politics demands subtlety, but the man doesn't strike me as the type to lie. If subtlety failed and his involvement came out, he'd own it.

Vanessa starts accusing Paolo of sending thugs to get revenge on her for not helping him 'make life hard for the kid.' I assume she means me. Which also means Paolo definitely tried recruiting support to act against me somehow. Jennifer Ruiz, Stefano, Paolo, and a handful of others all complain about an anarchist uprising. Discussion gives way to everyone trying to shout over each other—except for me and Aurélie. We stand there watching with the same expressions, like a pair of teachers making no attempt to stop a riot of second-graders in the cafeteria while thinking, 'screw it, they'll get tired eventually.'

Pascal Ivanov, Eleanor's close friend—and another Academic—brings the room to quiet by shouting his theory it could be anarchists posing as others to incite chaos.

"To what end?" scoffs Stefano. "What would they gain by this?"

"Anarchy, of course." Pascal grasps the lapels of his dull green blazer. Dude totally looks like the overly stereotypical 'nerdy' science teacher, except for being a little on the young side, barely into his thirties. "Their only goal would be to watch us turn on each other and laugh as society burns."

"Or it's what Wolent thinks we'll assume," mutters Stefano.

Once again, everyone gets quiet, expecting a fit of rage.

Arthur Wolent remains calm, though he isn't making eye contact with anyone. No, it isn't guilt. He's totally vibing like the Mafia boss who's smiling and joking with a guy who's not going to see another sunrise. Or, maybe in the case of vampires, a man who *will* see the next sunrise.

Oh, hell. Here goes nothing.

I storm across the open space in the middle of the circle, right up to Stefano. "Twice, I've been attacked by people claiming to have been sent by you."

He sighs out his nose while frowning at me, then makes a face at Aurélie like a manager would give a woman whose toddler is trashing the store.

"No, I'm not going away. I have something to say here." Must resist jabbing my finger into his chest despite wanting to real bad. Don't need any more broken bones this week. "Both times vampires attacked me, they claimed to be working on your orders… and I believe they lied."

He seems ready to bite my head off, but stops himself, head tilted in a 'do my ears deceive me' stare. The man looks me up and down.

"Sorry, skipped the fancy gown tonight. Look, everyone knows you think I'm being disrespectful to 'tradition' by not cutting ties with my family—but I also know I'm nowhere near important enough to be the reason all the elders start trying to kill each other. Sure, I'm living with my mortal family… who cares? Paolo's hair helmet is more offensive to vampire tradition than me."

About half the vampires in the room chuckle.

"Two nights ago, a pair of vampires attacked me and left me chained to a tree to hug the sun. They said Stefano ordered them to 'teach me the meaning of respect.'"

Everyone—except Aurélie, Stefano, and Paolo—gasps.

Aurélie already knew. The other two guys are just dickheads.

Stefano's angry glower backs off to the sort of expression one would make when watching an idiot pull on a push door.

"Exactly." I gesture at him. "You *know* why it's stupid. If you really wanted to destroy me, you wouldn't have done that… and I don't think you want to destroy me."

"One does not murder a child for being insolent," says Stefano. "It is an overreaction."

"And men like you used to consider women who wore pants as 'insolent.' My family is not hurting anyone." I look around the circle of vampires. "I've been attacked by someone pretending to be working for Stefano. It's a lie. Someone, maybe even a vampire among us, is trying to set off a bomb. They hoped I'd freak out and go crying to Aurélie to tell her you tried to kill me, expecting she'd come unglued and effectively throw Seattle into open war. But… if the guys who attacked me lied about it, there's a really good chance the guys who have attacked all of you are also lying about it."

Murmuring starts.

"St. Ives, too!" I yell.

She raises an eyebrow at me.

"You are accusing her of doing this?" Stefano scoffs. "What evidence do you have? Other than you stealing from her twice."

"Argh." I facepalm. "No. I'm not accusing her of anything. And I didn't steal from her. Another group attacked my home. Mortals under mental command. Dalton looked in their thoughts and found memories of being programmed by people who discussed working for St. Ives."

"Oh… Dalton Ames." Paolo laughs. "Did you ever stop to think he's the one behind all of this? Not only is he an anarchist, he doesn't even have a home territory. Did *you* look into their minds or are you taking him at his word?"

"No." I scowl at him. "I never stopped to suspect he's behind all this. I know him better than that. And, as you so imperiously pointed out, he doesn't consider Seattle his territory. Why would he give a toss what the elders here do?"

Know what's awkward? Having two dozen vampires all stare at me in total silence.

I face Eleanor. "Can you make zombies?"

"No," says Eleanor, without hesitation or emotion.

Stefano laughs. "Are you serious? Zombies? Child, you've been watching too much television."

"Okay, fine. Technically, they weren't zombies… merely

reanimated puppets remote-controlled by a vampire master somewhere else."

Eleanor raises a 'wait' hand to Stefano. "Don't laugh, Bianchi. Such things *are* possible. However, I do not dabble in esoteric ridiculousness. The methods are inexact and the results unpredictable, dangerous, or wholly inefficient. I am strictly a woman of science."

"Thought so," I mutter.

"Body puppets?" asks Vanessa. "Sounds horrifying."

"Look." I turn in place, eyeing everyone around me… but don't see anyone resembling the long-haired man. "Someone, maybe an outsider, maybe one of us, is testing weak points."

Stefano jabs a finger at me. "You did not imply I am weak."

Eleanor rolls her eyes.

"No. I'm talking about all of us as a whole. Like armor. Weak spots. Whoever is doing this knows information they would need to be close to us to obtain. They're aware of the friction between us. They're aware of me being at odds with St. Ives twice. They know Mr. Wolent is not fond of anarchists."

Stefano rubs his chin. "Yet they do not know certain things about you."

I'm sure he means my sunlight tolerance. Yeah. That. Stefano Bianchi is plenty old enough to read my mind whether I want him to or not. Must explain why he's being fairly cordial to me since I've basically defended him here. Six other vampires accused him of attacking them. Me saying I believe it's a lie casts doubt on their claims of his responsibility for other attacks.

"There's one more little detail." I concentrate on the brief image of the long-haired man I saw in the memories of Fred, Mike, and Mr. 'Snake to the Face.' "The humans commanded to kill anyone trying to help me escape sunrise were kidnapped and brought to a dark place. They didn't see much before blacking out except for a flash of a face, illuminated only by the glow in the man's eyes. Look at my thoughts. Does anyone recognize him?"

Having six or seven vampire elders all invade my head at once is super weird. Ever pluck a rubbery booger that feels like a strand wrapped around your entire brain peeling loose? Pretty much the same sensation.

Wolent, Stefano, Paolo, Aurélie, Pascal, and St. Ives exchange 'no clue' glances.

"It doesn't prove much. Their memories could have been tampered with." Paolo frowns. "The face could be manufactured."

"Agreed." St. Ives rubs the bridge of her nose. "Whoever did this may have inserted any image they wanted into those mortals' minds."

Pascal clasps his hands behind his back. "A red herring. The man those mortals believed they saw may not even exist."

Damn. I look down. "Okay. True. I have no proof he exists for real. But *someone* is still poking at sore spots trying to cause problems and put your names on it."

Wolent clears his throat, quieting everyone.

I scurry back to my spot in the circle beside Aurélie.

"It is time for caution." Wolent shifts left and right, looking at everyone, mostly the other elders. "This is likely an outside party attempting to initiate a war among us. Only, the war they're going to get is not going to be watching us tear each other's throats out."

Murmurs of agreement come from about a third of the crowd.

"But!" shouts Wolent, a hint of anger rising in his voice, face reddening. "If any of this turns out to be someone on the *inside* dicking with us, they're going to learn what it's like to experience unlife without skin."

A few gasps come from around us. Paolo can't resist an 'oh please' subtle eyeroll. I think it's less the man isn't afraid of what Wolent might be capable of, more an 'oh there goes the Fury threatening violence again' flavor of condescension.

Wolent either misses the look or ignores it. Given the mood he's in already, my money's on missed. When a Fury is naturally angry at something, it's quite easy for them to go nuclear. The trigger doesn't have to be related to anything. A car horn could sound outside and, next thing anyone knows, Wolent is throwing chairs through the wall. Fortunately, when the irrational rage hits a Fury and it's not caused by a specific person, they usually lash out at the environment.

So, I keep my gaze on the floor.

Wolent walks up to me.

Crap.

"Sarah. You get one of these sons of bitches, you lop their heads off and bring it to me."

He's gotta be reacting to me standing here holding a damn katana. Weird no one said a word of protest about it. Yeah, totally normal for a girl to attend a meeting carrying a freakin' samurai sword, right? And ack. Please mean vampire. Pleeeease mean vampire. If he doesn't specify, I'm going to assume he's not telling me to kill some mortal who's been controlled.

"Yes, sir." I nod. "Gladly. There's one with a blue mohawk I'd love for you to see."

Wolent spins away from me, pointing around the circle.

Whew. Out of the hot seat.

"That goes for all of us, not just the new kid." Wolent makes a neck-slicing gesture. "Next time someone gives any of you shit, bring their damn head here. Rest of the body optional."

More stares go around. Lots of confusion.

A true psycho would have no problem demanding we chop off the heads of his own minions. Wolent is neither a psycho nor sending minions out to attack other vampires. I don't think anyone here sincerely considers the man unstable enough to demand heads if he's responsible for any of the attacks. The quiet bewilderment must mean vampires are rearranging their opinion of what's going on, moving Wolent away from suspicion.

Then again, this could technically be part of his plan. I don't think it is, just saying… someone who really loves tinfoil hat websites might believe it. Wolent's hiding his plans for world domination right under the flat earth information.

Oy. I mean, there's 'lick a hot stove to make sure it's hot' stupid and then there's the flat earthers. They could probably play checkers against a literal rock and lose. Fluids in zero gravity environments coalesce into a spherical shape. They don't form into square, flat tiles. Planets are essentially the same thing, matter coalescing into spheres in a vacuum. Yeah, good luck debating a flat earth idiot. I'd talk about the mechanism of action for fluids in a vacuum and they'll think I'm talking about pouring water into their Hoover.

Before too long, vampires break into clusters for some 'after-meeting discussion.'

Aurélie smiles at me. "The official meeting is over, *cheri*. Go attend to your lover."

Ooh, I blush.

My 'lover.' Makes it sound so… I dunno, like we're characters in a regency romance novel. My father's betrothed me to the prince of Oregon, but I'm really in love with a poor boy from Seattle with no land or titles to speak of.

Aurélie laughs. "Oh, *cheri*, you simply must bring him to sit for a painting as soon as he is well."

… and she's in my thoughts. Heh, okay. Sitting next to Hunter for an hour is hardly a bad thing.

Tonight, though, I plan to sit next to him for a lot more than an hour.

21

OUT OF THE FRYING PAN, INTO THE WEIRD

I appreciate the 'irony of swords.'

Carrying one around made it unnecessary to have one. No vampires jumped me on the way home. Fine with me. Hunter and I didn't do anything more physically intense than lay in bed together holding hands watching a movie and/or talking. I know it's possible for a vampire to give a mortal some blood and it triggers accelerated healing. But, I didn't even bring it up, afraid adding even a few—literal—drops of weirdness into Hunter's life more than I do already by simply existing would make it worse for him.

If ever anyone specifically goes after him because of me, my policy will change. Boosting him a bit to survive a definite threat, I can do. My feelings on Dalton amping Sierra up remain mixed, the whole 'is the cure worse than the disease' conundrum. What side effects will it have on anyone, especially a kid, to partake of vampire-like strength and reflexes? Is it going to slow her aging down? Could she possibly become addicted to it? I've read about some fictional vampire settings where drinking blood from a vampire two or three times makes someone into a mind slave.

Aurélie laughed when I asked her about that. She'd know. Used to be, she had a small retinue of men in her company she routinely fed blood so they could 'keep up' with her in bed. They partook just a teeny bit more than three times and didn't become enslaved to her. She couldn't comment on the addiction since it became impossible to determine if they'd become addicted to *her* or the blood.

Power is addictive no matter what form it takes, so I'm going to assume a mortal *can* become hooked on feeling superhuman. Wait, no. I don't have to assume. Firsthand experience. Being superhuman is freakin' awesome. It stinks when I'm offline.

So, yeah. It's Saturday and I've gone a whole forty-eight hours without cutting a bitch. No, I'm not craving a fight. If this entire vampire war problem magically disappeared without explanation, I wouldn't complain. Or wait, maybe I would... purely because problems like this don't magically vanish on their own. I'd be too worried the red-eye man would be plotting some new scheme. By red-eye man, I mean the image from my three babysitters' minds.

Of course, now even their memories are suspect. Can't argue the suggestion it might be an illusion or a deliberate lie. If the dude I saw in their heads is real, whoever sent those three men to 'ensure' I roasted might have planted it there to fool me in case I escaped... or fool other vampires if they came to help.

Hold on... those three guys had been programmed to babysit me only until I immolated. Whoever arranged for me to hug a tree definitely expected me to turn into a screaming Roman candle as soon as the sun came up. Why would they feel the need to plant a fake image of a person in the heads of three mortals who wouldn't be anywhere near my remains when any other vampires found me? Those men would've gone back to their ordinary lives, never being aware they'd guarded a vampire execution.

Nah. Stefano's grasping at straws. Red-eye man has to be real. He might be a fooled proxy though, thinking he's working for Stefano but not. Or Stefano knows exactly who I saw and he's going to make sure the man dies for his failure. Assuming I'm wrong and he *is* really behind this, he'd have a reason to create doubt regarding the truth of what I saw in those guys' heads.

He's also a total asshole, so he might have said it purely to make me look foolish. Can't go letting the 'little girl' you accuse of being reckless and idiotic appear too competent in front of everyone.

Since I'm awake, I call Hunter. I want to spend the day at his house with him, if the Universe permits it. Gotta make sure he's awake, home, and it's still okay for me to pop over. As of last night, he wasn't sure if he'd be working or not. Having missed a few days, he really does need the money. It's *so* darn tempting to ask him to quit working at least until he's out of college, and give him money. After my 'adventure' in Ireland, I have a shameful amount in the bank. Freeing him from the need to work sounds pretty faerie tale, but there's a big problem. He'd feel extremely guilty. It would also make me feel kinda weird, too. Like I'm some stuck-up rich bitch who always gets what she wants, because money. He's been amazing so far, somehow not feeling inadequate as a man compared to me being all immortal and stuff. I'm afraid eroding all feelings of his self-sufficiency and independence could make him resentful.

And it's not like the leprechaun gave me *so* much gold I could pay for everything for both of us forever. Not talking millions here, just a few hundred grand. Aurélie thinks she can help grow it to a million or more in a couple decades with her tricky accounting stuff—as long as I don't spend it on bullcrap. It's all legal, merely way over my head… the kind of banking corporations do. And sure, barring emergencies, my intention right now is to kinda pretend the money doesn't exist. Let it grow and reinvest and grow or something. Whoo hoo. I guess I'm an adult now if I'm being responsible, right?

Wow, did I really just say 'leprechaun?'

So, yeah. Holding back on throwing money around unless it's an emergency. Like, if Hunter's mom is about to lose their house, I might… no, I'd mind-control bank people to leave them alone. Whatever.

I lounge on my bed and call him, one hand on the katana. Not like I expect hostile vampires to randomly show up in my room, but strange things happening around me seem to be the norm these days. Getting into a sword fight wearing only a long T-shirt is like totally Quentin Tarantino. I picture myself covered in blood in a Mickey

Mouse shirt, katana balanced over my shoulder, blood rolling down my bare legs from all the faceless dudes in suits I chopped to ribbons. A fine line exists between art film and schlock. Good thing I can fly, otherwise running barefoot in puddles of blood would turn it into slapstick.

I share this idle mental wandering with Hunter. He doesn't grunt when he laughs, good sign. His rib is still sore but not enough for him to show pain. In an effort to balance some family time in the mix, we decide I'll head over to his place after dinner time—assuming he ends up not going to work.

We're in the middle of talking about all the stuff we might try doing later if he doesn't feel too dizzy when someone knocks on my door. Taps are soft, so definitely one of the Littles. Can't be a crisis or they'd have barged in.

"What's up?"

My door opens. Sam peeks in, hesitant at first, as if he's afraid he might catch Hunter and me doing something he doesn't want to see. Realizing I'm here alone, he smiles and walks in. "Can you help me with something, or are you busy?"

"Is it important?"

"Kinda." He flaps his arms once. "Not life-or-death urgent, but it's maybe a little too much for me alone."

"Paranormal weirdness?" I ask.

"Yep."

"Someone threatening you?"

He shakes his head to the negative.

I sigh mentally. "Hey, Sam needs me for a bit. Can I call you back later?"

"Sure, hon. I need to finish up a bunch of stuff for school. See you tonight. If, umm, I end up having to work, I'll text you. But we can still hang out after."

"They really ought to ban working on weekends."

Hunter laughs. "Then no one could go out to eat, hit a movie, or have fun on the weekend."

"Oh, true. Okay. Love you."

"Love you, too." He smooches the phone.

I sit up, swing my legs off the side of the bed, and pat the mattress beside me. "Okay, bud. What's going on?"

Sam hops up to sit. "I've agreed to do a favor for the demon in my closet. Before you freak out, I know it sounds bad, but it isn't. He's not gonna like take my soul or anything if I don't do it."

"You made a deal with a demon?"

"Not exactly."

I raise an eyebrow. "Define exactly."

"This isn't him giving me something and now I need to pay for it. He just asked me to help him out with something and I said sure. I'm kinda like the C-Team."

"The C-Team?"

He nods. "Yeah. Like the A-Team, but I'm only a kid and I don't have guns."

I chuckle. Wow. How many nine-year-olds even know about a television series from the Eighties. Thanks, Dad. Eh, maybe it's not *too* weird. No worse than my father being a fan of the original *Star Trek* series.

"So, what's this favor?"

"It's not bad."

"Must be bad if you won't tell me what you have to do."

Sam holds his hands up. "I'm just getting you ready for it."

"That means it's probably bad but you've constructed a rationalization for how it's not as bad as it sounds. Any 'truth' you need to put someone in the right frame of mind before they'll believe is not truth."

He rolls his eyes. "Really, not as bad as you think. It's like how you didn't *steal* Coralie from the mystics."

"Uh oh." I rub my forehead. "You have to do something normal people would consider a crime but is really helping a ghost or something no one would believe exists?"

"Basically." He swings his legs back and forth.

"Spill it, kiddo."

Sam shifts to face me, one leg up on the bed. "Okay, so there's this museum, right? And inside the museum is a little vase holding another demon. She's not a bad demon. I don't even have to take the vase. Just break the seal on it to let her out."

I stare at him. "Oh, this couldn't *possibly* go wrong in any number of conceivable ways."

"It's a simple plan." He smiles.

"The simpler the plan sounds, the bigger it blows up in everyone's face." I smirk. "I'm a little concerned you're spending so much time around demons."

"Don't be prejudiced. They're just like us. Some are nice. Some aren't."

"Oookay. So, let me get this straight. You are here to ask me to break into a museum and smash a jar?"

He shakes his head. "Not exactly. *I* have to do it. Open the vase, I mean. It doesn't need smashing, just opening. I'm nine. I'll just pretend to be an idiot kid who touches something he shouldn't be touching. Not even gonna break anything. They'll think I picked up the lid and put it back down."

I flop over backward, staring up at the ceiling. "You telling me you don't have to break it proves it's going to get smashed. Most likely, the entire museum is going to end up on fire and covered in chocolate pudding."

He laughs. "Chocolate pudding?"

"Sophia didn't tell you?"

"No. What did she do?" He goes wide-eyed with delight. "Covered some place with pudding?"

"Technically… yes, but only one room."

"Nice. Was it good?"

"She didn't eat any."

He gasps. "What's the point of covering a room in pudding if you don't even have any?"

"I have no idea, but I'm sure there's a magazine dedicated to it somewhere."

"Huh? What's a magazine?"

I whistle. "Forget it. When you're a little older, ask Dad to teach you about George Carlin. You'll make his week."

"Noted." Sam nods once. "So, will you help keep me from getting in super deep trouble?"

"How do you know this demon in the bottle isn't bad?"

"Olmaz said so."

I sit up and furrow my brow. "Another demon. Did you consider he might be lying? And what the heck are you doing? Demons aren't Pokémon. You shouldn't be collecting them."

Sam laughs so hard he falls over on the bed and curls up into a ball. Unable to resist, I pounce and attack. Most guys who stray into a lair of a vampiress are in mortal danger. My brother escapes with a 'vicious' tickling.

A few minutes later, we're both laughing.

"I'm not collecting them," rasps Sam between gasps for air. "Just making friends. And yeah, I'm sure he isn't lying. Just kinda know he's telling the truth somehow."

Blix jumps up to perch on the corner of the bed and holds both thumbs up while murmuring incomprehensible demon warbles at me.

"He says we can trust Olmaz." Sam exhales hard, then pushes himself up into a seated position.

"What's going to happen if you let this demon out? Am I going to get kidnapped to Romania in six months by another group of angry mystics who put her in there?"

Sam laughs. "No. She's not a 'hurt people' demon. Olmaz said she helps people feel good."

Oh, crap. She's probably a succubus.

Wonderful. Just what my reality needed… *more* demons.

22

THE MOTHER OF NIGHTMARES

Sometimes luck and coincidence are awesome—and sometimes, they scare me.

At the moment, I'm talking about this museum my brother wants to burglarize. It's not a major museum full of expensive artwork, state-of-the-art security systems and an elite team of private security guards like something out of a *Mission: Impossible* opening sequence. The coincidence part is the place is really close—only in Olympia. Roughly sixty miles in a straight line.

The luck part involves the place being tiny. Like I said, no laser grids or pressure-sensitive floors. It barely has a website. I'm sure most people walking by it on the street mistake it for an antique shop. A group of three sisters and a brother have spent 'decades of their lives scouring the earth for the most eclectic assortment of rare paranormal artifacts imaginable.' Yeah, I'm sensing a big, steaming pile of tourist trap.

A few items highlighted on their website have descriptions so overwritten and melodramatic it's difficult not to laugh. They claim to have a dagger once owned by Alastair Crowley. Next image is an old iron candle holder they say belonged to a woman who called herself the 'Faerie Queen of Ireland.' She led a sect of now-extinct Celtic druids. *Iron* candle holder belonging to a faerie queen. Hmm. Something doesn't seem right about this story. Oh, here's the sacred spirit bowl responsible for General Custer's defeat… and a green-glass desk lamp once belonging to Winston Churchill, which is possessed by the spirit of an unnamed German secret agent who tried unsuccessfully to assassinate him. I half expect to see them brag about having King Tut's toilet seat or Cleopatra's G string. I hear she had a nice asp.

This isn't as much a museum as it's a tabloid newspaper in building form. Four slightly crazy people collected a bunch of pseudo-paranormal stuff and decided to show it to the public. Okay, before I surrender entirely to judgmental skepticism, my kid brother has the word of a demon stating another demon is stuck there in some manner of vase.

Stretching logic, it stands to reason if they have *one* possibly legitimate item, not everything in their collection is guaranteed to be total nonsense. However, I am not going to expect too much from people who think a group called the 'Witches of the Revolution' existed who are solely responsible for America winning the Revolutionary War against the vastly superior British Army because they cast spells. Yes, this 'museum' has the entire tea service these women supposedly used to work their magic. I'm not sure how brewing and drinking tea cursed England and King George into losing a war, but hey, these cups, saucers, and teapot apparently contain a bunch of spiritual energy.

I'm so excited.

In fact, I'm so excited about visiting this place, I'm going to be humming that song by the Pointer Sisters the whole way there. No, I'm not. I lied. No music plays in my mind. For the entire flight there with my little brother on my back, I'm questioning myself for doing this.

Why did I agree to help him jailbreak a demon? The consequences are probably far more severe than jailbreaking an iPhone.

So why are we flying to Olympia?

Because I am an emotionally needy sap.

Sam said he loved doing 'family stuff' with his big sister. He hit me below the belt when he said he's not going to be little forever, so he wanted to do fun stuff with me while he's still young enough to have adventures. Who says only vampires have mind-control powers? Kids have them too, but they only work on people like me with an overdeveloped 'aww' response to cute faces and big, pleading eyes.

As soon as the sun went down, we took off.

I probably should be worried more about my mother's response to 'we're going to rescue a kidnapped demon' being "That's nice, dear. Be careful, and don't make any deals for your souls." She also demanded I make sure Sam comes back *with* his soul. Either Mom thinks I'm amusing Sam by playing an imaginary game, she completely trusts me, or she's tuning out anything too crazy sounding. Probably a mixture of two and three.

Due to this errand, Hunter decided to go to work. He can't really help us out stealing a demon from a kitschy paranormal museum. No point in his sitting around at home being uncomfortable in bed. Hoping this trip doesn't take *too* long, but we did have to wait for sunset. At least the afternoon was fun. Spent it hanging with the family having a board game day. Yeah, yeah. I know. We are tragically lame. Oh, shit. Dad still wants to screen the two 'Escape' movies tonight. Dammit. I hate when the Universe sets me up for such hard, life-altering decisions.

Oh, easy fix. I'll invite Hunter over. Don't have to choose between him or family then. After the movies, he can spend the night in my room. Insert evil laughter here.

And wow. I'm really about to help my little brother commit a felony.

Well, possibly commit a felony. Is opening a demonic jar against the law? He *did* say we don't have to physically remove any item from the museum. So… just a stupid kid touching something he shouldn't, right? Also, this isn't a 'real' museum. They might not even care if people touch these obviously fake artifacts.

Winston Churchill's possessed desk lamp indeed.

I fully expect to walk into 'Aunt May's yard sale' disguised as a museum of paranormal curiosities. Them having one 'real' item doesn't mean anything... right? It should probably be more alarming Sam isn't the least bit nervous flying. Sure, I've taken him into the air at night before, but never sixty miles away from home, at 1,000 feet, or close to full speed. People don't *need* a motorcycle helmet on to tolerate 120-140 mile-per-hour wind in their face... they need the helmet to be able to see at those speeds. Since I am not a 'hover-cycle' and my little brother isn't driving me, it doesn't matter if he keeps his eyes closed. Maybe not looking is why he's not scared. Higher altitude makes *me* feel better since it gives me more time to intercept and catch him if he slips, but I figured it would freak him out.

My brother is scarily stoic.

Seriously. How many boys his age would find a demon portal in their closet and think 'ooh, cool! Let's see what's in there'?

A little over twenty minutes after takeoff, we land in a swath of trees beside the north end of Capitol Lake in downtown Olympia. We're not far from the 'House of Mysteries.' Seriously, they went with that for their business name. I'm wondering if one of their mysteries is how a place like this can generate enough money to pay the rent. Maybe the four owners are eccentric rich people who aren't doing it for profit but the lols.

Also, yay for short-term memory.

With Sam on my back, I didn't want to let go of his arms to check my phone. Before we left, I spent a few minutes staring at Google maps and navigated Olympia by sight. Downtown looks kinda like a scrabble board from the air. Neat, square tiles set in a perfect grid of road. One 'tile' contains a park of some kind, green with a weird glyph of pale sidewalks like some kid cut the initials DE into the side of a tree using only straight lines. Anyway, the museum is four tiles south from the green spot. Yeah, the giant lake is a big navigational assistant, too. Impossible to miss.

My little brother grins ear to ear as we walk out of the forest into a parking lot, then cross Columbia Street before heading down Tenth Ave. The place is still open for another two hours and fifty minutes or so, closing at midnight. You know, because haunted museums have much better ambiance after dark. From the outside, it could be easily mistaken for a fortuneteller's shop or maybe an antique dealer… if not for the sign saying 'paranormal curiosity museum' under 'House of Mysteries' in big gothic letters.

Pretending to be ordinary people interested in the place, we go in the front door… and whoa. I'm totally not prepared for the wave of supernatural energy smacking me in the face. There is *definitely* something here. It's weaker than the 'otherness' in the Aurora Aurea lodge where Sophia's been learning, but wow. More in this room than one demon-containing vase has to be authentic. Who'd have guessed? I spend a moment gawking around at various random items arranged on long tables, shelves, and podiums. Small signs or displays by each object undoubtedly contain information about it. The layout definitely says the place used to be some manner of retail store prior to becoming this museum. Maybe ten percent of the stuff is secured inside glass cases, most of it out in the open—just like a yard sale.

Stunned at the potency of the 'weird' in the air, I stand there by the doors, staring around.

"Hello, my dear" calls a short, black-haired woman in her fifties. "Welcome to the House of Mysteries! I'm Ruth Blackburn." She shows off an ouroboros medallion the size of a drink coaster in gold and black bearing the name 'Ruth' in a fancy 'Egyptish' font. "You must have a gift."

I glance left at the woman standing behind a standard glass sales counter loaded with kitschy souvenirs as well as T-shirts. Her dress, dark sweater, and wood-bead jewelry is somewhere between 'cool music teacher' and the aunt who's into new-age healing crystals and tries to sell some kind of multi-level marketing junk at every holiday gathering.

I remember reading about the owners. Three sisters and a brother. A grey-haired woman maybe a decade older than Ruth wanders on the opposite side of the room. She has to be Patricia Blackburn, the oldest sibling. She's playing tour guide, talking to a pair of twentysomethings. The guy looks thrilled. His girlfriend-slash-wife, much less so. No, she's not making faces like she wanted nice restaurant and got a trip to a monster truck rally. I think she's terrified.

"My sister sees dead people," says Sam, overacting a whisper.

I ruffle his hair, smirking. "The boy exaggerates."

"You must have some talent, dear. Not many people make a face like that when they first walk in." She winks.

"Hi. Found this place online. My little brother is super interested in paranormal stuff and ghost stories."

"Hi." Sam waves at her.

"You've definitely come to the right place." Ruth smiles. "We ask for a donation of $10. Kids under twelve are $2 each."

Sam stares up at her. "You sell kids under twelve for two bucks?"

Ruth laughs.

I grasp his shoulders and lean toward her. "My brother is a language nerd. Please forgive him. He doesn't mean to be sarcastic."

Sam gives me 'oh, I very much did' side eye.

Ruth misses his look or ignores it. "It's no problem, dear. The donation covers as much time as you'd like to spend here. All of us wearing one of these"—she tugs at her medallion—"are here to answer any questions you have about the items or tell stories if you care to ask us."

I can't justify mind-whammying her over twelve bucks. Besides, we're here to basically steal from her… sorta. And, the place *does* appear to be a little more legitimate than my expectations. You'd think being killed and turned into a vampire, seeing trolls, leprechauns, brownies, and magic would have made me less of a skeptic. Why is my initial reaction to a 'paranormal museum' to say 'yeah right'?

Whatever. I'm still trying to be normal. Most people doubt this stuff.

I pay… and we start wandering around. Sam isn't feeling a specific pull, so we head all the way to the left and follow the paths between tables like we've gone to Safeway, looking at everything from 'Jack the Ripper's knife' to a mortician's comb from the 1700s to seemingly ordinary—antique—household items. Their info displays claim the items came from haunted locations or happened to be present at sites of horrific events. A rusty lump is supposedly a lighter from a worker killed during the building of the Grand Coulee Dam. Stories claim people who have carried the lighter around have randomly died of suffocation, like it's original owner who ended up being covered in an avalanche of liquid concrete. Another rusted spar sits on a pillow next to a sign proclaiming it a handbrake from a train involved in a crash in 1903 where 314 people died.

Oddly, the 'lighter' gives me the creeps, but the brake doesn't.

The next table has a Damascus sword supposedly used by a 'crusader' to kill Abdul Alhazred, the author of the *Necronomicon.* It looks old and about as sharp as Bree Swanson. Wow. Someone needs to tell the Blackburn family they've been tricked. H.P. Lovecraft made that up as fiction. I am *highly* relieved not to sense any energy from the blade whatsoever.

Sam, predictably, finds everything fascinating and takes his time looking at all the signs and objects. Except for a doll, skull, crumbling left boot, and a few other things I can't see clearly from where I'm standing enshrined in glass cases, the items are out in easy reach. Most of this stuff looks like junk no one would want to steal. They don't have any signs up forbidding touching things. There *are* signs, but they say, 'touch at your own risk. Management is not responsible for dark energies following you home.'

Might be tricky if the vase Sam recognizes is in a sealed case, but if not… this should be easy.

Assuming, of course, we aren't making a galactic-level error by opening the demon jar.

"Achtung!" shouts a somewhat distant voice.

Neither Sam, Ruth, Patricia, or the pair of twentysomethings react to the voice.

I look around, but spot no ghosts. Shrug. We make our way to the end of the aisle and go around into the next one.

"Achtung!" yells the same voice. *"Du, Vampir-Mädel, komm her."*

Okay, either a crazy telepath is doing a spot-on impression of the fish from *American Dad,* or I'm hearing a spirit voice. I don't understand whatever language they're speaking, but 'vampire' is fairly obvious.

Again, I look around.

"Hier drüben! Komm rüber!"

Flickering in time with the voice draws my attention to a small desk lamp. The base and shade are made from greenish glass, the frame brass. It looks like something straight out of a 1940s war movie or a private eye's desk.

My jaw drops open. Oh, crap… Winston Churchill's desk lamp? Seriously?

"Ja du. Ich sehe dich mich betrachten. Hol mich sofort aus dieser Lampe!" shouts the lamp, its weak bulb flickering as it speaks… sorta like those red dashboard lights in *Knight Rider* whenever the car spoke.

"Whoa, okay… this is too weird."

Sam twists around to look at me. "What's weird?"

"Do you see that green lamp over there?" I nod toward it.

He looks past me. "Yeah."

"It's talking."

Sam laughs. When I don't start laughing along with him, he stares up at me. "Are you being serious?"

"Yeah. Do you see it like it's turned on? Flickering?"

"No. It's dark."

Whoa. Creepy. So, umm… wow. I leave Sam to wander the table where we were, and walk up to the giant wood desk near the center of the room. A sign beside the lamp indeed claims it to have belonged to Winston Churchill and sat on his desk during most of World War II. According to what they have written here, a German spy infiltrated Ten Downing Street and came close to assassinating him, but ended up being shot and killed before Churchill made it to the office one morning. Legend says the spy collapsed over the desk, smearing his blood on the lamp as he fell to the floor… and now his spirit is stuck inside it. Additional signs claim *this* desk belonged to Abraham Lincoln, the ashtray came from Al Capone, and the letter opener belonged to a guy named Robert Morgan, a rich pioneer who lived in the 1840s New Mexico and used it to murder nine prostitutes.

Eek.

Oh, yeah, the skull sitting next to it is supposedly one of those prostitutes.

Double eek.

It's all supposed to be haunted-slash-cursed, but only the lamp gives off any noticeable presence.

"Es ist nicht wahr. Ich bin kein spion," flickers the lamp. *"Wenn ich ein spion wäre, könnte ich Englisch sprechen. Dies ist nicht einmal Churchills lampe."*

"Wow, umm. Okay. I have no idea what you're saying."

"Sare!" whisper-shouts Sam.

I twist to look.

He's two tables over from where I left him, waving at me emphatically to come to him. He appears to be standing by an old-as-hell clay urn. Looks like something from the computer game *Diablo* characters can smash to find some gold coins or a healing potion. Or maybe a dusty clay pot recovered from a pharaoh's tomb.

"Sorry, lamp. Gotta go." I hurry over to Sam.

"Nein! Verlass mich nicht!"

My life just gets weirder and weirder.

When I reach my brother, he indicates the vase with both hands like a game show host. It's somewhat bigger than a volleyball, wider at the top than the bottom, dusty, light brown, and old. The facing side has a small rectangular border around writing that is definitely *not* English. It kinda looks Chinese, but not quite the same. I'm tempted to say it's probably a totally dead language. A tiny (comparatively) lid sits on top, sealed by what appears to be wax-caked rope. A few beads hang from the extra cord over one side.

"Great. You found King Tut's cookie jar."

Sam chuckles. "This is it."

The sign next to the urn claims it contains the ashes of a female assassin who attempted to take the life of Alexander the Great and was subsequently executed by being burned alive. The description text also alleges any man who spends too long looking at the urn will become sick, possibly die of a mysterious ailment—especially if they are named Alexander.

My BS detector needle is on eight, but my 'something's weird' needle's a solid ten. This urn is definitely throwing off some strong vibes.

"I'm still not sure how I let you talk me into this," I whisper. "This can't be a good idea. My siblings opening jars and letting stuff out has a *really* bad track record."

Sam nudges me. "Once isn't a 'track record. It's once. Sophia also didn't know what she was looking at. I know exactly what's in here."

Piano music abruptly starts up in the distant right corner. The twenty-something woman screams. I look over the table in front of us toward the commotion. A transparent, vaguely feminine, form has manifested as if sitting on a non-existent bench in front of the piano, playing it. I can't tell much about her appearance other than she's probably around thirty and from the late 1800s or possibly early 1900s. She's also laughing, clearly having intended to scare the hell out of the couple on a date.

The man's clutching his chest, gawking at the piano apparently playing itself while his girlfriend clings to Patricia Blackburn—who is also smiling like she fully expected the scare. If not for seeing the ghost, I'd have assumed it a rigged piano… which is exactly what the man begins saying as soon as he remembers how to breathe.

I again look at the urn. "Okay, what's your real story?"

A note of sadness comes from it. Whoa. Not expecting that. Demons trapped in jars for long periods of time get pissed off, not sad. Look at what happens when a four-year-old is stuck in a car for two hours.

Sam pretends to be studying other items nearby, reading their signs. After a moment, he elbows me, staring up and doing odd things with his eyebrows. I peek into his thoughts, which is what he was hoping I'd do.

Any cameras? asks Sam.

I look around, noting Ruth, Patricia, and the two other museum visitors. No obvious cameras. Can't believe I'm going to do this, but…

I give Ruth a prod not to pay attention to us for a few minutes. Patricia gets a prod to ignore everything going on around her except for the couple she's playing tour guide for.

"Coast is clear," I whisper.

Sam reaches out, grabs the small lid on the urn, and gives it a firm twist. The wax seal cracks open, emitting bright crimson light. A billow of white mist rushes out like he'd turned on a dry ice fog machine. Uh oh. This looks familiar.

The mist rolls off the table to the floor, rising into a column before taking on the general shape of a human body. Seconds later, it solidifies into a nude Middle Eastern woman on the younger side of twenty.

Eep!

I cover Sam's eyes.

He sighs.

"Thank you, Samuel." The woman looks at me. Her body language conveys no small degree of embarrassment, but also too much dignity to act like she's mortified. I can totally sympathize. It's exactly how I felt my first night as a vampire. "This is not by choice. These damnable essence traps do not capture clothing, jewelry, or anything else."

"Ahh." I nod, once, still not taking my hands away from Sam's eyes.

He folds his arms, tapping one foot.

"You had to deal with one night in a mausoleum." She stretches. "Try 450 years stuck naked in an empty stone room."

I blink. Whoa. "You know about that?"

She smiles coyly. "I hear things."

My brother raises a hand in greeting. "Hi. Sorry I can't see you. Sometimes, Dad lets us watch movies I'm not old enough for, but I have to look away at some parts 'cause there's girls."

The woman pats him on the head. "I owe you one, young man. More than one… being in there was absolutely dreadful." She clears her throat and adopts as regal a posture as a naked person can project. "I am M'Len D'Lar, once known as the Matron of Nightmares."

"You're doing the same thing Olmaz did," says Sam. "Can I just call you Mel?"

She smiles. "Can either one of you summon clothing?"

"Sorry, no. The only way I can summon clothing to where I am is by invoking the magic of Amazon, and it takes a couple days to arrive. I don't advise conjuring clothing that way. It's usually nothing like what you expect." I point a thumb over my shoulder at the door. "If you want to hide here for a bit, I can go grab you something to wear."

"Darn." Mel scowls off to the side.

"Umm, not to ask an indelicate question, but aren't you a succubus?" I raise an eyebrow. "Didn't picture one of you being modest."

Mel chuckles. "Don't seem so shocked. I am a succubus, not an exhibitionist. And the sign lies. I did not try to *kill* Alexander, nor was I burned to death. The urn didn't contain ashes, merely energy."

Right. Pretty sure any intended stabbing went in the other direction and didn't involve a knife.

"I believe you." Sam tugs at my hands in a testing manner.

Sorry bud. This part of your quest is R rated. You're only nine.

"Oh well." Mel frowns at herself. "I will find something. Thank you again, Samuel."

"You're welcome." He holds out a hand.

She shakes it, then disappears into a cloud of fog.

I let go of his eyes.

"Where'd she go?" asks Sam.

"Just poofed."

A tiny finger-snap comes from the floor, a crunch from my left.

I look down at Blix who's appeared out of nowhere. The wax seal on the urn isn't damaged anymore. Oh, neat. I didn't realize imps could un-break things. Assumed it's against their core nature. Granted, not many imps are more interested in video games than pranking people to death.

"This place is pretty cool," says Sam. "Can we look around more?"

"Dad's expecting us for movie night. We can come back here soon."

I force a smile. “Preferably after whoever’s trying to ignite a war in Seattle is gone.”

“Okay.” Sam grimaces. “Did Dad show you the picture?”

I sigh. “Alas.”

“Russel in the bushes.” Sam biffs himself on the forehead. “It might be time for an intervention.”

After a brief conversation with Ruth, informing her we enjoyed ourselves but ran out of time—and definitely planned to return, we head for the exit. The lamp yells something at me in German, but I don’t quite make it out. Releasing a demon from a jar is enough risky stuff for one night.

Having a conversation with a desk lamp never ends well.

23

NOTHING CAN TRULY BE ABSURD UNTIL THE GOVERNMENT GETS INVOLVED

Two figures approach from the left as soon as we exit the museum.

I experience a surge of panic-anger. Panic at being attacked while my kid brother is here and anger at myself for leaving the katana home so I didn't drop him. Fortunately, I recognize the two people walking up to me before making a potentially painful mistake.

Agent Kendricks and Agent Han: The Persons in Black. Both are mid-thirties. He's about as generic as a guy can be in terms of appearance. Looks like the dad from every 1950s TV show. Agent Han gives off seriousness like plutonium gives off gamma rays. Still haven't figured out why her thoughts are walled off to me, but after meeting Damarco the vampire hunter, I have somewhat of an idea. She is probably wearing an enchanted amulet, ring, or a similar mystical item.

They couldn't be any *more* conspicuous in dark government-issue raincoats.

I overact looking around.

"Expecting more friends?" asks Agent Kendricks.

"No, looking for the cameras. Feels like we're filming a scene in *The X Files.*"

Kendricks fails to hide a lip twitch. Han's eyes give off a sense of amusement, but she keeps a straight face.

"Got a minute?" asks Kendricks.

Ninety-nine percent of the time, when a fed asks, 'got a minute,' they're politely ordering you to talk with them. There's no way in hell they've become aware of a secret deal my little brother made with a demon in another dimension... right? I mean, how the heck did they find me here in front of this museum? Still, they don't really look like they're intending to give me a hard time.

"Sure." I put an arm around Sam. "Our parents are expecting us home soon for movie night but they won't mind a slight delay."

"We are concerned about a significant increase in unusual activity in the Seattle area," says Han. "It would seem disputes among certain segments of the population have escalated to the point where they are no longer... subtle."

"Wow. Been a while. I was wondering when you guys were going to show up."

They smile.

"Right, so... an unknown party is attempting to stir things up. I have no idea who it is or what they really want. They've attacked me a few times, claiming to be acting under the direction of another individual, but as far as I can tell, the other individual didn't send them. This person or group has also attacked several elders, trying to make it look like everyone's messing with each other. I'm guessing they want to start a war."

"Interesting." Han purses her lips.

A soft *whump* goes off half a block from the museum as a streak of glowing yellow light rockets away from a large, black sedan, leaving a faint smoke trail hanging in the air. Seconds later, a loud *splat* comes from out of sight behind the Subway place across the street.

Kendricks pivots to look at the car. "Something tried to tamper with it."

Han smiles. "It won't make the same mistake again."

Sam winces. Oh… poor Blix. I hope he's okay. Wait, no… he's clinging to my brother's back. Something else got launched away from the car. Ugh, I hope we didn't miss any imps.

Agent Han peers down at Sam with an odd expression. No idea what she's thinking, but I'm hoping she doesn't somehow sense the imp's presence. I'm sure the PIBs would have a *ton* of questions for why my little brother is hanging out with a demon. Technically, he's a daemon—which is the weakest form of demon. And yeah… my father told Sam he should've named him Matt instead of Blix.

Matt Daemon.

That one made *Mom* throw a piece of bread at him.

"Any ideas who it might be?" asks Kendricks.

"Nope. Whoever they are, they know enough about us to exploit history. Like, this pair of buttheads who don't like me for breaking tradition, another who I refused to give a stolen mummy to, and this super creepy twisted woman who tried to destroy me for stopping her from ruining some poor dude's life." I flap my arms. "Honestly, I'm such a minor part of the organization here, it's freaky whoever is doing this knows about my, uhh, problems."

Han nods. "It sounds like it might be coming from within. Or they have a spy."

"Yeah. Thought the same, too." I wince. "If there *is* a spy, they're not going to be happy soon. Pretty sure I've opened the elders' minds to the idea it's an outside threat, but they're not totally ready to believe it isn't some elaborate scheme."

"Any proof?" asks Kendricks.

"Unfortunately, no. Only suspicions and hunches."

Kendricks opens a file folder and shows me some pictures of burned buildings. I don't recognize any of the locations, specifically. However, I confirm to him that some of the vampires complained of attacks like this. When he shows me a photo of Shogun West's parking lot littered with bodies, I gasp.

"Did they order the fugu?"

The PIBs stare at me, unamused.

"You recognize this?" asks Agent Han. "Were you part of this event?"

"No... I mean..." I point at the photo. "I recognize the restaurant. We had dinner there for Sierra's birthday. No idea they scheduled murder sprees in addition to cheesy birthday music."

Han shakes her head. "We believe this restaurant to be owned by a holding company linked to Arthur Wolent."

"Whoa. Seriously? Small world." I blink. "Didn't know he had anything to do with restaurants. Explains why something weird happened. Uhh, why did they kill a bunch of people?"

"As far as we know, the bodies in this photograph were dead before they arrived at the restaurant. Multiple funeral homes in the Pacific Northwest reported break-ins and missing bodies in a surge last week." Kendricks shows me another photo showing several guys in suits loading the dead into a van. One of them—who's carrying two bodies at once—is pretty damn obvious: Aziz. Wolent's massive bodyguard. The guy Aurélie refers to as 'The Moroccan Hulk.' Dude's so big he verges on being a cartoon, like Maui from *Moana*. It's a Beast thing. "We managed to match one of the stolen corpses to some remains found in the parking lot of Shogun West."

I tell them about the 'zombie' attack on my house. "This looks like the same thing, only eight or nine instead of three."

"Probably sent them to smash up the restaurant," says Sam.

"Zombies..." Agent Kendricks whistles. "Please tell me you're pulling my leg."

Han glances at him like 'yeah, it's possible,' but doesn't say anything.

"Not strictly like you're thinking. Supposedly, a vampire is using them like a kid with a remote-control car." I shrug. "Don't know how it works."

"Right." He closes the manila folder. "If the situation in Seattle continues to escalate, it is going to become difficult to keep out of the public eye. I am sure your people don't want that either."

"Umm." I fidget, tempted to deny 'vampires' are my people. But...

my 'membership' on Team Wolent *is* official. Gotta own it, even if I'm not personally invested in politics. "No. They don't."

"Do let us know if you discover any information." Agent Han half bows at me. "I realize your people are suspicious of our motives. However, we are willing to offer assistance if things get out of hand."

"We would appreciate you sharing any information you can." Kendricks tucks the manila folder under his arm.

"Yeah, sure. Will do."

The agents nod at me and walk off together toward the black car. I stand there watching them go. Han pauses to glance in the direction the yellow light smear went, but doesn't appear to spot anything worth her time to investigate, and gets into the car.

"Why was she looking at me like that?"

I pat Blix on the head. "Maybe she felt his presence, or the jar left some spirit residue on you. I got the feeling she didn't really understand what she sensed."

Sam peers up at me. "So are those guys our friends, or should we be afraid of them?"

Follows Rule Girl would say yes. Vampire me is a little more skeptical. I mean, decades of movies don't make 'shadowy government agents' the bad guys for no good reason. The general vibe I get from them isn't too concerning. "Mostly friends, but I do have an almost unhealthy tendency to trust authority figures. My gut says those two are generally okay, but we should be careful. C'mon. Hop on. Let's get home before anything else weird happens."

"Awesome!"

24

FIRE IN THE SKY

It should have been a warning sign we set a demon loose from a jar and nothing caught fire.

From the moment we left home tonight for this crazy 'side quest,' I expected some big ol' failure dragon would take a giant bite out of my butt. Nothing in my life wants to be simple anymore. Lo and behold, we found our way to the museum, located the imprisoned demon, and released her. Other than a desk lamp shouting German at me, the whole trip went off without a problem.

Too easy. Nothing involving demonic liberation ever happens easy.

Also, I didn't cover Sam's eyes to protect him from the succubus doing anything specific to him. He's merely too little to see full frontal. Not sure if 'Mel' would have devoured a grown man who opened the jar. Honestly, after centuries of captivity, one would expect her to get a little fiery wrath going. Torch the museum, maybe steal some souls… a little reasonable light demoning, so to speak. I hated being trapped in a tiny mausoleum for one day. Can't imagine multiple centuries. I'd say if it had been me, there would've been some wrath to be dispensed, but a vampire can't go so long without blood. There wouldn't be anything left of our former psyche, assuming we didn't become a pile of dust. Then again, people don't usually fit inside jars the size of watermelons… so I'm guessing something a little unusual happened.

Her disappearing quietly definitely surprised me.

Blix is an imp who only pulls pranks when asked to. We have an apparently domesticated hellhound in the yard. I suppose it makes total sense my brother would run into a modest succubus. Maybe all demons aren't created equal. Or, maybe my folkloric understanding of what a succubus is came from misinformation—or D&D. Though, D&D borrowed it from 'real' lore. Prior to my death, I wouldn't have believed demons seriously existed at all.

Live and learn… or *die* and learn.

Whatever.

So, back to the jinx.

Our mission, the one I expected would end with lots of burning and screaming, plus a heaping dose of regret, turned out super easy. Too easy. The Universe took note. So, here we are flying home to Cottage Lake from Olympia. Sam's on my back. Blix is clinging to Sam's back making tiny *wharblgharblblblbl* noises by shaking his flappy lips in the wind like a dog sticking his head out of a car.

Roughly fifteen minutes into the flight, a voice below and left shouts, "Hey, she's one of Wolent's people. Get her."

In no context I can think of do the words 'get her' ever mean anything but trouble.

I look toward the voice. Two long-haired dudes in denim jackets, arms at their sides, race up toward me like a pair of ground-to-Sarah guided missiles. At this point, I am required by virtue of being my father's daughter to point out how surface to air missiles are often abbreviated as SAMs, which is the same as my little brother's name. Surprisingly, the reason I know this is not my father, but Sierra. One of her PlayStation games is sort of a flight simulator. I say 'sort of' because it's not going out of its way to be a realistic recreation of flying. The game is more arcade than realistic. Only so much they can do flight sim wise on a console. Anyway, it has SAMs. It also has an 'automated warning voice' that would say 'SAM lock' about fifty times a minute.

And yeah, I'm hearing the same voice in my head now.

Blix screeches something unintelligible.

"He says we have incoming," shouts Sam.

"I noticed. We're a little low on chaff and flares."

"Want me to fart?" asks Sam.

I blink. "You can fart on command?"

He shrugs. "Dunno, but I can try."

"Umm. I don't think it'll help."

There is no way I'm going to get into a midair claw fight when I'm carrying my brother. Even if we survive, Mom would kill me. If anything happened to Sam, I'd be a total freakin' mess… like worse than Charlotte, the Innocent I met in England. Her mind is gone. Poor woman acts like she's maybe six years old despite having been twenty-one when turned.

I pour on speed, pushing myself as much as possible. Sam's wrists dig into the front of my neck. No big deal. Air is not one of my needs. The fastest I've ever managed to go—while holding my iPhone to check—is 140 miles an hour. A normal person can tolerate similar windspeed on a motorcycle, so I'm not worried about hurting Sam by speed alone. Many vampire powers are linked to emotion, so my desperation to keep my brother safe *does* seem to be increasing my top speed. However, the two guys are still creeping up on us.

An Innocent pushing themselves into 'redline' is still slower than some other bloodlines can fly. Like Glim? I think he can do 180 or so, which makes no sense. The man can 'shadow gate' places. He doesn't *need* to fly. Why does he get the golden flight plan? For him, a trip from Olympia to Seattle could legit take two minutes in the shadow realm. Also, Sam is contributing weight and drag.

Blix is not contributing weight and drag—because he's gone.

Not sure when he lost his grip, but he disappeared. Maybe he let go on purpose to harass the guys chasing us? Once the two dudes are at the same altitude and no longer need to climb, they start catching up to me alarmingly fast.

Shit!

I can't outrun these guys. They *will* catch me and do something bad to both of us. Since a fight is unavoidable, my best chance is to get on the ground fast and eliminate the possibility of Sam plummeting to his death. He gurgles when I abruptly dive; his weight lifts off my back, all of it pressing into my throat. I'm flying downward faster than free fall, pulling him with me like a living cape.

At least I'm doing so until one of the vampires chasing us comes out of nowhere beneath me, crashing into us with all the fury of a hockey player pissed off over a bad referee call. I now know how a bird trying to fly across a road but getting hit by a speeding truck feels. And by truck, I mean his shoulder. A *bwawk* like a drop-kicked goose comes out of me as I fold in half over him.

The severe impact breaks Sam's grip on his wrist and sends him careening off into the sky.

"Sam!" I shout, sprouting claws. Rage and worry burn in my veins as I go for the most prominent target in sight—this dude's butt.

I grab both cheeks and sink my claws in as deep as possible. He shrieks in agony, as loud as if he'd sat bare-assed on the grill table at Shogun West. Extreme pain overrides reason, causing him to freak out, abandon his bear hug and hurl me aside. I tumble once before righting myself and scanning the skies for Sam. Fortunately, the human eye is drawn to motion. I spot him right away. My brother plummets toward the earth, still moving laterally at over a hundred miles an hour.

A second after I dive to chase him, the other vampire grabs me. I get a nice close up view of the crow tattoo on his left forearm. The bird, not Brandon Lee. Alas.

"No! Get off me! Sam's just a little kid! You asshole!" I struggle to break away, flailing and shredding at any part of him I can reach.

Sam's already a hundred feet down. Blix appears to be diving after him, too. But those tiny wings aren't going to make much difference to a fall from this high up. I've got mere seconds left before it's too late and I'll never catch up to him. Snarling, I ram my elbow back, catching the vampire in the side of the head. He grunts, but doesn't lose his hold on me.

My brother yanks his shirt off—and sprouts a pair of demon wings, arresting his fall to a casual cruising glide.

Stunned, I stop struggling and stare. "What the shit?"

Crow Tat stops trying to crush my ribs, staring over my shoulder at Sam. "Whoa. That's messed up."

"Do we really have to do this whole fight to the death bullshit right now? I'm babysitting my little brother."

"Are you trying to reschedule your ass-kicking?" Crow turns his head to look at me. He's late twenties. Kinda looks like one of the metalheads from my old high school, plus a bit of goth. No, I don't know him. I mean he's got the same sense of style. Long hair, denim jacket, black band T-shirt with a completely unreadable logo. What is it with metal bands and *extreme* fonts?

"I guess. Honestly, I don't remember scheduling it in the first place. I'm just a newbie, and this is really a bad time for me. Can we do next Tuesday at ten? Or better yet, if you guys have a problem with Wolent, why don't you go tell him to his face how you really feel, or are you afraid of him?"

"You calling us cowards?" shouts the guy with ten holes in his backside.

I shrug. "Umm, considering you're attacking someone who isn't even one year old yet, yeah, kinda. No, actually. I am *definitely* calling you a chicken."

'Claude' snarls in rage and flies at me, his fist cocked.

Right before his knuckles crash into the side of my face, I hurl myself straight down. Crow is bewildered enough at the sight of my brother for his grip to come a bit loose, but not fail entirely. I end up in a headlock rather than in a grip like we're slow dancing—and 'Claude' wallops his buddy in the nose. Sounds like two sides of beef smacking into each other.

Crow goes fly-tumbling away. 'Claude' hovers nearby, stuck between 'aw, shit, sorry man' and angry at me. I take the opportunity to add a few fashion slices to his shirt—and chest. He takes a swing for my face. I duck. The other one zooms back into the fray. Brawling in three dimensions is freakin' weird. Our ability to fly around is much slower than vampire reflexes allow us to dodge, so it's more difficult to evade punches, grabs, and kicks if an opponent gets close. Gliding around feels like slow motion to my amped up speed, but their attacks still look normal. It's like we're a bunch of martial artists doing wire work, only with more upside-down parts, no stunt doubles, and no food truck outside.

These two aren't as skilled as Mohawk—who I am sure had actual training in like jiu-jitsu or something. They are, however, much better at brawling than the idiots who jumped me at the parking deck. I focus on defense, attacking with claw swipes sparingly, aiming for sensitive spots. Every time one of them hits me, I go flying off to the side and they have to chase me again. I've totally lost track of where Sam went, but no point stressing out over him since the guys don't seem interested in him at all. I mean, callous disregard for making me drop him isn't much different than *trying* to kill him, but still.

"So, uhh, what are you guys planning to do here? Kill me or just deliver a beating?"

'Claude' grabs for me. I zip out of his way—right into the other guy's foot. Ow. Fish is okay. Not a big fan of filet of sole when it's attached to a Doc Marten. I go tumbling head over heels a few times from the force of the hit, hoping my neck didn't snap. Blood drips from my nose into my mouth, but my body isn't numb. Good sign.

After a momentary battle trying to get their pants to stay up—thanks, Blix, for trying—they chase. I flip over and fly at them. Crazy electrocuted kitten technique works for a moment keeping them back, but I can't score a hit before Crow grabs my right wrist and swings me.

"Hey, can we just call my ass kicked?" I shout while he spins me around and around. Oh, dammit. Now *that* song is stuck in my head. "I really need to be somewhere. Parents are waiting for me. Already gonna get in trouble for fighting."

'Claude' zooms at me, doing the 'Superman' flying punch thing. Crow's about to swing me into the guy's fist. Oh, this is going to hurt.

Fortunate anatomical fact: my legs are longer than his arms. I swing my feet up, planting both sneakers in 'Claude's' face, stopping him cold before his knuckles reach me. His nose explodes in a shower of red. The hit spins me behind Crow, but he's still got my wrist. A quick claw slice across the backs of his knees makes him yowl and let go of me.

Crow screams in rage and pulls a huge knife from a sheath strapped to his leg. It's definitely long enough to take a head off. Dammit. I try running (well, flying), but it's again obvious they're so much faster than me, I'm stuck in combat until they decide to go do something else or I knock them out. The three-dimensional brawl resumes.

For a couple minutes, it feels like I'm holding my own. The dudes are unusually clumsy—again, thanks, Blix.

I get overconfident and go for a claw swipe at Crow's throat despite thinking it too easy. Yeah. When something appears to be too easy, it usually is. 'Claude' gets me from behind in another bear hug, pinning my arms to my sides.

"Chin up, hon. Just gonna put you in a box and send you to your pal. Not gonna stay dead." Crow sizes up my neck for a slice.

Growling, I thrash, panic pouring energy into my muscles. On an intellectual level, I understand having my head chopped off is not going to kill me. However, there is no way in hell anyone—vampires included—can see a knife coming for their neck and not freak the hell out. 'Claude' is stronger, but I'm not defenseless. He's really got to work to hold me still enough for his buddy to saw my head off. Again, Crow's pants fall down to his ankles, causing him to delay stabbing me to fix them.

"Get off her!" yells Sam, from a fair distance away. "Last warning!"

Both guys laugh.

Crow grabs a fistful of my hair, pushing my head back. I kick him in the balls hard enough to shatter his pelvis… and break my foot. His face turns red, his eyes bulge out—and he explodes into a shower of ash, embers, and a few loose, smoking bones, which tumble toward the ground along with his huge knife.

Wow, I know some dudes get *really* pissed off if something hits them in the nuts—but exploding? That's new.

'Claude' stops wrestling with me, frozen in bewildered fear. Yeah, same here. The sight of a vampire *bursting* into flaming bits in an instant is the sort of thing capable of terrifying any other vampire witnessing it into derpy silence. Even if I wanted to destroy him, something about fire…

After a few seconds to process the sight—just enough time for any remaining sign of Crow ever having existed to fall out of view—'Claude' tightens his grip like a hostage taker, putting me between him and Sam, who is hovering about thirty feet away, flapping his little crimson wings.

He's kind of adorable, actually.

"Dude," I say. "Are you taking me hostage or cowering away from a nine-year-old boy?"

"Umm."

"I get it, man. Really. Split-second immolation is pretty damn terrifying. Don't think anyone would blame you for hiding, but if you want to go with using me as a body shield instead, I'll keep your secret."

Sam points at 'Claude.' "My name is not Inigo Montoya. You didn't kill my father, but prepare to die."

Screaming, 'Claude' lets go of me and rockets away in a steep dive, heading for the ground.

I tense, bracing for the blast of fire, but nothing happens. Sam's expression goes from 'evil wizard mastermind glare' to a huge, goofy smile. He casually flies over to hover beside me.

"What the hell happened to you?" I pat him to make sure he's real, then touch one of his wings close to his back. The dark red skin feels like warm leather. "Mom is going to freak out. She's still not totally cool over having a kitten in the house, and she doesn't even know about the dog yet."

"Relax." He grimaces at the blood on my face. "They're a temporary summon. I'm still Sam. It's only magic."

I whistle. "Wow… Uncle Hank called you a little hellion, but he has *no* idea."

"Ugh." Sam rolls his eyes. "You are turning into Dad. And demons aren't all evil."

"Do I even want to know how you made Crow explode?"

He scrunches his nose. "You knew those turds?"

"Nah. Guy had a tattoo of a crow on his arm."

Sam tilts his head. "Actual crow or Brandon Lee?"

"The bird."

"Oh." Sam scratches idly at his shoulder. "I didn't make him explode. Mel did. I asked her to help you."

Mel? Oh, ack. The succubus. I look around. No sign of her.

"She left already. I couldn't make the other guy blow up, but *he* didn't know that." Sam flashes an innocent smile.

"Great. My li'l bro's a gargoyle."

"Am not. It's a buff spell, like I said. Temporary. Remember the beastmaster class?"

"We are not in a video game."

"Could'a fooled me." He zips around me in a circle, playing with his wings. "And the beastmaster isn't from a video game. It's from Dad's campaign."

Duh. I facepalm... then check him over for horns. Nothing. Seems like he's the same old kid brother I'm used to having except for the wings. The skin on his back where they sprout doesn't look any different. Like someone glued dark red pool noodles to him. Okay, yeah, they're probably a temporary spell. My brother didn't mutate.

"Why didn't you tell me you could summon wings? I practically crapped myself when you fell."

"I didn't know I could." The color drains out of his face. "Olmaz gave me wings like this for a little while 'cause Ronan fell down a place in the demi-plane. I had to go get him. He said he'd show me how to use them whenever I wanted if I helped him free Mel. But, I haven't turned in the quest yet, so I didn't know if they would work."

"Turn in the quest?"

"You know, go back to Olmaz to tell him we freed Mel."

"Didn't you say life isn't a video game?"

He raspberries me. "I was kinda scared at first. Thought you'd come catch me, but the guy had you. So… I hoped Olmaz was watching and asked for help. Glad I didn't go splat."

I grab on, squeezing my little brother close. The surge of panic from when he first fell hits me hard without the adrenaline of two vampires trying to kill me. It's *so* much worse when I realize he didn't even scream. Is he really *that* brave or did he silently accept his imminent death?

"I'm okay."

"You didn't even scream when you fell. How are you so damned brave at nine?"

"I dunno. Didn't think about it. Umm. I had to try the wings. I probably would have started screaming if they didn't work."

He's obviously freaking out a bit, hiding it well. How do I know? The boy has wings and isn't flying in circles while cheering, playing around, and making a ton of noise. He shouldn't be this subdued. So, yeah, he's freaked. Another big clue, he's clinging to me pretty tight. We hold each other in midair for a few minutes until the 'holy crap' aspect of his almost falling to death stops ruling our thoughts.

"Should I fly myself or do you want to carry me?" whispers Sam.

"Umm, can you keep up?"

"Dunno."

"Race ya?" I smile.

"Deal!" He does a midair 'Bugs Bunny about to run' pose, then darts off.

He happens to be going in the wrong direction, but he's trying.

It's easy for me to catch up, barely feels like walking to me. At a guess, he's cruising along at somewhere around fifty miles an hour. I roll on my side and prop my head on my hand like I'm lounging in bed while gliding up beside him.

"Show off." He laughs. "Okay, you're faster."

"Home is also northeast. You're going west."

"Oops." He slows to a hover. "You should probably carry me. We're already late for the movie."

"Hop on, kiddo."

Sam lands on my back. His wings disappear into a faint cloud of brick red smoke. Perching on me is a bit too wobbly for him to put his shirt back on, so he holds it for now.

"Where's Blix?"

"He's chasing the other guy. Going to make him regret attacking us. He's pretty mad."

Oh, wow. I would not want to be 'Claude.' Imps having casual fun was bad enough. What are they like when pissed? "Hope he's careful. Little dude's not exactly difficult for a vampire to kill."

"He knows… he, uhh, saw you pop some of his friends."

"Sorry."

"It's cool. I didn't mean friends like real *friends*. Other imps. He's more mellow than them."

"I noticed."

Still shaking from emotion, I haul ass home. Question being, shall we ruin movie night by telling the 'rents what happened, or shall I stew on it until after?

Hello, my name is Sarah Wright and I am a lousy liar.

Here I am, lying in bed, staring at my ceiling and feeling like a horrible person.

I managed to pull off a multi-layered logic gate to prevent my parents from losing their minds. This let me walk around the truth without technically lying, so my guilty conscience didn't give me away. Sam has wings, or at least a magical ability to fake it enough. Having him knocked away from me is not my carelessness or incompetence. I didn't 'drop' him. Our being separated in midair turned out to be no risk to his life. The risk to Sam's life came from two vampires, which I successfully kept busy and away from him. We got into a fight with vampires on the way home. Not mentioning the fight took place in the air vs. the ground is not a relevant factor, given that both Sam and I can fly.

Before the movie, we told Mom and Dad two vampires attacked us over the current 'issue' going on—not personal. Sam said, 'we kicked their asses,' which the 'rents took to mean I did the ass kicking while Sam watched.

My guilt is about half from not telling the parents about Sam's ability to enchant himself with magical wings. He has no idea how often he can do it, if it only works in a serious emergency—like falling from 1,500 feet up—or if he can use them whenever he wants. I'm sure he's not going to waste time before trying to figure it out.

I'm also anxious as heck over this new development. My brother is expanding his 'demon army.' Good grief, I made a joke about Pokémon before, but he's really doing it. He's already got Blix with him pretty much constantly. We have a hellhound in the back yard. Olmaz is living in his closet, and Mel came out of nowhere to get all flamey. Does that mean he can ask them for help whenever and wherever he is, or do they have to be nearby? Also, will they exact some kind of payment for doing favors?

Not worried yet. Mel said she owed him 'a few' for releasing her. Crisping one butthead vampire probably didn't put her out too much. Also, she crisped a butthead vampire in an instant. I probably should be extremely careful around her. Don't want to piss her off.

I want to scream WTF at the top of my lungs, but Mom would yell at me for swearing.

So, instead, I stare at the ceiling and mentally scream WTF.

What is happening to my family and how much of this is my fault? Sam's odd connection to demons appears to have started with the imps arriving, which happened because of Sophia. Technically, the mystics 'activated' her when they subjected her to magic. Kinda like a superhero origin story. She got exposed to 'arcane radiation' and developed powers. I could blame the mystics for Sam and Sophia. Of course, the mystics wouldn't have turned Sophia into a human spy drone if I hadn't been a vampire who Coralie contacted for help recovering her remains from their vault.

Bad—or morally grey—people doing bad—or morally grey—things is not my fault.

I repeat this to myself a dozen times.

It's like Dad says… a mushroom vendor problem. Who has the better morels?

If a cop recovers stolen goods and the criminal shoots him for it, it's the criminal's fault. Not the cop's fault for doing his job or even becoming a cop in the first place. My becoming a vampire is not to blame for everything to happen after it.

Exhale. I almost believe myself.

Honestly, kids are expected to grow wings eventually… just not so literally. I swear if Sophia sprouts angel wings next month, I am going to lose my mind. Pare it back, Sarah. Pare it back. Anxiety goblins are manageable. Sam didn't seem to mind this new development. Kids are usually pretty good at sensing bad guys and he's not the slightest bit afraid of any of his new 'friends.' Once he put his wings away, his back didn't have any unusual marks or protrusions. No horns.

Really hope the demons are as nice as they're claiming to be. Sam can be naïve and trusting—not as much as Sophia. My brother does have a reasonably keen ability to smell BS.

I'll have to trust it, at least for now.

Surprisingly, the 'rents didn't press for too much detail about the vampire attack despite Sam being with me. Maybe because he seemed unfazed by it. Dad thinks it's an adventure, and Mom's started treating all the crazy stuff like normal, everyday goings-on. Take Sophia to dance class on my way to have a diplomatic meeting with a woman who's 357 years old. You know, ordinary stuff the eldest daughter is expected to do. It's Mom's way of dealing. Technically, this stuff *is* normal—to us.

Sam said demons are more like humans than our folklore would suggest. They're not all diabolical and evil. Who knows? Maybe he's right. Wouldn't be the first time bad public relations has done serious damage to an entire group.

Look at pitbulls.

Ugh. Come on sunrise. Hurry up and knock me out so I can stop roasting in the fires of my guilty conscience.

25

DUTIFUL

Everyone has a demon or two in their closet, but my brother takes it to a whole new level.

Given the craziness of what happened, I stayed home all day Sunday. Yeah, my weak self caved in and told the parents about the museum, the succubus, and the wings. Predictably, Mom started to declare I'm not allowed to fly with my siblings anymore out of fear of attack and dropping them until Dad pointed out Sam could apparently now fly. I decided not to mention the kids going through the mirrorverse is technically *more* dangerous than flying with me. Without Blix to guide them, they might never find a way out and spend the rest of their lives wandering endlessly in a bizarre, confusing landscape incomprehensible to mortal minds—like they'd become separated from the parents at Ikea.

I *did* say this current warfare going on wouldn't last forever—or hopefully much longer. Once random vampires are no longer trying to start problems between Seattle's elders, it won't be a problem for me to carry them around... at least until they grow up a bit more. Taking a pigeon to the face at 120 MPH hurts, but it won't make me drop one of my siblings. Eventually, however, they'll become too big to carry. I gave Ashley a ride once and… let's just say 'graceful' is not the word to describe it.

Talking about the chances of random attack get me wondering what the hell a pair of agitator vampires were doing halfway between Olympia and Seattle. 'Hey look, there's one of Wolent's people' is what the guy yelled. I don't believe they came after me specifically. They happened to be there and spotted me. So, what the heck were they doing so far south? Maybe the 'red-eyed-man' I saw in those mortals' heads lives down there? Honestly, I know thing zero about vampires in Olympia. Could be, whoever is stirring this pot of poop lives there and those two had been on their way north to Seattle intent on causing problems.

So, despite having Hunter over Sunday night, as soon as it became dark enough to think Wolent would reasonably be awake and ready to receive a phone call, I did what any dutiful new employee would do… and told the boss. He sounded concerned as well as angry in equal parts, and wanted to see me right away.

Argh. Seriously, universe? What do you have against me spending time with Hunter?

Arthur Wolent meets me in the foyer of his giant house.

It's nice having Aziz behind me watching the door. Normally, I'm not a violent person, but it would be awesome to watch him slap the hell out of 'Claude.' No, it's not his name. I just call him that because it sounds like 'clawed.' Hope the dude has trouble sitting down for a couple days.

"Sarah… tell me what happened." Wolent walks up to me and does this odd European type greeting where he kinda sorta kisses me on the cheek but not really.

I do have dignity, but I'm not above liking this guy treating me like a daughter. Being an Innocent doesn't give me a wide variety of powers, but I might as well use the ones I've got. Supernatural cuteness isn't going to be useful everywhere. If it endears me to a man like Wolent and makes him protective of me, I'll take it. Wish it worked on jackasses like Mohawk. Guess it means Wolent is really not a bad guy inside. And no, I'm not afraid of *him*… just the Fury button. It's like having your grandpa—who you trust completely—walk around always carrying a live hand grenade he brought back from the war.

We move into the living room. I sit on a vast burgundy couch, Wolent facing me on the other side of a coffee table in a plush wingback chair. Feels like I've stepped into a crazy movie where they're recreating Bram Stoker's Dracula as this hybrid mix of 1800s and modern world. Kinda like the Shakespeare movie with DiCaprio. Anyway, I give him the whole story starting with my little brother asking me for help.

"So what happened with these two miscreants? Where did they go?" asks Wolent.

"One ran off back toward Olympia. The other… he's probably still in my clothes."

"Pardon?" He tilts his head. "In your clothing?"

"Yeah… as a fine dusting of ashes."

Wolent's eyebrows almost wind up on the back of his neck when I describe 'Crow' exploding to cinders in an instant. Hopefully, I'm not giving him any ideas of recruiting my little brother as a weapon.

"It's a strange situation I'm still trying to wrap my head around. It's kinda like a little kid having a dangerous assassin for an acquaintance." I smooth my hands down my jeans until I'm gripping my knees. "He can ask her for help but no guarantee she will… or that she won't demand some kind of payment from him. Unpredictable."

Wolent nods once. "Demons…. Interesting. You'd likely be best off not letting Eleanor get wind of it."

"Oh, yes, sir. Trust me. Not planning on it. Besides, she'd reject the existence of demons because they're not sciencey." I chuckle. Can't say it isn't tempting to tell Stefano and Paolo my little brother could potentially ash them over in an instant in hopes it keeps them away from my family… but doing so could blow up in my face. Better they think I—and my family—are harmless.

Wolent leans back, rubbing his chin. "Olympia… there are a few vampires there. Mostly anarchists, which fits. A small group of civilized vampires dwell there also. None I can think of who'd gamble with their existence to destabilize Seattle."

I sit there in silence, having nothing further to add.

"I appreciate you bringing this to my attention." Wolent pats the armrests of his chair before standing. "At least we have a place to start looking. Go on and have a nice time with your boyfriend."

"Thank you, sir." I turn to leave.

"Oh, Sarah?"

"Hmm?" I peer back at him.

Wolent smiles. "I have no plans to involve your young siblings in our affairs. That said, if ever a situation arises to threaten us in the most serious of ways, do you anticipate he would be willing to offer whatever assistance he might be capable of?"

Yeah, I am naïve and have a strong tendency to trust and be loyal to authority figures, of which Wolent is one. He's been nothing but nice to me and my family, so yeah… I imagine Sam would be willing to involve himself—technically asking Olmaz or Mal for a favor—if something seriously dire happened. Since I'm involved officially now, if another vampire faction *does* make open war on us, they'd see me as part of this 'crew' and come after me, too. By extension, my family as well. As soon as I think of him as 'part of my family,' Wolent smiles.

"Probably if it's serious," I say. "But you know he *is* only nine."

Wolent nods. "I wouldn't ask. Leave it to yours and his judgement. Merely saying if something out there ever looks like it might destroy us all…"

"Definitely."

Hopefully, I can absorb whatever demand or payment Mel makes of Sam instead of him.

26

A BIT TOO MUCH FOR MOM TO HANDLE

Speaking of succubi, I came close to being one Sunday night.

Hunter crashed pretty hard after we finished, and spent the night in my bed. It almost felt as if I'd drained his energy. In the remaining hours before sunrise knocked me out, I divided my time between schoolwork and wondering about the true nature of succubi. Human folklore is starting to seem notoriously misinformed. It's almost like certain political groups made up stories completely out of their butts in order to convince people to hate demons, vampires, and other supernatural beings blindly.

I mean, a succubus being *embarrassed* about having no clothes on? Maybe the whole sexually charged thing about them was made up by horny monks hundreds of years ago. I mean, you lock a bunch of dudes away from society and forbid them from going near women, their frustrations are bound to come out in other ways. Gawd, hope it's all exaggerated about succubi. My kid brother having Mel on supernatural speed dial is a straight up *Weird Science* scenario. Not so bad now, but in like five years when he's a teenager? Looking at her is going to have an entirely different effect on him.

Even if she doesn't have charm powers.

Who knows what succubi are really like? Maybe all it means is a demon who is both female and looks exactly like a human—instead of having like wings and hooves. People in the Middle Ages were *not* exactly progressive when it came to gender equality. Being female at all was seen as evil to some people. Temptresses and so forth. Men who had no willpower blamed women for their inability to control themselves.

I'll back-burner my anxiety over a succubus hanging out with my brother until I know more about them.

Anyway… Wolent has people going to Olympia to look around. He hasn't asked me to do it, thankfully—probably because he's being protective or wants to send more of an ass-kicker to deliver the sort of message one can't write on an old timey scroll. Someday, I'll be able to handle those deliveries, too. It's out of character for me, but I do kinda look forward to being more of a badass even if all it's ever useful for is self-defense.

It's Tuesday now.

I turned in my Poe paper yesterday. Fingers crossed the grade is decent. Professor Connolly dumped some sixty pages of reading on us for bio tonight. I've been home from class barely five minutes, enjoying the freedom of escaping my pants. Since my plans do not include going anywhere tonight, I changed into one of my long T-shirts. Weird. I don't remember the exact moment the idea of wearing pajamas or a nightgown struck me as 'lame' or childish. Sophia adores nightgowns. No surprise there. The frillier, the better. You'd think Sierra would go for PJs, but she's also kind of a fan of the nightgown, though not so much for the frills. Sam's a coin flip between pajamas or briefs to sleep in. Depends on how tired he is before bed. Sometimes, he's just too tired to finish changing.

Right. I have homework to do.

At 10:13 p.m., the ghostly form of Coralie appears next to me, still in the same black, quasi-frilly 1900s style dress I first saw her in. Lucky for her, she's a ghost and wearing the same outfit every day for a century doesn't get funky.

"Sarah!" Coralie attempts to grasp my arm but only turns a spot cold. "Sierra is quite likely to die if you do not help her."

"Shit!" I jump out of my chair. "Do I have time to get dressed?"

She nods. "Yes. And bring your sword."

Craaaaap. Sierra, what are you doing? I rush into a pair of jeans and trade the long sleep shirt for a normal tee. While I'm scrambling into my clothes, Coralie pokes a finger at my iPhone, which unlocks itself and opens Google Maps. She stares at the phone, watching the app scroll to a location and highlight it with one of those orange pointer things.

If a 189-year-old woman can work an iPhone, Grandma Sheridan has no excuse.

The phone indicates a warehouse near the docks next to West Queen Anne.

I pick up the phone. "Thank you!"

Coralie makes an urgent face at me. She's worried about Sierra, too. I don't even stop to wonder what the hell my twelve-year-old sister is doing all the way in downtown Seattle at this hour. As the news guy always asks, it's after 10:00 p.m. and I *do* know where the child is. Problem being, she's somewhere she shouldn't be.

I drop an F-bomb, grab the katana, and run out into the basement, up the stairs, and straight out the patio door. Sierra's life is in danger. No time to tell the parents where I'm going or grab my sneakers. Sword in one hand, phone in the other, I fly so fast my clothing ignites. Just kidding. Feels like the wind is about to rip my shirt off, but it doesn't. Yeah, fear and worry *definitely* affect my flight speed.

The general vicinity of my destination is easy to spot from the air. Two giant 'prongs' stick into Elliot Bay at the north end. Coralie put a map marker on a warehouse type building a little east of it across the train tracks.

I land on the roof beside a small, raised outbuilding and approach the single door. It's tiny, only big enough for a stairway so maintenance people can access the HVAC equipment up here. Male voices inside sporadically shout things like 'check over there' or 'she couldn't be far.'

My heart races. They're hunting my sister.

The door's locked. Big surprise there, right? I could be quiet and try to nudge the retaining bar aside with a claw… but making noise will distract whoever is chasing my sister away from her. So, I go full barbarian. Whenever Dad runs D&D for us and we encounter a locked door in a dungeon, Sophia wants to be careful and quiet, check for traps, and make sure no one gets hurt. Sierra usually ignores her and kicks doors down. Sam usually stands twenty feet back in either case. Can't help but think it's appropriate to use her methods when her butt is on the line.

Kicking a steel door that opens outward isn't a great idea. I'd make a ton of noise, but it wouldn't bother the door much beyond denting it. I grab the knob and pull until the latch plate breaks out of the doorjamb. Not the loudest possible way to open a door—no, the *loudest* way to open a door involves plastic explosives—but if the people hunting my sister are vampires, they definitely heard me.

Strangely, the searching shouts don't stop. Maybe they think one of their guys bumped into something. I rush down a switchback stair to another door and emerge on a catwalk overlooking a huge warehouse. Most of the room below me contains massive two-story-tall steel shelves piled high with pallets of various consumer goods. This is not an abandoned warehouse. None of this stuff looks old. Vampires tend to have a fairly loose grasp of property rights. They likely helped themselves to the building.

From my elevated vantage point, I spot about half a dozen people searching the aisles between shelves and checking forklifts. A late-twenties woman in a black sweatshirt and BDU pants stands guard at a door all the way at the other end, holding an AK-47. She appears to be the only one carrying a firearm. A few of the others carry collapsible batons, knives, or pipes. Three don't have any visible weapons.

Sierra's nowhere in sight, which is both freaking me out and reassuring. Unfortunately, I *can* smell her. No, she doesn't stink. Vampires can pick up human scents but not as well as dogs. It's a real pain for us to follow a scent trail, but if someone's nearby and hiding—or has been in a room recently—we can detect their presence.

Coralie materializes next to me and points toward the back, left corner. "She's hiding under the shelf of cat litter."

"Thanks."

I fly along the catwalk to avoid making noise. Upon reaching the rear of the warehouse, I dive over the railing, flip on the way down, and land between two tall shelves. Frightened sniffling coming from under several pallets of Fresh Step beside me stops. While it's perfectly understandable for her to be scared, this is the first time Sierra's ever *sounded* terrified. She didn't even react like this to the five-headed nope-a-saurus in the mirrorverse. Maybe that thing went so far over the top she dismissed it as not being real. A bunch of vampires hunting her in a warehouse is scarier for being less outlandish.

Crouching, I peer under the shelf. Sierra's flat on her front, pale as a ghost, wide eyed. Her face is smudged dark, like she got a little too close to a laser printer toner explosion. Like me, she's barefoot. Curiously, she's wearing a nightgown—but has her sword. Should I be worried it doesn't seem too weird to mention my little sister *has* a sword of her own? Is it weirder Dad got it for her as a Christmas present?

"Sare!" whispers Sierra.

All trace of fear evaporates from her. She scoots out from under the shelf, jumps up, and grabs my arm. "Boost me!"

"What?"

"Blood stuff. If you don't make me stronger and faster, I'm gonna die."

I point up. "We can go out the roof."

"And what? They come after us and catch us in midair? I'm not Sam. I don't have wings!" She stomps, her foot clapping on the smooth concrete.

"Over there!" yells a woman about five aisles away.

Crap. Double crap, in fact, since Sierra has a point. Odds are, at least two of these vampires can fly. Better odds say none of them are Innocents. Yeah, they'd catch us easily, especially while I'm slowed down by extra weight.

I nibble on my lip. "Dunno... I don't want to mess with you."

"It's not permanent. I trust Dalton." Sierra shakes me. "Would you rather buff me now or turn me into a vampire after these morons kill me? I'll take it, but I'd rather not be stuck at twelve for eternity."

Footsteps race toward us.

Oh screw it.

I extend my fangs and nip a small cut on my left wrist. Like the world's cutest little leech, Sierra clamps on and suckles from the wound. Her facial expression is definite 'eww this tastes horrible' which reassures me a little. I've loaned Glim the ability to tolerate mortal food—primarily so he can enjoy beer again—but this is my first time giving blood to a living person to 'buff' them. Since the Transference is largely based on desire, I apply the same logic here and concentrate on wanting my sister to get faster and stronger.

She doesn't take much... barely two teaspoons' worth.

I lick my wrist clean, sealing the cut a second before several vampires appear at either end of the aisle we're in. Two above us.

Sierra leans her head back, shuddering like a cocaine addict after taking a hit of potent stuff. "Listen up, buttheads." She pulls her sword from its scabbard. "We can do this the easy way or the hard way. I'm only gonna warn you once. Leave us alone and no one's gonna lose body parts."

The vampires laugh. One woman even 'awws' at her.

Admittedly, a wispy twelve-year-old in a nightgown is not exactly the most intimidating sight. Hell, I'm not much more fearsome. Becoming an Innocent didn't make me any shorter... well not much. Mostly, it altered my appearance to make me seem younger. These guys look like a street gang. I'm sure they're not the least bit intimidated by me.

"Well, two-for-one," says a spiky haired guy in a pleather jacket—with decorative chains on it.

I glance at him. "Duuuude. Is someone filming a retro Eighties movie? You guys look like generic 'bad guy punks.' Seriously. Time to update your style. Please tell me you're not going to start blasting Mötley Crüe or something over the fight scene."

Sierra cackles.

He snarls.

I point the katana at him. "Wait a sec. *Why* are you trying to kill my sister?"

"Wolent's tired of you breaking tradition," says a woman on the left.

"Dumbass," whispers another woman next to her. "That's the Stefano guy. This bitch works for Wolent."

About half of the vampires surrounding us sigh at the ceiling or facepalm.

"Look, I know it's all BS. You guys aren't even from Seattle and are just trying to manipulate the elders into starting a war."

Pleather jacket guy shakes his head at me. "She knows too much. End them both."

"Not gonna work." I narrow my eyes at him. "The elders already know what's going on."

"Whatever. Killing the two of you is still gonna be fun." He grins, then runs at me.

I'm not sure what the dude expected to accomplish, since he doesn't have a weapon. It's safe to say he did *not* expect me to know how to use a sword—as evidenced by his head coming off neatly to my first swing. His body keeps trying to grab me—blindly—until I stab the katana into the severed head, then he falls over.

"Dumbass," deadpans Sierra.

All freakin' hell breaks loose.

Three more vamps come at me from the right. Another group rushes at Sierra from the left. Without a word between us, my sister and I synchronize our movements, spinning around back to back in the middle of a swarm of vampires. It's freakish to see her keeping up with me. It *is* kinda silly for vampires to all speed themselves up when fighting other vampires. None of us really get an advantage over each other, since we're all roughly the same speed. Well, these guys are a touch faster than me because they're older, but none of them have the first clue how to swordfight.

Falling objects, exploding bags of cat litter from missed attacks, and other crap in the background seems to hang in super slow motion —but everyone fighting is moving at normal speed. Sierra isn't close to being vampire strong, though. Adding a supernatural boost to a scrawny kid her age makes her about as strong as an average adult man. Thankfully, she understands this and doesn't try to rely on any maneuvers requiring brute force. She capitalizes on her small size and agility, though two guys do learn the hard way what an abnormal amount of muscle power in a small foot does to a man's sensitive bits.

I lop off the arm of a guy swinging a giant wrench at me, spin into a thrust between some pink-haired bitch's boobs. My sword's momentarily stuck, forcing me to duck a knife slash before flinging the nunchuck-wielding woman off my sword. A stab to the heart from a relatively thin blade like a katana only incapacitates a vampire for a few minutes. She slumps to the floor and tries to drag herself away, acting more like she's too drunk to stand and doesn't have a hole through her heart.

Sierra hacks a guy's right leg off at the knee, then spins around behind him to parry a baseball bat going for her head. She swipes her sword across bat guy's throat, spinning on her toes like a ballet dancer before delivering a fancy thrust into the spine of the guy she legged.

I swear the girl has watched *Mulan* too many times.

Dalton definitely didn't give us Chinese sword techniques. Maybe she's merely improvising for style points and I'm imagining. A guy wallops me across the back with a chain. I let out an *oof,* but grab the chain before he can pull it back. Sierra darts around me, thrusting her sword two-handed up into his heart. An instant later, a blonde in a micromini and a T-shirt with an anarchy symbol rushes at her from behind, about to impale her on the end of a crowbar.

I abandon the chain, swat the crowbar aside, then body-block the blonde, knocking her into a stagger. Before she gets her balance back, I lop her head off. Six feet of blood sprays up from the neck stump. Ooh, she's going to be hungry as hell when she gets her head back on straight.

"Thanks," says Sierra, yanking her blade out of chain guy's chest and spearing the severed head so the body stops flailing.

"No problem."

Chain guy wheezes and sinks to his knees. Sierra tries to 'Voltron' him, cutting him in half from head to crotch, but her blade stops about eight inches in, at his mouth. Still, cutting his brain in half is sleepy time for at least eight hours.

Blam!

A bullet ricochets off the floor by my foot.

Sierra screams.

Blam.

I lean out of the way of a spiraling rifle bullet heading for my face. It's not the most effective thing in the world to fire a gun into a vampire fight *after* everyone's already got the agility dial up to eleven. This really is *Matrix* stuff. Bullets seem to be flying about as fast as thrown baseballs. Not super simple to dodge, but definitely possible.

"Wolverine me!" yells Sierra, pointing her sword upward.

A punk in a puffy, yellow coat—holy Eighties, Batman—swipes a switchblade at me. I parry it hard enough to send the tiny weapon flying. He ducks my retaliation and pulls a second, bigger knife off his belt.

Blam! A bullet clanks off the shelf near Sierra.

She flattens herself against the shelf closer to the person shooting at us from high up, snarling at me. "Sare! Wolverine me!"

I swat the combat knife out of Yellow Jacket's hand. "What?"

He goes for a handgun under his coat. Oh, screw this progressively larger-weapon escalation bullshit. I stab him in the mouth, twist the blade, and slash it sideways out of his skull above the left ear. Dude falls over with a flip-top head. Really is more efficient to chop into the head than cut it off at the neck.

Sierra ducks a woman swinging a baseball bat at her head, then kneecaps her. "Throw me up there to get the bitch with the rifle!"

The woman swings the baseball bat at her from the ground. Sierra blocks, but the vampire bitch is strong. My sister goes flying backward into a pallet of toilet paper. She bounces off and hits the floor on her front. I rush over and pounce on 'bat woman,' stabbing my katana down through her eye socket with enough force to gouge the concrete under her head.

Sierra emits a war cry, scrambles to her feet, and charges another vampire dive-bombing me from the top of the shelf. Bastard stabs me in the back before she gets to him—but Sierra proceeds to reenact a *Mortal Kombat* fatality on the poor son of a bitch. Her initial attack rips his knife arm off at the elbow. As he backpedals, she slashes his gut open. He makes the mistake of trying to grab her with his remaining hand—which he promptly loses. She hits him in the chest twice more before he slips in blood and starts to fall over backward. Sierra jumps over him, swinging a beheading stroke in midair before landing behind him. My turn to stab the head on the floor.

She looks totally *Crouching Tiger Hidden Dragon*... until her bare feet slide out from under her in all the blood. Still, the kid makes falling on her butt look smooth and intentional. Can't blame her. The only reason I'm not recreating my first time on ice skates is the power of flight. I'm hovering even though my feet are touching the floor.

Blam! A bag of dog food by Sierra explodes.

Damn good thing she fell.

"No way, kiddo!" I yell, then launch myself upward.

The pale goth woman in the black sweatshirt with the AK is up on the catwalk where I initially entered. She fires rapidly at me as I'm rushing up to intercept her. For the most part, I weave around bullets whizzing by me at the apparent speed of ping pong balls launched out of a leaf blower. While spin-rolling out from under an incoming head shot, I catch a glimpse of Sierra leaning out of the way of a bullet coming at her from the side before throwing her sword at a green-haired dude in a biker jacket. The hurled blade plunges to the hilt in his chest. Reeling, he fires a handgun wildly, his aim ruined. She runs at him, then jumps into a double-kick, planting both feet on his chest on either side of the handle as she grabs it, then springs away into a backflip, tearing the sword loose as he falls over.

I don't see what happens next due to rolling over and slashing at AK bitch.

And whoa... my sister is as fast as a vampire. Superhuman agility would make 'movie Legolas' jealous. What the hell am I doing? Is it a mistake giving her blood? Or am I going to rationalize it as our family is entirely messed up now? Sophia's got magic. Sam's got demon Pokémon. Sierra needs *something* to keep up. She *can't* stay normal, or she'll always be listed as 'child kidnap victim' in the end credits.

Sigh. Please don't have permanent bad side effects on her.

Contrary to what some weeaboos think, a katana will not cut an AK-47 in half, even with a vampire's strength behind it. She blocks, but staggers backward from the force of my strike. Yeah, I'm pissed. My right leg buckles out from under me when I try to land on the catwalk—ugh, she put a bullet in my thigh—so I keep fly-hovering while swinging at her. She's pretty fast, but parrying a sword using a rifle has a huge flaw.

I aim for her hands.

She screams as her fingers go flying. The rifle falls to the metal grating out of my way. She's got the nerve to yell 'stop' after shooting at me and my sister. I don't. My slice hits her on the shoulder by the base of the neck and stops about heart deep. Her fangs extend reflexively as her body contorts in a near-death rigor. Vast amounts of blood flow out of her. Generally, vampires retain blood even from nasty wounds… but cutting the torso almost in half is an exception. Holes in the heart tend to be… messy. Slicing the heart in half? *Way* messy. Decapitation's fairly geyserish, too.

I really ought to do worse than simply chop her open. She tried to shoot my sister. Unlike me or all of these jackasses, *Sierra* won't get back up in a few hours and feel sore. This whole thing looks gory as hell and on some level *is* disturbing. But, it's like a video game. No one stays dead. It's tempting to empty the rest of the rifle into her out of spite, but better not to leave my fingerprints on it just in case.

Sierra's waiting for me amid an assortment of bodies. Her nightgown is almost entirely red, stuck to her skin. The only part of her not coated in blood are her eyes, because she wiped at her face a little. More unsettling is her wired expression of exhilaration. I have to check her thoughts. Whew. Okay, she's not having a 'that was freakin' awesome let's do it again!' moment. It's a 'holy shit we're alive!' moment.

I land beside her, favoring my right leg. "You okay?"

"Yeah. Fine. I know this isn't going to kill them." She squats over one guy, wiping her blade clean on his shirt. "Should we light them on fire?"

Wow... I stare at her.

"What?"

"Kinda surprising me by the bloodlust."

She stands. "They *were* trying to kill me. You think they'll forget about it when they get back up? Just trying to be practical here."

"Umm. Maybe if we don't destroy them permanently with fire, they'll be grateful enough to leave us alone?" I fidget. Wow. I really am too nice. They were going to kill Sierra, and I'm sitting here feeling bad about the idea of lighting them on fire.

"They won't come after us if we burn them, either." Sierra shrugs. "Your call. I've already taken out my frustrations on them."

"Do you think they'd have killed you or just made you forget seeing this place?"

She taps her foot, making a gloopy *pap-pap-pap* in the blood. "Umm. Dunno. I don't think they planned to kill me until after you blabbed and told them we knew about their nefarious plans."

"Right... Wow. You are *covered* in blood."

Sierra looks down at herself. "Yeah. It feels pretty disgusting. So are you, by the way."

We look at each other for a few seconds before saying, "Mom's gonna freak" at the same time.

27

SURPRISE TENTACLES ARE NEVER FUN

I haven't seen this much blood in one place since my first period.

Okay, slight exaggeration. Let me rephrase. I haven't seen this much blood in one place since the nightmare I had in the weeks *before* my first period. Looking back, I got myself worked up for nothing. Leave it to stupid kid me to take things wildly overboard. In my nightmare, things exploded like a damn ruptured fire hydrant right in the middle of class. Probably Dad's fault for letting me watch a really cheesy horror movie where people had arms cut off and like super soakers of blood squirted everywhere.

My child mind applied the same logic to what periods would be like. And of course, it had to happen in an extremely public, extremely embarrassing way. I expected it would. Reality ended up being much tamer, but still unpleasant.

On the list of things I do *not* miss about being mortal, the monthly visitor is in second place… right after not having to be scared to go anywhere alone after dark.

Whew. I whistle. "Impressive. I can't believe we took on… were there eight or ten?"

"I lost count." Sierra kicks a severed forearm away. "Maybe twelve."

"Are you hurt?"

"No."

"Sore?"

"No."

"Really? You were zooming around like something right out of an anime."

She laughs. "So were you."

"Yeah, but I'm a vampire. You're still alive. How the heck did a little sip of blood give you so much of a boost?"

"Uhh." Sierra starts to scratch her head but stops, cringing. "Eww. Blood's everywhere. Umm. Dalton said your boost would work better since we're closer. It's supposed to be stronger if the vampire loves the mortal, or some sappy BS like that. Plus, we're actual family. Don't feel guilty or get all worried. If I'm going to have your back, I gotta be able to keep up."

I wipe down my blade, then retrieve the scabbard and put the katana back in it. "Dammit."

"What?"

"Coralie told me to come here. Those guys *were* going to kill you. Dammit."

"Why are you saying dammit? They didn't kill me."

I look at her. "Because I'm starting not to feel guilty about the idea of burning them to death."

"*You* don't have to do it." Sierra shrugs.

"You're not playing with matches. Mom will freak," I say to the little girl covered in blood who just chopped helped me chop a dozen vampires into pieces.

She laughs. "No, not me. Call Wolent. Have him send people here to clean up. These guys are basically enemies on his territory, right? Whatever he decides to do to them is not your fault."

"Good point. Hey Siri? Send a geotag to Arthur Wolent." She beeps acknowledgement. "Hey Siri, send a text to Arthur Wolent." I wait for the beep. "Bad guys at this location. They kinda fell to pieces. Will give more details later."

"Oh..." Sierra pokes me. "Before they saw me, I heard them talking about a guy named something weird. Sounded like Anselme Ernoul."

I blink. "Isn't he a snob chef from some TV show?"

"Umm, no idea. He's a vampire in Astoria. I think he's their boss, too. Sounded like a big group of vampires want to take over Seattle. They're kinda frustrated the elders haven't started ripping each other apart yet."

"Good." I smile. "So, we have a name for this guy now."

"Yeah. He sounds like a butthead."

I glance at her. "Now for the big question. What the hell are you doing here?"

Sierra gives an exasperated sigh like she's late for work because she got stuck in traffic. "Soph was trying to use magic to scry and find out who's causing all the trouble."

"Scry?"

"Yeah, you know... crystal ball type stuff? Anyway, let's just say things didn't go quite the way she wanted."

"Shocking."

Sierra chuckles. "Tentacles may have been involved."

"Uh oh."

"I ran to grab my sword so I could cut her loose, but when I got back to her room, they were gone. So was Soph. I opened the closet to look for her... and a tentacle grabbed me around the head. Next thing I know, I'm here."

Oh, that explains the black stuff on her face. Dried void tentacle slime. Eww. And crap. Sophia might be in trouble somewhere. The girl really needs to stop trying to mess with opening gates.

"They didn't notice me right away, so I crawled under a shelf to listen. They were talking about stealing a whole bunch of dead bodies so some dude named Anselme could send them to 'mess stuff up.' It's not just our family being attacked. They want the old vampires of Seattle to fight each other."

"Yeah. I got that feeling."

"Over here!" Sierra runs off, the patter of bloody feet echoing in the now-silent warehouse.

It's kind of a miracle no cops have shown up due to the guns firing. Pretty sure the police won't come in quiet, at least not quiet enough to escape *my* ears. I should have plenty of time to grab Sierra and make a roof exit if they do.

She leads me to the other end of the warehouse where six garage doors line the wall at a loading dock. Multiple cafeteria style tables are set up around some forklifts. A pair of zoned-out security guards sit handcuffed to one forklift. Probably snacks for the vampires. It wouldn't surprise me if the vamps intended to kill these two guys later to be used as 'zombies.'

"This is where they hung out before." Sierra points at a laptop. "The woman who had the gun seemed to be the one in charge. She kept looking at the computer when talking about the places they planned to attack."

Hmm. This is definitely not their lair, most likely a temporary staging area for a campaign of misdirection. It's probably not a great idea to spend much time here. Looks like someone got the stupids and forgot to lock the screen when they noticed Sierra and everyone began searching for her. After changing the admin password to the word 'password' so we don't get locked out for good, I grab the laptop to take with us. Oh, oops. Sec. I snap the handcuffs off the security guards and—damn. The mental command in their heads to stare into the ninth dimension is too potent for me to overcome. Hopefully, whoever Wolent sends here to clean up can take care of them.

"Uh oh." Sierra gestures at the trail of bloody footprints we left.

"Compared to the mess in the back of the building, that's mild."

"Yeah, but my tracks are small. They're going to know a kid was here."

"Relax. Wolent's people will take care of it. C'mon. Let's get the hell out of here."

She nods. "Promise me one thing."

"What?"

"Don't fly too high, and if some dickhead decides to attack us, sprint for the ground. I'd prefer to fight instead of fall."

"Okay. And I won't tell Mom you said 'dickhead.'"

She frowns. "Are you going to tell her I sliced up a bunch of vampires?"

"Still debating."

Sierra laughs.

28

BLOODBATH

Greg Miller, a boy in my class from high school, liked to go to the firing range with his dad.

He used to say shooting targets was a lot of fun, but cleaning the guns afterward sucked. Sierra loves going to her sword fighting lessons. Being covered in blood is kinda like the annoying chore after the fact. Thankfully, she hasn't come home from there looking like she jumped into a blood lake. I'm almost certain Mom would pull the plug on those classes if Sierra routinely had to slice up vampires. To be fair, she adores sparring. *Actual* fighting, she gets no real thrill out of. Awesome. Much like me, the whole time she's in a real fight, her brain is basically screaming an endless stream of profanities and hoping to walk away alive. She's not a small psychopath.

Defending herself from vampires is way different from stabbing a living person.

She may or may not hesitate to slice a living guy trying to hurt her, but either way, doing so would probably leave a mental scar—unlike what we just did. My sister has filed it away as no more traumatizing than shooting fake people in a video game. It helps to know nothing either one of us did with our swords tonight is permanent. All those vampires will get back up in hours… provided Wolent's people don't leave them out for the sunrise. Heads don't roll back in place all on their own. Those vamps will have some fun trying to maneuver their bodies around blind looking for the head.

Ya know what looks *super* weird? Sticking a sword into a head and the flailing decapitated body fifteen feet away drops unconscious. However, headless bodies running around and pouncing blindly is definite nightmare fuel even if I completely understand what they are.

My sister is pretty quiet on the flight home. It doesn't take long, only a few minutes, so we have no real time for a deep conversation. Upon arriving at the house, I don't touch down and glide into the kitchen via the patio door. I hover for a second, debating between the basement shower stall and the upstairs bathroom. Heck, I'll drop her upstairs and use the one in the basement. She's a little too old for sharing a shower. Maybe if we'd been covered in poop she wouldn't care, but yeah, this is only blood. Sierra lifts her head off my shoulder to look around. Before she can ask why we're floating like a gory pinata in the kitchen, I drift forward across the house to the upstairs bathroom, careful not to brush against any walls or furniture. The two of us are so soaked we'd act like a permanent marker writing in blood. Still hovering, I set Sierra on her feet in the bathtub.

Sierra sets her sword on the rug, blushes a little, then shrugs. "You gonna go downstairs?"

"I was planning on it… umm, unless you don't really want to be alone."

She smiles, looking relieved, blush fading. "Nah, I'm fine. Swordfights, please always help me if you're there. Showering, I can handle myself."

We stare at each other for a moment. Sierra's expression shifts from defensive to guilty to adoring. I can't help but read her thoughts. She's feeling bad about how she used to scream 'get out' at me if I tried to walk into the bathroom when she was already in there, as if I did it on purpose. My almost-death has 'slightly rearranged' our family dynamic. Sierra won't yell at me now, but accidentally barging in on her still embarrasses the hell out of her. She was really hoping I didn't plan to stay here and shower in the same tub.

And she knows I'm looking. Guess my emotion's on my face.

"What about poop?"

"Eww." Sierra grimaces. "If we got covered in poo, it wouldn't matter if we shared a shower... because you would be erasing the entire memory from my head."

I chuckle.

"Careful going downstairs, don't drip."

"We're not dripping anymore. The blood's dried enough to be tacky."

"Wearing blood is *always* tacky." She grins.

"Oh, no!" I facepalm. "You've got it too."

"What?" Sierra goes wide-eyed.

"Dad's pun genes."

"Noooo!" Sierra fake wails.

One does not simply witness a bloody apparition drift through the house and not go to investigate. Mom skids to a stop in the doorway, staring at us. Once she realizes she didn't witness a strange multi-limbed floating blood golem and, in fact, it was only me giving Sierra a piggyback ride, she covers her mouth to hold back a scream of worried confusion. "What happened?"

"Well..." I gesture at Sierra like a game show hostess. "She's getting older. A girl's bound to end up covered in blood at a bad time sooner or later."

Sierra gasps. I think she's blushing. Difficult to tell.

Mom smirks, unimpressed.

"Seriously, though," I say. "Some vampires attacked us. We had to cut a few bitches."

Sierra laughs. "Sare, you are way too normal and suburban to ever say 'we had to cut a bitch.' It's as cringey as Dad quoting lyrics from rap music."

"What?" gasps Mom, jaw open.

"It's true," says Sierra. "Dad listens to rap sometimes."

Mom stares at her. "No, I mean… attacked? Why are you in a nightie? Please tell me what the hell happened before I lose my mind."

"Nothing in the house, Mom." I'm seriously getting tired of standing here covered in blood. It's tempting to peel my clothes off so the sticky sensation stops. Nothing Mom hasn't seen already and my sister would look away.

"We, umm, had a magic oops." Sierra shakes her head.

"Speaking of…" I look at her. "Where is Sophia?"

"I dunno. Kinda lost track of her when the giant tentacle wrapped around my head and yanked me into the closet."

Mom rubs the bridge of her nose. "Why does Sophia have a giant tentacle in her closet?"

I cringe, resisting the urge to go for the cheap joke. "Uhh, not touching that one with a ten-foot-pole." Okay, maybe I didn't resist it well enough.

Mom's turn to blush hard.

Sierra scrunches her nose at me. "Huh?"

"Why are there strange creatures from the void lurking in your sister's closet," says Mom in her 'I'm angry but keeping myself composed' voice.

Sigh. "I'm guessing she tried to open a teleportation gate again and didn't quite pull it off."

"She's not old enough to drive. She shouldn't be trying to establish pan-dimensional gateways." Mom looks at us again, exhaling in disbelief.

"She didn't." Sierra points in the general direction of Sophia's room. "She just wanted to scry, you know… look at stuff. Get information."

"Mom, I need to start searching for her as soon as we don't look like a walking crime scene. Gonna head downstairs and clean up. Uhh, Sierra, you want me to just take your nightie and toss it in the laundry?"

"Ugh. Okay." Sierra turns the water on and pulls the shower curtain forward to hide behind it.

"You know, Sarah, a fun evening out with your little sister isn't supposed to end with the two of you covered in blood."

"I know, Mom. Sorry. I didn't mean to bring her to a sword fight... but you should be proud of her. She kicked ass."

Sierra peeks around the shower curtain, grinning proudly.

Mom whistles. "And what are you doing outside at this hour?"

"Accident. Tentacle, remember? I didn't *want* to go anywhere." Sierra lifts one foot into the gushing water. "It's warm enough. Gonna start showering now. Can I please have the bathroom to myself?"

Her bloody nightgown comes flying over the top of the shower curtain. Easy catch.

"I... don't know how to handle this." Mom rubs her forehead again. "Grandma said motherhood could be rough sometimes. She had no damn idea."

"C'mon, Mom." Without touching her—due to blood all over me—I sorta shoo her out of the room. "Mind getting the door? My hands are a mess."

29

VAST INTERDIMENSIONAL NON-SPACE

Showering off semidry vampire blood is a chore.

This stuff is stickier than normal blood. It's like someone dumped a bucket of cherry pancake syrup over my head and it hardened into a lacquer. Much scrubbing needed. Fortunately, it's mostly on my face, arms, and hair. It didn't soak through my shirt or pants much. Note to self: next time I end up a bloody mess, don't wait so long to clean up. Once I'm back in my bedroom, I finish drying off, then grab a clean T-shirt and pair of jeans.

It's unnerving Sierra showed more discomfort at the idea I might have tried to share the tub with her than she did at chopping up a bunch of vampires. Yes, she had a total non-reaction to a swordfight as gory as a Quentin Tarantino movie. If my unlife continues like this, I may need to buy a weird yellow jumpsuit. I've already got the katana. Did I mention it's a 'real' one? Not a Home Shopping Network cheapie. According to Coralie, the sword does not have a soul trapped in it, which is good. Nah. Forget the yellow track suit. It wouldn't look good on me. Besides, it's difficult to get bloodstains out of bright colors.

Somehow, Sierra views 'killing' vampires like stepping on bugs, but she doesn't regard *me* as a creature. Not sure how she's processing the contradiction, but hey. I'm not a meaningless creature. Go me. I am, however, prepared to deal with the possibility Sierra's going to have a nightmare or two in the near future. She's like the ballsiest twelve-year-old in the world, but she is still a child. Neither one of us acknowledged how scared she had been while hiding under the shelf before I got there. Kinda like two grown men in the middle of a combat zone catching each other crying from fear—they just accept the moment and move on like it didn't happen.

Right, I can worry about helping Sierra manage the pieces of a potentially crumbling psyche tomorrow. Sophia's still missing. I'm almost to the basement steps when her voice comes from the second floor.

"That totally sucked!"

I rush upstairs. The 'rents and Sierra are slow-motion walking across the hall from Sierra's room. Thanks to my accelerated speed, we narrowly avoid jamming together, squeezing into the room at roughly the same time. Sophia's room is empty.

"What the heck?" I spin to look at the parents. "You heard her, right?"

"In here," calls Sam.

We scramble across the hall again.

Sam and Ronan—both in pajamas—stand on either side of Sophia, who's got both feet in an orange plastic beach bucket a short distance in front of the closet. I can't tell what Sophia's wearing because she is a silhouette, as if someone dipped her in a vat of black paint. The substance drips down her body, explaining the bucket. Klepto is pasted to the top of her head like a lumpy toupee with eyes. Both Sam and Ronan look like they stood a little too close to a cartoony explosion, having smears of black stuff on their PJs and faces.

"Totally sucked," mutters Sophia.

Klepto emits a miserable sounding "Mew."

"Do I even want to know?" asks Mom.

"What happened, Soph?" I ask.

"Things that cannot be unseen." Sophia shivers.

"Looks like she had a negative experience with void energy." Dad gingerly swipes a finger at Sophia's forehead. He sniffs the gunk on his fingertip. "Doesn't smell like anything."

"It technically smells like *nothing*." Sam holds a finger up. "It's liquid nothingness."

"I don't like tentacles," says Ronan in a flat tone.

Dad pats him on the head. "You are normal. People who like tentacles are considered strange."

The kids all look at us, confused.

"Not now, Jonathan." Mom exhales. "Will someone please tell me what's going on?"

"Uhh." Sam wipes black smudge off his cheek. "Olmaz helped us get Soph back from the non-space where the black tentacle thing lives."

"It hit me." Ronan scrunches up his nose. "Like getting smacked with a baseball bat made of Jell-O."

"You had to fight the giant void octopus to get Sophia back?" I ask.

"No. It just kinda flailed at us like we were mosquitos buzzing around it while we pulled her out." Sam chuckles. "He wasn't trying to kill us. I think he's afraid of humans."

"Good instincts." Dad nods. "If the void starts tolerating humans, next thing you know, there'll be Starbucks, McDonald's, and KFCs all over intra-dimensional non-space."

Mom sighs.

"I was trying to scry to figure out who's causing all the trouble for the vampires." Sophia wobbles, almost losing her balance from standing in a bucket. "I kinda saw this big room with a bunch of shelves and stuff. Tried to get a closer look, but something went wrong and my closet popped open. Tentacles grabbed me. Sierra ran to get her sword, but the void monster pulled me into the closet… and slime."

"They grabbed me when I looked in the closet." Sierra folds her arms. "Tossed me into the warehouse."

"Oh no," whispers Sophia.

"Blix saw them go into the closet and said we needed to help." Sam pats the imp on the head. "I didn't know what to do, so we went to ask Olmaz."

"What's an Olmaz?" asks Dad.

"He's the demon who cured Ro when he got paralyzed."

"Demons now..." Mom looks at Dad.

"Dad." Sam smiles. "Think of them as an extraplanar race. They're not creatures of evil. It's a little more common for them to be dark than us. Some *are* buttheads, not all."

"So... they're insurance adjusters?" Dad raises an eyebrow.

"Not *that* evil," mutters Mom.

I lean close to my littlest sister. "Are you okay?"

"Yeah, just annoyed." Sophia grumbles. "I think an outside force messed with me. All I tried to do was scry and the magic went all sorts of crazy. The bad vampire is probably a mystic, too."

"Mew," says Klepto.

I bite my lip. "Well, they made corpses get up and walk, so... yeah. Good chance they're a mystic. Might want to hop in the tub."

"Is this gunk going to wash out of the carpet if it gets anywhere?" asks Mom.

"Good question. Don't think the stuff you use is rated for solidified nothingness." Dad chuckles. "We could test on a small inconspicuous area of rug."

Mom smirks at him.

Sophia looks down. "Stare too long into the void, and the void shoves you into a random body cavity of a giant octopus."

Mom, Dad, and Sierra shiver.

"Let me carry you." I gingerly grab her under the arms. "Mom's not gonna like you tracking gunk across the house."

"Is she covered in nothingness slime or ink from a giant void octopus?" asks Dad.

"Squids make ink," says Sam. "It was a void octopus, not a void squid."

"Look at Sam, kraken wise," mutters Dad.

"Oh, dear." Mom facepalms.

I grimace. "Ouch, Dad."

He examines his fingernails. "What can I say, I'm a sucker for a good octopus pun."

Sam and Ronan exchange 'kill me now' glances.

"Duh, what am I doing?" Sophia rolls her eyes.

She waves her hands around like a wizard for a few seconds. The black gunk peels off her, revealing her pink nightgown. Strands of ooze gather into a floating glob of ink jelly. Poor Klepto gets pulled away and trapped in the amorphous mass—until she reappears in a flash of teleportation sparkles once again standing on Sophia's head, slime free.

"Can I flush this?" Sophia guides the floating mass toward the door.

"No worse than anything Sam did to the toilet," says Sierra.

The boy laughs.

"Wait, no. It'll clog." Sophia gestures at the window, which opens by itself. She sends the void slime ball outside, then flings it off at blurry speed.

A man screams in the distance.

"Oops," says Sophia.

Blix looks a little too innocent.

"Hey, Soph?" I ask. "What happened to the super sticky slime you threw out the window when you de-gunked Ronan?"

Sam rushes to the window and leans out, feet off the floor.

"No clue." Sophia shrugs.

"Hah." Sam snickers. "You got Mr. Niedermeyer right in the head."

"What's he doing in our yard?" asks Dad.

"He's not. He's in *his* front yard." Sam ducks back in the window and closes it.

Sophia starts walking for the door, but I grab her.

"Where are you going?"

"To apologize." She makes a sad face at me. "I didn't want to hit anyone."

"Apologize… and what? Admit to having magic? You can't."

She looks down.

Damn. Now I'm going to feel guilty for a week. Making Sophia upset is as emotionally damaging as drop-kicking bunny rabbits.

"It's just ink. He's fine. It'll wash off." Sam yawns. "It's almost eleven. We should go to sleep."

Mom and Dad exchange a look like they aren't sure if anyone here ought to get grounded for anything. Dr. Spock never offered advice on how to deal with void octopi or accidental teleportation.

"Yeah. Go to bed." Dad pats the girls on the shoulder. "You two okay or do you need to decompress?"

"I'm fine." Sierra shrugs.

"I guess." Sophia keeps staring at her feet. "It's mean to throw slime on old people."

"Soph." I hug her. "I know, but think about it. You didn't intend to hit him. And, how are you going to admit to being responsible without creating a whole bunch of trouble for everyone? The harm possibly caused by telling Niedermeyer about the supernatural stuff is way worse than having a face full of goop he can easily wash off."

She exhales. "Okay. You're right. I'm okay. It *was* kinda funny watching Klepto try to fight an octopus bigger than our house."

Klepto snarls playfully.

"Okay, everyone—except Sarah. Bedtime." Mom claps twice. "Sophia, no more scrying after dark."

"But, Mom! It wasn't my fault. The vampire messed with me."

"We'll talk about it tomorrow." Mom guides her out of Sam's room into the hall. "Go to bed."

Sophia looks at Sierra, who shrugs in an 'ugh, sure, okay' manner. Sophia follows her into Sierra's room. She's a little upset, doesn't want to sleep alone. At least I know she's not truly scared or she'd be asking to stay with me.

I'll take any wins we can get at this point, even if they're small.

30

A BRITTLE ALLIANCE

A promise is a promise, even if it's potentially evil of me.

Not going to hurt anyone directly. As soon as the 'rents deescalate from DEFCON 1, I pull my sneakers on, grab the katana, and fly to Petra Stanovaya's house. It's not a place I ever wanted to go again. Good chance she has human captives in there. This woman is the sort of vampire responsible for medieval peasants burning us at the stake.

However, I'm too young to do anything about her, no matter how much her activities horrify me. The best I can do is hope she remains afraid enough of the Shadows to keep her need for revenge against me set aside.

Whatever she may do in response to the information I have doesn't bother me too much considering the man who's causing all this trouble tried to kill me and my family multiple times, plus attacked various other vampires I consider my friends.

I approach the front door of her mansion. Coming here is more nerve wracking than being on stage at my high school talent show. In fact, it's like being a geeky kid forced to apologize to the bully who almost killed them because the bully smashed their hand while kicking my ass—and their parents are going to sue mine if I don't. I'm not paralyzed in fear. Even if Petra decides to freak out and attack me, I have a sword. Also, considering I want no part of a fight with her and no intention to go inside her house, it should be easy for me to get away.

Jaw clenched, I ring the bell.

A moment later, a tingle runs down my spine like I'm being watched by something malevolent. The feeling fades in seconds. Not long after, the door opens to reveal Petra. I must have interrupted her doing something 'special' since she's wearing a robe and likely nothing under it. She's so pale she looks fake, like department store mannequin white.

The woman gives me this irritated 'what do you want' glower until she notices the katana and switches to making a 'really?' face.

"Please don't mind the sword. I'm only carrying it in case the idiots causing trouble jump me again. Sorry to bother you, but I told you I'd let you know as soon as I found out who was responsible for the firebomb."

Her expression brightens to a scary sort of gleeful. "Oh? Which one of them did it?"

"No one in Seattle. There's another vampire somewhere by the name of Anselme Ernoul. He's trying to make everyone here turn on each other and start a war."

"I've heard of this man." Petra narrows her eyes. "From the Old World. If he really is involved, it may be time for me to find another city."

I blink. Uh oh. If someone as twisted as her is afraid of him, not a good sign. "Wow… that bad?"

She nods once. "The old ones have secrets you cannot even imagine. Look, it's been a long time since I've had a charitable thought toward anyone, especially a person who ruined my art, but I'll say this. If I were you, I'd collect my little family and stay well away from whatever Anselme wants."

"Yeah… I wasn't planning on being involved. Thanks. Oh, umm… just to clarify. It's not Wolent, Stefano, Paolo, Aurélie, the Shadows, or any random punks who are messing with you."

"I appreciate you keeping your word even though we are not friends."

What can I say? It's hard for me to consider taking delight in completely ruining people's lives and turning them into hollow, shattered shells a 'form of art.' I give her a weak smile. "Only doing my part for vampire peace… or something."

"Do you have any idea where he might be? Just so I know where *not* to go."

Petra taps her foot. "Even you aren't stupid enough to go after him."

Wow, is she showing some concern for my wellbeing here? "Honest. Not my plan."

"Ferreting out information like a good little girl for her boss."

Shrug. "Guilty as charged."

"As far as I am aware, he and his associates live in the Cathedral Tree Cemetery."

I raise an eyebrow.

"Not *live.* You know what I mean."

"Sorry, wasn't questioning the semantics of life versus dwelling. Never heard of Cathedral Tree Cemetery."

"Oh." She waves dismissively. "It's on the outskirts of Astoria, in Oregon. Can't say I've ever been there. I find graveyards woefully depressing."

This coming from a woman who ruins lives until people want to die.

Ack. Crow and 'Claude' weren't from Olympia. They had to have been flying to Seattle from Astoria. Yeah, total by chance meeting. Also, crap. I woke up chained to a tree outside Astoria. Dammit! Missed an obvious clue. Why didn't I even think to question the location? Guess I figured a couple of random idiots just went to a patch of remote woodlands.

"Okay. Thanks."

Petra regards me with an odd sort of look. Fingers crossed it's her way of trying to imply she's considering us to be 'over.' As in, she's gone from wanting to destroy me and only hesitating out of fear of retaliation to simply disliking me and having no further interest in my utter ruination.

Works for me.

"Night..." I take a step back.

She recedes into the house, closing the door.

Whew. Time to get out of here. It's not often a field mouse survives having a chat with an eagle.

31

NO LONGER MY PROBLEM

After making a quick stop home to grab the laptop, it's time to fly to Wolent's mansion.

Yeah, old vampires all seem to have mansions. So what? I don't care. Big houses don't impress me. They're a pain to clean and a person can only be in one room at a time, so what's the point of having fifty of them? I'd make a comment about property taxes, but I doubt Wolent—or any vampire—pays them. Then again, who knows? It might be less hassle to deal with it than have to re-mind-control someone every few decades.

Even though I have zero interest in ever owning a mansion, it pleases me a little to note Wolent's house is bigger than Petra's. They say there's no money in art, but how profitable can draining people's lives away to nothing be? Oh, wait. Really profitable… but she doesn't work for the healthcare industry.

Aziz greets me at the door. I spend a little while chatting with him. He's a sweet guy despite his size. No idea why people expect giant dudes to be either dumb as a rock or nasty. Admittedly, he *is* a Beast, so he can sometimes lose all control and turn into an uncontainable engine of destruction. No, not a toddler… a literal force of nature.

He must be good at controlling it since no one here ever seems afraid of him.

Anyway, I eventually go inside. One of the mortal assistants tells me Wolent is busy, and ushers me off to a sitting room to wait. I drum my fingers on the laptop. The silent room gets me worrying about what Petra said. If this Anselme Ernoul guy is a mystic and a vampire, he might be able to do that 'scrying' thing and realize I'm the one who's handing over this information to Wolent.

Petra being frightened of him is impressive, but she's also frightened of Shadows. Not dark spots. I mean the vampires. My sister Sophia is frightened of actual shadows. Or used to be. Petra might be afraid of Sophia if she knew about her talents. She'd *definitely* be afraid of Sam. Well, not so much Sam but Mel the succubus. Pretty much any entity capable of snapping their fingers and causing the instantaneous combustion of a vampire into sparkly bits is something to be afraid of. Rumor has it excessive amounts of disco music can also cause vampires to explode in flames.

For whatever reason, the woman appeared to be afraid of vampires from the 'Old World' as if they're some mythically powerful creatures. Hopefully, she's referring to Europe when she says 'old world' and she hasn't gone full Cthulhu. You never go full Cthulhu. Granted, my sister's closet is occasionally home to giant void tentacles.

Can't get in much more trouble by giving the laptop to Wolent than we're already in. If Anselme really did notice Sophia attempting to magically spy on his operation, he's already going to be regarding her-slash-my family as a threat. Maybe he already did, which explains the zombie attack. Why poke us though? Did he expect those zombies to succeed or were we a trial run? Suppose it hurt his ego when my kid sister killed three of them 'herself.' I doubt he saw the hellhound. Explains why the next time zombies happened—at the hibachi restaurant—he sent a small army of them.

I really shouldn't call them zombies. It's not accurate, but it's much easier to say than 'remote-operated ambulatory corpses.'

Hmm. Might as well check out this laptop. I open it, log in, and start poking around. One folder—created right on the desktop—holds files containing notes on various Seattle vampires including me. Their photo of me is from the night the two idiots attacked me in the parking garage at the school. One of them must have taken it before asking me to kick their ass. They have a photo of Sophia as well, apparently taken via a long-distance lens as she walked from school to her bus. I have to laugh at the big red lettering spelling out 'dangerous' across the bottom of the image.

Few things say 'deadly threat' like a twig of a blonde tween in a pink dress wearing a pink Hello Kitty backpack.

No photos of Sierra, Sam, or my parents. Every other picture in the folder is a vampire. I notice they don't have any photos of the elders, or any Shadows regardless of their age. The text documents *do* have info on everyone, including the elders (no Shadows though). It's weird and spotty. Lists of random facts contain stuff like 'had a legal battle with so and so in 1934' or 'hates the new girl.' The comments on Eleanor St. Ives mention she 'had past discontent' with me. Apparently, Paolo Cabrini regards me as an 'insult to vampire kind.'

Well F you, too, asshole.

The Exxon Valdez called. They want their oil back. I'm talking about his hair. I swear it could deflect bullets. How the heck did they find out so much secret stuff? All the elders suspect Aurélie of lying about not having any interest in politics. Most of them believe she's really in control of the city by virtue of charming Wolent. *His* notes don't support the idea. Despite her being way older than him, he regards her as a 'young, delicate woman.'

Stefano thinks the Shadows are really pulling the strings despite their claims of being neutral observers.

Curious the files have zero info on any of the Shadows.

Notes on me are pretty limited, too. Mostly pointing out my issues with Stefano, Paolo, Petra, and Anatoly Zharkov, the vampire who owns the Abaddon night club. Stupid spyglass. Why I ever agreed to help Dalton steal it, I still don't really understand.

The last item in my section says 'beware Fuzzydoom.' Then, WTF is 'Fuzzydoom.'

Done.

I cackle.

Once I recover my composure, I keep reading. Looks like this laptop contains an incredible amount of information about Seattle vampire society. Properties, businesses, homes, comments about who deals with who, who hates who, and so forth.

How did they get all this stuff? How could anyone *possibly* know about Fuzzydoom?

Oh, duh. I slap myself in the forehead. Anselme is a mystic. He must be scrying for information, getting it from the spirit world. Hmm. Wonder if the reason he has nothing on the Shadows is because their hidden hall is shielded somehow from supernatural spying? Seeing the note of 'dangerous' on Sophia's picture makes me slightly less afraid of Anselme. He's probably still a total badass, but if a kid with some barely controlled magical abilities is a threat, the man's probably not untouchable.

"Sarah," calls Wolent as he enters. "Sorry for keeping you waiting. I wish the fools told me who wanted to see me."

He doesn't mean to imply I'm any sort of VIP. More like I'm working on an important assignment he's keenly interested in. "I have information."

"Excellent." He walks over.

I stand at his approach. Might as well be formal. We sit at the same time in facing chairs.

"The man responsible for these attacks is a vampire named Anselme Ernoul." I offer the laptop. "His people have collected a ton of info on us here."

Wolent's eyebrow ticks a slight bit up. Something about his expression gives off a sense he knows of him but either doesn't remember much about him or only heard the name in passing. "A computer?"

He already knows about Sophia since it's literally impossible for me to keep secrets from a vampire so much older than me. I explain the messed-up scrying, Sierra getting yanked unintentionally across Seattle to a warehouse, the resulting fight, and everything she overheard them talking about. Without a doubt, he's watching it all unfold in my head. No problem. It's not because he doesn't trust me, he's probably looking at faces to see if he recognizes anyone. Plus reading thoughts is like a hundred times faster than speaking. He's certainly sent people to check out the warehouse already, but it's not obvious he's learned much from it yet. Perhaps the meeting he'd been in when I arrived involved the vamps he sent to check on the place.

"I spoke with Petra before coming here tonight."

"Isn't she trying to destroy you?"

"We're not friends, really. This all started—at least for me—with her showing up to threaten me for firebombing her house. She assumed I did it. To keep her from shredding me, I promised to share whatever information I found about who really did it. She knows of Anselme, said he lives in Astoria, at Cathedral Tree Cemetery. He's also a mystic, which explains how he's turning cadavers stolen from mortuaries into weapons. Also makes sense how he got this information. Must be from scrying or snorting tea leaves."

He glances at the laptop.

"It's got notes, photos, information, many secrets." I lean forward, lowering my voice. "I think Anselme is using magic to pluck secrets out of the spirit world. All these comments sound like things he can use to set the elders against each other."

"Interesting. What did you read?"

"Are you implying I know nothing of this or seriously asking?"

He smiles. "I'd appreciate your confidentiality. However, the question was sincere."

"Most of it is stuff like who had a dispute or bad blood with who. Things an agitator could use to exploit. Like… how the elders think Aurélie is controlling you and running things by proxy."

Wolent chuckles. "It doesn't take strange mystical means to pick up on that old rumor. I'll let you in on a little secret." Wolent taps his head by his right eye. "Furies are really damn difficult to charm. Comes from being hard-headed."

I smile.

"All right, kid." He pats the laptop. "This is a great find. Stay alert and keep your head down. The waves are going to be getting a bit choppy around here soon."

"Yes, sir."

He escorts me to the door personally, wishes me well, and walks briskly back inside.

Something tells me I may have launched the vampire equivalent of an ICBM at this Anselme guy. Nah. Not my fault. Dude whacked a hornet's nest. It's time for him to get stung. Hmm. Is *starting* a war the best way to go about stopping one? Fingers crossed we're not about to see an all-out vampiric shitstorm between Astoria and Seattle.

32

THE WALKING DERP

Other than carrying a sword at all times, my life is quiet for a few days.

Mom and Dad think the 'forces of evil' have gotten bored with me because I'm not politically significant and they've already failed to leverage the animosity certain parties have over me as a useful tool to create instability. Dad suggests Anselme didn't have a particular problem with me, merely thought I'd be a means by which he could get Aurélie and Stefano/Paolo going at it. Since it didn't work, no further need to mess with me.

Here's hoping.

Unlife goes on, as they say. Okay, no one says that. *They* say 'life goes on,' but the sentiment is the same. So, yeah. School, homework, taking Sophia to Dance class or Sam/Sierra to Taekwondo when Mom gets stuck at work, hanging out here and there with Ashley, Michelle and/or Hunter is a nice change of pace. I'm afraid to feel too normal because it will piss the Universe off. I'm *definitely* not letting my guard down about the Anselme situation until Wolent or Aurélie tell me it's over.

By now, maybe some of Wolent's people went to Astoria and pounded Anselme and his associates into a thin red paste... but no one's said anything yet. Oh, Mr. Niedermeyer ended up being interviewed by a paranormal YouTube guy due to his claim aliens threw 'an unidentified black substance' at him. The dude was so pissed off at 'kids pranking him,' he legit called the cops. They tested the slime and couldn't determine what it was. I heard their lab equipment did some *funky* things after exposure to the stuff.

Yeah, the PIBs found out about it. Yeah, they paid me a visit.

I also brought them up to speed on what I knew about Anselme. Not sure whatever department they work for has the resources to deal with vampire-related unrest, but they appeared content to hear my information and leave—not before asking me to make Mr. Niedermeyer forget the black goop entirely. They also had the YouTube guy in their van. Yeah, I had to erase his memory of the interview, too.

Honestly, it didn't bug me to do since it's not a conspiracy capable of hurting anyone. Bothered me more they had the guy handcuffed and hooded. Kidnapping a dude is totally icky. I would've gone to the guy's place to erase his mind. But I guess the government's obliging about delivery mind alteration. Right to my doorstep.

It's once again a Wednesday night. Strange thing about days… they recur every week.

Dad declares a spontaneous movie night after dinner when all the friends have gone home.

He puts on *Maximum Overdrive.*

Interesting premise. Various machines somehow come to life and try to kill people. Everything from toasters to trucks. Sierra thinks it's hilarious. Sophia's scared. Great, she's probably going to be hesitant around appliances for a few days. The movie makes Mom and Dad nostalgic looking at various gadgets like they had in the house as kids. Blenders, wall phones, radios, and so on.

Right around the time the people take shelter in the building while all the cars surround them outside, I get this sudden weird feeling. The air in the room gets heavier, almost like a house-sized beach ball is resting on my head.

Dad apparently notices an odd look on my face and pauses the movie. "Sare? You okay?"

"Fine, but I'm picking up some kind of odd telepathic energy." I concentrate on the unexplained feeling, reaching out mental feelers in an attempt to make sense of it. *Hello? Who or what is this?* After a moment of not getting a reply, I shrug. "It's like I'm trying to make contact with an entity of some kind nearby, but whatever it is doesn't feel truly conscious. It's possibly alive, but like, only at the edge of being sentient. It might not even be aware of its own existence."

"Is Kanye at the door?" asks Dad.

Mom covers her mouth, holding back a laugh.

"Or Uncle Hank," deadpans Sam.

The girls laugh.

"Uncle Hank is definitely aware of his own existence, and he's determined to punish everyone for it," I mutter.

A splintering crash comes from the back yard.

Sam perks up, looking toward the kitchen.

"Even *I* heard that. Probably a deer crashing over the fence." Mom gets up and heads to the kitchen to look.

A loud shattering of glass precedes Mom screaming.

I grab my katana—yes, I had it with me for movie night—and leap over the back of the sofa. I have a clear view through the dining room into the kitchen at the patio door, which is in a million pieces on the floor, smashed open by a pair of 'zombies' forcing their way inside. Mom jumps back from a hand trying to grab her.

Three of them push past the frame of the patio door, bending it inward. One gets caught up in the twisted metal and falls on his face, his two pals walking over him toward Mom. I run to the kitchen, going after the zombie closest to my mother. He doesn't react at all to my approach, giving me a nice easy shot at his neck. A swipe of my katana launches his head across the kitchen into the sink. I rear back and punt him in the chest, throwing the body out the door into the yard.

Dad grapples the second standing corpse, struggling to pin him against the wall where the patio door used to attach. Klepto appears on his head in a flash of teleportation sparkles, dangling a red headband from her mouth. Once she notices my father's hands are a bit occupied, the kitten puts it on for him.

"Thanks, kitty," growls Dad in between grunts.

I chop the head off the corpse who got tangled up in the frame of the door. Oh, damn, he stinks. The body isn't rotting… just the dead blood dribbling out of his neck stump smells astoundingly nauseating to vampires. It's worse than a bag of potatoes forgotten in a drawer until they decompose into dark liquid. I grab the body and toss it out the door.

Another corpse jumps on me from behind and bites me on the side of the neck.

Some idiot vampire forgot he's piloting a dead body without fangs.

Splat!

Brain matter showers over me, covering Dad, the wall, the floor. The arms around me lose strength as the body goes limp and collapses. I sheepishly turn to look behind me and there's Mom, examining the bottom of her two-handed iron skillet.

"Oh, dear…" Mom cringes at the gore on the walls. "Is that going to wash off?"

My D&D-loving father considers the skillet an enchanted weapon he calls 'Imp's Bane.' Doesn't matter it couldn't kill an imp. They're surprisingly resistant to blunt force trauma. Need superhuman strength to make them burst open. Mom *did* knock a few loopy enough to leave them vulnerable to being caught and stabbed, but the skillet didn't directly kill any.

"Maybe." I put the katana to the throat of the body Dad's holding against the wall and slice the head off.

He tosses the corpse outside, then gasps for breath.

"Didn't think I hit him that hard," mutters Mom.

"They do seem to be a little squishy," I say.

"What are they?" asks Mom.

"Zombies." Dad nods once. "Obviously. More are coming."

I look out into the yard. At least fifteen stumbling dead people shuffle toward us. One steps on Sam's soccer ball and wipes out.

Another literally clotheslines itself on Mom's clothes line, and falls over backward, arms flailing. Two crash into each other and get tangled in something like a sloppy kiss.

"Wow, it's like watching remote control robot wars if they gave the controllers to the visually impaired." I chuckle. "They're not a serious problem. More annoying than dangerous."

Sword high, I jog out to confront them before they get into the house. Loose brain matter is much less of a cleaning problem on grass than in the kitchen. Dad runs around the swarm, heading for the tool shed. Eep, he's going for the weed-whacker I bet. Zombies start chasing him. Dad barely managed to hold one off. He's not going to handle four at a time.

"Mom, guard the doorway!" I yell before racing over to keep them away from my father.

It occurs to me, in addition to the ones walking around, the yard's littered with the remains of about twenty more bodies already torn to shreds. Never thought I'd say this, but having a hellhound is *really* handy. Equally effective at stopping random zombie invasions and door-to-door salesmen.

The buzzing of the weed whacker engine starts up in the shed. Dad appears at the doorway, headband flowing in the wind, weed-eater held high and revving. He's a combination of Chevy Chase and Conan, heavy on the Chevy but way closer to Egon.

Know what's really bizarre? Watching someone decapitate zombies with a weed-eater.

These bodies *are* unusually squishy. Since Dad appears to have things under control, I slash my way back to the door where Mom's playing whack-a-rat. They might have overwhelmed her if not for how they keep tripping over their fallen brethren.

Shouts at the other end of the house tell me the Littles are fending off a frontal assault. Oh, dammit… I'm about to panic until I realize they don't sound worried. Mostly Sierra yelling 'one over there' and Sophia chiming 'got him' every like fifteen seconds. Blix occasionally emits a war screech.

I can't even call fighting these things 'fighting.' It's like practicing my katana technique on bundled straw mats capable of wandering around. Sure, they're *trying* to cave my face in, but they're kinda slow.

A few seconds after the sounds of battle fade, a flamethrower blast goes off in the yard, lighting three moving corpses at once.

"Whoa!" yells Dad over the idling weed-whacker.

Seeing no more moving bodies, I walk over to him. "You okay?"

"Yeah, fine." He holds his gardening tool with the bravado of a soldier carrying an M-60 machine gun. I imagine his headband wavering in a breeze. Pity the wind's calm.

"I'm impressed. You overpowered a zombie."

He wags his eyebrows. "My family was in danger."

"Still… Those things are abnormally strong."

"Well… you know how parents can sometimes lift cars off their kids in times of crisis. I had a lot of motivation."

Oh, no… what sort of supernatural craziness is going on with my Dad now? Is Dalton giving him hits of blood on the sly, too?

Another flamethrower blast lights up some body parts.

Bewildered, Mom wanders a few steps out from the smashed patio door. "Sophia? Are you using magic past your bedtime?"

"She didn't do this," I say.

A moment later, Sophia appears in the gaping hole of our former patio door. "This wasn't me… and you guys said it was okay for us to stay up a little late to watch the movie." She points back over her shoulder into the house. "We have dead people in the living room."

Mom groans.

"Don't freak out. There's no stains on the rug. Sierra didn't have to use her sword. Mr. Anderson's suggestion worked! Dispelling magic turns them off." Sophia smiles. "Easy."

I crouch to wipe gore off my blade on a dead guy's sweat pants. "Yeah. They're basically remote-control toys. You're shutting down the signal so they go back to being ordinary cadavers. The greatest crime here is someone wasted new clothes on walking corpses."

"I'm glad they did… this would have been ten times more horrible if we had to fight a hoard of naked zombies." Mom shudders.

Both of my sisters chime, "Eww!" simultaneously.

"Some of them still have ID bracelets." Dad holds up an arm. Yes, it's still attached to a body on the ground. "They raided a morgue this time."

"Oh, Blix lit one on fire," says Sophia, "but the curtains are out now."

A sheepish imp warble comes from deeper inside the house.

Mom points at the burning patches. "What is going on? Where did that fire come from?"

Sam appears in the doorway beside Sophia. He looks like he's expecting to get in a ton of trouble. "It's Max."

"Max?" asks everyone at the same time.

"He's my friend." Sam forces a big smile. "Please don't be mad."

Mom and Dad exchange an 'oh, what now' glance.

33

SORTA, ALMOST, BUT NOT QUITE CANINE

Oh, the hellhound. Right. He named it Max.

"I don't see anything." Mom stares at the burning body parts littered around the backyard.

"He's invisible." Sam walks out to stand beside Mom.

"Careful, hon. You don't have shoes on. Watch where you step." Mom puts an arm around him.

"Invisible?" asks Dad.

"Aren't you a little old for an imaginary friend?" Mom rubs Sam's back.

"Allie, 'imaginary friends' don't breathe *real* fire." Dad cuts the weed-eater's engine, leans it against the shed wall, and cautiously approaches Sam. "You didn't happen to bring a dragon home, did you?"

Sam chuckles. "No, Dad. He's not a dragon. He's nice."

A heavy grunt emanates from the back corner of the yard.

Mom stiffens, looking toward it. "Samuel, what is 'Max.'"

"Umm." The boy grinds a toe into the lawn. "He's kind of a dog."

"Define 'kind of,'" says Mom.

Sam looks down.

A minute passes.

"Sam?" asks Dad.

"Umm, he's a..." the boy mumbles 'hellhound.'

"What?" Mom cups a hand under his chin, lifting his gaze to make eye contact. "Please don't mumble."

"Promise you won't freak out?" asks Sam.

"Oh, this is going to be bad." Dad appears to be fighting the urge to laugh.

"He's not bad. I just don't want Mom to get crazy angry and not think about stuff." Sam hugs her. "Please? Just be calm."

"Okay, Sam." Mom exhales. "Tell me what Max is."

"He's a hellhound... but it's not bad."

"Hell... hound." Mom's right eye twitches.

Dad glances at the yard's far corner. "Is he housebroken?"

"Jonathan!" Mom gasps at him.

"Uhh, technically, yes." Sam scratches the back of his head. "He hasn't been in the house yet. But if you mean will he pee or poo inside, it's not possible."

Dad seems to finally realize the girls are standing in the doorway. "Careful, you two. There's broken glass all over the floor and neither one of you has shoes on."

"Why do you sound so surprised?" asks Sierra. "Shoes in the house is a class-A felony."

Mom flattens her eyebrows.

"Drat. This is gonna be expensive." Dad sighs at the wreckage of the patio door. "Sare, will you give me a hand hanging a tarp for the night?"

"Yeah, no problem."

Sophia gives off a faint cloud of light. She swipes both hands upward as if tossing a tennis ball for a dog to chase. A storm of twisted metal and glass bits rush into the air, swirling around for a few seconds before reintegrating into an intact sliding door as if we watched video of a bomb destroying it played backward. The sound coming from the metal frame as it bent itself back into place nearly makes my over-amped ears bleed.

"Never mind the tarp." Dad blinks.

"Neat trick," I say, still cringing from the high-pitched squeal.

Sophia grins. "I've figured out how to selectively reverse the time stream for only one object. Reality considers 'the patio door' to be one object, so it got all the different pieces in one spell."

"Not enough wine in the world," mutters Mom.

"You don't drink that much." I nudge her.

"Another few years of this and I might start."

"Aww." I hug her.

Dad opens and closes the sliding door. "Amazing."

"Uhh, we still have a bunch of body parts in the yard," deadpans Sierra.

"Oh, I'm sure the hellhound will devour them," says Mom, heavy on the sarcasm.

"No." Sam shakes his head. "He doesn't eat physical food. Max feasts on the discontent, misery, and suffering of mortals stuck in an endless cycle of an unfulfilling existence from which they cannot escape."

The 'rents stare at him.

"Well then." Mom blinks. "I better not take him to the office. He'd get fat."

Sierra snickers. "Oh, he's going to *love* Uncle Hank."

"Yeah." I smirk. "The way most dogs love Snausages."

Dad laughs.

Mom swats at him. "You're not supposed to laugh at that."

"Why not, exactly?" I tilt my head. "Hank *is* miserable and discontent. It's not making fun of him to state fact."

"So, umm…" Dad quirks an eyebrow. "Shall we drag all the bodies out here for cremation?"

"They're people." Mom flicks her skillet, tossing a bit of hairy scalp off to the side. "Stolen bodies. We can't simply destroy them all."

Dad rubs his chin. "Do you have a good excuse to give to the police why we have thirty corpses on our property?"

"More like forty." Sierra points at the house. "You're not counting the pile in the living room."

"*Pile?*" asks Mom.

"Yeah," say the kids at the same time.

"They kept walking in the door and falling over as Soph dispelled them." Sam laughs.

Sophia smiles.

"Straight out of *Looney Tunes.*" Sierra shakes her head. "I didn't even need to use my sword. They just walked in and dropped dead in a single-file line."

My parents start debating the idea of Max incinerating the bodies or not incinerating the bodies. After a minute of them discussing it, I cut them off.

"Guys. Idea." I hold up my phone. "Let me call the PIBs. If you don't want to burn the remains, I'm sure Kendricks and Han will be able to deal with the bodies and get them back to wherever they came from without anyone being the wiser. They can smooth it over."

"It's probably a better idea. Someone might find bones in the yard later and suspect us of being serial killers," says Sierra.

Mom looks at her. "What kinds of TV shows are you watching, young lady?"

"The news." Sierra's delivery is so straight-faced I can't tell if she's serious or being sarcastic.

Dad chuckles, then nods at me. "Yeah, call the PIBs. See what they say."

"Okay."

As if on cue, my phone rings before I can open the contacts app. Uh oh. It's Wolent.

I swipe to answer. "Hello?"

"Sarah. I'd like to speak with you as soon as you're able to get here. It is important."

Good: the tone of his voice doesn't sound like I'm in trouble. Bad: he's probably going to want me to do something.

"Yes, sir. I'll be right there."

"Now what?" asks Mom.

"Wolent wants to see me." I swipe to dial the PIBs. "Give me a sec to get this started, then I gotta go see what he wants."

Mom and Dad exchange nervous glances.

A weird noise comes from the back of the yard.

We all turn to look.

Sam's waving his arms around as if skritching and petting a dog tall enough to be eye level with him. Max emits a series of noises somewhere between happy puppy and the mating call of a demonic whale being sucked backward into a black hole—or as most people know it, dubstep.

Wow… my life.

"Kendricks," says a voice on the phone.

"Umm, hi. It's Sarah." I head inside so he doesn't hear the dog. "Got a minute?"

34

SOMEWHAT LESS CORDIAL

Calling someone to have dead bodies removed from your house on the quiet is weird.

It's not something I ever imagined doing for real. When did I end up in a Tarantino movie? Surprisingly, Agent Kendricks understood and agreed to help. They seemed almost *too* interested in helping clean it up. They're probably going to rubber-glove the bodies from a supernatural standpoint. To them, this is like Agent Mulder finally finding a dead alien body.

They understood I had to run an errand and may or may not be there when their crew shows up.

On the flight to Wolent's estate, I debate the attack on my house. Why were those zombies so squishy and uncoordinated? Maybe Anselme tried to control too many at once, so couldn't focus too well. Doesn't explain their odd squishiness. I suppose 'magic does weird things' could be a factor. Might be the mystical version of microwaving a Hot Pocket too long. Wait no, bad example. Nuking a Hot Pocket too long produces the hardest substance known to science. Similar principle though.

The big question is, did Anselme send these as a serious attempt to kill us, or is he waving his ass at us and daring me to do something?

Could the attack have been the mystic vampire equivalent of TP-ing my house as a middle finger for messing up his plans? Aurélie didn't seem too worried about him. This is going to sound crazy, but one of her dolls said he's afraid of her.

Might explain why she hasn't been targeted by any attacks. Also, living way up off the ground in a penthouse apartment accessible only via flight or a secured elevator helps. Even for someone with vampire strength, it's a pain in the ass to throw a Molotov upward thirty-six stories.

My guess is, Anselme is afraid of her due to her charm aura. It's unlikely she could kill him with it, but she'd definitely be able to shut anyone down and send them away. I still have no idea how old this guy is or if Petra simply meant Europe by 'Old World' or specifically *Medieval* Europe. She seemed terrified of him, but it's understandable. Even watching Sophia has me highly worried about what mystics *might* be capable of.

I don't figure anything out before arriving at Arthur Wolent's estate.

Aziz opens the door for me. "Hello, Sarah. He's waiting for you in the study."

"Thank you, Aziz."

He groans.

"What?"

"Sorry. Ever since that movie *Fifth Element* came out, I hear 'thank you, Aziz' in my sleep."

"Oh. Duh. Sorry. Wasn't trying to…" I smile cheesily.

He chuckles. "It's fine."

One rule to a long, healthy unlife: do not piss off a man who has biceps as big as your torso.

When I arrive at the study, I'm surprised to find Vanessa there, as well as Henry Arnold and a handsome thirtyish black guy in an expensive shimmery blue suit who I don't recognize. Guy feels like a mortal, but still has a noticeable aura of power. Has to be enthralled. Bet he's connected to some company Wolent owns. More than likely, he's the inside man there to keep an eye on things.

I nod in greeting to everyone. "Sorry I'm a couple minutes late. Had a mess to clean up at the house. More guided corpses."

Grimaces and noises of distaste come from everyone.

"Sarah." Wolent walks out from behind his desk to do the usual handshake plus not-quite-kiss greeting. "Good of you to come. You know Vanessa, of course. This is Tyrell Bray, an associate of mine."

Tyrell bows in greeting.

"Hey." I wave.

Vanessa smiles at me.

I return her smile, then look back to Wolent. "You said it's important. Happy to help whenever I can."

He clasps his hands in front of himself like he's about to give me important or bad news. Fingers crossed it's important. "I would like you to take advantage of daylight to deliver a little present to Anselme Ernoul."

Can't help but stare at the duffel bag. Uh oh. What's in there?

"My people have located his lair." Wolent gestures at a TV screen on the wall, which comes to life showing a photograph of a typical looking old, ivy-covered mausoleum crypt. Moss fills in the grooves of the engraved name 'Barnaby' above the entrance. Based on the scale of the door, I'd guess the building is about the size of an old one-room schoolhouse.

"Looks kinda cramped. Do they just sleep in there?" I raise an eyebrow.

"As you should know by now"—Wolent winks—"looks are often deceptive. The crypt contains a concealed entrance to an underground complex where roughly forty vampires dwell."

"Wow. Forty?" I blink.

"Exactly. I fear a direct fight would be entirely too messy. Roaches like this deserve to be stepped on."

I eye the duffel. Yeah, pretty sure it's a bomb. "All right. I'll do it. Can I ask a question?"

Wolent nods. "Of course."

"I'm curious why you're sending me and not a mortal thrall who's like a pro at demolition."

He grins, patting me on the arm. "No need to be nervous, Sarah. It is a fair question. I have several reasons. One, vampires can smell mortals more easily than other vampires. If a mortal entered the lair, their presence would disturb the vampires and wake them. You would have to create a disturbance in order to stir Anselme and his associates from their diurnal slumber."

I nod.

"Two, once you are inside underground in the dark, you will have a much better chance of survival should anything go wrong. A mortal thrall would be far more vulnerable. Three, it's easier for you to cover your trail. If any mortal authorities end up investigating your involvement here, you can personally make them remember whatever you like. Reason four, the complex is hidden under a large stone too heavy for a single mortal to move."

"Wow," I whisper.

"Five..." Wolent's grin broadens. "I trust you more than a random mortal thrall."

I smile back at him. "Sounds good. I'll do my best."

When I reach for the duffel, Wolent waves me off.

Tyrell lifts one of those pale grey metal suitcases out from behind the desk. It's pretty big, like a full-sized suitcase. He sets it flat on the desk, turns it to face me, and opens it. Inside are mostly packages of grey stuff like modeling clay. The stuff doesn't look exactly like movie plastic explosives, being sparkly, as if fine bits of metal are infused in it. Way too small to be shrapnel pieces, more like shavings. A small keypad and display screen at the front of the case looks straight out of a spy movie.

"Sarah..." Tyrell gestures at the panel. "The device is reasonably simple. If you've used a microwave oven, you can operate this. Type in a number representing minutes and seconds from one to ninety-nine minutes. The system won't accept a value lower than one minute, so it's pretty hard to blow yourself up."

I chuckle nervously. "Well, that's good."

"Insert the key here, turn it as far to the right as it will go. Engaging the key turns on the number pad. After you enter the time, lift this safety guard and push the red button to arm the device. The timer will start when you remove the key." Tyrell taps a plastic shroud over a square button. "At any point before detonation, pushing this same button three times rapidly will pause the countdown. If you put the key back in and turn it all the way left while the countdown is paused, you will disarm the device."

"Okay."

He hands me a keyring with two keys. One's got a round, hollow end like for a vending machine, almost like a tiny socket wrench. Other key is normal. Guessing it goes to the locks on the suitcase.

"I suggest you be far away from it when it goes off." Wolent squeezes my shoulder. "Don't underestimate the amount of time you need."

"All right."

Tyrell closes the case.

I grab the handle and—after giving myself a mild strength boost—pick it up as easily as an empty plastic box. A bomb is most likely only going to piss Anselme's people off, but maybe a couple days of digging themselves out will change their mind about messing with us.

"I'll get it done tomorrow."

"Excellent."

"Be careful, dear," says Vanessa. "That's not a firecracker. It's a bit like you. Appears small to an untrained eye, but is surprisingly potent."

Heh. I smile, trying not to feel patronized. Vanessa has no problem with me at all. She's a little catty with Aurélie but it's purely a jealousy thing about beauty. "Understood."

I make my way out and head down the hall to the front door.

Gee. Wolent's sending me to deliver a message again, but this one's a little less cordial.

35

FATHER DAUGHTER PROJECT

When I walk in the door at home, I'm shocked to see everyone still awake.

Sierra's in the middle of a top-down fantasy type game on the PlayStation. Sophia's reclining on the sofa, playing with Klepto. Sam's absorbed in his PSP. The 'rents are both reading. My father's munching on something.

"Wow, it's after eleven. Can't sleep?" I ask while kicking my shoes off.

"We waited for you to finish the movie," says Dad. "C'mon over."

I head for the kitchen, pausing behind the couch. "One sec. Gotta put this downstairs."

Dad looks back at me. I notice he's eating a Devil Dog.

I stare at him.

"Sorry," he mumbles past chocolate cake. "Got a sudden craving."

"Wow. Dad, you're a walking pun."

"We know this, but what do you mean?" asks Sierra.

I point at the snack cake. "Devil Dog… hellhound?"

Sam smiles. Sierra biffs herself in the forehead. Sophia gives him a 'wow, Dad, really?' look.

Blix perks up to look at me. Chocolate residue marks his lips.

Doesn't look like the Littles have had any. Probably a good idea not to give them sugar before they go to bed. Not wise for Dad to have one this late either, but as they say, 'it's good to be the king.'

"Blix." I pat the case. "Please do not mess with this."

He emits a high-pitched, "Ee-ooba."

"Blix says he won't," says Sam, not looking up from his handheld game. "Wants to know why you asked."

"It's a powerful bomb."

Mom nearly drops her book. "Young lady! What did I tell you about bringing destructive devices into this house?"

"You let Sam's butt inside," deadpans Sierra.

My brother appears proud of himself.

I shrug. "Technically, Mom, you never actually said we weren't allowed to bring thirty pounds of plastic explosives in the house."

Sierra gawks at me.

Mom almost throws her Kindle up in frustration. "Sarah! That's not normally the sort of thing parents *have* to specify. It should be assumed."

"Holy shit," whispers Sierra. "Thirty *pounds?*"

Sighing, Mom gives her side eye.

Sierra pauses her game, jumps to her feet, and gestures at me. "Sare's holding thirty *pounds* of Semtex, and you're going to get mad at me for saying 'holy shit'? She's carrying a bomb big enough to put our house into orbit. If it goes off, the biggest piece of our home left will be a toothpick."

"Sierra." Dad raises an eyebrow at her. "I'm a little concerned you know what Semtex is."

"Oh, come on." Sierra points the controller in her hand at the TV. "It's in *Call of Duty.*"

I glance at the metal suitcase. "I'm honestly not sure what kind of bomb this is. There's a strange metal powder mixed into the plastic explosive. It's gotta be something really nasty if Wolent thinks it's going to be effective on a vampire nest. Only thing I know for sure is I *don't* want it going off inside the house."

"Neither do I." Mom stares at me. "Are you sure about this, Sarah?

Remember what happened last time you tried to bomb a vampire den."

I hold up a finger. "Wasn't me. Dalton did that. I got caught in the fallout. Besides, I have Wolent's blessing for this. It's an official operation, not a private vendetta. We will have backup if the poop hits the fan."

My mother lets out a defeated sigh. "We're really talking about this."

"We are," says Dad. "It's okay, dear. Kids will eventually grow up, get a career, plant huge bombs in dens of dangerous vampires. It's normal. The way life goes."

Mom stares at him.

"So, uhh, Dad..." I rock heel to toe. "Can you help me with an afterschool project? Err, technically a before-school project?"

"Sure. It'll be nice to have some father-daughter time. Been a while. What's the project?"

I pat the bomb. "Bad vampire nest needs gone."

Mom facepalms.

"Absolutely!" Dad practically shouts, dripping with eagerness.

"Jonathan!" Mom grabs him.

"Relax, Allie. She's just going to ask me for a ride because she can't fly during the day, and doesn't feel safe driving when she can barely see."

I blink. First, he breaks even wrestling a zombie, now he's reading minds? "Umm, Dad? Whoa. Are you psychic now?"

"Nope." Dad smiles. "You said 'before school,' which means during daylight. Also, the only reason I can think of it making any sense for Arthur Wolent to have his most junior person do a mission like this is your unique talent."

"Yeah. Okay. True." I heft the bomb. "Gonna go stash this in my room and be right back."

Wow. Tomorrow can *not* show up fast enough. I really don't like having a giant bomb in the house.

36

MISSION HIGHLY IMPROBABLE

I wake up at 2:12 p.m., the earliest my eyes have opened in months.

Apparently, enough stress *can* affect a vampire's circadian rhythm, or whatever it's called for us. To calm myself a bit, I think about the notes questioning what the hell Fuzzydoom is. I haven't told Sophia about the picture marked 'dangerous' or the comment about her nightmare monster. She'd be terrified if she knew someone took her picture from afar, and mentioning the giant pom-pom of annihilation might tempt her to try summoning it to get rid of Anselme. Considering most of her attempts to use magic end up going awry, her summoning Fuzzydoom into the real world would set off a chain of events likely to destroy the entire planet. Not worth risking.

Yeah, I'm nervous, but having the bomb in the house makes me way more nervous than what I'm expected to do with it. Despite it being 'early' for me to be awake, I spring out of bed and throw on some black leggings left over from a former waitress job, a black T-shirt, black hoodie, and my darkest brown hiking sneakers. The only black shoes I have are 'starter' high heels. They're a bit formal for a bombing, I think.

The leggings are a bit iffy, too. If I'm going to end up doing crazy stuff like this, maybe I should get some baggy military style pants in black. Skin tight isn't really practical. Whatever. Don't have the time to worry about it now. This bomb needs to be out of the house ASAP. I rig the katana on a cord across by back, add a pair of sunglasses, pick up the suitcase, and head upstairs. Kitchen's a little warm, but I'm too nervous to care.

"Dad?" I call.

"Yo!" comes from his computer room.

"Ready to do this?"

"Sure am." He hurries out of the small room. The white polo and khakis are totally secret agent level gear. "Wow... you look like an urban commando."

"Yeah. I know. Pretty silly, right? It's bright out and I look like a hole in space. Even underground, black won't help. If they wake up, I'm going to be easy to spot."

He grins. "Well, don't wake them up."

"Yeah. That's the plan."

We go outside together to the Sentra. It's seriously warm, but I don't feel like someone stuck me in the microwave. No smoke either. Unfortunately, the brightness still messes with my eyes. Despite sunglasses, the world is way too intense for me to drive safely. According to my phone, it's going to take us three hours and eighteen minutes to reach Astoria. We'll probably get there around 5:30 p.m. If it takes me ten minutes—ha, I should be so lucky—to drop off Wolent's present, it'll be around nine before we get home. Expected sunset time is 8:01 p.m. If I leap out of the moving car and fly, I could potentially make it to class a little over an hour late. Staying in the car all the way home would make me miss two thirds of the class, so no point bothering.

Dad encourages me to grab my books so I can depart a moving vehicle. He even offers to pull over to let me out. Sweet of him, right? Okay, fine. He thinks school is important, and I did miss Professor Heath's class last week.

Can't help but remember the Peters brothers firing a flare into the basement of a funeral home full of kill-feeder vampires. The Universe sure does have a weird sense of synchronicity. This is a bit more extreme, but Anselme and his buttheads started it. Heck, maybe me telling Wolent about blowing up the funeral home gave him this idea. Or maybe bombs are the best practical solution for a vampiric problem.

We talk about random stuff like we usually do on long car rides. I sit scrunched down in the seat, wearing sunglasses, but otherwise, I'm not too uncomfortable. Dad eventually starts cracking jokes about how goofy those animated corpses looked. We geek out—obviously since my father is involved—and make jokes about inept necromancers rolling poorly on their 'summon undead' skill check. It's funny until I randomly think about those corpses being someone's relatives. It's not like Anselme killed them, but still feels wrong to laugh at *real* zombies. In a movie, video game, or D&D campaign, they're generic 'dead people.'

"... like something right out of *Shaun of the Dead.*" Dad whistles. "Wonder what the point of it was."

"Dunno. I couldn't figure it out. I mean, you killed them with the weed-eater. This scary Old World vampire couldn't possibly have meant them as a serious threat. Or they're underestimating us big time."

"Hmm. Hon?" Dad glances over at me. "Think some other entity out there is trying to send all the vampires of Seattle after this Anselme guy?"

"Whoa. *Inception* level stuff." I purse my lips. "It's hurting my brain to even think about it. Maybe I shouldn't blow him up if it's an elaborate misdirect. I do so hate becoming a pawn in someone's Machiavellian schemes."

Dad snickers. "Happens to everyone as soon as we take our first day job. Good point though."

I mull over the idea for an hour.

"Nah. Don't think anyone's doing that. The storm of derp zombies didn't have any effect on Wolent deciding to send a gift. Also, some other party trying to turn the Seattle Elders into assassins to get rid of

Anselme would have had no way to know Sophia would bork a scrying ritual and catapult Sierra into the middle of their staging ground so she could overhear them. The only reason Sierra ended up there is she decided to open the closet. No one could've predicted it." I hold a hand up when Dad opens his mouth. "And before you *Inception* level three me by saying someone somehow managed to arrange all of it on purpose, making sure Sierra landed there *to* overhear everything, it doesn't explain why the people in the warehouse tried to kill us. And they *definitely* did. Coralie warned me about Sierra."

Dad's quiet for a while.

Yeah, hearing Sierra had a brush with death upsets him.

"Unless Coralie is in on it," mutters Dad. "Or being compelled."

"Are you joking?"

"Not sure. Weird random ideas. Probably taking conspiracy theory nonsense to new heights."

"Just a bit. Coralie doesn't have the ability to mess with Sophia's stuff and fling them across the void. I also feel quite strongly she wouldn't lie about imminent harm to Sierra."

Dad squeezes the wheel hard. Yeah, he's angry someone almost hurt Sierra. "Place the bomb well, sweetie. Make sure none of them crawl out of that hole."

"You got it, Dad."

Things I never expected my father to say for $800, Alex.

Another twenty minutes later, the gloom's lifted and Dad starts humming *Mission Impossible* music. Yeah, I'm the world's dorkiest secret agent. Gotta get a ride from my parents to the scene of the mission. We pull up outside Cathedral Tree Cemetery three hours and twenty-six minutes after leaving home. Got caught in a little traffic and needed gas.

"Well, here it is, hon." Dad chokes up a bit exactly like he did when I started kindergarten. "Your first day at bombing places."

Heh. He's totally acting.

"Thanks for the ride, Dad." I hug him. "If I'm not back in twenty minutes, don't come after me. Wait for dark and find Glim."

Dad grabs my arm. "Don't make me worry so much."

"Not planning on it." I pull the red headband he got me for Christmas out of the hoodie pocket and put it on.

"You remembered!" Dad beams.

"Yeah." I smile. "Back as soon as I can."

"You're getting good at this."

"Umm, this is the first time I've done anything like this."

"No, I mean the daylight thing. It's pretty bright out and you're not even smoking."

"Wow. Yeah." I look at my hands. "Maybe I leveled up after spending a whole day tied to a tree."

Dad makes a suspicious face at me. "The master of this grand misdirection planned it on purpose to prepare you for this moment."

"Ugh. Dad. No. This is not a setup. No Illuminati."

I bite my lip, thinking about Aurélie. Perhaps 'illuminaughty.' Someone like her could scheme this whole thing to get rid of Anselme if he'd somehow wronged her years ago. But, nah. She's way more direct. Right? Besides, she has no way to mess with a scrying spell Sophia used. Who knows what kinds of information all of her haunted dolls might be providing, but it still wouldn't let her tweak magic. And there's no reason whatsoever for her to send zombies to our house.

No, Sophia's power is *so* weird and unpredictable, there's no damn way *anyone* could possibly have engineered it to specifically throw Sierra into that warehouse and shove Sophia headfirst into a giant void tentacle beast's body cavity. I'm totally confident in her horrible luck to entertain any doubts Anselme is responsible.

Unfortunately, in broad daylight, I can't make myself stronger and I don't even have the benefit of the 'always on' strength boost. Lugging a metal suitcase with thirty pounds of bomb in it is a chore. Heavy and ungainly big. Grumbling, I trudge into the cemetery, looking around for the mausoleum marked 'Barnaby.'

Gargoyles, not angels. Gargoyles not Angels.

Most of the mausoleums here have little angel statues. The one I'm looking for has gargoyles and looks older. One good thing, I still can't get tired despite being offline. It takes me a little while, but I eventually reach the deepest part of the cemetery where the bulk of the mausoleums cluster together. This area is steeped in eeriness. Graveyards don't usually make me feel weird, even post-vampire. I'm sure this is an aftereffect of continuous strange rituals taking place nearby.

Darren Anderson's lodge also felt odd, but not gloomy. Combine magic with whatever nastiness Anselme is up to—going to call it necromancy, even though the term's from a game. He made the dead walk. To anyone who's ever played D&D or any sort of fantasy-based computer game, he's a necromancer. Same logic might make Sophia a wild mage. Heh. Or the child apprentice who keeps misreading scrolls.

Ugh. Focus, Sarah. Gotta be serious for now.

Upon spotting the 'Barnaby' mausoleum, I drag myself over to it as fast as I can lug this huge suitcase. Admittedly, it's not abnormally huge. I'm not exactly big. Dad could carry this easy, and he's a nerd.

It's a bit of a project to get the door open, primarily due to me being kinda on the noodly side and not too strong at the moment. Turns out it's a trick latch and not a case of the mausoleum door being sealed. Obviously, the vamps who live here come and go all the time. It wouldn't be bolted or welded shut. Once I find the little button to push, the lock releases. Whew. As soon as I shuffle into the crypt, the air goes cool. I push the door shut, trying to be quiet.

Online.

For a second, it's as if the suitcase disappeared. I have to look to make sure it's still in my hands. It went from burdensome to insignificant in an instant. Yeah, it's good to be an undead.

Eight concrete boxes surround me, four on either side. They're big enough to hold two coffins apiece, stacked. Most have two plaques, but two are single-occupant. All the names end in Barnaby. Giant stone slabs seal each one. Other than saying I had to move a stone too heavy for a mortal to lift, Wolent didn't give me a lot of detail about *where* the slab would be.

Either he erred, didn't know, or figured it would be so obvious he didn't need to mention it.

Option three. Vampire eyes are *really* sharp. A trail of wear in the stone floor goes past all eight burial vaults to a big square hunk of rock by the rear wall, directly opposite the door in. Two metal rings embedded in the front corners show signs of frequent use as well. Yeah, this is definitely intended as a 'door' only vampires can open.

I set the suitcase down, grab the loops, and pull.

The stone is not light, even to my vampiric strength. Grunting, I heft it up a few inches and shuffle backward, dragging it enough to open a gap big enough for the suitcase. No need to pull it all the way. As quietly as it's possible to do, I ease it down, cringing as the big slab teeters, balanced on the edge of the hole. No one comes flying up from underground to kick my ass, so I'm probably in the clear.

Good idea to listen for a bit.

I crawl around to the opening and peer in.

A shaft leads straight down four-ish stories to a concrete floor. The wall closest to the crypt exit has a ladder, presently blocked off by the hatch cover sticking a bit more than halfway over the hole. Fortunately, I don't need the ladder.

Suitcase in hand, I fly up, squeeze past the stone slab, and glide down to the bottom, entering a chamber the size of a small room. It's empty, smells like dirt, and has one way out: a corridor going straight ahead maybe a hundred feet to a larger room.

It's utterly silent. Quiet as a tomb. Thanks, Dad. Ugh. Puns are in my blood. Good thing I can hold my breath forever. It would be loud in here. I ponder the oddity of being a vampire who has to consciously think about holding her breath. Most vampires are the reverse. If they don't think about breathing, they don't breathe. Such a small thing, but it's neat to me.

To remain as ninja-like as possible, I float up off the ground and glide down the hallway. As an extra precaution, I keep my legs bent up at the knee in case they have trip wires or laser beams. Sure, I'm not playing D&D right now with a tricky game master who puts ten traps in thirty feet of corridor. This is the real world. Well, as 'real' as vampires, mystics, and imps can be.

The 'room' at the end turns out to be a round chamber from which seven other corridors span like the spokes of a wheel. An assortment of old, battered chairs, two sofas, a couple tables, and dozens of mismatched rugs fill the area. Definitely looks like a vampire 'hang out' spot. Sorta. It's kinda boring, really. No computers, television, or anything to do. Maybe they have the fun stuff down one of the other hallways. Probably hard to pick up a decent WiFi signal forty feet underground.

Right. I need to get the serious hell out of here as fast as possible.

This room looks like the middle of the complex. It's probably the best place to plant the bomb, being the center. Even better since I don't need to get any closer to sleeping, dangerous vampires. I select one of the randomly placed carpets, a purple-and-gold one, and lift it aside to hide the case under it. A giant lump is going to be suspicious, but less so than a big steel suitcase. Couldn't be any more obvious if they wrote 'this is a bomb' on it.

I ease the case down and open it, then look around at the various corridors leading away. Empty, quiet. Each passage has multiple doorways on either side. Can't tell from here if they have recessed doors in them, or are merely openings. It's kind of like being in an ancient tomb with slightly better interior decorating. The hub chamber is part *Lost Boys,* part hippie commune. Having random skulls placed around is a nice touch. Yeah, definitely a bunch of shiny, happy people living here.

This is going a lot easier than I expected, which means it's going to go super wrong. Or not. It might've gone pear shaped if I forgot the katana. Or the headband. Guaranteed, if I didn't bring my sword, I'd have gotten jumped already.

Right. Focus.

I insert the special key, giving it a turn fully right. Red numbers appear as 88:88 on the display screen for a second before reverting to 00:00. I hope whoever made this device isn't an idiot and button pushes don't beep like a microwave.

Hmm. A hundred feet of corridor to a vertical shaft. I could fly it in seconds. Maybe I could get away with setting the timer for one minute. Wolent said not to be too aggressive though. Hmm. Okay, fine. It's super quiet down here.

I type in 3:00. Thankfully, the keys do not make beeps when pushed. I blink, open my eyes and sanity check the display. Three-zero-zero. Not thirty minutes, not thirty seconds. The number of the counting shall be three minutes. It shall neither be two minutes nor shall it be four minutes.

Ack. I shouldn't make myself want to laugh.

Here goes. I lift the button shield and push the arm switch. A red LED by the timer comes on. You'd think a serious bomb maker would label it 'armed' or some such thing. No, this guy puts 'boom boom' by the red light. Points for being literal, I suppose.

The glowing red numbers remain at 3:00, flickering faintly.

Slow exhale.

Gingerly, I turn the key back to the middle position and pull it out.

2:59

2:58

I close the suitcase and take full advantage of my vampiric speed to lock the two clasps and pull the rug over it for concealment.

Easy peasy. I stand, turn to face the way out—and a flying dude tackles me. We sail across the chamber until my back crashes against the wall. Dude's holding me off the ground by two fistfuls of my hoodie. We're eye-to-eye and my feet are dangling a little past his knees. He's like a goth metalhead, but muscular, long black hair and a partially stoned, partially not-quite-awake fog in his eyes. Guy's looking at me as if he can't figure out if he should break my neck, pet me like a stray cat, or try to eat me.

Uh oh. Three minutes might not have been enough after all.

37

CALORIES ARE FOR LESSER MORTALS

Used to be, I thought the scariest clock in the world was the one on the wall in school.

Having twelve minutes left in a test period with twenty questions remaining unanswered has nothing on a three-minute bomb timer. This is a great way to handle educational anxiety. I think every college student should be trapped in an underground chamber thirty feet away from a massive bomb while a half-awake vampire holds them down so they can't get away.

If I get out of here, no test will ever intimidate me again.

Wolent's voice mocks me. Yeah, I should have set the timer for like fifteen minutes.

So, yeah. Back to this giant dude pinning me to the wall. He totally looks like a real-life version of Nathan Explosion from *Metalocalypse*. Oh, Universe, you have an awful sense of humor. As in, there's about to be an extremely real explosion here. Before I became a vampire, if I had an almost seven-foot-tall long-haired bodybuilder holding me off the ground, I'd probably have fainted. I'm still kinda close to having a panic attack. Two things keep me in control of my emotions.

One, I'm a vampire. Two, this guy doesn't look like the lights are on upstairs.

No, I'm not calling him stupid. He's literally out of it. Except for Innocents, we *really* don't like being awake during the day. He's running on fumes with the faculties of a drunken housecat, fumbling around in the dark at anything he thinks might be moving and edible. Basically, he's operating at the mental level of a television network executive—you know, like the bastards who cancelled *Firefly*.

I look down at my sneakers. It's not too unnerving anymore to see them so far off the ground. But it is when I'm not flying. Shit. 2:40 or so left on the timer at a guess. Dude's a mental grapefruit right now, so there's no way he's going to be able to process what a bomb is even if he realizes the huge bump in the carpet shouldn't be there. I don't have to worry about defending the device… just getting the hell out of here before it incinerates me, too.

Seems the guy is confused because I don't smell like a mortal.

What the hell did I do to wake him up? Can't think of any noise I made.

He might be huge, but he only weighs so much. I grab his hands, peeling his thumbs away from my hoodie while planting my feet in his chest and shoving as hard as my legs are capable of. Having my back against the wall helps. 'Nathan' flies back, losing his grip on my sweatshirt. Awesome. I much prefer not running outside topless. Honestly, I'm not sure what would be worse… sitting in the car with my Dad like that or dying in a blast down here.

I zip away heading for the exit… but *shit*, all the corridors out kinda look the same. Which way is it?

Seconds later, the dude comes after me, grabbing my ankle as I attempt to fly off. Growling, I roll over onto my back, kicking at his hand. He's so mentally blank at the moment, he just holds on, oblivious to my sneaker smashing into his fingers. I'm almost afraid to sprout claws and slash him. Extreme pain might set him off like the Tasmanian Devil. He's presently unaware of me as a *threat*, and my continued existence is highly dependent on allowing him to continue not knowing what to think of me.

If this dude goes full feral, I'm going to be in multiple pieces. It's really damn difficult to run away from a bomb when one's legs are detached from their body. Around and around I go like an angel trying to fly with one ankle chained to a stone pillar, frantically searching for the way out. Everything looks the same. I'm about to try dragging the dude to the case so I can disarm the bomb, but ooh! I spot a corridor without any openings on either side. That one *has* to be the way out. Every other passage leading away from this hub room has multiple doorways.

Screw it. Gotta have less than a minute left on the clock.

I draw my katana and size up his wrist for a slice. The instant I make the decision to hack his hand off, he growls and hammer-throws me by the leg into the wall. Ouch. Not sure what hurts more, my face, my probably dislocated hip, or my ankle.

His snarl of rage is all the motivation I need to push off the wall and fly like hell for the exit. There's no time for a fight in here. 'Nathan' is on my ass, flying behind me, grabbing at my legs. Going full speed down a hundred-foot corridor isn't the wisest thing I've ever done. I can't stop in time to make the ninety-degree turn going straight up.

I smash into the wall.

'Nathan' crashes into me.

Oh, there's a rib or two. Or maybe it just hurts and nothing broke. Didn't hear any crunching.

The hit seems to disorient him a bit as he's struggling to process difficult concepts like why we can't fly through solid stone. Dude does not have the strong motivating force of knowing there's a big ass bomb about to go off. I launch myself up the shaft. He follows. Cringing, I fly straight into the slab still half-covering the top, flinging it upward like a tiddlywink. Alas, hitting the stone causes me to slow down a crapload.

Dude catches me, grabbing my legs around the knees in a hug.

Ack! I don't even think about anything beyond getting the hell out. Probably would be smart to stab him in the head and knock him out, but I'm sorta panicking. He's got a hold of me… and nothing else. My flight power is enough to drag him across the mausoleum.

I cross my arms in front of my face an instant before zooming into the door.

We burst out into broad daylight. It's like going from nice air conditioning to Arizona desert August in an instant. My flight power cuts out in an instant, dumping me on the ground. 'Nathan' screams. Smoke billows out from under his shirt. His face and forearms blacken in seconds. He's no longer trying to hold me back, merely clinging in some kind of animalistic response to excruciating pain… and I'm freakin helpless, not strong enough to drag him anymore.

Growling, I grab at the damp stone pathway, tearing up moss, struggling to pull myself forward, but I might as well be encased in concrete from the thighs down. I've become Sarah-calibur, the vampire stuck in the stone.

Panic rises… but somehow, my thoughts don't go crazy.

Desperate, I twist back and slash the katana one-handed at his burning face. The top of his head breaks open, pouring glowing embers onto his back. Flames erupt, racing down over his ass to his legs. My sword hitting his head sounds like I'm whacking a bag of Doritos, dry and crunchy.

His arms break apart, weak as kindling.

Trying not to scream, I kick my way loose and scramble to my feet, hastily backing off a few steps. Out of sheer morbid curiosity, I stand there watching this big dude shrink into a vaguely human-shaped black log of burning matter. Wow. First time in my life I'm glad a guy *didn't* last three minutes.

I back up a little more and glance down at my hands. No burning. It's a bright, clear day and I'm feeling only slightly microwaved. Whoa. Maybe I *can* get better at this sun thing after all. It's definitely *not* comfortable. Kinda like listening to Gilbert Gottfried's voice. Won't kill me, but it's to be avoided if at all possible. As a test, I concentrate on 'fighting' the sun… and the pain lessens to tolerable discomfort. Holy cow. It works! My body is definitely burning 'vampire power' at an extreme rate to keep my composure in the day. Probably will need to feed off two people later tonight, but small price to pay.

Right. Time to get out of here.

I sprint most of the way across the cemetery. Seconds before Dad and the Sentra come into view, I slide my katana into its scabbard and slow to a Hollywood walk. Cue the cool explosion behind me as I nonchalantly stroll away from death and destruction.

Dad spots me.

I stop, pull my sunglasses out of the hoodie pocket, and put them on.

Guess you could say, those vampires had a real blast.

Boooooom!

A dragon's breath of blinding white flames shoots out of the open mausoleum door. I shudder at a sudden wave of *icky* supernatural energy. Not sure if the bomb had some extra spice to it or if a bunch of vampires dying at once released a spiritual supernova. Maybe Anselme kept some magical artifacts down there. I imagine there are probably some bizarre components needed to animate corpses. Meh. Who knows? Pretty sure ordinary bombs don't release a tidal wave of overwhelming dread as a matter of routine.

Half smiling, I attempt the 'cool' walk back to the car, but can't take myself seriously at all and end up laughing. After only like six steps, I break into a run, eager to get out of here. My katana gets tossed into the back seat as I jump in and slam the door.

Dad starts the engine. "Damn, it feels good to be a gangsta."

I chuckle, glancing sideways at him. "No… just, no. Sierra was right. You shouldn't quote rap."

He fake scoffs, then peers past me. "Is that white phosphorous? Damn. Guess Wolent's not messing around."

"What's white phosphorus?"

"An incendiary chemical weapon. Keeps burning underwater. Very hard to wash off. Super painful. I think it's been banned by the Geneva Convention." He pulls around in a U-turn and begins the drive home.

I blink. "How do *you* know what it is?"

"Your sister isn't the only one in the house who plays video games."

"Ugh." I slouch in my seat, pulling the hood up to hide from the sun. "I think the bomb relied on something slightly more involved than ordinary chemistry."

He nods. "Yeah, you're probably right. So… good guys win?"

"More like the less bad guys won."

"Not sure I follow."

I shrug. "Vampire groups competing for territory reminds me of gangs during Prohibition shooting at each other. Yeah, I'm on 'Team Wolent,' but I'm not really sure we count as the 'good' guys. More like 'as good as it's possible for vampires to be'. Then again, I am naïvely idealistic and probably trusting them all way more than I should."

He laughs. "True, but how many other summer jobs let you practice demolition work?"

"Wow." Can't help but laugh.

"So yeah, the less bad guys won." Dad drums his fingers on the wheel. "Sort of like shades of grey."

"No. Dad. Please never say those exact words in that exact order ever again."

"Huh?" He looks at me for a second, then blinks. "Oh. Duh. Right. I meant morality."

"Yeah, I know. Just don't want to think about you or Mom reading one of *those* books."

He laughs. "Don't worry. We won't. But, you know… we're not innocent. It's happened at least four times."

"Gah! Dad!" I cover my ears.

My father smiles broadly, pleased with himself. Grr. Why is it fathers take such delight in embarrassing their kids?

"Thanks for helping me with my, umm, project."

He bumps his fist into my shoulder. "Hope you get an A on it."

I stare at the car roof. "Ugh. My life is *so* weird."

A few minutes pass in silence before plastic crinkles.

Dad offers me a snack cake. "Care for a Devil Dog?"

"Sure." I take it. "I'm no longer beholden to calories."

38

THEY'RE NOT READY UNTIL THEY STOP SNARLING

I love bombs.

Bath bombs, that is. The explodey kind, I'm totes happy staying away from as much as possible. It's been a few days since our trip to Astoria, and Seattle has quieted down. I did end up flying to philosophy class as soon as it got dark, leaving Dad to drive himself home. He insisted, saying my education was important. I'm sure he would have preferred delaying the bombing until the weekend so I didn't miss class at all, but Anselme's people *were* doing damage and needed to be stopped. Being an hour late to class is trivial by comparison.

Professor Heath accepted my excuse, even seeming flattered I'd rush to get to his class after having a near-death experience.

Wolent gave me a big ol' back pat. He did find me going to class before meeting him amusing, but it didn't bother him. Yeah, got the feeling the elders view me going to college in the same light people look at kittens or puppies doing something pointless and cute. Whatever. No one told me what, exactly, the bomb was made from, but Wolent's agents haven't observed any activity going on around the cemetery related to Anselme. As far as Seattle's 'official' vampire society is concerned, I'm now a 'real' vampire who's willing to play by the rules. Go figure. If they wanted to know that, they could've talked to any of my former teachers. Even Stefano and Paolo have backed off a little in their contempt. They *still* think it's a mistake for me to be living at home, but it seems they are now at least willing to wait for me to actually screw up before they complain about my existence.

I let the PIBs know about the situation so they could help keep the lid on the explosion. The compound being so far underground prevented any visible destruction from reaching the surface beyond the interior of the mausoleum being charred black.

Dunno if the place caved in or merely experienced a 'cleanse by burning'.

Hunter and I are going to visit Aurélie this Friday to sit for a painting. It'll probably come out looking like the cover for a romance novel set in the 1800s. Admittedly, I'm a tiny bit uneasy at how he's going to react to her presence. Even if she works hard to contain her charms, it's like asking the sun to be less warm. It took Ashley months to return to relative normal after being exposed to her. Then again, they did a lot more than simply exist in the same room.

Mom's even adjusted to the hellhound in the backyard. I guess his helping fend off an attack of walking corpses kinda endeared him to her. Predictably, driving me to a bombing has set Dad off on a marathon of 'spy' themed Eighties movies. He's planning to go through them once a week, but hey, it's fun.

We're creating memories.

The kind of memories that'll make me cry in a hundred years, but still. I'd rather have them than not.

Me? Right now, I'm enjoying the quiet normality of a Pomegranate Fantasy bath bomb. Must be in a good mood since I'm not hiding completely underwater. It's a Tuesday night and there's nothing pressing on my schedule beyond some studying, which I have plenty of time for.

"Sophia!" shouts Mom downstairs. "I'm not going to say it again! Please get these mushrooms out of the sink! I will not be growled at by fungus in my own home!"

A small person runs by the bathroom door, heading toward the stairs.

"Mom!" calls Sophia. "I can't move them until they stop growling, or they'll explode. Do you want the whole kitchen permanently dyed glowing rainbow?"

Laughing, I stretch my legs out and enjoy the warm embrace of pomegranate-scented bathwater.

Awesome. We have snarling fungus in the sink, but at least no one's trying to kill me.

My life is back to normal.

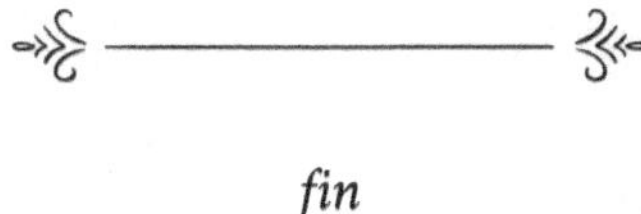

fin

ACKNOWLEDGMENTS

Thank you for reading the eleventh book in the Vampire Innocent series!

Much gratitude to Lee Sheridan for editing and Alexandria Thompson for the cover art.

Additional thanks to Jan Moulding for helping with the German translation.

ABOUT THE AUTHOR

Originally from South Amboy NJ, Matthew has been creating science fiction and fantasy worlds for most of his reasoning life. Since 1996, he has developed the "Divergent Fates" world, in which *Division Zero, Virtual Immortality, The Awakened Series, The Harmony Paradox, and the Daughter of Mars series* take place. Along with being an editor at Curiosity Quills press, he has worked in IT and technical support.

Matthew is an avid gamer, a recovered WoW addict, Gamemaster for two custom RPG systems, and a fan of anime, British humour, and intellectual science fiction that questions the nature of reality, life, and what happens after it.

He is also fond of cats.

Visit me online at:

Facebook: https://www.facebook.com/MatthewSCoxAuthor

Pinterest: https://www.pinterest.com/matthewcox10420/

Goodreads: https://www.goodreads.com/author/show/7712730.Matthew_S_Cox

Email: mcox2112@gmail.com

OTHER BOOKS BY MATTHEW S. COX

Divergent Fates Universe Novels

Division Zero series

- Division Zero
- Lex De Mortuis
- Thrall
- Guardian
- Harbinger
- The Shadow Fixer
- Neuroshock

The Awakened series

- Prophet of the Badlands
- Archon's Queen
- Grey Ronin
- Daughter of Ash
- Zero Rogue
- Angel Descended

Daughter of Mars series

- The Hand of Raziel
- Araphel
- Ghost Black

Virtual Immortality series

- Virtual Immortality
- The Harmony Paradox

Prophet of the Badlands Series

- Prophet's Journey
- Prophet's Mercy

Divergent Fates Anthology

(Fiction Novels - Adult)

The Roadhouse Chronicles Series

- One More Run
- The Redeemed
- Dead Man's Number

Faded Skies series

- Heir Ascendant
- Ascendant Unrest
- Ascendant Revolution

Temporal Armistice Series

- Nascent Shadow
- The Shadow Collector
- The Gate to Oblivion
- The Queen of Discord
- The Burning Alchemist

Vampire Innocent series

- A Nighttime of Forever
- A Beginner's Guide to Fangs
- The Artist of Ruin

- The Last Family Road Trip
- The Phantom Oracle
- How Not to Summon Demons
- Ordinary Problems of a College Vampire
- A Vampire's Guide to Surviving Holidays
- An Introduction to Paranormal Diplomacy
- A Vampire's Guide to Adulting
- How to Stop a Vampire War in Six Easy Steps
- Ancient Vampire Death Cults and Other Annoyances
- Hunting Vampires for Fun and Profit
- A String of Seriously Unlucky Events
- The Summer of Completely Usual Strangeness
- Demonic Crisis Management for the Modern Vampire

Standalones

- Wayfarer: AV494
- Axillon99
- Chiaroscuro: The Mouse and the Candle
- The Spirits of Six Minstrel Run
- Sophie's Light
- The Far Side of Promise anthology
- Operation: Chimera (with Tony Healey)
- The Dysfunctional Conspiracy (with Christopher Veltmann)
- Of Myth and Shadow
- The Girl Who Found the Sun

Winter Solstice series (with J.R. Rain)

- Convergence
- Containment
- Catalyst
- Catacombs

Alexis Silver series (with J.R. Rain)

- Silver Light
- Deep Silver
- Silver Quarrel
- Silver Crucible
- Silver Heart

Samantha Moon Origins series (with J.R. Rain)

- New Moon Rising
- Moon Mourning
- Haunted Moon

Vampire For Hire series (with J.R. Rain)

- Moon Master
- Dead Moon
- Lost Moon
- Vampire Destiny
- Infinite Moon
- Vampire Empress
- Moon Elder
- Wicked Moon
- Moon Blade

Maddy Wimsey series (with J.R. Rain)

- The Devil's Eye
- The Drifting Gloom
- Dark Mercy
- Primal Wrath

Samantha Moon Case Files series (with J.R. Rain)

- Blood Moon

Immortal Operative (with J.R. Rain)

- Broken Ice
- Broken Wing

Four Elements series (with J.R. Rain)

- The Elementalist
- The Black Rose
- The Wakefield Curse

Witches series (with J.R. Rain)

- The Witch and the Hangman

Zeb Clemens series (with J.R. Rain)

- The Beast of Devil's Creek
- Wanted: Undead or Alive

Young Adult Novels

The Eldritch Heart Series

- The Eldritch Heart
- The Cursed Crown
- The Sapphire Soul

Evergreen Series

- Evergreen
- The World That Remains

- The Lucky Ones
- Nuclear Summer
- The Nuclear Frontier
- The World We Make
- The Threat Unseen

Progenitor Series

- Out of Sight
- Out of Mind

Diary of a Teenage Fey

(Short story series)

- Elder Horror
- The Hag of Barrow Falls
- Babysitter's Nightmare
- Lharakki
- Bauble for a Soul
- Simulacrum
- Amorphous
- Manticore

Standalones

- Caller 107
- The Summer the World Ended
- Nine Candles of Deepest Black
- The Forest Beyond the Earth

Middle Grade Novels

The Adventures of Ubergirl series

- My Dad is a Mad Scientist
- Aliens Ate My Homework
- The End of all Halloweens
- Dr. Infinity and the Soul Smasher

Tales of Widowswood series

- Emma and the Banderwigh
- Emma and the Silk Thieves
- Emma and the Silverbell Faeries
- Emma and the Elixir of Madness
- Emma and the Weeping Spirit

Standalones

- Citadel: The Concordant Sequence
- The Cursed Codex
- The Menagerie of Jenkins Bailey

www.ingramcontent.com/pod-product-compliance
Lightning Source LLC
Chambersburg PA
CBHW030605180626
46816CB00005B/1689